MARK OF THE WITCHWYRM

A monstrous tale of axes and alchemy by
STEVE VAN SAMSON

Standard Paperback Edition
First Printing, 2021
ISBN 978-1-5136-8083-5
Cover art by René Aigner
Jacket Design by Steve Van Samson

Rough House Publishing
PO Box 3232
Worcester MA 01613

www.RoughHousePublishing.com

For Madeline.

May you always find a little of yourself in Rivka.
She has your hope, your heart, and just a tiny bit of your courage.

~Love Dadeline

EVERY JOURNEY IS A DAMNED CIRCLE...

FOREWARD & ACKNOWLEDGMENTS

The book in your hands represents roughly three years worth of work, but the story goes a bit farther back than that.

For over two decades I've had the components and characters of this world swimming around my head, though I had always planned on a different member of the Belmorn lineage taking center stage. A character who I have always thought of as "my Conan". My roving adventurer who walks through a world of myth and plague. It was only in late 2017, when I began plotting everything out, that I decided to set this particular story much earlier. That the book which I originally titled "Black Ouroboros" would in fact be a prequel to those other stories... which could come later. And they will.

A big scaly thanks go to my intrepid readers: Ken, Desiree, Jordan, & especially to my brother Tim For helping me hammer out that ending. Also to Derek Rook for all of his incredible work, bottomless enthusiasm and for believing in this project (and this writer) enough to take a chance on publishing his first novel. A novel which, by the way, would be in much worse shape if not for my wonderful editor and dear friend, Trisha Wooldridge. In addition to cracking the reins whenever I got any of the horse stuff wrong, she gifted me the beautiful poem which you will find printed on the following page.

~**Steve Van Samson**

One Thing Unchanging

A will o'wisp trail leads not quite to home,
through uncanny valley, steaming sea foam.
Mythic multiverses tell tales restyled,
and echo-skewed stories twisted to poem.

When common knowledge redefines truth,
overlapped maps remark known paths, forsooth.
Familiar cities, alien gods...
Death and life change in the flash of a tooth.

Hungry fantasies shift solid, then fray.
Reality scarred from wytch magic's sway,
where real teeth bite flesh and tail stingers tear
holes to a realm where bones of victims lay.

Between bard call and book, tellings compiled,
Truth changes currency, value defiled.
Yet unspoiled, unchanged, steadfast and true,
is ever a father's love for their child.

By Trisha Wooldridge

PART ONE
CROWS & PAWNS

1-1

Flakes of white drifted down and down, between leafless branches, frosting all with sleepy indifference.

So this is snow. To the man upon the long-legged horse, the exotic precipitation weaved a kind of magic. He was a stranger to these cold northern woods--a traveler from a region where the daring speared and hauled slime-slick beasts onto damp, waiting banks.

Before now snow had existed solely in tales--the sort of thing that might pass between travelers on their way from one somewhere to the next. But in this foreign place, those tales at least, were manifest. Feeling a burgeoning shiver at the base of his spine, the rider turned away from a gust of wind.

Circling his head, was a leather band with several burnished medallions. As well as a pair of long black heron feathers, the band held in place a dark headscarf. The garment was black as the hair beneath it--with long, tattered tassels that whipped in the breeze behind.

There was also a collar which lent the bearings of a rogue. It was turned up and large enough to hide a strong nose, harsh jaw, and almost omnipresent frown. Of the man's face, all that could be seen were a pair of eyes which glared with the fatigue of nineteen long weeks. They were grey, those eyes. Determined and full of storms.

Rander Belmorn was an imposing man with a prodigious weight upon his sun-beaten brow. He was descended from a proud, nomadic tribe who'd once hunted enormous elk in the shadow of the Karaggash Ridge. Almost two centuries ago, those copper-skinned people were forced to abandon their plains for a new home. Settling at last upon the banks of a massive, uncrossable river. A brackish body of water which not only bisected the continent but teemed with the sort of prey most were too afraid to hunt. Taming the gigantic horses they found there, these people carved out a new existence--not as hunters or fishermen, but something in between.

Rander Belmorn was a man of the river--what some called a blackfoot. And he was far, far from home.

SNAP!

A crisp rending of twig pulled the man's attention. He glared between trees that were taller and more dense than he had ever known possible. But beyond the snow dusted trunks, Belmorn saw nothing. No beast or villain to hinder his progress, and so he relaxed. Settling back into the rocking movement of his horse.

After a long, quiet moment, the stallion shook its head, causing the bridle to whip and jingle. Like all of its breed, the animal was immense. As big as any draught horse but longer of leg. Its coat was nearly black--the color of rain-kissed soil--except the legs, which looked to have been painted of pure alabaster. Where the two opposing hues met, light attacked dark in the manner of bold, horizontal stripes.

An adamandray would be an exotic sight in all lands save the Black River region where it had dropped so unceremoniously to the ground. Though he was much younger then, Belmorn could still recall the sight of that ungainly foal blinking up at him, wondering what in the world had just happened.

It has been said that, against its will, an adamandray is harder to move than the tallest oak. Yet for the past nineteen weeks, the stallion served his oldest friend well--bearing the man down roads of stone and pressed earth, past villages, cities and markets where men swallowed flaming swords or shouted their wares.

Magnus was the horse's given name, even if it was seldom used anymore.

"Sorry, Old Man." The blackfoot spoke with a dry rasp, his vocal cords not yet accustomed to the climate. "Drifted away there for a second."

Belmorn patted the horse's neck, and for a fleeting second, he considered glancing behind. South. Back over the travel and toil of nineteen weeks. All the way back home. To a small riverside village called Grael.

"I bet you're hungry."

The horse coughed up a cloud, flipping its long black mane. After coming to a stop, Belmorn swung a leg over the saddle horn and dismounted. Thumb and forefinger worked at the collar button until the flaps of leather parted. With his face now woefully exposed, a sudden shiver racked the man.

He had never worn a beard before, nor had his hair ever come so near his shoulders. Such trappings were burdens to men who pulled enormous eels and worse out of those black southern rivers. As he scratched the obscured line of his chin, Belmorn's mind yearned to wander again--to slip backwards along the road.

What would Malia think if she could see him now? Would she fancy this leaner, hairier, more hollow-eyed version of her husband? Belmorn frowned, suddenly feeling very cold.

His gaze fell to the flakes gathering on the black fur of his cloak. The bear pelt was a recent acquisition, purchased from an eight fingered merchant in Britilpor. Only a few weeks back, he had scoffed at the idea of spending good coin on anything that could not be digested. But now, as the hairs of that cloak collected more and more snow, he regretted not spending a little more on something with a hood.

The adamandray whickered impatiently, nudging the rider back into the moment. With something like a smile, Belmorn slid his hand down the animal's neck to a small satchel. A potent aroma asserted itself as he extracted three pale stalks, each terminating in a conspicuous white bulb. He had been carrying the leeks for three days and nights, ever since discovering them growing on the side of the road.

The musky bouquet caused a pang to twist in the man's gut. Gripping one of the leeks between his teeth he snapped the stalk in two. Keeping the white half for himself, he fed the greens to Magnus.

"Sorry there isn't something better." After watching the stalks disappear, he patted the animal's neck. "Don't worry, Old Man, we'll find more soon. The city can't be far now."

Belmorn chewed his final bite slowly, imagining the leek was a bit of roasted eel fillet with dill gravy. The beautiful musing caused the man's stomach to twist and complain. He couldn't help but lament finishing the last strips of dried rabbit two days earlier. It had tasted good enough, but with the meat gone, these pale stalks were among his most prized possessions. If he was wrong about being able to find more food and soon, both horse and rider were going to be in a bad way.

No--it wouldn't come to that. They just had to reach the city.

Magnus' ear twitched and rotated. Without warning, the stallion coughed up a puff of steam and a series of nervous grunts. Something was in the air. Something subtle but steadily gathering above the snow. Belmorn could feel it too and so they both stood as statues--just listening. To the man's surprise, he could hear the snow as it fell around him. But there was another sound. An under-sound.

Birds, Belmorn thought. His gaze shot to the path, and then, straight through the trees.

The sky flashed bright white and rumblings of thunder weren't far behind.

"Steady, Old Man," said Belmorn, reassuring his friend with a firm pat on the neck. "Steady. Just a little lightning, that's all. Usually it follows rain... why not this?"

Again Belmorn found himself staring between the trees to the right of his path. The echoes of thunder were gone, but he could still hear the other sound--the birds.

"Crows," he muttered. "They sound mad. Frenzied."

There was something about the cawing racket that seemed important. But what? The man's mind tried to produce an answer, but it felt frozen and slow. Then, just as a new pang of hunger pulsed in his gut, Belmorn remembered something.

"Crows," he said with sudden understanding. "Crows scavenge."

Hanging from one side of the saddle were a series of sturdy iron rings--all square, all mounted to a long leather strap. Stepping into the first of these, Belmorn leapt back into his saddle. Shifting his legs almost imperceptibly, the blackfoot clicked his tongue, which spurred the beast into a gallop. In a veritable blur, the trees of the forest rushed past. The tall, branchless things were not especially tightly packed. Moving between them on the back of most horses would be considered idiotic at best, but Magnus was far from most horses.

As the pair bounded headlong past brush, over fallen trunk, the cawing din grew louder--closer. Sensing this, Belmorn slowed to a trot. There was definitely something up ahead, just through the trees. And whatever was happening was happening there. From such a close proximity, it felt as if the chorus of birds were scraping the inside of his skull.

4

Another flash lit the heavens. It was brighter than before and a peel of thunder was directly behind. The lighting was getting closer, but what did that mean for a snow storm? Belmorn didn't know, and he didn't care. Nothing mattered beyond the prospect of having something in his stomach besides onions and day-old bile.

Fluidly, the blackfoot slid from the saddle to the ground. Then, keeping his eyes on the clearing, he led the adamandray over to a tree--looping the reins around its trunk.

At this, Magnus gave an angry snort.

"I'm just going to have a look. This..." He pulled the reins taught so the horse could see. "This knot is not my best work, okay? You understand?"

The horse chuffed, regarding the clearing with one bulging eye.

"Listen... I don't know what's in there. If things go bad... you'll hear--you'll know." Belmorn gave a small tug so the horse could see the looseness of the knot. "If that happens, don't come after me. Okay? Just break this and go."

The horse stamped a rear hoof on the forest floor and received a reassuring pat on the shoulder. The Blackfoot's hand slid then to the first of a pair of axes mounted on his saddle. Gripping the handles, he pulled them free--turning them in his palms until the blades faced the ground.

"Oh stop worrying. Remember... Rinh is with us."

Belmorn turned toward the squawking cacophony. Stealth would be a wasted effort, he knew. As he stalked toward the noise, his fingers tightened around the two axe handles. Like the man who held them, the axes were Graelian--each supporting a massive, wedge shaped head. These tapered down to a keen, crescent edge which spoke more of scythes than axes. The weight of the weapons felt good in his hands. Powerful. And more, they felt a lot like home.

The sensation hit him so hard, he could almost smell the riverland of his birth. And the raging waters--dark, brackish and full of fury.

1-2

Back pressed against a trunk, Belmorn peered around and into the cacophony. Birds--they were everywhere. There had to be a hundred or more--big, black and all riled into a frenzy. The biggest crows he had ever seen. At least twice the size of their black river cousins.

The man stared into the cawing legion that seemed more like a great swarm of insects than birds. He tried to grasp some sense of what he was witnessing, but the racket pressed into his ears, making it hard to think.

Suddenly and all at once, the cloud of crows swelled, parted. It all happened fast, but not too fast for the blackfoot's eyes to see and understand with terrible certainty. That inside that swirling storm of feather and claw was a man.

Belmorn retreated a step. The pair of Graelian axes suddenly felt very good in his hands.

The crows' victim wore a hooded cloak of darkest blue--a shade just past proper midnight. Some of the birds circled above like half-sized vultures; the rest were on the attack, reaching out with sharp talons and thick, powerful beaks, screaming their ugly, sour notes.

Amidst the racket, Belmorn could hear the swipes of the hooded man's stick slicing through the air. Bizarrely, the hand that wasn't brandishing the feeble weapon was held straight out--perfectly parallel to the ground. For some reason, the man had been tethered where he stood. Around one of his arms were loops of a thick, greenish rope which ran in a taut line to a tree.

Belmorn stared agape at the scene before him. And the longer he did so, the more certain he became that rope was rather a braid of slithery vines. That the hooded man was not tied to the old tree. That in fact, he was ensnared by it.

"Is this the best you've got?!" The hooded man roared above the noise. Then his stick connected, mid-arc, with one of the crows. The strike sent the bird careening through the air. After hitting the ground head first, its wings flapped feebly while hand-sized talons raked the ground.

"Ha!" The hooded man's voice roared with satisfaction. "That's what you get! Every last one of you!"

In answer, the feathered maelstrom seemed to darken. The flapping, cawing mass moved as if possessed of a single mind. More school than flock, it regrouped then fell once more upon the tethered man, who managed to cinch up his hood at the last possible second.

Belmorn couldn't have said what was going to happen next, but he knew he could not in good conscience remain idle. His grip tightened on the axe in his right hand. His throwing arm. The crow on the ground, still dazed, never saw it coming.

THUKK!

The effect was as explosive as it was instantaneous. No sooner had the axe struck the ground, then the panicked crows scattered in all directions. By fives and tens, the birds came to roost. Lining high branches, a safe distance away, the scowling things muttered softly amongst themselves.

Chaos momentarily abated, Belmorn looked about like a fox searching the grass for wolves. He could see that only two of the birds remained, though not by choice.

At this distance, Belmorn could see the greenish ropes were actually thorn-covered vines. Strands of the initial braid had apparently released the hooded man's arm and now gripped the two remaining crows. One of the birds pecked its way free and flew off to join the retreated flock. The other did nothing but flap its wings and scream the way only crows can. The pathetic sight brought to Belmorn's mind images of a child's kite in a hard wind.

Snow-covered leaves crunched as the blackfoot approached. His gaze remained fixed on the hooded victim. And for many long moments, the two strangers stood in silence, neither wanting to be the first to look away.

Without a word, Belmorn scooped up the crow he had killed and pulled his axe from the ground.

The hooded man was leaning backwards at an angle so severe, it would have been impossible without the tether. It seemed clear that a constant struggle was going on. That the man was actively fighting to keep his current footing. It was almost as if the vine were trying to reel him in.

Belmorn looked once more at the massive knot wrapped around the old tree and had an unsettling thought. That the way the bark was bulging out over the vines, it looked very much like the tree were being slowly strangled. He shuddered. He didn't like this. Not one damn bit.

The still tethered crow continued to squawk and gyrate in the air-- caught like a fish on an ever shortening line. The end of the vine had already crept up the bird's body and looped around its neck.

Then, with a final squawk, the crow dropped--hitting the ground with a pathetic squeak. The living lasso continued to coil around its prey--mummifying the bird in thick coils of its own length. By the time the body reached the tree, there was no crow--only a thorny green pod. This was pulled up the trunk about three feet, where it was then secured by more creeping tendrils.

"Rinh." Belmorn was the first to speak. His voice was low, full of revulsion.. "What sort of tree is this?" He stopped there but meant to say more. Unfortunately, words seemed to be breaking on his tongue.

"That?" the hooded man grunted "That's a pine. Forget the tree. It's these damn vines you have to watch out for!" Losing a step, he slid a little closer to the knotted trunk. "Ever hear of a vampire rose?"

Belmorn shook his head. Now he could see the vines were reaching most of the way up the man's arm, barely inches away from his neck.

"It's a creeper vine. Predatory. Latches onto a tree and sends out these damned ropes under the leaves and snow. Anything touches one, it reacts like a flytrap," the man grunted as he was pulled forward a step. "And if you'd like a firsthand demonstration of how it feeds, by all means, continue to stand there and do nothing."

Belmorn's eyes flashed.

SNAP!

With one quick strike, the axe blade passed through the vine, sending the hooded man tumbling back on his ass.

Having lost their quarry, the vines began to shrivel back toward the old pine. Gripping the axe handle tighter, Belmorn fought off a shiver.

He couldn't help but imagine the sort of scars such a hideous embrace would leave behind. Lowering his eyes to the ground, he chose his next step with care.

On the ground, the stranger's hood had fallen to reveal a pale, weathered face. The man wore a pointed beard and hair that was unkempt and black with a fair share of silver. Without a word, he scrambled to his feet and began brushing snow from both legs and backside. With a scowl, he turned from Belmorn to regard the trees. Then he hurled a stick at the nearest crow-lined branch.

"Damned feathered shrews!"

The stick went wild, soaring just under the intended branch and through the trees beyond. After throwing a rather obscene hand gesture, the man composed himself. Then he spared a single word for his rescuer.

"Thanks."

Belmorn watched speechless, as the man in the hood stormed off. Though perplexed, he could suddenly feel the weight of the crow which would be his supper, tugging at his hand. Enough of this hooded stranger, Belmorn had troubles of his own. Besides, he had instructed his horse to leave if it heard trouble. If Magnus had done so, the road ahead had just gotten a hell of a lot longer.

He turned to leave the hooded man to his business, but something made him stop and look back. What he saw made one eyebrow stand up. Against all good sense, the hooded man was marching straight for the old oak tree that had nearly been his grave.

"What in the hell are you doing?" Belmorn blurted out.

"Exactly what I came here for," grumbled the hooded man, lifting his feet oddly as he moved. "I don't suppose you have an unlit torch on you by chance."

Belmorn raised an eyebrow. Said nothing.

Upon reaching the old oak, the hooded man carefully wrapped his fingers around the handle of something sticking out of the trunk. Then, with a single, firm tug, he pulled it free. It was a knife--long and thick, with a wicked curve to the blade. Belmorn hadn't noticed the thing before, but now it seemed the most important object in the glade. He watched intently as the now armed man rounded the tree, and the sinister knife passed from sight.

After that was when he heard them. Wet, squelching sounds. The insinuations of living things being cut.

"Finally!" The word hung heavy with relief. "Halfway round the world nine times and the answer was here. Right here, all along."

When the man appeared again, there was something new in his hand. Something small but apparently worth courting death for a second time to retrieve. Whatever it was, he secreted it away into an unseen pocket. The knife though... that, he held at the ready.

As the hooded man approached, Belmorn frowned behind his collar. The notion that he might be improperly paid for his efforts occurred. Stopping a few feet away, the hooded man's eyes narrowed into slits, as though he were taking in the look of his rescuer for the first time.

"You're still here," he said in an uninterested tone. "Fair warning... I've got no way to repay you for what you just did. And if you were thinking of robbing me... you should know that the others already took all the good stuff."

"You've got me wrong, friend. I'm no thief. The only thing I'm after tonight is supper," Belmorn held up the bird. "I'm on my way to Roon. And past it."

The other man said nothing. If his face wore an expression, it was obscured by the shadows of that midnight hood. There were numerous long, black feathers sticking out of his cloak--all at odd angles like the quills of some half-bald porcupine. Finally noticing this, the man began to pluck them out, one by one.

"There is nothing past Roon. Not anymore."

Belmorn's eyes widened, but he had no chance to respond.

"Have you ever eaten a timber crow before?" the other man asked.

"No." Belmorn shook his head.

"Better than starving outright, I suppose," the hooded man took a deep breath, rubbing the length of his arm that had been constricted. "Fair warning... the meat tastes like dead leaves and worm-asses, but if you can keep it down, boon for you."

"I'll... keep that in mind." Belmorn's eyes moved off the shabby bird carcass to sweep around the area. As far as he could tell, the hooded man was devoid of any resources, save for whatever might be stashed in the folds of his cloak. A man alone and effectively naked in the middle of a cold, dark forest.

"You say there were others? That you were robbed?"

"Robbed. Taunted. Left to die." The hooded man shrugged. "I believe that was the order. Must have been an hour ago. They found me just like you did, though there were less birds at that point. Bastards killed my horse, took all of my wares, and left me to feed the rose. They thought it was hilarious."

The story struck a chord in Belmorn. "I'm sorry." He frowned in distaste. For one brief moment, he considered bending his cardinal rule--the one about never investing in business outside of his own.

"Not your problem." The hooded man's tone was dismissive. "People are cold in these parts. Though I have to admit... the ones that left me to die didn't look half as nefarious as you, friend."

From behind his high collar Belmorn's head tilted back. He looked the man up and down--wondering where that curved dagger had gone to. Eventually, he let out a little sigh. Slowly, his eyes drifted back to the vine covered trunk--to the squirming pod that had once been a very large crow.

"We've got flowers back home," Belmorn swallowed hard. "Ours don't eat people."

"Most don't, as it happens." The hooded man stormed past, finding a spot of ground where the snow had been disturbed recently. "The vampire rose is unique. The thorns are hollow. It uses them like fangs. To feed. To drink."

The man spoke clinically. Matter-of-factly. As if he had not, barely five minutes ago, been caught in the clutches of the very monster he now described. As such, Belmorn couldn't help but wonder if the man's ordeal hadn't caused him to go a bit mad.

"This specimen is still young, which is why I chose it," the hooded man was rubbing his forearm. "Eventually, if it feeds enough, flowers will grow. Big ones. They do look a bit like roses from a few paces back. Give you one guess what color." Without waiting for an answer, the hooded man fixed a glare between the trees. "Ah..." He looked suddenly pleased. "I got you, you son of a bitch."

"You've got... ?" Belmorn looked at him in confusion. "Not the men who robbed you!"

"Who else?" The other man sounded preoccupied. "Mannis Morgrig--an ugly name for a rat who fancies himself a wolf. I knew this bit of wood fell under his pissing territory, but I've only recently returned to these woods. Before tonight, I'd be fortunate enough to know the man solely by his reputation." As he spoke the word, the hooded man seemed to dwell on the unsavory taste of it. "The rest of his merry band are just flies, but Morgrig, well... he's the shit they've gathered around."

With that came another flash and rumble. In the weird light of the clearing, Belmorn stood and stared as thoughts turned inside his skull.

"Snow lightning is a bad omen," said the hooded man with a flat, distant look. "Bad... but for who?" He said this strangely, as if speaking to a third party only he could see.

"You can't go after these men." Belmorn's voice was grim. He plunged forward a series of steps until the hooded man was within arm's reach. "Alone, you'll be at their mercy all over again."

"Alone..." The hooded man locked eyes with his savior. "Alone is my truest state. My only state." The man's voice had become low and deadly. He turned his back to Belmorn, inserting a hand into his cloak. "And before you go offering something both of us will regret... a bit of advice. When you wake up... please be on your way. Nothing here deserves one second more of your time. Just get back to the path. Roon is shit as destinations go, but it isn't far."

Confoundment twisted Belmorn's face. He started to say something, but the man in the hood moved fast. His arm thrusting forth a handful of what looked like very fine sand.

Muscles clenched, joints locked in their place, and the body of Rander Belmorn became rigid as stone--dropping most unflatteringly to the snow-dusted ground.

1-3

There was no light, only black--and black were the sounds.

Surrounded by a copious void, Belmorn became aware of a vague sensation--like something pulling at the back of his mind. The longer he concentrated, the more it summoned the notion of something unfinished. Something of the gravest importance. But before he could recall what the something was, a shimmering silhouette appeared before him.

The light made Belmorn wince in pain. This new something, hurt his eyes. Beholding it was not unlike staring too close to an open flame or directly into the sun. Though the silhouette was not well defined, he knew it to be the outline of a child. Belmorn felt himself reaching out, but the child--the boy, he knew somehow--was far beyond his reach.

Suddenly, he wanted to scream, to tell the boy not to go. But in this land of nothing, his voice was like everything else. It did not exist. Unable to stop it, the child-like shimmer did a fine impression of time and slipped away.

Time. The word formed in his mind. On this errand, time was his greatest foe.

When his true eyes opened again, for a split second, Belmorn assumed he was dead. High above, trees stretched like great featureless columns--all reaching for a single vanishing point. He tried to move his legs, his arms, even his tongue, but all felt as pliant as stone.

Deep inside, the man felt a gathering panic. He tried to think, to remember what had happened, but a dark shape darted past his vision. The first crow was soon followed by others, emboldened by their brother's tenacity. Belmorn gaped in impotent horror as more and more of his field of vision was invaded by wings and beaks and talons. Negative space bled into and asserted itself over the positive.

Utterly frantic, the stone man poured every ounce of will into a single action. To move his hand. To swat away the bird that had just landed on his leg. Gods--the size of it. Practically eagles, these timber crows. The bird's head twitched--rotating in short, mechanical increments. It hopped forward onto the man's crotch, twitching its head back the other way. Belmorn's effort to move was colossal, monumental--the hooded man's attack had done its work. Whatever magics dwelt within that strange dust had severed the connection between body and mind.

This is why, he thought, *you never bend the damned cardinal rule.*

Again the crow hopped--this time onto Belmorn's chest. Its eyes seemed to contain no malice or ill will of any kind, but something far worse... a black, bottomless hunger. The first strike shot a jolt of white pain, but this was merely exploratory. The second was worse.

When the bird pulled back, there was something in its beak. Something pink and wriggly like the tip of an earthworm. Belmorn watched, frozen in revulsion as the bird threw back its head, gulping down the tiny morsel that had once been part of his lower lip.

In his head, Belmorn bellowed--raged--battling the spell of the hooded man he had spared from a fate that now seemed deserved. But no matter how hard he fought, no fist would form from his lifeless fingers.

Something occurred.

Perhaps his initial assumption had been correct. Perhaps he really was dead, and this was simply what all men experienced after their time was up. A torture among tortures, unlike any recorded. For none who experienced it had the means of forging it into a warning. Trapped in a shell called self--forced to watch, whilst a pitiless world spun on.

Again, the crow's head flicked into a new angle. From hungry to curious. There were more of them now. Belmorn could see others on and around his useless limbs--each armed with a terrible beak and the unmistakable air of greed. Having sampled a bit of lip already, the boldest crow pointed its beak directly at the man's left eye socket.

Belmorn did the only thing he could do. He prepared himself. In his mind, he could see two faces--a dark-skinned woman with long black hair and a small boy that had his father's grey eyes. The emotions that swelled were powerful. Even there, lying in the snow, they warmed him. Exchanging fear for a profound sense of regret. And worse... of failure.

He could hear the woman's voice.

"Don't go," she said. "Don't you dare walk through that door."

Sudden movement flashed to the frantic blur of dark wings. The birds parted in his vision--screaming their dissonant, off-key chorus. Forgetting his state, Belmorn tried to crane his neck, but just as before, the man's body ignored his commands. And so he continued to stare in the only place he could. Watching snow and feathers as they drifted gently down.

Then he heard them--the repeating crunch, crunch, crunch of footsteps coming steadily closer. It was a familiar sound, and the longer Belmorn listened, the more certain he became. These steps were not human.

A long face appeared. One that terminated in a pair of enormous, black nostrils that gaped and fired clouds of hot steam. At the sight of his oldest friend, Belmorn practically burst.

"Magnus!" The word surprised the massive horse far less than the man lying in the snow. "Can't move. Some damned spell..." With this, one of his fingers gave a sudden twitch. "Wearing off... I think. Just don't go anywhere. Damn feathered shrews."

The adamandray snorted in agreement. Then he pawed at his friend's chest with a huge hairy hoof, stroking as gently as one might ever dare hope from an animal of such an impressive size.

In all, it was close to an hour before Belmorn was able to reach a full sitting position. And a few minutes more before he realized that he was not so far from a small, but healthy campfire. The sight of the thing was inexplicable, but he could hardly protest. And so, he allowed the flames to do their work, reveling in the warmth as it moved through his limbs, into his bones. Though his body was stiff, muscles were beginning to recall and slowly resume their purposes.

Both the snow and strange, out-of-place lightning had passed... and with them, the light of day. Despite his pragmatic nature, Belmorn had held out hope to spend this particular night in a bed. A real one, with neither stone nor root to prod and torment him into the small hours. Roon, the fabled city at World's Edge, was close now. He could feel it. But whatever else he was, Rander Belmorn was no fool. He had been on the road too long to risk travel by moonlight.

In the snowy glade, serenity had settled. The crows had all flown away, and aside from the gigantic horse, Belmorn was alone. He sat basking and listening to the fire's gentle pops, and for the moment, he was content.

Not for the first time, his tongue inspected the triangular gap in his lower lip. The pain had been sharp at first, but was worse now. The area felt hot. Dangerously so. As soon as possible, Belmorn knew he was going to have to sew the wound shut. He possessed both thread and needle but the thought of what he had to do was too much to face just yet.

And so he resolved, just for a while to brood on the hooded man, and what he might do if they ever crossed paths again.

He turned to see his axes had been propped against one of the numerous pines not ensnared by a carnivorous plant monster. The only crow he could see now was on the ground. It was the one he had split down the center. Its tattered feathers were flecked with dark red and a fresh frosting of snow. He noticed the bird no longer had legs. More alarming than that, it had been eviscerated.

As he realized these disturbing details, a uniquely pungent smell pulled his eyes downward. On the front of his coat was a most peculiar thing--a sort of macabre corsage fastened in place by a long pin. Small yellow flowers and pale twigs wrapped around what could only be his supper's missing legs and intestines. The talons, whether by reflex or design, were now curled into tiny fists. With the sweet musk of decay in his nostrils, Belmorn tore the talisman from his chest and flung it away.

"Rinh!" he spat, checking himself for further tokens of the hooded man's appreciation. "If I ever see that damned wizard again... so help me."

Belmorn needed to stand--to shake off the sensation which now crept and crawled up his spine. He cursed himself a fool for ever feeling even the slightest shred of compassion for the man.

Stiffly, he walked over to collect his strewn belongings. He returned the axes to their homes beneath his bearskin cloak. Aside from the missing legs, the body of the dead crow appeared untouched.

The eyes of the blackfoot narrowed as he wondered again about those legs. What part they played in the hooded man's spells? For a second, Belmorn thought better of cooking the bird. But hunger was no beast to be reasoned with. And so, with a frown, he grabbed the bird and with stiff fingers, started plucking.

Another hour had passed--or near enough to make no difference.

Belmorn was reclining against a tree with one arm behind his head. With the crow meat now in his stomach, he could say with certainty that the hooded man's warning had indeed been a fair one. That said, it had also been the best meal Belmorn had eaten in almost two weeks. He glanced over at his companion. The horse that had saved his life.

The head of the massive adamandray drooped close to the ground. Its teeth clicking and nibbling at what looked like more wild leek greens. Seeing this, Belmorn's brow softened.

"No more forks in the road, Old Man." Belmorn hunkered down a bit more, buttoned up his prodigious collar and closed his eyes. In his mind appeared the familiar image of a dark-haired woman who was his wife. The apparition was so potent, so indescribably beautiful, seeing it hurt his heart.

Then he saw her expression. The anguish in her eyes. The accusation.

No--this was not the time for that. Not when he was so close. Not when a barkeep in Fengaal, the constable of Staghardt and nearly half dozen others, had all given the same answer to his only question. One word, spoken with tight, trembling lips.

"Jayce."

The thought brought an unbidden throb of heat to his mouth. The pain was sharp and his tongue shot out stupidly, making it worse. He had tried to keep the wound clean, but the crow meat had been greasy stuff. Removing a glove, Belmorn cupped a handful of snow until it began to melt, proceeding to wet the blood-crusted gap in his lower lip.

The act was excruciating. Forcing his trembling hand to its work, the man cried out. The sound was too loud, but there was nothing for it. The lower half of his skull had become a pounding drum--almost too brutal to bear.

Tears in his eyes, Belmorn looked up to see the horse was showing signs of distress. Magnus' hooves came stomping down as his massive head whipped from side to side.

"Sorry, Old Man--" He winced, tasting blood. "Didn't mean to wake..." His voice trailed off as he realized that the horse's stress was not fueled by his outburst.

Out there, between the trees and in a dozen pairs... Eyes all looked his way. His mind raced to the crows, but these were different. Larger. Brighter. Each shone in the dark like some earthbound star.

The hand of the blackfoot flew back for an axe but a blinding impact stopped him. He saw a flash. Pain the color of starlight.

It was an accident, he managed as a coherent thought. Magnus had turned his head in surprise. And when near one hundred and fifty pounds of horse skull connects with a freshly cleaved lip, the result is undeniable. The man careened backwards--toppling and crashing into unconsciousness.

1-4

The sun filtered down through the canopy in long, unbroken rays. Covered in snow, the woods were almost too pristine to be real. The world shimmered like some misplaced childhood dream. Belmorn had trouble believing his current surroundings could be part of the same world as one containing man eating crows, vampiric plants, and an army of flaming eyes.

Pain throbbed where the crow had begun to eat him, but this was far from the man's chief worry. His tongue prodded gently, inspecting the thread which now connected the halves of his bottom lip. The taste was sharp. He touched the area and, to his horror, withdrew a vile green paste on his finger. Belmorn spat, looking in revulsion at the mossy phlegm-wad that hit the ground.

The stitches appeared remarkably well done. At its zenith, the pain had been crashes of lightning behind his brain. But now, the sensation had been reduced to a dull, rhythmic thrum that pulsed in time with his heart.

Aside from the lingering taste, Belmorn knew he was doing better than he had any right to be. The problem that twisted his gut was the fact he had absolutely no idea who had sewn his face back together.

Had the spirit of his Black River smiled down from so far away? Or had this been the work of the man in the hood--returned perhaps with a sudden stroke of conscience? Though it pained him to admit it, Belmorn had no way of knowing, so he resolved to focus on what really mattered.

Time--his true adversary. It was still slipping away.

The path stretched in a winding white line, cleaving the forest, showing him the way. With more than the usual effort, the blackfoot climbed up into his saddle and rode on. Feathered hooves tramped ground laden by leaf and snow. The adamandray's head hung low. Magnus had looked remorseful all morning, like someone who had just smashed his already injured best friend in the face.

Far from oblivious, Belmorn smiled. He stroked his friend's neck. "It's alright," he said. "I'm alright. Not sure why, but I feel okay. You really saved me back there. But if you had taken any longer, there might not have been more than a dirty skeleton for you to rescue. I really did not like those birds."

Magnus snorted. Shaking his head, he arched his back, jutting up the saddle uncomfortably for a moment.

"Not that I'm complaining." said Belmorn with a sudden lilt to his voice. "And believe me, I've learned my lesson. No more breaking the cardinal rule. To hell with these northerners. Our business is all that matters." He sighed with frustration. "Whoever that damned wizard was, he said Roon wasn't far, and that is the news we needed."

The city of Roon represented more than an opportunity to purchase life sustaining wares. Much more. Roon was one of the last remaining steps on his journey. Nineteen weeks of riding and seeking, of hunger and saddle sores and exquisite heartache had all added up to a single sum. The proverbial 'X' which marked the spot. The blackfoot's coveted treasure was close now.

Jayce.

After discovering the name, Belmorn proceeded to wave it like a banner at every city and town and for every stranger in between. From what he had learned, the village was the definition of remote. Allegedly it was situated across the High Veld--in the shadow of Mount Einder. The mountain's scant arrangement of peaks was said to approximate the silhouette of a castle. What made Jayce so difficult to find was how completely it was ignored by modern cartographers. A curious thing. In the last nineteen weeks, every map Belmorn had laid eyes on made no mention of any settlements past Roon.

All but one.

It had been expensive, that map, but possibly, hopefully, worth every damn penny.

Belmorn's heart tripped.

There was light ahead--finally an end to the forest road he had been following for so long. Whether the stallion had entered a canter of his own volition or by some cue from its rider, Belmorn could not say, but with a boisterous shout he did intend, he urged Magnus into a full gallop.

A sudden widening of the road ended at something Belmorn had not expected. Halfway between defensive wall and sculpture Roon's outer wall was a sight to behold. Squinting at the white stone as if it were giving off light, Belmorn tilted his head. His gaze moved up and up, trying to locate where it all ended, but the top of the wall was lost amidst the overgrown branches of trees.

The horse whinnied with an excited head shake.

"Yeah," was all Belmorn could muster. His eyes devoured the series of oversized figures which stood shoulder to shoulder, in a rigid line that wrapped around the wall in both directions. As he approached, Belmorn could see that every stone man held an enormous shield and was probably over twenty feet tall.

"The Roonik Guard." He spoke with reverence, having heard the term many times in the preceding weeks.

The road led to the only break in the stone figures that he could see. In place of a door, there was a single portcullis--a sliding gate made of criss-crossing metal bars. Belmorn had seen the like before--usually at the far end of a castle's drawbridge, but such things were antiquated. From another, older age... just like Roon itself.

Belmorn had heard it called the last of the great shield cities; now he had an idea of what that meant.

Unlike his ultimate destination, Roon had been depicted prominently on every map. The place served as a gateway to the vast northern expanse which men called the Veld. Raised in the waning years of the last millennium, before the green-haired raiders crossed an ocean of ice in their dog-faced ships--in a time when the legendary Venomancers of Zanhaziib yet held sway over their now-lost domain.

If one believed such things.

Belmorn pulled Magnus to a halt, dismounted, and walked closer to the gate. The pattern of the bars was unique. Not vertical and horizontal but crossed in stark angles like an iron latticework. He placed a gloved hand upon the surface, then pulled it away to inspect the red flakes.

"Definitely iron." He hadn't meant to say the words aloud. His speech elicited an unexpected snort. A man stood just inside the gate, a guard, who was trying his best to look as if he had not been caught asleep at his post.

"You there... Highwayman." The man's accent was strange, similar to the only other north man he had met. The one he should have left to the crows. "Never seen you before."

Slowly, Belmorn unfastened the buttons holding up his collar.

The guard stepped forward. That was when Belmorn could see that the man was gripping a black powder rifle.

"True," said Belmorn in the most pleasant tone he could muster. "I have never been here before. I am... looking for something."

"That so?" the guard scoffed, raising an untrusting brow. "And what might you be hoping to find?"

Though loathe to spill his story to this lone sentry, Belmorn knew that any hesitation on his part would come across as suspicious--even deceitful.

"Only rest and supplies," he said calmly, truthfully. "And if I can find one... a guide."

"A guide to where?" The guard snorted again. "Hate to disappoint you, friend, but past Roon, there's nothing worth finding. The road ends here."

Belmorn lowered his head and grinned a knowing grin. "Unfortunately for me, it goes a bit farther on, I'm afraid. I'm headed for a small mining village called Jayce. Do you know it?"

Hearing the name caused a subtle shudder in the guard. Attempting to recompose, he nodded. "I do. But as I said, it's not worth finding. Silver stopped flowing near ten years back."

Belmorn flashed a scornful glare. "Didn't come all this way for silver."

The guard coughed up a laugh. "Nothing else in Jayce--never was. Just a dead mine, an empty mountain and a town full of ghosts. Take my word on this, friend... you came all this way for nothing. Even if there were treasure left in those veins, you'll find no one here mad enough to show you the way. It's too far into the Veld. Past the moat, almost to the mountain. And that road, well... it belongs to her now."

Belmorn raised an eyebrow. His face hurt and was losing his

patience. "Her who?"

The guard pushed his face closer to the bars. Close enough so that Belmorn could see the bloodshot white of his eyes. "Why, the Veld has a witch. Slithered into these parts about the same time the silver stopped flowing." The guard studied Belmorn's face. "I promise you this, friend... run afoul of that one and you'll spend every night of the rest of your miserable life begging and pleading for one thing and one thing alone..." Yellow teeth flashed in a crooked grin. "Forget what you're after, friend... death will be your new treasure, and she'll make you beg for it. Problem with witches... They tend to keep their victims alive for as long as possible."

Belmorn's jaw tightened. From the proximity, he couldn't help but smell the guard's breath. Sweet and revolting like maggoty beef. From a pocket, he produced something small and circular--roughly the color of gold. Holding the coin between thumb and forefinger, he pushed it forward enough so the guard would reach for it, and then pulled back.

"Let me in," Belmorn said firmly, quietly. "I'll cause no trouble and will be gone by morning." He looked past the guard, tried to glean something of the city itself.

The guard licked his lips, then managed to compose himself. Straightening his back, the man scowled through the bars. "Fine. I need a name and where you come from."

"Rander Belmorn of Grael."

"Grael?" the word sounded misshapen on the guard's northern tongue. "Never heard of it."

The blackfoot shrugged. "Well, I've never seen a female diplocaulus. Doesn't mean the males have taken to laying the eggs." He held the coin higher so it gleamed in the light.

The guard looked confused, but his bloodshot eyes followed the trajectory of the coin. "Gone by morning?"

Belmorn gave a slow nod.

After another moment's consideration, the guard pushed a hand through the bars. The palm of which was promptly filled with a golden coin. After biting the thing, the man seemed satisfied, then went right back to annoyed. Gripping the spoke of what looked like a large wagon wheel, the guard pulled, but this only resulted in a high metallic squeal. Looking emasculated, the guard tried again, harder this time, forcing unseen machinery to wine back to life. Slowly and with visible effort, the wheel was turned on its axis, slowly raising the latticed portcullis with each rotation.

When able, Belmorn led his horse by the reins beneath the gate. At the last second, he looked up to see the many angled points of the portcullis and urged Magnus on a little faster.

"A place this big must have an apothecary," he asked without asking.

The guard grunted, scratching behind an ear. "Kuhn's," he was out of breath. "But... if I were you, I wouldn't bother. Not tonight."

Belmorn stopped. "Why not?"

"Because by this hour Graden Kuhn will be far too deep in his cups to be of any use. For a peddler of wellness, the man is as cordial as a viper when drunk." The guard frowned. "Better to try in the morning when he's only hungover. Shop won't be open but if you bang hard enough on the door you may get lucky. As for tonight, find The Folly."

Belmorn gave a look of confusion, much to the guard's amusement.

"Roon's still got two working taverns, but that's the one you want. Ask for Ottma. She'll set you up with a bit of food. Maybe a bed if she's in the mood." Again the guard bit down on the golden coin. "Head down this main road here. It widens about a quarter mile down into a square. By this hour, it will be the only place with the lights still on."

Again, Belmorn felt his lip throb. After sparing a semi-grateful nod for the guard, he moved away from the gate and into the last of the great shield cities.

PART TWO
THE ALCHEMIST

2-1

It was always strange, seeing the dust do its work.

The body of the stranger first became rigid, and then it toppled--landing hard on the snowy ground with a dull thud.

The act had been impulsive, and in truth, Tenebrus Kro didn't feel great about it. After all, the stranger had appeared out of thin air--first rescuing him from the crows, then the vampire rose, and then promptly demanding nothing in return. Nothing but some greasy crow flesh for an empty belly.

The alchemist regarded the green glass bottle and the fine powder it held. For a fleeting moment, Kro could picture a remote island. The home of a strange, veiled woman who had shown him firsthand what the stuff did to a body.

Gorgon dust was among the rarest of ingredients he had ever come across. Truly an effective remedy--both for time-wasting conflicts and banal, unhelpful conversations. All who breathed it became temporarily incapacitated but suffered no lasting harm.

The man on the ground would be fine in about an hour. Kro knew that. Still... perhaps he had been too hasty--dusting the tall stranger who had just saved his life.

No. It's fine. He'll be fine, Kro thought, firmly. Stay focused on one thing at a time. Forget the last four hours; they were worth it. You got what you came for.

He reached into his cloak, stopping just over a hidden pocket.

Through the fabric, he could feel tiny objects inside--the spoils which he had so carefully, surgically removed from the damnable plant that had held him prisoner for so many hours. Like tiny disembodied hearts, they pulsed in the perfect dark of his pocket--barely alive, not quite ready to die.

Kro had crossed an ocean before realizing that what he needed most grew just outside his own front door. And after making the long trek home, the last ingredient was finally his. Now that he possessed all of the tools, only one thing remained. The very task he had set his mind to so many years ago.

The Goddamned witch had to die.

Above, amongst the falling snow, a dissonant choir was gathering again. He had forgotten about the damn birds. Soon enough, their hideous racket would be at its previous volume.

Kro sneered at the vine of the vampire rose. The severed tendril that had gripped him for so many hours was slowly shriveling--retracting. It coiled into small loops as it shrank closer to the old oak which served as its host. He could still feel the thing creeping up his arm, closer and closer to his throat.

A conspicuous green pod caught his eye, secured to the tree by a growing number of tendril-vines. As he watched the thing, Kro saw it pulse. Just once, like an unborn babe kicking at the inside of its mother's belly. Even now the timber crow was alive as hollow thorns drained what remained of its life's blood. A pitiable fate to be sure. One which Kro had cheated only by the intervention of a stranger.

The man who had just been turned to stone for his troubles.

With a sigh, Kro pressed his thumb and forefinger into his temple and rubbed. He knew he couldn't leave the stranger as he lay. Not even he had grown that callused. The effects of the gorgon dust weren't permanent, but that fact hardly mattered to the hungry murder of timber crows circling overhead.

"Damn it." He unleashed a defeated sigh.

Kro gripped tighter the knife in his hand. Then he stalked over to a crow which lay in a bloody mess on the forest floor. It had been cleaved, probably by one of the stranger's axes. Kro's first cut severed the bird's legs; the second opened its belly. He proceeded to extract every inch of ropy pink intestines. He cut again, wincing at the sharp, fecal smell. Working as fast as he could, he wrapped the intestines around the severed legs, securing them in place with a knot.

After a moment's inspection, Kro placed the grisly thing upon the stranger's chest. He thrust the cleaner of his hands into his cloak. Careful fingers explored pockets before emerging with a steel pin. That was when he froze.

"Wolves..." His mind raced. Shifting between justification and objection. "No. Don't be thick. There haven't been wolves--actual wolves--in these woods since..."

He stopped, feeling a sudden wave of panic. His girls. What would they say if they knew? If they could see him right now? His hand red with guilt and shame. Even now he could see them. The cheeks of his youngest were rosy--chapped as ever by the unkind northern winds. But when the lips of the girl parted, her voice was a biting caw.

The sound grated against the man's bones, harshly ripping him back to reality.

Throwing anxious looks into the dark spaces between the trees, Kro sighed. With an audible huff, he stormed toward the tree line and began rifling through the brush there. The so-called herb-of-grace wasn't especially rare in these parts, but summer was two weeks gone. As such, it was almost fifteen minutes before he found one that still possessed open blooms. The bright yellow flowers possessed their own unique aroma. Taking care not to let the blossoms touch his skin, the alchemist plucked the flowers, stem and all. After quickly wrapping these with the rest of his makeshift talisman, he placed the tiny bundle upon the chest of his unconscious savior, fastening it in place with a pin.

"There." He frowned, only sparing a partial glance for the man. "Waste of time though. There aren't any damn wolves, but that should keep the crows away."

He felt like a villain. Why had he reacted so badly? Throwing the dust without cause or consideration? The stranger had been warning him of the obvious. To track down Morgrig by himself would indeed be a very bad idea. The irony was plain. For the coming work, Kro was going to need as many hands as possible. And if they could wield axes, those hands might prove especially useful. Invaluable even.

Part of Kro wanted to deliver a swift kick to his own be-cloaked ass. He looked down at the stranger's face, at the copper hue of his skin.

What sort of business might call a black riverman here to this forsaken edge of the world? He wondered, already knowing the answer. The sort that is not easily put aside.

"I told you..." The alchemist's voice was low--solemn. "People this far north are a cold lot. Cold as the wind. Whatever you're seeking in

Roon... I hope you find it."

2-2

Few men had traveled farther, searched deeper or tracked down as many hidden quarries as Tenebrus Kro. He was always a seeker of hidden things and rare ingredients, but for the last seven years he had taken this mission abroad. Crossing oceans and lands untold--all to answer a single, brain-cracking riddle.

How do you kill a witch?

As far as Kro was concerned, it was the last question, the only question. And for seven long years it seemed to him the only endeavor worthy of his attention. Tonight however, all of that changed. The moment he made the acquaintance of a man called Mannis Morgrig.

Kro had been ensnared by the vampire rose for the better part of an hour when he first heard the sound. Sliding through the perfect silence of the woods at dusk, it was a long, bone chilling howl. The sound was so startling, it nearly caused Kro to lose the footing he was fighting so hard to keep.

"Over here!" a voice shouted through the trees. "This way. Someone's there!"

At first, the voices were sweet music. After all, Kro had little hope of being rescued from his predicament. The hour was late and even the closest road hadn't been well travelled in years. On top of all that, no one was searching. Not for him.

Even as he'd struggled and pulled and battled at the end of the thorny tether, about all Kro dared hope for was a quick death. The vampire rose had him, and it was not letting go. With every twist and tug, the vine crept a little more up his arm.

Again came the howl. Longer and louder than before. And this time, it brought more than cold dread for the man's stomach. This time, it brought crows. Dozens at first, then more. All of them, greedily cawing and croaking and filling the air and branches above.

Kro swore into the cacophonous night. Why the hell hadn't he brought a torch? He possessed the materials. A bit of rag, a drop of oil... they were in his saddle bags and his horse wasn't far. Kro had secured the animal to a tree--his standard practice when foraging for things liable to bite back. He could have been there and back with the materials within half an hour... maybe less. He was in a forest; there were sticks everywhere. Why the hell hadn't he listened to his gut instead of rushing in like some brainless novice?

"Must be the rider," came another voice, slightly more jovial than the first. "We'll have to thank him for all these fine gifts."

A familiar whinny was quickly drowned out by cruel sounding laughter. Every ounce of hope that had risen in the rose's victim plummeted. Worst of all, his horse was screaming. Hearing that, Kro's heart gave a painful throb.

He really liked that horse.

"Just through there!"

To the west, Kro could make out movement through the trees. A few seconds later, a man with wide eyes stumbled into the glade. When he saw Kro, he thrust out a finger.

"Just like I said, Mannis! If that's not the rider, I'll eat my boots."

A group of no less than fifteen men poured out of the same entry point into the glade. One, he noticed, held a blowing horn not far from his lips. They were, each clad in a random assortment of leather and armored plates--the sort worn by Roon's guard. Tarnished silver but incomplete--a gauntlet here, a spaulder or a helmet there. Most wore a smear of red paint--across the nose, under an eye.

Bizarrely, one was wearing a plague mask--the sort used by doctors. The thing was a filthy shade of pale. That man was holding two swords like long butcher knives. He had ropes of long black hair and stared directly at the alchemist.

Kro, feeling a crawling like spiders up his spine, suppressed a shiver.

The final pair of brigands crashed in after the rest. Each holding a short length of rope attached to a chestnut mare with a fully white face that looked as if it had been painted. The animal fought for all it was worth--rearing, bucking, lashing out with its front hooves. Kro recognized the wildness in its eyes as one of the more primal breeds of fear.

"Let her go!" Kro fired the demand. His voice was raw with emotion.

The crowd stopped what they were doing and turned to look--all of them blinking dumbly. After a few long seconds, it became obvious that someone from the back was pushing their way through.

"Oye! You hear that boys?" This new voice was deeply unpalatable to Kro's ears. Equal parts gravel and slime with a low caste, country accent. "The man wants his filly back. P'raps we should offer him a bite, aye?"

The resulting laughter hit Kro like a wave of pure, sadistic glee. He watched as the brigands parted to reveal a bearded man with long red hair pulled back into a horsetail; both sides of his head were shaved. Kro had seen men wearing that style years ago in the west, amidst the remote hinterland townships beyond the Karaggash Ridge. The man was vast, with hands large enough to strangle a bear. His motley, silver-white ensemble was more complete than the rest. Both legs sported grieves, while his right shoulder carried an ornate, wolf-faced pauldron. The chest plate he wore did cover most of the man's chest but was open in the center. Inexplicably, the metal flared outward in dangerous edges. To Kro's eyes the piece looked as if it had been ripped open by unthinkable claws.

"I'm afraid I'm going to have to agree with the lads on this." Red beard looked directly at Kro, scarred lips twisting into a lopsided grin. "Besides, it's not like you're in a position to be making demands, now are ya?"

Kro frowned, seething beneath his hood.

"Either way," shrugged the big man. "It's not as if a company of wolves is likely to relinquish its supper, now is it?" As the crowd agreed, their leader's grin widened.

"Wolves?" Hissed the alchemist through clenched teeth, again yanking at the unyielding vine. "Wolves?"

Why hadn't he just gone back for that damned torch? He would be halfway to the moat by now.

"Why yes, wolves! Of course!" said Red Beard with an exaggerated flourish. "What's the matter? Did the howls not give it away?"

Once more, the men erupted in laughter.

"I see no wolves here," Kro sneered. "Just some very lost rats." Against all good sense, a mad smile formed on the alchemist's lips. "Filthy ones, by the smell."

Red Beard stopped--folded his arms. Suddenly, he looked the way one does when recalling the punchline to a filthy joke in church.

"The tongues of damned men are looser than their bowels on hangin' day.' My mum said that once. Right to my old dad. Right before the hangman sent him kicking."

"Hmph," grunted Kro, pulling still tighter on the vine. "Charming."

Red Beard raised an eyebrow--adopting an expression that was difficult to read. "We had our moments. But... if I were in your position..." He stepped slowly, carefully judging the distance between the predatory plant and himself. "I would consider my next move very carefully, friend. From my vantage, it looks like you've stepped in something."

Again, laughter roared from the crowd. The sound was so oppressive, Kro could practically feel the force of it pressing against his skin.

"Never saw the point of flowers," Red Beard was circling the old oak that supported the tangled mass of hungry vines. He shrugged. "But the vampire rose gots my respect. Lethal as any wolf, that one. And what she catches, she holds tight... at least 'till she's had her fill."

Just then, came a combination of sounds that drew all eyes back to the horse. It was on the ground, writhing on one side. Bellowing not from fear but agony. Kro twisted to see the men who had been leading it along were cursing in frustration. Then, one of them hauled off and kicked the animal right in the neck.

The eyes of the alchemist lit up with rage. He pulled furiously at his bonds--desperate to fire off the steaming tirade of profanity which was now lodged firmly in his craw. But no words came. Only a bellow of such primal intensity, hunters a mile away might have thought it the anguished wail of some unlucky beast caught in a snare.

Which is exactly what it was.

"Kill me." Kro knew damn well these men could offer him little better. And what was a knife in the back compared to what waited for him at the end of this damned rope? "You hear me, you filthy parasite?"

"Kill ya?" said Red Beard, feigning offense. "After you provided us with such a feast?"

In answer, the crowd cheered, sounding almost lustful. Ravenous maybe. The two men holding the horse ropes forced the animal's head to the ground and began to laugh. Kro shouted unintelligibly and pulled harder than ever. Even as the green ropes bit into his skin he could not feel them. Inside the alchemist raged a fierce conflagration-- as out of control as it was impotent.

"I know who you are, Red Wolf. Word of your plague has reached as far as Fengaal. They say Mannis Morgig and his rats never leave survivors."

The look on the Morgig's face was a serious one, but it did little to faze the alchemist.

"So," Kro had adopted a smug expression. "Why don't we get on with it, you putrid sack of dog shit! Pay me the same price for my horse as if you had found me riding it."

Clearly sobered, Morgrig said nothing. For almost a full minute he simply continued his trek around the old oak.

"Fengaal you say?" The large man spoke quietly, though there were no other sounds to pose a challenge. "That's pretty damn far."

Gone was the low country accent. The man sounded almost like an entirely different person. Having taken great care with his footfalls, Morgrig faced the hooded man's back.

"Even so close to the World's Edge, men have the ambition to survive. Sometimes that means building something. A city, an army-- the thing itself is immaterial. But without the right reputation, men will not follow, and then the thing will fail. Crumble into rubble and dust. Out here most of all, reputation is everything."

Morgrig leaned in close. His words came softly. Like insidious whispering worms.

"Call me filthy again," said the Red Wolf. "Do it until you're blue-- won't matter. Won't work. Believe it or not, friend, I am a fair bit smarter than I look." Kro couldn't see the man's face, but he could tell Morgrig was enjoying the music of his own words. "The thing is, killing you straight out would be a mercy. And, speaking as a filthy parasite, I'm afraid such things just aren't good for business. I'm sure you understand."

A thin sound appeared. That of a blade sliding from its sheath.

"But since I'm not entirely devoid of compassion, I'm going to give you something a whole lot better than mercy. Something rare enough in these troubling times."

"That so," Kro spat.

"Yes," Morgrig's whispering had turned to slime. "I'm gonna give you a sporting chance."

Bright steel flashed beside Kro's face.

The knife was thrown hard and true. It spun through the air, hitting the trunk with a dull wooden sound. And there it remained, roughly a foot below the mass of killer vines.

Still struggling, still doomed, Kro couldn't have been more than ten feet from the old oak. And though he willed them not to, his eyes drifted from the knife, up to the writhing knot of thorny vines.

Keeping himself away had been a constant struggle--a marathon-like test of strength and endurance. As time passed, the vine had increased its leverage by wrapping around itself. Resisting the constant pull had taken every shred of the alchemist's energies. But now, as exhaustion loomed, he shifted his focus back to Morgrig's knife. The first few inches of the blade had been pushed into the wood. The rest looked sharp. Very sharp.

"Whatever slack you give, that vine is going to use against you," Morgrig spoke very seriously, in genuine warning. "Within seconds, it will loop around your neck--attempt to cut off your air. Then you'll feel them. A thousand thirsty needles, entering your arms, your chest, across your neck... even in your eyes."

Kro felt a hand on his shoulder,

"So what do you think, Rose Man?" More whispered words. "Think you can get to that knife? Maybe cut yourself free before that happens?" Morgrig's voice became playful "Or I could always help things along. Maybe, give a little push."

A broad hand slapped Kro on the back, almost causing his footing to slip. The others, of course, found this hilarious. Kro wrenched his neck around, wanting in that instant, to tear a chunk out of Mannis Morgrig.

The bandit leader simply stood up straight. "Well then. Looks like maybe you've got some fight left after all." These words were the last spoken in the secretive, refined voice. What came next was shouted in the heavy accent Kro had first heard the man use. "Come on, boys. We're done here. This one's got a full night of screaming planned. Best we leave him to it."

The brigands parted, allowing their leader to pass between them. Before disappearing through the crowd, Morgrig stopped to regard the mewling, struggling mare.

"Oye, Voss!" Morgrig shouted, sounding suddenly furious. "What'd you do? Just look at that leg. Damn thing's broken!"

The man looked up, guiltily. He was dressed differently than the rest. Sporting a long jacket that billowed like a cloak--black with silver trim and a badly misshapen collar.

"S--Sorry Mannis! Really!" stammered the man called Voss. "We didn't see the rock. The thing was fighting and it came right down on it. The foot slipped and--"

The sputtering was cut short as the bandit leader raised a hand. "Shut!"

The single word said all that was needed. The tone of it was as sharp as the dagger he had thrown.

"Stop your whining. Get those bags off before the damned thing destroys whatever's inside--hear me?" Morgrig's voice was iron wrapped in velvet. The men wasted no time, hurriedly fumbling with buckles and straps. When the bags were off the animal's back, Kro could see that Morgrig was still not pleased.

"Slagter," he barked. "If you will..."

The man in the plague mask nodded. He moved swiftly, almost without a sound, lifting one of his ugly cleaver-swords high into the air.

When the horse screamed, Kro felt the sound in his bones--as if all the marrow inside had turned to ice.

"Better get going. Voss, Dirk," barked Morgrig. "It's you two who'll be dragging it back... and ya better not be late." Morgrig opened a pocket watch then snapped it shut again. "Dinner's gonna be a spectacle tonight."

The two men who had been wrestling Kro's mare each seized a leg. Around them the other bandits filed past--back through the same gap in the trees from which they had come. And like a shepherd tending an especially ugly flock, their leader was the last to go.

Wearing a look of extreme weariness, Mannis Morgrig turned to the alchemist. "You see what I have to deal with?" he sighed, pinching the bridge of his nose. "Sorry you had to see that, but you had to know. Up here, there's no one to buy a horse for a hundred miles. Might as well enjoy the spoils, yeah?"

Kro stared back, seething, hating, willing destruction with his every cell.

Just then, a bright flash of white light lit the heavens. For a few seconds, neither man said a word. Both stood firm--an invisible line of malice between them. The thunder rolled in a few seconds later. It was soft at first--distant.

The alchemist said nothing. He only pulled at his bonds and glared.

For a moment, something in Morgrig seemed to shift. Maybe even, to give. "Snow lightning," said the brigand. "Bad omen in these north woods." His voice was flat. "But bad for who I wonder?" Morgrig had grinned then, displaying rows of yellowed teeth.

Narrow with disdain, Kro's eyes flicked to the dagger. It was still many feet away, still embedded in the trunk of the old oak. He wanted nothing more than to bury it in the chest of this man.

This despicable, red-bearded leader of rats.

There were more memories than this and each burned like an open flame. No matter how the alchemist willed them away, they would not leave his side. As he followed the trail through the snowy wood, Tenebrus Kro made a decision. If he could not stop the bombardment of memories, then he would burn them for fuel.

"Just look at that leg. Damn thing's broken!" The voice of Mannis Morgrig was almost as infuriating in echo form as it had been in person. "Dinner's gonna be a spectacle tonight."

Again and again, Kro could hear the parting scream of his horse as the masked man's cleaver-sword opened its throat. The mare had been with him for almost two years--ever since purchasing her off that one-armed trader in distant Eos. All reddish chestnut but for a white painted face, Cinnabar had been a good horse, but she had also been Kro's friend.

His very last in all the world.

2-3

Out of his robes, the alchemist produced the dagger he had pulled
from an old tree.

Morgrig's gift.

The blade was curved--nine or ten inches long with a fine handle
wrapped in leather. Kro turned it over in the fading light, musing on
just how close he had been to becoming plant food. What Morgrig had
presented as a sporting chance Kro knew for what it was. One last kick
to the ribs from a sadistic bully. Both men knew there would have
been no way to reach the dagger in time. Not before the damned rose
slid its coils around his neck for the final goodnight.

And yet...

Kro tested the edge with his thumb, stopping at the first hint of
pain. It seemed a fine little weapon--one he could imagine few wasting
on a cruel joke. And yet, here it was. His fingers tightened around the
handle as a wicked sneer curved his lip.

The alchemist knew he had to return to what he had been doing
before a single, stupid misstep had caused his night to go so horribly
awry. He still had the oil and now, after all he had suffered through...
he had the seeds. Nothing in the world mattered more than his true
quest. And now, finally, the answer to that brain cracking riddle was
in his hands. After so long he was so damned close.

For seven years he had searched, scoured, tracked, experimented.
Surely, he had earned this one tangent. The right to reclaim his stolen

property. And maybe, to bring a little devastation to the filthy vermin who did the stealing.

The question was not if he could find Morgrig's camp. Judging by the state of the trail, the men moved with all the stealth of drunken mammoths. But beyond a nebulous need to make them pay, Kro had no idea what he was going to do when he got there. One man against at least fifteen bandits, cutthroats and brigands--any one of which was more than his physical match.

As he trudged through the snow on a path toward probable self-destruction, the alchemist frowned. Kro needed a plan and he needed one now. It was time to take stock.

The unseen pockets of his cloak held things which the alchemist deemed most irreplaceable. A few seeds, a vial of strange, dark oil-- these occupied the spot over his heart. Another pocket held a pair of goggles and two small bottles. The green one held what remained of the Gorgon dust. With some help, he had harvested the stuff on that abandoned spec of an island off Hellas from a species of lizard with very special eyes. For some yet-unknown reason, upon death the animal's eyes calcified and could be ground into a fine powder. A powder with incredible properties. Truly, gorgon dust was potent stuff but he did not have enough to petrify an entire camp.

The interior of the second bottle was covered with what looked like soot. Inside were three objects, all coal black. The first was crooked, segmented, roughly two inches long; the others were small like pebbles. As Kro turned the bottle, the bone shifted to create a dull tink against the glass. Once, it had been the smallest finger of a hand from a child whose name he had never learned. Kro had come to think of him as the kindling boy.

It was easier that way.

All accounts agreed that the mother and infant sibling had perished in the infamous blaze. They had been buried with low spirits and high emotions on a small hill, far from their village.

What was left of him who the villager's claimed had invoked the wrath of their harvest God was an anathema--a reminder of what can happen when worship is allowed to wane. The father had acted quickly and in secret. Wrapping what was left of his son in a bit of burlap, then leaving the remains on an oceanside cliff, beneath a pile of stones. A place where the boy could surely do no more harm to his people.

Spontaneous combustion had fascinated Kro for years, and he wasn't going to miss a chance to study a body firsthand. Though it had taken many days, he located that shallow, clifftop grave--and with no discernable guilt, the alchemist had exhumed what was left of the boy who had turned three quarters of his own family into piles of smoldering ash. Three fingers, part of a rib, and some teeth were all the burlap held.

The bones, he'd found, were shockingly abnormal--nearly hollow like those of a bird. Along the marrow cavity, inside pockets too small for the naked eye to see, Kro had discovered a reflective substance, like crystalized tar that proved to be as volatile as it was impossible to extract.

Kro did not believe in harvest gods. The kindling boy, by some accident of birth, had simply been born wrong--not a boy at all but a living powder keg. One equipped with an invisible fuse that time had quietly run all the way down.

The alchemist stood in the snow, just remembering, transfixed by the small, ashy bone. It was easier to think of things as components-- ingredients. How callously he had pulled the remains from where they had been laid to rest by a frightened father and husband whose entire world had been burned to the ground.

Thief. He thought with a twinge of shame. *Just another label you've tried on for size. Alchemist, collector, merchant... and thief. But why stop there, grave robber?*

As often happened in the darker hours, black thoughts were drifting to the surface. Thoughts about balancing the scales. About fate and its cruel tricks, and the sort of world where a child could be born with tar in their bones. Or could be stolen away. Vanished--winked out of existence by some monster.

Or a witch.

"Daddy..."

Kro could hear the voice of his daughter as if she were standing right beside him.

"What's that? What did you bring back?! It looks like a funny rock."

"A rock?! He had laughed." No Lishka..." His voice rang with the trembles of a heart so full it was overflowing. "Look again. Look at the shape. How one end is bigger than the other. Can you see?"

"Ohh..." The girl had said, her eyes alight with recognition. "It's... an egg?" she squealed, throwing her arms around her father and burying her face in his warm belly. "It is! Oh daddy! I love it!"

Even in his memories, the words were muffled by the fabric of his cloak.

"Do you think it will hatch soon?"

Kro drew the back of one hand across his face. Past and present--neither tired of tormenting him. Once he had been happy. A man with two perfect girls.

He would be with them very soon.

Kro had been telling himself this for a very long time but somehow, the promise felt truer now than ever. Was this just another of fate's tricks? His scientific brain spun and worked. Always needing to discern--to understand the why, the what, and the how. Always.

Secretly, it was the part of himself he hated most.

He clenched his teeth, unintentionally pinching the inside of one cheek. And as Kro continued down the trail, he became aware of the coppery taste of blood.

2-4

Ahead, light flickered through the frosted woodscape. Someone at the end of their rope might have taken it for an oasis. A place of salvation. But as Kro stood in the isolated gloom of near dark, his eyes focusing on the orangey glow which could only come from a roaring campfire, all he could feel was the cold.

He gripped the ashy bottle, turned it to hear the familiar tink as the tiny finger and teeth shifted. The remains of the kindling boy had not held the secret to the prime element of fire nor any other cosmic abstract. But, as fate would have it, the bones did possess one trick, and it was a splendid one.

Already the rib had been frittered away, bit by bit--along with three other teeth. Each time he had decided to call upon the kindling boy, the child had helped him--even saved his life once.

This fact was the only thing able to keep Kro's guilt in check. The nameless child whose only crime was being born different had been granted a new legacy. Not fiery death, but the preservation of life.

The alchemist reclined his head to look up through the canopy. What little he could glimpse of the sky looked empty--felt empty. It always did.

A different man in his boots might have thought to pray--to beg whatever god might be listening for a blessing--but not Tenebrus Kro. He was a man who believed such acts to be the definition of futile. The gods were gone, if they were ever there at all.

Kro had always believed only in what could be touched and dissected. Still, part of him yearned for the fantastic. Little else could have pulled him so feverishly across half the world--scouring in dark places for things only named in whispers.

Vampiric plants, gorgons, size-shifters, and enormous black birds able to pull lightning from the sky--they had all been real. Had all been true. And there had been more. So many more.

Willingly or not, every last one had given something of themselves for the cause. For the one mission. For the riddle.

Almost reverentially, Kro lifted the bottle, touching it to his forehead. There were no prayers within, no promise of victory, only a threadbare notion he dared call hope. He looked at them--the final remains of a small boy he had never met. Just a little finger, a few teeth. Not much, and yet... he did not despair.

After all, on at least one occasion, he had faced worse with a hell of a lot less.

In the brush ahead, it was all too easy to make out where the thieves had dragged their supper. A lovely red-brown mare with a white face. Anger threatened to flare again, but Kro shook it off. Morgrig's camp was close now. Close enough to smell.

There was movement ahead! Someone else was on the trail!

Panic surging in his throat, Kro backed up to a massive tree and synched up his hood. Standing like that--still and silent, his snow-laden cloak acted as natural camouflage. As he watched the scout step ever closer, his eyes narrowed into hateful slits. Earlier, the dagger had felt so cold in his hand--as if sculpted from ice. Now it was a part of him. An extension.

Morgrig's gift. The thought pulsed as fingers tightened into vice like grip.

The scout was barely ten paces away now. Kro's heart pounded in his chest, behind his throat. He was sure that at any second, it would all be over. That he would be discovered, and the scout would call out to the rest of Morgrig's merry band. Fortunately, the man didn't seem especially interested in anything that wasn't in the bottle he kept raising to his lips. And so, as quietly as he could, Tenebrus Kro drew in a long, deep breath and watched as the scout stumbled another step in his direction.

Finally, when the alchemist could hold the breath no longer, all he knew was release.

PART THREE
COLD AS THE WIND

3-1

As Belmorn took in the buildings and sprawling streets, all the leagues and months on the road melted away. There were a handful of people about--mostly men, none looking under fifty. All drab of dress and quick with the hairy eyeball, they moved in the opposite direction of the strange man who had just ridden through their gate.

Magnus' shod hooves crashed small thunderclaps on the stone road. Gone were the muted thuds of the forest floor. The sounds made Belmorn feel a bit too conspicuous. Though as eyes squinted toward him and the giant horse, the blackfoot reminded himself that his purpose had little to do with subtlety.

People... Belmorn recalled the words of the strange man in the hood. Cold as the wind in these parts.

He couldn't help but wonder how many of these north men would leave him to the mercy of a murder of timber crows, a man-eating rose, or something equally horrible.

A witch, for example.

When a breeze hit his face, no shiver came. Roon was cold, but far less so than the forest had been. Belmorn glanced up the street. Every dozen or so feet stood a tall post which terminated in an ornate lantern of glass and silver. These glowed with a golden light. The hue alone made him feel a bit warmer and left him wondering if that was indeed the intention.

All around, architecture stole his breath. There were steeples and spires, topping immaculate stone structures of palest grey. He could see yawning gargoyles, sprawling staircases, and reliefs depicting battles he did not recognize. Wherever his eyes moved, they feasted. But as he walked, Belmorn began to focus on what lay in between those ancient wonders.

In the negative spaces, he began to notice doors, carved wooden signs, and windows. Some were wide, others had been made small and circular, but all were covered in the same lattice pattern used in the portcullis.

Are these the homes of the proud people of Roon? Belmorn wondered briefly.

Up ahead, the cobbled street widened just as the guard claimed it would. Further down, in the center of the square, stood a tarnished statue of incredible size and detail. Nearly twice Belmorn's height, the silver man stood rigid amidst a small garden that had been built around him. One hand of the figure held aloft an actual glass lantern that glowed and flickered. But the statue seemed to gaze beyond his light source, as if searching for something.

The tarnished figure had been rendered with plate armor of a bygone age. Appearing both decorative and functional, the surface was embossed with intricate scrollwork and finished with a series of buckles, though this covered only half of the figure's chest. Bizarrely, the other half was bare. More striking than that, however, was the longsword protruding from where the silver man's ribs would be.

After walking around the statue, Belmorn saw that the blade extended a good three feet or more out of the statue's other side. It was a strange sort of sword. Not straight, but long and narrow, with a wicked curve.

"He fought like that for two days. Did you know?"

The voice came with no warning. It caused Belmorn to reel around as massive, hairy hooves clopped in place. Standing there was a small, waifish thing. The child was gripping an old horse blanket, using it as a sort of hood. The fabric was tattered and filthy. Even from a few feet away, it made Belmorn's nostrils curl.

"I'm sorry?" Belmorn heard himself say. "Fought like what? With a sword through his chest?"

"Yup," Said the child, matter-of-factly. "Run through with his own blade. Can you believe it?"

Holding onto the reins, Belmorn smirked. "I guess that depends. Who was he fighting?"

"A monster," said the child with reverence.

The kid looked to be roughly ten or eleven, but it was difficult to tell. The face was filthy with grime and across the bridge of the nose was a dark smudge. But what Belmorn noticed most were the eyes. Like emeralds, they were full of something. Not storms, but something better. Hope, maybe.

"This world is full of monsters, kid."

He couldn't tell whether this was a boy or a girl. Not that knowing the gender would have stopped him from keeping one hand on his coin purse. Rander Belmorn may have been a simple riverman, but Roon was far from his first big city.

"Monsters, sure, but not like this one," the kid continued. "The Teng-Hu came from far away. Somewhere in the east. It had had hands like talons, wings as black as midnight and three children which it carried in the folds of its robe."

"Huh." said Belmorn.

The child nodded. "They had ugly names. Fever, Infection, and Death."

The blackfoot was staring in disbelief at how articulate this kid was. He felt almost certain this was a boy, but perhaps a boy educated by books and school masters, not of a life spent begging for scraps on the cobbles.

"That's the reason the bird-men came. And why they've been here ever since. It's... how you know it all really happened." With a slight shudder, the boy took a step back into the long shadow of the silver man.

Belmorn looked up at the statue, at the hard, beardless jaw and the stern brow. "Never heard that one before. That's quite a story," he said, meaning it.

For an instant, the boy's eyes met those of the tall stranger. "There's more. Before him, a lot of brave warriors tried to kill the Teng-Hu. Dozens. And they all died."

"All of them?" Belmorn sounded unconvinced.

"Yup..." The boy looked around before dragging the back of one hand across his nose. "All but him," he indicated the statue.

"So who was he?"

"Depends who's telling the story." The boy shrugged. "Some say he was a soldier named Gabriel--first killed while defending his king in some old-time battle. But others say he was never mortal to begin with. That his true identity was actually that of Charon, the fabled boatman whose duty it was to guide lost souls across the black rivers of the afterlife."

The phrase triggered something in Belmorn. Something which brought him instantly home. "Black rivers..." he said under his breath and then said no more. It had taken until now, but the story was beginning to sound very familiar. He could remember a legend he had heard as a boy. Of an unkillable warrior known only as the Wanderer. He noticed a small plaque affixed to the base. Two words had been carved--

THE GRAVELESS.

"Such is the way, I suppose," Belmorn said this dreamily. "The older a thing is, the more guesses people manage to attach to it."

"That sounds right," said the boy with another shrug. "A name isn't so important though. Not when you can do what he could. See... the one bit all versions agree on is that whoever this man was, he couldn't die. That's the important thing. Why he could fight a monster for two whole days with a sword through his chest. Get it?"

Belmorn looked to the statue's tarnished silver face. "Favored by the spirits. The Graveless Wanderer..." Belmorn's voice was distant. "I do remember this story."

"It's my favorite," said the boy, wiping another sniff away. "I like your horse."

"Oh?" Belmorn smirked, stroking the animal's neck.

"He's big. Why are his legs so long?"

With a chuckle, he looked between Magnus and the boy. "Ever heard of a river ghost?"

The boy shook his head.

"Adamandray are a special breed. Their legs have to be so long and powerful to feed upon the saltgrass which grows beneath the powerful current of the river where I come from."

The boy took a step closer, but when the horse clopped the ground with its front hoof, he stopped. His eyes were as wide as saucers. "It looks like someone painted his legs."

Belmorn raised an eyebrow. "It does," he tried unsuccessfully to lower his smile. "But my people say, long ago... Rinh, the great river spirit, grew angry at these horses. For, you see they were the sole creatures it was powerless to carry away. So, in a rage, Rinh stole away all of the color from the legs of these special horses and gave it to the river itself--making murky black what once was clear..." Noticing how utterly enthralled the boy was, Belmorn began to smile. "We call them ghosts because of how they appear when wading out amidst the rushing waters. There's often a bit of white just above the surface." He stroked Magnus' shoulder--moving his hand down to where the shades of dark and light mingled and became stripes. "Just enough to make it seem that instead of walking, these horses are floating out there."

"Wow." The boy looked to be imagining this very thing. He shuffled his feet, nervously inching closer to the gigantic horse. From beneath his blanket hood, the child's mouth had become a tight line. "River ghosts," whispered the boy. "I like that."

A strange feeling had grown in Belmorn. One he could not quite categorize. The purse under his hand seemed to pulse like a living heart. He knew perfectly well that the coins inside were few, and since he possessed nothing more to pawn, they were going to stay that way. Just as he knew that he could not get involved with any business that did not directly assist him in reaching his ends.

By Rinh, it was already September. Time was running so thin; it was far too terrifying to think about. He looked down at the raggedy boy and his horse blanket hood. Belmorn had seen countless others like him. Passed by them in the streets. Waifs, urchins, children of the cobbles--whatever the local moniker, cities always possessed more than their fair share. And just as in all those other places, in Roon, Rander Belmorn was a stranger. It was not his responsibility to spend his concern, nor his charity.

Remember the cardinal rule, he thought.

"His name is Magnus," Belmorn's voice was so deep it practically rumbled. "He won't hurt you. Especially not after such a fine swapping of tales. Speaking of which... yours was better." He flipped forward a coin--a golden twin for the one that got him past the gate.

The boy caught the small metal disc by clapping both hands together. He looked up, appearing quite surprised.

"The guard back there," Belmorn shot a lazy glance behind him. "He mentioned a place. Something called the Folly?"

"Oh. Yeah. The Hag's Folly." For an instant, the child's eyes flitted to the left, then dimmed. "They don't like me there." He shrank away. His body language was practically screaming a desire to run.

"Is that so?" Belmorn folded his arms. "Why not?"

"Because little leeches ain't good for business, are they?" The gruff voice spun Belmorn around. Armored men were storming his way with swords drawn. He recognized one as the guard from the front gate.

"That's him. Bribed me with a guilder. Don't see them much."

Belmorn could feel panic flushing into his cheeks, but also fury.

"A guilder, aye?" said the man who had spoken first. "Well stranger, it seems you've got deep pockets. But where pray tell are you intending to spend it? I fear our whores won't be nearly expensive enough."

Belmorn said nothing. He counted the men. Five. On his best day, he might be able to take three, but this particular day was about as far from his best as he had known. Crow flesh had staved off his hunger, but he was days past exhausted, and the effect of that damned wizard's powder yet weighted his limbs.

"I have come a long way. I seek no trouble, only a single night's rest and the right to spend some coin restocking my provisions," Belmorn's voice was low and steady. It took some effort, but his words offered no aggression.

"That's shit," the tall guard spoke up again. "He told me he was looking for a guide to take him to Jayce."

At this, the five Roonik Guards burst out into a fit of laughter.

"Oh-ho! Jayce is it?" Sputtered the leader "Well, boys! Looks like a proper madman has wandered into our fair city! Either that or a liar, and you know how the captain feels about them. Where did he say he was from again?"

"Place called Grael, Sir. Never heard of it."

"Probably 'cause he made it up! Either way, it's too late for this. The captain can sort it out in the morning. Let's go stranger, you're coming with us."

The Roonik Guards stepped forward, but Belmorn only tensed. His mind racing madly, running through the course of action left to him. He had no intentions of occupying a jail cell but resisting would surely prolong that stay. Perhaps indefinitely. No. Better to go along quietly and make his case to the man in charge--the captain.

"No!" The voice was thin--youthful but firm. "Leave him alone!" Quite unexpectedly, the boy leapt in between Belmorn and his attackers and was standing with both hands held out. The selfless act caused a second round of laughter to explode from the five guards.

"Out of the way, leech!" One of the other guards thrust out a steel boot which was caught by the boy's stomach.

The small body doubled over pitching forward. Teeth clenched in pain as little hands released the dirty blanket. Belmorn watched all of this unfold in a series of truncated, slower than average motions. By the time the boy's face ricocheted off the stones, fields of white pressed into the sides of his vision. The man's hands were no longer hands at all, but hard things--hammers of solid iron.

This was the last rational thought the riverman would retain of the evening. Everything after was lost in a blur of fever and rage.

3-2

Darkness returned, bringing the faint glimmer that approximated the shape of a young boy. A boy of about nine.

As the vision had been in the woods, the form remained blurred, shifting, as indistinct as mist. The face though. Belmorn's heart thrummed at the sight. It was a face he missed more than feeble words could express. He reached for that face--wishing beyond all reason that the shimmering flesh would become solid when his fingers reached it.

That was when distance stopped making sense.

The inches between them stretched and grew until the boy-shape was almost too distant to see at all. Belmorn squinted hard, refusing to blink even as tears welled and streamed.

At first, the phantom boy had held out a hand of his own, reaching for his father. All too quickly though, the limb began to turn--changing until Belmorn could no longer recognize it as a piece of his son. The hand twisted into a horrible hooked thing. Like a tool for digging or perhaps a weapon. Before Belmorn could act, the boy began to claw and rake at his own throat--digging in with sharp fingers of living light.

"Sasha!"

Jolted awake, Belmorn sat up in the cold and the dark. He blinked unconsciousness away. Tried desperately to see, to understand.

Where am I?

The room was dark and small--lined with straw that smelled awful. The walls were stone, as was the floor. Beyond these mundanities, the only thing he knew for certain was that this was no dream. Pain never felt quite the same in dreams as in real life. And wherever he was, there was plenty of pain.

He couldn't see them, but Belmorn knew the bruises were there. His jaw pounded like a percussion section. Fractured? Possibly. But how? By who?

His last few memories were muddy and too large, as if they had swollen to an abnormal size--in that other place. The one with the boy trying to tear his own throat away.

No! He thought. *That won't help you now. Put it away and get off your ass.*

Belmorn stood up, but too fast. It felt a little like his head hadn't risen with the rest of him. With a sudden wave of vertigo, he pitched forward, slapping one hand flat on a stone wall. Then he promptly emptied the contents of his stomach onto the floor.

When the retching subsided, Belmorn dragged the back of an arm across his mouth. White pain exploded from his lip, leaving him reeling, almost out of breath. After a few moments of heavy breathing, his tongue inspected the only injury he remembered getting. The triangular gap in his lower lip was still sewn shut, but the pain that radiated from the spot came in great pulses of heat reaching into his stomach.

"Never made it to the damned apothecary." He laughed without thinking but ended up sucking air through his teeth. "Never made it anywhere."

It didn't take a scholar to know where he was--at least in the general sense. Three of the walls were identical; the fourth was comprised of a latticework of iron bars. Beyond the bars, the gentle glow of torchlight kept the darkness from being complete.

Belmorn smirked, recalling just enough. That last night, after reaching Roon at long last, he had done something stupid. Something that very well may have undone all he had worked for.

Nineteen weeks of keeping to the plan... for what? So you can break the cardinal rule twice in two days?

"Sasha," Belmorn said the name again, this time tasting the full brunt of the coppery pain it brought. He bounced both fists off the iron bars. Time was his enemy, that was true... but time had an endless number of allies to throw in his path.

"Oy! You hear that?" The voice was distant.

"Yeah. Sounds like he's awake," came another voice. "I'll get the captain."

The hushed voices were followed by a series of footsteps that echoed and shrank. For a time, Belmorn heard nothing beyond his own breathing. In, out--in, out. It was a ragged, monotonous sound and he hated it. If he had to listen to that long enough, he might just go mad. And so he resolved to focus on something else.

His feet were cold. Hell, they felt more wood than flesh. Intrigued by this, Belmorn looked down to see a pair of stockinged feet.

"Where are my boots?" His shout echoed, but quickly died.

He wanted to punch the wall. Instead, he cupped the top of his head. Neither his headscarf nor leather band were there. Gone also were most of his trappings--coat, gloves, coin purse, and the bear pelt cloak he had just purchased in Britilpor. They had stripped him of everything but pants and shirt and locked him away for... For what?

He could almost remember, but a crippling throb of pain pulsed behind his forehead, stopping him from trying. Tears streamed down his cheeks in hot lines, but they barely registered. Belmorn shut his eyes tight--tighter. His lids felt as if they were covering smoldering bits of coal. But why? Why the hell had they done this to him?

As if in response, a sudden vision flashed across his mind. A vision of dark feathers and a long stabbing beak. As the fractured memory replayed, Belmorn flinched. Then he understood.

"Hold it together, Lord Belmorn," he spat. "This... is not where your journey ends. Can't be. He wouldn't do that to you."

He who? Came a petulant voice in his head. You mean your river spirit? Rinh can't help you here, blackfoot. No one can.

Suddenly, a new sound rose above the incessant in, out--in, out of his breathing. Footsteps. Heavier, surer of themselves than the ones he had first heard.

From beyond the bars, the glow of a lantern registered. Next came voices, a harsh clunk of metal on metal, and the whine of hinges. Belmorn tried to make out what was being said, but his head was throbbing, pulling him down, down to the filthy straw. Whatever was about to happen, he wasn't ready for it.

He watched as two armored guards entered his cell followed by a third. All had blades pointed at the prisoner, but only the last one wore a smug look of satisfaction. Not especially vexing at first but as soon as Belmorn glanced down, a sneer pulled at his throbbing lips.

His missing boots suited the guard remarkably well.

Belmorn wanted to lunge right then. Unfortunately, just remaining upright was taking the lion's share of his energy. When the fourth and final man entered the cell, he moved slowly, with a deliberate, confident gate. Behind him flowed a regal cape of a perfect shade of black--the sort only velvet can manage. This man carried an air that the others lacked. Tall and broad of shoulder, he was garbed in a pale suit of armor--ornate but not overly so. Belmorn noted a conspicuous hole in the center of the chest plate--circular with a reinforced rim-- revealing dark fabric beneath.

The man wore no helmet, though his head was crowned with a thick mane. The pale, golden locks swept into waves and wrong turns, recalling words like "wild" and "untamed." With the way the other guards gave him space, there could be no question to the man's identity.

Here, stood the captain.

3-3

Unlike the three men he'd sent in, Captain Henric Galttauer was unarmed save for a large, brass lantern. In lieu of a verbal order, he cleared his throat upon entering and dutifully, the guards took another step back--lining the far wall.

The captain hung his lantern on a hook, and then, with a flourish of cape, he fixed the prisoner with an ice-blue stare. Surprisingly however, the man on the floor said nothing. Didn't flinch nor shrink the way so many in his position had before, but simply stared right back.

His eyes--there was something about them. Something dauntless. Tangled black hair disappeared into a wiry, untrimmed beard of the same color. The man's skin was a coppery brown as foreign as the headdress his guards had taken from him. Whoever he was, the prisoner was no north man.

"Good morning," said the captain in a tone of melted chocolate. "I trust whatever fight you have left has calmed since last night. That... was quite a display."

"Where am I?" The prisoner spoke evenly, voice measured to not sound threatening.

An amused smirk curled the captain's lip. "In a very tight spot, I'd say. Out here, we may be within an ace from the world's edge, but this is still my city. And those stones under your ass..." He leaned in, towering like a giant above the helpless wretch on the floor. "Well, those are mine too." Still smirking, Galttauer searched the man's face, but it was like trying to read a book written in an unknown language.

"Why am I here?" asked the prisoner.

Was this man joking? The captain smiled more to hide his own confusion. "Why?" He snorted dismissively. "The Roonik Guard is an ancient order--nearly as old as these stone walls. For generations, the citizens of Roon have looked to members of my family's line for protection. It is a duty my father passed to his son--one I shall keep gladly, until the spirits decide to call me home. And when a stranger appears at our southern gate with a monstrous horse and a questionable point of origin, my guards--even those who are easily bribed--know to alert their Captain." Galttauer leaned in, even closer, velveting his voice with confidence. "And when this stranger proceeds to incite a six man skirmish in my city square, well..." He shrugged. "Here we are."

Lines creased the prisoner's brow, and the grey in his eyes churned like storm clouds. A frown began on his lips, but the man winced ever so slightly. It was then that Galttauer noticed the crudely stitched split in his lower lip.

"Perhaps my men were a bit overzealous last night... but these are trying times. Let me start again." The captain straightened to his full height, taller than most men he knew. "I am Henric Galttauer, Captain of the Roonik Guard and oath-sworn protector of this city." He stopped to see if the prisoner appeared impressed. But the copper-skinned man said nothing--did nothing beyond glare right back from his spot on the floor.

On the captain's face there grew a subtle expression. One that might almost have been offense but for a secret curling of the lip. An expression that, on one side at least, threatened to become a smile. Galttauer was intrigued by the man in his cell. Despite the ungodly hour, he was almost enjoying himself.

"I will admit," He began again, "etiquette is not exactly a prime concern out here, but in my experience... introductions generally arrive in groups of two or more. You are... ?"

But instead of responding, the prisoner began to look around the cell. His eyes flitting from place to place, came to rest on the boots of Guardsman Kürsch. Boots, Galttauer noted, which the man had not possessed before the previous night's arrest.

Either goaded by the unwanted attention or looking to show off, Guardsman Kürsch stepped toward the prisoner. "Are you deaf?,"

Kürsch demanded. "The captain just asked you a question."

"You want my name?" hissed the prisoner through clenched teeth. "I left it at the gate."

Kürsch kicked the stranger in the stomach, knocking him almost a foot back. The prisoner coughed, grasping his stomach, then looked up at his attacker. As the seconds passed, the man's gaze steadied and intensified. By Galttauer's estimation, he was studying the guardsman the way a hunter looks at prey--weighing all options, working out the most efficient kill.

The captain observed all of this without a word--standing back while his men moved to redraw their swords. Then he noted the extended hand of guardsman Kürsch, and how it trembled.

"That's enough." He said at last. Galttauer's command came from the depths of his chest. As such, the words reverberated in the close space like those of an angry god.

Appearing truly rattled for the first time, the prisoner looked up, though his eyes did not meet those of his captor.

Knowing exactly what he was looking at, Galttauer presumed the man was trying to understand the meaning or symbolism of the small, deliberate hole in his breastplate. The one which so many generations had worn before him, as tribute to their patron saint. For a moment, the captain felt wary. Wondering if the prisoner was considering, with those predator eyes, if the aperture might be a possible weakness. But then, like a passing thundercloud, the man's hard expression melted away.

The prisoner rubbed the top of his head as muscles in his jaw unclenched, relaxed. Then, looking far less fierce than only seconds earlier, he met the captain's eye.

"There was a boy." The prisoner's voice trembled with quiet rage. "What happened to the boy?"

"A boy?" Galttauer exclaimed. "What boy?" The question was surprising, though the captain tried to keep this from his expression. "One of our little street pigeons, perhaps?" He shook his head to refocus. The stranger's concern gave him an opening at least. "I assure you, if there was a boy involved in last night's affair, he is in a better spot than you, my friend. Now let us try this once more..." The captain extended a hand to the man on the floor. He spoke his name in a tone to inform the prisoner that this was his last chance for a civil conversation.

"Henric Galttauer."

Something unreadable flashed across the prisoner's face. But he swallowed hard and accepted the offered hand. The man rose slowly, straightening his legs and spine with care--both attempting and failing to hide a tremble in his left knee. At his full height, he was imposing indeed. Slightly taller than Galttauer himself.

"Rander Belmorn," said the prisoner, calm forced into his voice. "Of the Black River people. My village is one of a few along the Eastern bank of what is known as the lower trunk. A place called Grael." There was a slight waver as he spoke the name of his home.

"The Black River?" Galttauer asked, trying to recall seldom used geography.

Belmorn nodded. "You know it?"

"I know of it." The captain let the smirk return to his face. Now he had information with which he could weigh this prisoner. "Tales sometimes take longer to reach us here in the end of the world. But yes... I seem to recall something about dark-haired, red-skinned hunters--how they would supposedly ride out into the rushing waters of their river aback giant horses..." Galttauer continued to pull out memories of the stories from the far south. "Grael." He rolled the word over his tongue--tasting it. Then he pulled a sharp breath in through his nose. "If memory serves... that is a long way from here."

"Yes," said Belmorn. "A long, long way."

Clearing his throat, the captain offered a firm nod to his subordinates. The three guards responded appropriately, and in unison, lowered their weapons.

"It would seem that a more... private conversation is required here..." Galttauer watched his guards swap uneasy glances. "Leave us."

"Captain..." Kürsch began. "Sir. Is that wise? This one... last night, it took four of us to--"

"Guardsman," The captain's voice was sharper than any blade. "Your concern is noted but unwarranted. You have your orders."

"Yes, Sir. Of course." The guard licked his lips, and then nodded to the other two. The momentary fear of his captain's wrath melted into concern. "We'll not be far." Kürsch shot one last sneer at the prisoner before exiting with the others.

Mirroring the expression as it exited, Belmorn turned with a deep scowl that might have shaken a lesser man. But Captain Henric Galttauer had seen many things in the last decade. Things a hell of a lot worse than this foreigner. And so he smiled.

3-4

"So... you are a fisherman."

Hearing the question that wasn't, Belmorn's focus blurred for a moment. Maintaining his composure was becoming a labor. Every thrum of his nervous heart pulsed in his face--in his swollen, mysteriously mended upper lip.

"A fisherman?" he balked, only slightly out of breath. "Fishermen poke at minnows with sticks. I... am a blackfoot. Master of the adamandray and of the brackish course. The diplocaulus, the salt lion, seven species of greater eel, even the dread nautiloth--they have all known my steel."

"Ah. A blackfoot." Galttauer looked as if something had just slid into place. "So... this is why you fought my men with such vigor. Such staunch determination. What are a handful of Roon's finest when stacked against beasts of such a caliber, eh?"

Belmorn said nothing, though poison coursed in his glare. His hands closed, forming empty fists that ached for their missing axes.

"Be careful." Galttauer's voice took on an edge. "Do not forget where you are, blackfoot. It has been said that my patience is a gracious but fragile thing."

The threat in the captain's words didn't ring half as loud as the one in his tone. Belmorn's face throbbed as a bead of sweat traced a path from temple to jaw. He had battled monsters and had always won, but this foe before him was no mindless mass of shell and slime-slick tentacle. And this cell was far from the undulating pitch-dark waters of the battle ground he knew.

So impossibly, unthinkably far.

"I have never been to your river," said Henric Galttauer. His voice returned to its previous amiability. "But then... I have never been anywhere. Roon is my everything, my everywhere. And I would do anything to protect it. Do you believe me?"

It took a second before Belmorn realized he was expected to answer. And so he relented a nod.

"Then we are on even ground, and that is a good place to begin. Here..." The captain produced a small wooden stool from just outside the cell. After setting it on the ground, he gestured for Belmorn to sit. "Please. You look ready to fall over."

Belmorn's eye went wide, then very narrow. That stool might as well have been a rare eel flank steak with onion gravy. He wanted it so badly, his bones hurt.

"What is this?" He heard himself ask.

"That..? A marvelous invention guaranteed to hold your ass about a foot off the ground." Galttauer stepped toward the lantern and gazed into the flickering glass. His voice sounded distant. "Just one of our amenities for you to enjoy."

Before Belmorn could convince himself that he didn't need the damn stool or that the cell's gravity wasn't twice as strong as anywhere else in the world, he found that he was already sitting. Through the intense wave of relief, Belmorn opened his eyes to find the captain still at an eye level. It took a moment to understand that Galttauer was sitting as well.

"How many of these things do you have out there?"

The captain's smile bloomed, and for one brief instant, Belmorn could see that it contained no malice. "As I said, I have never been to your river, but I know that it is a long way off," said Henric Galttauer. "Must have taken you three months to travel here."

"Closer to five," said Belmorn--feeling as if those ice-blue eyes were trying to read his own. "Galttauer..." The name came without thought. "Let me go." Another bead of sweat trickled and tortured down his face. He wanted to swat it away. "Last night, there was a boy. Just a harmless..." He shook his head, refocusing. "We were just talking... discussing your statue. Then your guards appeared and..." Belmorn stopped, swallowing back the rest of his dark musings and tasting bile on the way down. He could still picture the kid--still smell the reek coming off his blanket. And hear the sound a boot makes when thrust into the soft stomach of a child. Behind all those memories, a small voice sang from somewhere in the far back of his brain. It reminded him of another boy. A boy he loved more than life itself.

Belmorn could tell that Henric Galttauer was not the sort to suffer demands. If he ever wanted to see his family again, he was going to have to choose. His son, or a poor vagrant he'd known for five minutes.

"Roon..." Belmorn began, allowing the rest of his body to become as unclenched as his hands. "... will suffer no further disturbance from me. Let me go, and I'll be on my way."

Galttauer's face had gone deadpan. For a time, he simply seemed to consider the offer.

"I believe you." The corners of the captain's mouth turned downward. "Authenticity is a rare thing, but I know when I am sitting across from it."

Suddenly, Belmorn became aware of flickering lantern light and how it played on the man's wild, blonde hair.

"But tell me, blackfoot. Why do I have to let you go? Are we keeping you from pressing business? What could possibly have made you cross so many leagues only to find yourself cast in a cell for a crime as base as brawling? Tell me, but know that if your answer is less than authentic, I will know." With hands on his knees, the powerful-looking man leaned forward, crooking his head to one side. "Believe when I say that these ears have been sharpened by a thousand well told lies. And that any you tell, will not be suffered."

Belmorn's head dropped into his hand as locks of hair--long and unwashed--fell against his wrist. The sensation caught him off guard and he pulled away violently as if from the revolting tickle of an insect in mid glut. Through a fevered haze, he stared at that hand. Was it truly his? Those gnarled digits, half frozen and caked so thoroughly with grime? Under such filth, the scars from a life spent battling river monsters were hardly visible. How many times had Malia ran her perfect fingers along those callused lines? And how many times had she scowled when he brought a new one home for her to dress?

He used to know.

"Okay," he began, then paused. The decision was no longer what to tell, but rather how much. "I am here because of my son." The words burned like smoldering coals upon his tongue. Once he began, Belmorn found that he could not stop them from flowing. "He is willful, strong... and far more charming than his father..." A smile tugged at the corner of Belmorn's lips, but he smothered it. "My son is a good boy. His name is Sasha Belmorn. He will be ten at the end of the year, and he is dying."

3-5

For a moment it seemed Belmorn could not continue.

"We call it the purple sickness. It is an old disease, and as effective as they come. The sick can suffer for a long time as their throat swells a little more, day by day--hardening into something closer to wood than flesh. Over time, breathing becomes hard as the body slowly strangles itself. It moves faster in some people, but others can live with it for as long as a year." His voice sounded as if it were coming from a great distance away. "But the end is always bad. Either they go crazy from lack of sleep or, if their hands haven't been tied down... sometimes victims will claw at their own throat. Until there's nothing left."

"God." Galttauer wore a look of revulsion.

Seeing this, Belmorn nodded.

"It's why the smart ones just drown themselves in the river." He stopped for a moment, shook his head. "Because if the disease is allowed to run its course, in their final moments eyes bulge half out of the skull, red and full of the same terrible thought. That the tiny bit of air in their lungs... is the last they'll ever have."

Silence grew in the cell. Swelling until it touched every stone--every strand of reeking straw.

"I see," Galttauer began with a pang of genuine regret. "My heart goes out to your son, blackfoot. I hope you believe that. Though I cannot help but wonder... if you truly loved the boy, why you would choose to spend so many of his final days galloping farther and farther away from his bedside."

Belmorn looked at the captain with daggers in his eyes. "*If* I loved?" His breathing was deep and ragged. He rose ominously off the stool and glared."If?!" The pain in the man was naked, escaping like steam from every pore.

Suddenly, Henric Galttauer experienced something like shame. Not for what he had said, but for the unsavory decision he was coming to. For the plan that had been knitting itself together in the back of his mind.

"Had I stayed," Belmorn forced a flimsy calm over his words. "My Sasha would have had no chance. But there is a cure for the purple sickness. I have seen it."

"Seen a cure? Here?" The captain's curiosity was piqued. "What would give you the idea that such a thing could be found in my city? There is no sickness in Roon! Not for a hundred years and even then, nothing like you describe. I am very sorry to tell you this, blackfoot, but most of our doctors have moved on and our best apothecary is also the town drunk."

"Roon was never my goal." More heavy breathing filled the cell. "Jayce. I need to reach Jayce. I have a map. Only another day's ride... maybe less. For the love of pity, man... Just let me go."

"No one goes to Jayce. It is..." The captain stopped to find the right word as an unexpected and unwanted ache pulled at his heart. "... inaccessible. If what you are seeking is there... I'm afraid it no longer exists."

"I'm not seeking a what," growled Belmorn, ignoring most of what had been said. "I'm looking for a man. A traveling merchant who once roamed this country--peddling a most unique stock of wares. The sides of his wagon were purple and decorated with a bold black ring. Though unmistakable even at a distance, the symbol, like the merchant himself, was more than it seemed. Up close, you could see the ring was a snake eating its own tail. What some call... the Ouroboros."

Galttauer's eyes flashed then, though he did not speak.

"Always in the spring, every year or two, this merchant brought trinkets and goods like we had never seen. He never gave a name, but... in Grael, he became known as the brushman."

Forgetting himself for a moment, Galttauer snickered unapologetically. "'The brushman', you say?"

Even Belmorn released a small chuckle before continuing. "The fact is this... Among those exotic wares and medicines were the finest horse brushes we had ever seen. Each was unique--handmade by the man himself. With handles of bone and bristles we were never able to identify. You see, Captain... our horses are everything to my people. Without the adamandray, we would be poking with sticks, praying for minnows. Unfortunately, river fleas can be a problem." Belmorn pinched an inch of air. "Tiny shrimp-like creatures. They can infest even the biggest horse in a single afternoon--afflicting it with something far less pretty than mange. I think that's why he kept coming back--this merchant. We were good customers. Emptying his stock of brushes almost every time."

"I see," said the captain with waning interest. "And is that how you expect to cure your boy? With a horse brush?"

"You're not listening." Belmorn's voice was low but steady. "This man sold many things. Certain... ingredients--tinctures, ointments and drafts that would make any apothecary green with envy. Among them was a substance labeled Witch Tears."

"What?" With a swift jolt, the captain stood--causing the small stool to skid back across the stone floor. "What was that?"

"Witch Tears." Belmorn repeated the words firmly.

Hearing this, Galttauer repressed a scowl, annoyed at himself for reacting so explosively. Clearing his throat, he gestured for the prisoner to continue.

"I've never forgotten the name," said Belmorn. "Fowl, milky stuff. Stored in little bottles and kept in a locked chest. Was probably the most valuable thing he had... though I never heard him name a price."

"This 'brushman'..." Galttauer's words lacked their previous confidence, and he hated that. "How do you know he was not a fraud? That his medicine was genuine?"

Belmorn sighed, rubbing his temples with thumb and forefinger.

"Two years after my son was born, the brushman returned to Grael after being away for almost sixteen months. In that time, a woman in a neighboring village contracted the purple sickness. The first case in nearly three decades. She was a mother of five--all between the ages of eleven and four. Children who would have been orphans. But... somehow, the brushman heard about her. He found the woman's home and made her a broth sweetened with a single drop of his medicine. A single, perfect tear." Belmorn stared down his jailor. "That woman was Nikta Bergen. The first and only person known to have overcome the purple sickness."

Henric Galttauer stared with wide eyes that did not blink.

"But..." Belmorn continued with weary regret. "That was the last time any of us saw the brushman. He never returned, and not a soul knows why. Common sense says he must be dead, but my wife says I never had much of that." Belmorn wore a smirk now. "So I have been tracking him these past nineteen weeks. Asking after at every possible turn, hoping such a man would have made an impression wherever he might have gone. Don't you understand? All of my searching has led to this. To the place he calls home."

"Jayce," Galttauer said, only partially aware he was speaking at all. He sighed, shaking his head slowly. "Tell me, Belmorn. If I did release you... is there anything I might say that would stop you from going to this place? Anything that might convince you to turn around? To go back to your river? And your boy?"

Belmorn's face was frozen in a grimace of outrage. "No. Only death will stop me from finding this man. Do you understand?"

Turning his back to the prisoner, Galttauer stormed out of the cell and slammed shut the door with a loud metallic clang. Then, looking through the iron bars, the captain said, "I understand. And... I am sorry."

"What?" Belmorn exclaimed. "What are you doing? Sorry for what?"

"For what must happen tomorrow." Galttauer lifted his head but could not pull his eyes from the floor. "My heart goes out to you, Rander Belmorn. And to your boy. Your journey has been a noble one, but it has been for nothing. There is no cure here, and the man you seek no longer exists. He suffered the same fate as Jayce. Just one of hundreds to fall victim to our witch." Spite and fear hung on the captain's voice, but he no longer cared. "She appeared seven years ago and the Veld had lived in her shadow ever since. I promise you this, blackfoot--she will shed no tears for your boy."

Belmorn opened his mouth, but no words came.

"But the witch is not my only concern," Galttauer went on, straightening his back but still unable to meet the other man's storm-grey eyes. "Not anymore. Not since those damned wolves infested our southern woods. I am in something of a spot, you see. All roads to and from my world are thoroughly blocked by monsters. Roon is the last of the great shield cities, and it was built well--with good bones and strong walls. Unfortunately, with all trade cut off, our resources grow dangerously thin--more so every damn day. Our goats are spent, and everyday our hunters come back less and less. Time is our true enemy, you see. No matter what we do, it ticks on. Soon, the people of this great and ancient city will be no more. Not at the hand of a bandit or the teeth of a witch... But safe behind our good walls, with empty, distended bellies." A smirk, this one mirthless, lifted the corner of the captain's mouth.

"I..." Belmorn seemed to be searching for words. "I am... sorry."

Snorting at such a ridiculous response, Galttauer finally looked the man in the face.

"But..." Belmorn continued. "I don't understand. You have able soldiers. You have rifles. Why do you not fight?"

For many long moments, Galttauer said nothing. His gaze wandered to bruises, a swollen cheek, the split lip that curved with a sneer... anywhere but the blackfoot's sharp, grey eyes. "Sometimes it is the simple questions that require the most complex of answers." He smiled wistfully, and then pinched the bridge of his nose. "But you, blackfoot... you are a stranger here. I do not expect you to understand."

"Just... Let me go. Let me continue on my way. If I die, so be it. But you should know, I have no fear of bandits. And as for your witch... my axes have tasted worse. Do you hear me? We can help one another."

"We can." The captain flicked a speck of something from his cloak. "Just not in the way you think. Your bravado is refreshing, but misplaced. Make no mistake, blackfoot, if I were to release you, it would be a death sentence that would serve no one. Not your boy and certainly not the citizens of Roon. But... perhaps you can provide them with some small measure of relief. Perhaps..." Galttauer let his voice trail off, as his eyes looked to potential near-futures. "These people don't know your face, nor can they account for your inexplicable presence here. What you have shown them is a man who, minutes after arriving, beat the hell out of five of my guards. Roon's people cannot stomach more hardship. Not a single drop. Already they are starved for relief. And tomorrow, their addled minds will be eased. That is how we help each other."

Taking and releasing a breath, the captain moved away from the iron door. "Tell me, blackfoot... in your vast travels, have you ever heard the name Mannis Morgrig?"

A sharp intake of breath answered that question.

The captain pulled keys from his belt, locked the cell door and walked away. A heavy clang against the bars followed him.

"Galttauer! Stop!" Belmorn roared. "Who is Mannis Morgrig?"

At this, Henric Galttauer stopped. "As of tomorrow..." he said with no pleasure whatsoever, "you are."

PART FOUR
COMEUPPANCE

4-1

Mannis Morgrig looked up from where he sat resting in his tent.

Men were shouting outside. His men. They sounded panicked, frightened. Standing, he reached for the knife that usually weighed down his belt. The scabbard was there, but empty. It took a second before he remembered where he had left it. There had been a tree. An old one strangled by dangerous vines and a poor wretch whom he had taunted and left to die.

No. Morgrig thought feverishly. *It's not possible. Even if that bastard managed to cut himself free, he wouldn't come here. No man would do that. At least, no sane man.*

Morgrig glanced at the saddlebags that sat on the table where he typically dined alone. He hadn't looked inside them yet. Something outside popped--then came a shrill, jarring sound like the initial clap of thunder. Hissing an inward curse, the large man stormed out of his tent with sword in hand.

The world outside was filled with smoke and chaos. But mostly smoke.

The campfire billowed a pillar of ash colored liquid. Only it wasn't liquid. Nor was it the usual sort of smoke produced by a usual fire.

FLASH!! CRACK!!

Unlike the first, the latest crack sounded as if it were made up of many smaller ones--as if someone had thrown a handful of black powder into the flames.

Morgrig's hand flew to his eyes, but it was too late. He had to fight through searing pain to keep them open. Through a blur of tears, he could see more of the strange smoke. Now two rivers of the stuff were pouring out of his campfire! Smoke didn't do that. Nothing did.

"Voss!" roared the Red Wolf. "Dirk! Slagter! The hell is going on here?"

"Mannis!" came a voice he could not place. "We're under attack, Sir! Someone is--ert!!"

Morgrig clawed the tears away from his eyes, battling to see something--anything. Then he wished he hadn't.

There were ghosts in the smoke, silhouettes and shades. They moved in and out of existence--stretching into shapes that no man could make. *Snakes*--this was his first thought. Whipping, lashing about inside the smoke. It was ludicrous, but he could see them growing, looping around and over one another as they assaulted his men. He could see neither heads nor tails, but the panicked shouts assured Morgrig that he had not gone mad. Whatever this was--it was actually happening.

Bellowing with rage, Morgrig lashed out at the things in the smoke. His blade sliced through coils and lengths of the phantom whips. A pain punctured up his arm. Bitten, his mind screamed, but wrongly. When he looked, he saw a length of thorny vine there--wrapping around his arm. With a cry of disgust, he ripped the coiling thing away, leaving a bloody track on the exposed flesh.

Not snakes, he realized. Vines!

The injured tendril wasted no time in attempting to insinuate itself around the hand that gripped it, but Morgrig acted in time. Hurling it to the ground, he stomped until only green pulp and thorns remained. The man turned, every inch of him a wild, raw nerve. The smoke was thick, but through it shadows flickered. Silhouettes of more parasitic vines--undulating, cracking like phantom whips. They were in the air and on all sides, and as far as Morgrig could tell, he was the only one who wasn't screaming.

All of this--somehow it had to be work of the man in the hood. The one he taunted and left to a most horrible death. Maybe the man had been some sort of wizard. Or maybe he had risen to Morgrig's dare-- had moved fast enough and actually used the knife to free himself. Neither option seems likely, but deep in his gut, Morgrig knew it could be no one else. Whatever this was, didn't feel like an attack. It felt like retaliation.

"Rose man!" Morgrig's voice was ragged, unhinged. "You'll not catch me in a snare! You hear me, worm? I'll find you and by whatever Gods are watching, I'll tear you apart!"

There!

Someone was rushing towards him through the smoke. The silhouette was indistinct, but at the last second, he saw a telltale flap of cloak.

Bearing his teeth, the Red Wolf thrust out a fist. The attack contained all the will to shatter stone, but only smoke felt its wrath. In frustration he roared, following with a furious, horizontal slash of his broad, twice-edged sword. The second attack fared better and his opponent went down. Following this there came a hirking, gurgling sputter that sounded a little like music.

"Voss!" called Morgrig into the chaos. "Oye, Voss! You hear me?"

The brigand stood over his victim--glaring with triumphant, bloodshot eyes. He waved a hand, but the smoke would not be dismissed. His eyes burned and stung, but he fought to keep them open. Morgrig needed to see the dead man. The face of the son of a bitch who dared to attack him in his own camp.

"Fucking smoke!" he shouted. "Voss! Get your ass over here!" With that, Morgrig began to cough. Only a single bark at first, but quickly the fit doubled the man over.

From behind rang a shout. Someone else was rushing through the smoke. Morgrig spun, lashing out with every bit of force he had left. His sword clanged, sending reverberations up through his arm. Jolted, Morgrig recognized the shadow of a beaked mask. The one worn by his so-called butcher.

"That you, butcher?!"

The beaked face gave a nod.

A smile pulled at the corners of Morgrig's lips, and slowly, the shouts of his men returned to his awareness. More than a dozen panicked voices had melded into a single sound, like the drone of panicked wasps.

Of the two torrential rivers of smoke that had flowed so improbably from the campfire, only a lone tendril now trickled.

Suppressing a fresh cough, Morgrig looked down. The dead man's face was almost visible. Again he tried to wave the smoke away, but it was persistent stuff, swirling back into place almost immediately.

It was all so damned confusing.

Using his shirt, the Red Wolf wiped at his eyes. God, how they burned. All around, more and more shapes were appearing, slowly becoming men he knew. Men he commanded. Men whose bodies were now horribly bent and constricted. He wanted to count them, but his eyes kept slamming shut--each time with a new burst of pain.

"Plague of fucking whores--Voss!" he shouted into the chaos.

"It's Dirk, Sir," answered a voice. "Thank the gods you're still alive!"

"Never mind that, where is Voss?"

"Don't know, Sir. Hard to see anything in this."

"What the hell happened?" growled Mannis Morgrig.

"Haven't seen him since the first flash. We was lying about, waiting for the horse to cook, when all of a sudden, there was this bang like thunder. And then came the smoke. The smoke and the..."

"Vines." Morgrig frowned. "I can see that, Dirk. Got the bastard that did this, too. Got him right here." He looked at the man on the ground; his pallid face was almost visible.

"But sir..." objected Dirk. "Begging your pardon, but our attacker... He ran off."

"He what?" The Red Wolf shot an angry glare at his man.

Dirk nodded nervously. "Saw him myself, sir. Son of a whore was wearing a long cloak with a hood. Think it was that guy we left for the rose."

Morgrig felt like his insides were about to boil. He looked back down, finally able to see the pale man on the ground who wore a look of surprise. In a pool of blood lay Alberg Voss, Morgrig's most dependable lieutenant, still dressed in his long jacket. A single horrific slash to his neck gaped like a slanted, second mouth.

Morgrig was transfixed by the wound--confounded by it. For a few moments, he could only watch the gushes of red empty out of the man. Pulsing in a series of slow heaves.

"Sir?" The questioning voice belonged to the man called Dirk. A northerner neither the mental, nor physical match for the man on the ground. His hair hung in long greasy strands, and there were eight red lines painted on his face--four on each side.

"Mannis?"

Hearing his name, Morgrig looked up, inhaling a cold draft in through his nostrils. He scanned the camp. The smoke had cleared enough to reveal a scene no less grisly than the one at his feet.

His pack of wolves was bloodied. Broken. A half dozen bodies-- some squirming, some still--were strewn about the camp. They were thoroughly wrapped in coils of thorny green ropes that all had the same origin point. From the still raging fire, flickering like an apparition in the flames, was a horrendous, bulging mass, a tangle of unburnt vines that approximated a sort of body. From this, the rest of the tendrils had grown. And it was to this that the man-sized pods were giving the contents of their veins.

How could this have happened? Morgrig's mind raced. *How could it have grown so fast?*

But there were no answers to these questions.

His bleary, groggy eyes settled upon a single perfect flower growing from the tangled mass. The petals slowly peeled and spread to reveal a center as red as blood. It looked like the inside of a heart, and like a heart, it was beating.

It was all too much. Something snapped inside the Red Wolf of the north woods. Morgrig threw back his head and howled. The sound travelled far, coursing with anguish and with mindless, bestial rage.

4-2

As the sound reached his ears, the alchemist froze in place, pressing his back hard against a tree. Kro had heard the fury and chaos, but to him, the howl sounded like something worse.

There were brass goggles over his eyes and a dark maroon cloth wrapped around his face--obscuring both nose and mouth. These he pulled off, allowing the cloth to fall to its usual place around his neck. Hungrily, he took a deep breath of clean air. The camp was on the far side of the forest. As such, he could feel the cold breeze coming off the lower veld, through the trees.

Around the tree trunk, Kro looked toward the still raging commotion. Then he looked down at the tiny, soot-dusted vial. At the meager bits of bone that remained, trying to understand and process what had just happened.

The plan had been to steal back his saddle bags amidst a cover of chaos and of smoke. As they ever had, the bones of the kindling boy worked like a charm. The kiss of an open flame was all it took to create a vast river of liquid smoke.

But something else had happened. Something Kro had not expected. Just after the first kindling bone had popped in the fire, he had felt movement in his breast pocket.

It must have been the proximity to the fire. The extreme heat had caused an unexpected reaction in the unnatural objects.

Panic had thrust him back to his traumatic imprisonment mere hours earlier--choking his very breath away. The seeds had become a writhing ball of vines, growing at an improbable rate. Heart in his throat, Kro had mindlessly seized the thing and hurled it like some hideous spider into the roaring campfire.

The men around had been shouting about the smoke. But quickly, those shouts turned to screams.

Even for a man of his experience, there were many things in heaven and earth that Tenebrus Kro could not claim to understand.

The vampire rose was an exceedingly rare, wholly unnatural thing. The creation of man's effort to improve upon what nature had made perfect from the start. Until a handful of hours ago, Kro had always given the plant a wide berth. But he had dreamed up plans for those seeds. Vital plans.

Something wicked stalked the Veld. The creature had earned her death many times over. Unfortunately, such things are not so easily hastened from their perch upon this mortal coil.

The seeds of the vampire rose had been vital. Half of a solution to a riddle he had spent nearly a decade trying to solve. The last question. The only question.

How do you kill a witch?

Tenebrus Kro had risked his life, not once but twice in a single night for those seeds. Then he had secreted them to the safest place he had. Stored in the breast pocket of his cloak, alongside the other half of the riddle's answer.

The small mass was a gland, shriveled and purple, like a dried out plum. He had discovered it quite by accident on a stretch of beach on the other side of the closest ocean. The seeds were treacherous to harvest, but that gland was irreplaceable. Perhaps it had been the combination of the two ingredients reacting to the heat of the fire or the strange liquid smoke. In truth, all Kro knew for a fact was he had wasted seven years of his life. Blown them all on a single night's worth of impetuous decisions.

His stolen property had not been reclaimed, but what was the point anymore? His last hope had gone up in smoke. Literally. To enter the camp again would be suicide, and while Kro felt little desire to go on, he would not allow the wolves to be his executioners.

There was only one place left to go, a poison sanctuary if there ever was one. Tenebrus Kro sure as hell didn't have friends in Roon. Not anymore. No one would even want to sell him a horse. But none of that mattered.

As far as he could see, his well of options had officially run dry. And so, the alchemist cinched up the edges of his hood and started walking. If he moved quickly, he might reach the northern gate in a couple of hours.

"It'll be morning by then." He said to the dark woods. Offering a shrug. "Wonder if The Folly serves ale for breakfast."

PART FIVE
NORTHERN HOSPITALITY

5-1

Rander Belmorn was ushered at rifle point toward a crowd that parted as he approached.

The chains connecting his hands and stockinged feet forced his gait into a stunted hobble. He gazed at the gathering masses and frowned. How plainly they hated him. Eyes judged, even before any imagined crimes could be hung around his neck.

Belmorn wanted to scream, to vomit his outrage upon every face in that crowd. But one of the guards had gagged him with a red sash before they'd exited the barracks. They had clad him in his own coat and cloak, though the act was no courtesy. Belmorn had no delusion of how his dark garb made him appear. It had been his own idea, after all. Looking like a ruffian may have come with downsides, but it had warded off plenty of other trouble.

Not that any of that mattered now.

Belmorn tried to conjure an image of the two he loved most, they who he had failed. But as the stock of a powder rifle prodded him onward, he could see nothing but the gathering, scornful faces.

Turning his head, the blackfoot glared at the tall blond man responsible for his current predicament. Galttauer stood rigid, dressed in his finest armor and long velvetblack cloak. From an impassive face, his ice-blue eyes were fixed upon the crowd. He never saw the prisoner's naked hate or how it assaulted him with abandon.

Belmorn's feet felt stiff as those of a statue and could no longer detect cold, only different degrees of stabbing pain. As he lumbered from the stone courtyard onto the first wooden step, the pain lessened somewhat. Another jab from behind sent him stumbling up onto what felt, to him, like a stage.

He looked up to see a man with a lopsided hat, clutching a book to his breast. Shivering and numb, Belmorn put up no fight. Allowing the guards to lead him between three conspicuous posts.

Just part of the set decoration, he scoffed inwardly as his tailbone was pressed against the middle post, the tallest of the three.

With the turn of a key, each hand was disconnected from the ring between his feet. The guards stretched out his arms and attached both hands to the posts--each positioned slightly behind the middle. Once upright, Belmorn's back was pressed firmly and flatly against the central post. If the man had ever felt vulnerable before, such feelings now seemed quaint.

On either side of the stage was a row of empty seats. Seven on one side, seven on the other. They looked heavy--made out of the same pale grey stone as most everything in this damnable city. The sides and high backs were decorated in relief style carvings of what looked like winged wolves. Belmorn looked at these through a haze of fury and frustration, wholly unable to appreciate their beauty.

As if on cue, the crowd went silent, then parted--making way for seven robed individuals. Like a line of silent monks, they appeared to glide toward the stage. All were garbed in long black robes and birdlike masks. One by one, they filed onto the stage and stood before the seven seats on the left.

"The high court of Roon does recognize the Seven of Hraaf. By their eyes no truth may go unseen." The man with the book declared this with a knifelike voice.

The crowd shouted a phrase in almost perfect unison, "Let them see!"

Belmorn's head swam as he tried to take in the whole scene. His arms felt on fire. If he leaned too far to the left or right, the opposite shoulder threatened to pop out of its socket. He had heard of cities that enjoyed public torture, but this was his first personal experience with the concept. As a hot tear streamed, the sound of footsteps on wood pulled his attention back to the stairs.

A second line of robed figures were now taking the platform. These wore similar robes, but white instead of black, and their masks sported the snouts of dogs. Or something like dogs.

First crows... now wolves, Belmorn thought with a look of sardonicism. *But they've got it backwards. Wolves come first. The birds just claim the scraps.*

In spite of himself, Belmorn was grinning. It was the only sane thing he could do.

The man with the book stepped forward. "The high court of Roon does recognize the Seven of Vaarg. By their ears no lie may go unheard."

"Let them hear!" replied the hungry crowd.

"If they who keep order are prepared to watch and to listen... I ask them to sit." The man with the book looked solemn. As the fourteen mask-wearers took their seats, he began to walk from one side of the stage to the other.

The crowd had swollen since Belmorn passed through it, but every head was trained on the same individual.

"Before you..." said the man, "is he who has been charged with crimes most heinous." He opened his book and raised an eyebrow. "Infiltration of your sacred city, which as of the present time remains shut. Wanton violence against five members of your Roonik Guard. And before that..." The man's eyes widened in abject horror. "No less than three years of fear-mongering, aggravated thievery, and murder. Are these not the charges as written by your own hand, Captain?"

Belmorn found the face of Henric Galttauer not far from the stage. His cold eyes were rimmed with red veins, but they remained unreadable.

"It is so," said Galttauer, ushering a swell of shock and awe from the crowd.

"Very well. And the accused..." continued the man with the book. "Can you tell the court his name?"

"I can."

At once, the crowd gasped.

For a moment, Galttauer looked about to change his mind on something. But that might only have been Belmorn's imagination. "His name is Mannis Morgrig."

The racket of outrage and bile hit Belmorn hard. He knew what came next, had known it was coming since the night before, when he had spoken with Henric Galttauer. Either too incompetent or cowardly to apprehend the true perpetrator, the good Captain had decided to pin Morgrig's rather extensive list of crimes upon the chest of a stranger who's face no one knew. A man whose only crime had been the hope of purchasing food, medicine, and a night's sleep off of the ground.

The rest of what was said washed over Belmorn like a gust of cold wind. He glared at the masked judges who clearly had no more power to hear and see lies than the post at his back. Then he glowered at the crowd--the furious, spitting crowd.

"Roon's people cannot shoulder more hardship. Not a single drop more. They are starved for relief. Tomorrow, their addled minds will be eased. That is how we help each other."

Galttauer had claimed his people were beset on both sides by monsters. That they were slowly starving to death. Was any of that true?

Belmorn did not know. All he could say for sure was that very soon, his arms were going to be as numb as his half-frozen feet.

No. There was another truth. One other thing he knew with absolute certainty. His quest had failed.

Nineteen weeks on the road, of seeking and scouring and tracking and sleeping on dirt and subsisting on wild onions... All of it had been for nothing. His boy would die a thousand miles away with a purple face, strangled and murdered by the swelling of his own throat.

Sasha. The name of his son sparked in Belmorn's mind and stuck there like a thorn.

With renewed desperation, he scanned the faces of the onlookers, despising them in turn. He didn't give a cold damn for their plight. Witches and cut-throats were too good for this lot. He turned to the captain, willing eels to burst from behind those accursed, ice-blue eyes, and then...

And then, a light flashed from the crowd. It had been brief, but blinding. So bright that new pain lingered behind his eyes. Belmorn looked around, but could not locate a source for the inexplicable flash.

The light, he thought with disdain, *perhaps it's just the first sign of madness. Of your mind collapsing in on itself.*

The man with the book was talking again, addressing the row of bird masks who all looked towards each other, and then, in unison, gave an ominous nod. Belmorn lunged, only causing pain to explode in his left shoulder. The sensation was dizzying. His head lolled to one side--just in time to see a skewed vision of seven dog-faced figures adding their nods to the rest.

The crowd erupted with overwhelming approval. Apparently, justice had been seen, heard, and decided. Not that this scripted tragedy had anything in common with true justice.

The flashing light returned. Once, and then quickly again, causing fresh spots to bloom before his vision.

Seething at this final indignity, Belmorn squinted at the crowd, leering, scanning. He located a man off to the left, near the back. He was holding something reflective--a small mirror perhaps. When the man realized he had the attention of the condemned, the object was put away. Slipped into the prodigious folds of his cloak. His face was obscured, this man--hidden by the shadows of a prominent hood.

It was him.

The son of a bitch he should have left for the crows. Even as the guards reappeared and began to release his bonds, Belmorn's eyes did not release him. The man with the mirror. The man in the hood.

Feeling slack in the chains, the blackfoot lashed out. Accomplishing nothing beyond angering the guards. The stock of a powder rifle connected with his chest, knocking the wind from his lungs. Even as he folded, gasping for breath, Belmorn's eyes remained fixed on the man in the hood. Then, through hot tears, he watched that man extend a finger and lift it to where his lips would be.

"Shh," said the gesture.

5-2

Hours passed in solitude as the cloak of night descended over day.

Belmorn had been taken to a different room than his previous accommodations. Three of the walls were made of wood rather than stone, with a fourth of familiar iron latticework. The room was less than half the size but it had a bench on one end--more akin to a stable than a proper holding cell.

They had allowed him to keep his clothes, even returning his gloves and a pair of boots he did not recognize. A strange sort of thing, Belmorn thought. *A scrap of dignity for the condemned ?*

The clothes had been delivered by a familiar guard, the one who had recently acquired a pair of fine, Graelian boots.

"Compliments of the captain," the man had all but growled. "Can't have you freezing to death before morning."

Though Belmorn had wanted to reach through the bars, he instead did nothing, said nothing. He'd simply accepted his property with a secret, silent gratitude that burned like acid in his craw. And for the hours that followed, dark thoughts swam around inside his skull. Darting from corner to corner like a school of frenzied minnows.

Dawn was in the saddle and riding fast. He could smell it. And for him, dawn was the end. The final act of Rander Belmorn was folly. Farce. Woefully executed for crimes that did not belong to him.

It had all been made clear by the man with the book. The city Magistrate of Roon had calmly explained in his cutting voice just what the court's decision meant--what every man, woman and child in the crowd was already celebrating. That, bathed in the first rays of morning, the condemned was to be given the Test of the Graveless.

It all came back to that patron saint of theirs. The tarnished silver statue Belmorn had been accosted beside in the first place.

Come dawn, a special sword--long and curved--would be slid through the heart of the guilty. As the logic went, if the decisions of the Hraaf and the Vaarg were somehow made in error, then whatever Gods floated above this place would know. And in that unlikely event, by their grace, Belmorn would live on despite his fatal wound, just as the fabled Charon the Graveless was said to have done so many centuries before.

It was all a steaming pile of horse shit, but to Belmorn's reasoning, no more so than his mummer's fart of a trial.

The blackfoot sneered, more in disgust than despair. He tried to steer his mind to better days, toward his wife and son. But the more he tried to summon those faces, the blurrier they became, because the sight of another kept overtaking the rest.

The hooded man in the crowd he could see clearly. He who Belmorn had saved in the woods. What the hell had he been doing in that crowd? Signaling him... but for what possible reason? Had he come to taunt his savior? To further pay his debt with even more trespasses? Or could it be something else?

"Bastard," Belmorn growled. If he ever saw that damned wizard again, he was going to... to...

To what?

There was no time for this pointless wallowing. By Belmorn's guess, he had three hours at best before the pomp and circumstance. What had Galttauer said about time?

"Time is our true enemy, you see. No matter what we do, it ticks on."

To hell with Galttauer too. Belmorn wouldn't waste his final hours on him either. With an effort, he shut his eyes, not to sleep but to remember better days.

"Dad? This spring... I think I should pick out a foal." Sasha approached his father as he was riding back from the river.

"Oh?" Belmorn asked in the considerate voice of a father. "You do, huh?"

"Definitely. Yeah." The boy folded his arms, the same way his father was known to, his voice very matter-of-fact. "I'm almost nine, you know."

"Nine already? My goodness, I must have lost track." Belmorn paused to look at his son with amusement while Magnus lowered his head, sampling some inland grass.

"Be serious, Dad. Nine is practically double numbers. Do you remember Garrick from Hallabard? The blacksmith's son?"

Belmorn pretended to consider this for a second or two. "You mean the same blacksmith's son who is four years older than mine and nearly five inches taller?"

"That's him," the boy continued undeterred. "He got to pick a foal-- three springs ago."

"Is that right?"

"Yeah, Dad. A stallion." The boy gave a pointed look at Magnus. "Named him Arauder, I think. Should be big enough to begin to ride next year."

Belmorn smiled. "Probably." He plucked off a flea trying to swim in the Old Man's mane. Flicked it away.

The boy bit his lower lip, looking about ready to keel over from the burden of waiting for his father to say more on the subject. "Well? Can I?"

"Can you what?"

"Pick out a foal this spring?" Sasha's face was so screwed up with frustration, it was practically blue.

"Oh, my son." His father sighed long and looked longer. "I know this can be a difficult business, waiting to grow up. But do you remember what I told you about a blackfoot's work?" He gave a nod to the lowering sun.

The boy looked miserable. In fact, if his body language could be believed, the prospect of responding was a labor equivalent to emptying the entire river with a bucket.

"Yes." He forced the word out with an exaggerated sigh. "That it doesn't end when the sun goes down."

"That's right," said Belmorn, privately brimming with pride. "River work has a way of following a man home. It sits with him at the supper table, lays in his bed, even colors his dreams. And do you remember why?"

"Because the river bites hard."

"And... ?"

"And it doesn't let go."

"Believe that, son. Every word and with all your heart. Because once you wrap a haresh around your head, once you climb into that saddle, ride out, and feel the brackish course between your toes, it will be a very long while before you climb back down again."

As Belmorn said this, he considered the possibility that he had gone too far. There was yet more to say, but his son was just a boy. Not even nine. There would be plenty of time for him to come to grips with the life ahead of him. Decades if Rinh was kind. Belmorn pulled on his stallion's reins and offered a weary, surrendering smile as he continued walking.

"You'll understand one day."

The boy refolded his arms, trying and failing to look cross. "Even if I never learn to ride?"

Belmorn shook his head and smiled. "Definitely." The man winked at his son. "And one day, before you know it, you'll ride back home after a long, wet day, but it will be an old man who steps from your saddle. And you'll look down to see a small child standing there. A girl or perhaps a boy who must certainly be secretly drinking magical potions for how fast they grow. This child will look up, and they will see you. See you the way no one else can. And then they will start asking about foals."

"Dad..." The boy looked unconvinced of something. "You're not old."

"No?" Belmorn mocked astonishment.

"No."

"Hmm..." He considered this. "Well I feel old."

Belmorn could almost feel the shared laughter shaking his body. His arms twitched with an acute muscle memory of a father scooping up his son--holding him in his arms and squeezing. It was difficult to endure. Not at the time, but here and now--as he sat, waiting for the bells of morning.

The last he would ever hear.

5-3

A clamor jolted the man's bones, hitting like a bucket of ice water and banishing the vision of his son.

Just outside his cell, a shout had been cut short. Then came a series of heavy, clanging thuds. The dropping of a stack of cook pots was the first thought to enter Belmorn's brain. Inclining his head, he peered through the lattice.

There! Another thud was followed by a dull sliding, as if something was being dragged. Desperate to see, Belmorn pressed himself against the bars, but the angle was bad. He strained but had no power to see around corners. Whatever was happening was near. In the direction of the posted guards.

Seconds later, a figure appeared. Dark, cloaked, and more importantly, hooded.

"You?" Belmorn hissed, taking the only step back the small enclosure allowed. As the moment passed, surprise gave way to anger. "What are you... ?"

"Maybe not a friend," said the hooded man. "But the closest thing you have." Raising a ring of keys, the man tried them one at a time.

"Not close enough," Belmorn growled. "I've already tasted your idea of gratitude. Should have left you for the crows."

"Yes, well... perhaps so." Three keys into the ring, the hooded man was beginning to look nervous. "Warned you, didn't I? That folks up here are a cold lot."

Belmorn's frown became a scowl. He made his hands into fists, certain that they would fly soon.

The hooded man worked hurriedly, throwing a glance toward where the noises of commotion had come from. As the fifth key clicked with a deep metallic whine, the door swung open.

Belmorn reached through the iron doorway, grasping cloak and slamming the hooded man against the wall.

"Wait!" The man's voice was thin, choked. "Look--your anger is justified, but there's no time for it. We have to go before..."

"We?!" Belmorn slammed him against the wall again. "There is no we!"

"There is if you want to get out of here!" sputtered the hooded man, real fear in his expression.

For a long moment, Belmorn's grip did not loosen. His fury felt good. Better than that--righteous. He had fantasized about such a moment, a last chance to extract some measure of pain from this one.

"Sasha." Belmorn hissed the name through his teeth.

Bewilderment colored the hooded man's reddening face.

"You killed him, you son of a bitch!" Ferocity shaped the blackfoot's words. "You've killed my son!"

The hooded man's struggles were feeble--meaningless against the blackfoot's considerable rage. Registering as little more than the resistance of water weeds against a river's swell and flow. Within seconds, his face went to a shade of purple as his eyes bulged from their sockets. He opened his mouth but all that came was a squeaking hiss of air. The last breath he would ever take.

The sight hit Belmorn like a kick to the gut.

Realizing what he was doing, he dropped the hooded man. Both horrified and ashamed, he took a step back--gasping as if he had been the one nearly choked to death.

5-4

Dimming light rushed back in an explosion of color and shock.

The alchemist gasped, hungrily gulping down air that both froze and scalded his lungs. Kro's mind raced, but one thing was certain: He wasn't dead yet. He'd been gifted with mercy once again by a tall stranger whose name he hadn't bothered to learn. And now, that man was stepping toward him, frowning deeply.

Clutching his bruised throat, Tenebrus Kro held up a submissive hand. "Wait!" His voice gave way to a bout of dry coughs.

The tall man stopped. Anger melted into concern across his dark face and grey eyes. "I almost--"

Kro waved away the rest of the man's sentence. "Forget it," he said. "Had it coming. Look, I'm probably the last person you'd like to trust right now, but if you want to get out of here..." He threw a nervous glance towards the only way out of the narrow structure. "But we have to move quickly. Not out of the woods yet, so to speak."

Still looking guilty, the tall man pick up the bear pelt from where it lay near the cell's gate. As he threw the garment over his shoulders, Kro remembered what he'd seen and grabbed on his way to find this person who kept stubbornly intersecting with his life.

"Here. They had the rest of your effects in a box outside." He offered the headscarf and a leather band with several burnished medallions. As Kro pushed these forward, a beam of moonlight landed right on a small inscription carved into the inside of the headband. "Lord

Belmorn?" Kro read this with as much amusement as surprise. "Are you from a noble house?"

"No." The newly-freed prisoner took the ornament and slipped it over the marbled black fabric of his headscarf. "Just a bad joke. Forget it. Let's go."

Kro nodded and led the way down the hall, past the two guards he'd treated to a pinch of Gorgon dust.

"You froze them," the large man said loudly. "Like you froze me."

Warily, Kro looked around, searching for new arrivals and other unwanted surprises. "That is the wrong word for it. Think of it this way... If you imagine every muscle in your body as a hand..." He held up an open hand. "The Gorgon dust turns them all into fists." He clenched to demonstrate. "Typically, consciousness fades fast, like snuffing out a candle. As you can attest, the effect isn't pleasant." He turned to regard the men on the ground. "But they'll live. And that is more mercy than those masked idiots will spare us if we are caught again so, if you don't mind."

Kro headed out to where two horses--a chestnut gelding and a silver mare--had been tied to a pair of posts.. With a pleasant smile, he quickly freed the mare and checked her temperament. The horse was lithe and lovely, turning her head with the slightest touch of rein.

"So sorry to ask this of you, lady," Kro spoke gently, offering the back of his hand for her to sniff. "But I need your help." After ensuring her girth was secure, he stepped into stirrup and eased himself onto the saddle. His smile grew as she accepted his mount--turning willingly when asked.

Noticing the larger man had not even approached the chestnut, the alchemist called, "What are you waiting for? We have to go."

"No," the man growled. "Not without the horse I rode in on. He doesn't belong so far from his home. From the river. And he sure as hell doesn't deserve this frozen city. I'll not leave without him."

"Aah! A riverman, blackfoot maybe. That explains a lot." Kro nodded with the realization. "Damn," he said. "So we are talking about the big one, yes? The adamandray?"

Surprise widened the eyes of the other man as he stared back at the alchemist.

"River men and their horses." Kro sighed. Pleased with his revelation but now aware of new challenges, he shook his head. "He's right where you left him. Just go fast."

"What do you mean 'where I left him'?"

"Town square. By the statue. They built a makeshift corral around the beast. From what I've heard, not even a battalion of guards could move him." Kro gave a chuckle, unsurprised in the least from what he remembered of those horses.

The riverman's face flushed with pride. "Well done, Old Man."

"Just be aware..." Worry crept into Kro's voice as he recalled the set-up in the square. "You may have to fight for him. There were three guards posted earlier. One more than they spared for you here! Some or all may be occupied with other matters. It's possible. I did buy us some time, but little of that remains at this point. So get your horse and meet me there, at the north gate." He pointed. "Opposite direction of all the smoke."

"The *smoke*?"

"You'll see it." Kro couldn't keep the grin out of his voice. This rescue plan, at least, was unfolding as efficiently as he'd planned it. "Hopefully, I'll have the gate open by the time you get there."

The riverman relieved one of the frozen guards of his long sword. Pulling the blade from its scabbard, he tested the weight as he asked, "What if you can't get the gate open?"

"Well," Kro shrugged. "In that case, Roon's executioner is going to have a busy couple of days. Now move, riverman." With this, Kro rounded his horse and began to gallop away.

"Hey!" The voice of the man boomed. "Who are you?"

"Call me Kro," the alchemist called without looking back. "Pleasantries later. Just go!"

5-5

Rander Belmorn gripped his stolen longsword. Though he was glad for the weapon, the weight felt strange in his hand. Alien. He hoped he could use it well enough, if it came to that. By Rinh, what he wouldn't give to hold his axes again.

Just as he finished rounding a corner, Belmorn stopped and sniffed. Upon the night air hung a dangerous, unmistakable scent.

Smoke.

He glanced to what he regarded as south. The streets of Roon were utterly empty. Was the hour so late? Or was this due to something else? The work of this new hooded ally?

Shouting came from a distance, from the same general direction as the smoke.

Belmorn ducked into the shadow of a small overhang. Approaching from another direction was a garrison of mounted soldiers. *Five or six*, he thought. They were riding hard toward him. Heart in his throat, Belmorn pressed his back against a wall, willing his body to flatten. He became acutely aware of minute details regarding the sword in his hand--from the weight down to the texture of the grip.

What if the blade caught some errant beam of light and proved his undoing? Quickly, quietly, Belmorn positioned the stolen weapon in between his body and the wall. He held it there, too nervous to even breathe.

On the stone street, the coming hooves pounded a terrible, chaotic rhythm. In a great gust of air, the soldiers thundered past, pushing their horses not fifteen feet from where Belmorn stood. With a mixture of horror and relief, he watched them go. Riding off and away, in the direction of the shouts and smoke.

It took a moment before the man in the shadows dared move again. Then he ran. Ran for all he was worth. Cold wind blew through the street, filling and freezing already chilled lungs. Still he pushed, forcing his legs to keep their pace. Ahead, Belmorn could see a familiar intersection. He had passed it the night before. Or had that been two nights ago?

Ignoring the meaningless question, he dashed out of the safety of the shadows to where he'd last seen his oldest friend.

The silver man with the sword through his heart stood as proudly as before, one hand holding out a flickering lantern. From such a distance, the tiny light seemed almost alive--like the careless glow of a candle fly. Kro had spoken true. By the statue was a fence that hadn't been there before. It was a sort of corral, hastily built but nearly five feet high. Inside was a sight for sore eyes.

"Magnus!" Belmorn's shout caused the horse to swing its massive head in his direction. Unfortunately, the call had a similar effect on the pair of armed guards outside the corral.

"Oy!" one guard shouted as both men unsheathed their long swords. Each was an exact duplicate of the one Belmont gripped. More than ever, the weapon felt strange, but he managed to block a hard downward thrust.

To his surprise, the attacks came rather clumsily. One from the front, and then a second from the side. These men, these Roonik Guards-- though their black and silver armor lent a fearsome aspect, they seemed hesitant. Even with such an ungainly weapon, Belmorn was able to block and move fast enough to prevent the guards from flanking him.

The fact was, his fighting skills had been honed battling slithering river beasts--pounding forearm-length harpoons into their hides. It was a prowess they celebrated back home, but hardly useful in his current predicament. So what then was giving the guards pause? Was it simply the Belmorn's size or the storm which raged in eyes? Or is it possible that his new false identity was actually doing some good?

If I ever meet this Morgrig person... thought Belmorn, deflecting another attack. *I may actually have to thank him.*

"You there!" One guard backed several steps away and shouted through panting breaths. "Go! Tell the captain! Mannis Morgrig is loose!"

KLANG!!

Sparks flew as Belmorn's sword clashed with another.

"Hurry, Damn you!"

KLANG!! KLANG!!

A misstep sent one guard lurching forward, just enough for an opening. Unlike the captain's metal, these guards' armor was designed to cover the shoulders and chest, leaving certain areas unprotected. Belmorn buried his fist in the man's stomach and the guard dropped to the ground.

"Behind you!" a voice shouted, high in pitch. The voice of a child.

Belmorn turned just in time to see the gaping end of a black powder pistol. The second guard was smiling.

BAOH!!

With a flash of light, the top third of Belmorn's sword disappeared. River man and Roonik guard stood frozen, mouths agape, eyes wide and white. Belmorn heard a terrible wailing. As if there were a miniature pipe organ in his skull and someone was holding down one of the high keys.

Looking at what remained of his longsword, he watched a tendril of smoke drift from the point of impact in a long, liquid thread. The world beyond, for a moment, faded to non-importance. Right then, reality was reduced to the ragged remains of this sword. This stolen weapon that had miraculously saved his life.

There came a great crack, the breaking of wood. The sound ripped Belmorn into the current moment and set his mind back on course.

The adamandray brought down its massive hooves, further splitting a section of fence. The boards had no chance but to be split and pummeled into a mass of wooden quills. Barking a deep, angry neigh, the horse Magnus leapt free of the enclosure he had, until that moment, chosen to abide. The huge animal arched its neck and lifted its tail.

The guard with the pistol turned just in time to see a flash of feathered hoof. The hop and strike happened faster than one would expect from such a massive animal. Like the boards of the corral, the guard's fate was sealed. His body crumpled lifelessly. And there on the cobbles, blood flowed from a new canyon in the man's skull. Within seconds, a pool had grown. A lake of the most vibrant red that Belmorn had ever seen.

Tossing aside the shattered, miracle sword, Belmorn looked into the large glassy eyes of his oldest friend. "You waited for me." He slid a hand up the animal's jaw--patting it firmly. "I only wish I had something for you. You must be starving."

The horse snorted into his human's face before sniffing at the man's forehead.

"Yeah," said Belmorn "They didn't feed me either." His gaze moved to the horse's flanks. To the intact saddle bags and, more importantly, the twin pair of Graelian axes, still secure in their sheaths. "Well done, Old Man." Belmorn practically bubbled with elation. "You didn't let them near you, eh? Of course you didn't. Come on, I think it's time we leave."

One hand was on the saddle horn, one foot already in the ladder of rings when Belmorn paused. There was a small sound. A weak whimpering coming from somewhere close by. It was a sound that right now, Belmorn did not have time for. Every nerve in his body was on fire with the need to ride. He recalled his cardinal rule, the one about never investing in business outside of his own.

"But--?" came a small voice from somewhere behind. "Can't... I can't..."

A distant battalion of armed guards was running their way. They were crossing the wide intersection now. They would be on him in under a minute. Much closer, however, was a small child. A waifish thing, draped in a smelly old blanket

Protruding from the small body, from the soft patch between collar, chest and shoulder was something that did not belong. Something long and thin that gleamed metallic in the light of the September moon. The object's identity clicked in Belmorn's mind as the blanket changed color from dirt brown to a deep, dark red.

"Sir? I... can't..." The boy looked at the shard of the exploded sword that had impaled him. In his eyes were questions, though Belmorn did not know what to say.

5-6

The adamandray thundered over the cold cobbles of the ancient city like wind born of a hurricane. The fur of Belmorn's bear pelt buzzed on either side of a prominent collar. The long, tattered ends of his haresh headscarf flapped behind like twin lashes. His eyes were hard, focused. They had to be. One hand was holding the reins of a galloping horse while the other cradled a small child.

The body was cold but still alive. Belmorn pressed the small, unconscious form to his side, willing a fraction of his own warmth to be of some benefit.

The one thing he refused to do was look down. To do so now, to see the length of cold steel protruding from such a small being would surely be his undoing. As he galloped over the darkened streets of Roon, Rander Belmorn accepted a silent, wordless oath.

He did not know this homeless boy, had never even asked for a name. Why had he gotten close when all other children shrank away from his villainous appearance? Not once but twice. Both times by that statue.

It didn't matter. The why seldom did.

Why would the purple sickness return after so long? Why had it affected only one child in all of the towns along the black? And if one child had to suffer, why did it have to be his?

Sasha. The name burned in Belmorn's throat--behind his eyes.

But nineteen weeks and who knew how many leagues separated

this man from his small, bedridden son. Sashander Belmorn needed his father. But in the last few minutes, something had changed. Another had needed him more.

Belmorn frowned; a stab of pain pulsing in his stitched lower lip. Urging his mount on faster, one thought burned in his mind.

To hell with the damn cardinal rule.

More hoof beats made him look behind to see three riders were approaching. Fast. Just not fast enough. Another turn set him directly toward the northern gate. The massive iron lattice work was already rising as wheels of varying size turned and moaned. The mechanical racket reached Belmorn in his saddle, even over the cacophony of hooves.

He glanced behind again. The riders were closing in. If it came to another fight, Belmorn would lose. He gripped the child more tightly in his arm and leaned into the speed of his horse.

Next to the sentry shack was the silver mare. It stood a few paces away from the gate, pawing at the ground, unsure what was happening. Not wanting to panic the animal, Belmorn urged Magnus to a slow trot. Inside the shack, a hooded man was furiously battling the control wheel. On the floor, the sentry lay stiff and unmoving, another victim of the wizard's dust.

"About time!" shouted the man. Belmorn remembered he'd called himself "Kro." He turned the wheel one last time with a loud, metallic clunk. "The mare! Get her out of here! I'm right behind you!"

Wasting no time, Belmorn transferred the reins to his other hand and whistled at the silver mare. As she looked up, he reached out for her bridle, then led her beneath the iron gate.

Once they were clear, Kro released the control wheel. With a guttural shout, he kicked a large, floor-mounted lever. The device gave a brief metallic squeal, sending the heavy gate outside into a free fall.

Dashing out of the shack, Kro spared a glance to the three approaching riders. In the lead was a man with a wild mane of blond hair, billowing like the open flame of a torch. Even from this distance, the ice-blue eyes of Henric Galttauer burned with terrible, freezing fire.

Stealing a final breath of Roonik air, Tenebrus Kro threw himself forward. Rolling beneath the descending gate and out of that city of fools for what he hoped was the last time.

Leaping onto the silver mare, he met the shocked eyes of the riverman as the gate crashed behind them. The sound spurred the horses into a full gallop. Slender mare and gigantic adamandray raced hard and fast away from the ancient city that had treated its guests so poorly.

Kro looked back over his shoulder and through the bars. Though the good captain was riding hard, it would take many minutes to get the gate open again. Not that he would. By Kro's guess, Galttauer hadn't left his city in a long time. Years maybe. Long enough for his southern roads to become thoroughly infested.

Mannis Morgrig was no wolf. Only a moth whose flame was the inaction of a coward. In the moment, Kro's judgment of Galttauer felt righteous but his conscience put a stop to that. It reminded him that the sins of the captain paled next to his own. Still, it felt good to look down on someone else for a change.

Allowing the rhythm of the horse to erase his rising guilt, Kro took a deep breath of forest air. Then he set his eyes on 'Lord' Belmorn. The riverman was imposing. His height exaggerated further by the enormous horse he rode. The animal had to be twenty hands high at least.

"I see you've picked up a passenger," Kro shouted.

At first, Belmorn said nothing, but tightened his arm around the child. "Not a passenger," he yelled back. "A patient. An innocent. Will Galttauer follow us?"

"Not likely--" Kro interrupted himself with a gasp. A terrible shard stuck out of the unmoving child like the blade of a hilt-less dagger. He composed himself enough to explain further and perhaps lessen the panicked worry in his tall companion's eye. "Henric won't dare leave his people. Not even to protect them."

Kro cast another look at the child. His mind trying to estimate the extent of the injury, how long they might be able to ride. This small patient needed immediate attention, but Kro was no doctor.

As the hooded-man looked at the child in Belmorn's arms, the wind caught the edge of his hood just right and blew it back. The man's face was gaunt, weathered. It was the face of one who had lived not one lifetime but many, none of which looked to have been easy.

Even in the low light, as he looked upon that face, Belmorn felt the distinct spark of recognition. He knew that nose, those high cheekbones, that curve of jaw. By Rinh, he did.

The hooded man pulled at his reins--slowing the mare down to a trot, then a stop. In a flourish of cloak he dismounted and held up a finger.

"Don't move." The man lifted his hood. "I'll be right back."

With that, he disappeared into the shadows between the trees. Seconds stretched into minutes and the adamandray snorted a cloud of hot, impatient air.

"It's alright, Old Man." Belmorn patted the horse's neck, scanning the woods on either side. Darkness prickled his skin along with the cold.

It would be morning soon. And despite their dramatic escape, dawn might yet be bringing death. Reluctantly, his eyes settled upon the metal shard protruding from the unconscious child whose name he did not know. An urge rose then--in his chest and in his fingers. He wanted to grip that piece of broken sword and pull. He lifted a hand to do so.

"Don't," said the man in the hood, stepping back onto the path without as much as a rustling footfall. "That shard could be on an artery. Here. Let me." Kro extended both arms into which Belmorn lowered the child.

Kneeling, Kro gently lay the precious bundle upon a patch of earth where the coating of snow was thinnest. Then he hunched over the body. His posture and long dark cloak obscured his work from the man on the horse.

Belmorn dismounted, approached, and then froze as the clang of metal shattered the near-perfect silence. He looked down at the bloody shard on the ground. It was long--unthinkably long. Ten inches at least and on one end, he could see a distinct blemish--pure black. Scoring from where the pistol ball had hit.

As he stared at the unlikely thing, snow began to gently fall. And where the flakes fell upon the shard, they turned from white to pink before going full red.

"One of the guards tried to shoot me from behind. But this child warned me just in time. I turned and... The shot hit the sword, perfectly. And it exploded."

"Well... you're in luck," said Kro without looking away from his patient. "Missed all the important bits."

Belmorn exhaled. It was strange. He hadn't meant to hold his breath. "Good," he managed to say. "That's very good." He took another step forward to see what was happening. The man called Kro was kneading something in the palm of his right hand while the left applied pressure to the wound. A sharp smell scratched his nostrils. Like fresh cut pine but mixed with something else.

Lemons?

"The bandana," barked the man in the hood. "Give it here."

Stunned, but only for a moment, Belmorn removed his leather headband and then the dark, marbled haresh he had so recently recovered. Strands of hair fell to the sides of the man's face, but he was too cold to feel them.

Kro pressed and worked whatever he had been kneading into the wound. Blood leaked out in a single gush, but was quickly stanched.

"What is that?" Belmorn stood there feeling useless. "Tree sap?"

"From the northern pine." The hooded man slowly transitioned from pressing with his palms to just his thumbs. "Should stop the bleeding. Bandana!" He thrust out a filthy hand, snatched the cloth, began to wrap it around the limp form of the child, under one armpit and around the opposite side of the neck.

"Damn it," grumbled Kro. "This is one hell of an inconvenient place to get run through. An arm or a leg I can dress. This?" He shook his head. "Listen... Belmont was it?"

"Bel-morn." He spoke slowly.

"Right. Well, I won't lie. This wound... is bad. Ugly. The shard has left slivers behind. I found two, but there's likely more inside. I've done all I can here, but if we don't get those slivers out..."

The statement hung in the air, incomplete and yet fully understood.

"I have a place. A safe place." Kro lifted the child, setting it back into the waiting arms of Belmorn. "Maybe five miles from here. In the thorns. If she lives that long, I'll do what I can."

Belmorn's eyes were wide as saucers. "She?"

PART SIX
INTO THE THORNS

6-1

Beneath a waxing September moon, two riders tore out into open country. The dense woodland had given way to a sprawling darkness that rolled away on all sides.

The terrain of the low Veld contrasted starkly from the forest but details were hard to discern. More than anything, Rander Belmorn was aware of a vast openness. For the first time in days, it felt like he could actually breathe.

Belmorn's eyes strained to adjust to the sudden increase in light, but slowly, blurry forms took shape. He could see strange, wedge-like protrusions, dozens of them--jutting up from the ground at angles that gave pause. As a blackfoot, Belmorn's thoughts went straight to the wellbeing of the horses. About the potential calamity that could be wrought by a single misplaced hoof.

"We have to slow down!" His voice boomed over the sound of galloping horse feet.

Kro turned his head in time to see the adamandray slow to a brisk jog. And though he urged his silver mare to do the same, the alchemist did not look happy about it.

"That girl..." His voice was slightly muffled by a dark red cloth that was covering his nose and mouth. "She doesn't have long, Belmorn. You must know that. If you want her to have a chance, we must move fast. As fast as we possibly can."

"We are." Said the blackfoot, in a tone that welcomed no argument.

"The light is bad and I don't like the look of those rocks."

"We call them giant's teeth," shouted Kro, pointing at a cluster of the ugly stone protrusions. "The crows peck at lichens that grow mostly on one side. Gives them that slanting shape."

"Good for the crows," Said Belmorn. "Bad for us. I won't put the horses in danger, and we've already pushed them too hard, getting away from that damned city. Right now, this is as fast as we go."

Hearing the logic and hating that he was unable to argue with it, Kro relaxed his seat, softened his posture.

"Have it your way, then. We're close enough anyway I suppose. Maybe another two miles. Ten or fifteen minutes at this pace providing we don't stop again."

"Good." Said Belmorn slowly riding past the man. "So what are you complaining about?"

Ahead, the road shot across about a mile of this hard, rock-laden country before swelling into a hill--the slope of which was only visible by its slight, moonlit edge.

As the breeze lessened on his cheek, Belmorn looked down to the small child who fit so well in the crook of his arm. She couldn't have been much older than his own son. Perhaps nine or ten. In the low light, it would be easy to mistake her lack of consciousness for sleep-- to hope that she was dreaming of better things than those he had given her.

What had she been doing? The question burned. Why had she not run away when the fighting began?

Still holding the reins, Belmorn adjusted the tourniquet with his thumb and forefinger. His marbled black haresh was still tight around her body and the flow of blood had not resumed. Small reliefs, but they would do. For reliefs were in short supply.

This child, this little girl... Belmorn knew right then that he would do anything to save her. But he could not forget his true purpose.

In a great, frustrated cloud, the man expelled the combined weight of too many burdens. He slid a gloved hand over the top of his head. Without the haresh, his hair had gone stiff, frosted and freezing into slivers of black ice. Once again he regretted not spending a little more on a better cloak. Specifically, one with a hood. With this thought, he turned to regard the man riding beside him.

"Why'd you do it?" His voice was flat but not unfriendly.

The other rider turned. In the stark moonlight, his face was lost in the shadows of his hood.

"Good lord, Belmorn, you really do know how to start a conversation. Do what?"

"Why did you risk your own life?" asked Belmorn. The storm in his voice was audible but restrained. "Freeing a man from prison--from a death sentence. A man you already left for the crows?"

"Ha," Kro scoffed in a tone that held no mirth. "I didn't leave you for the crows, Belmorn." His voice was low. "I just left you."

"Is there a difference?"

"Of course there is a difference! I made you a talisman, didn't I?" Kro looked for a response.

Belmorn's mind raced back, finding the past few days to be a blur. He could remember trying to move. The feeling of being trapped. Of perfect helplessness. And he remembered the crows, who had surely took him for dead. How bold they had become. Bold enough to sample his face. He pressed his tongue against the inside of his lip, tracing the stitches and tasting the faint traces of moss and blood. The area was still tender, but not quite so inflamed as it had been. Another small relief, he supposed. At last, he offered,

"What is a talisman?"

Hearing this, Kro couldn't help but laugh. "Feet, intestines, flowers. Pinned right to your shirt, it should have kept most things away."

The memory clicked. Belmorn had all but forgotten the strange bundle he'd found pinned to his chest upon waking from that sleep of dust. He had interpreted the thing as a further sleight. Some manner of pungent black magic.

"A talisman." He repeated the word. "So that's what that was."

"Think of it as forcing a skunk to notice its own reek," Said Kro. "No crow would touch you wearing that. Even added some wolfsbane, just in case... but it seems the only extant wolves in these woods do their hunting on two legs."

As Kro went on, Belmorn drifted a bit. Again his tongue poked at the cleft in his lip. He still had no idea who had mended the wound. However unlikely it was, someone had found him out there as he lay so exposed and helpless in the snow. *Someone or something.* With this unsettling thought, Belmorn could once again picture the last thing his conscious mind had been able to process. An army of stars had twinkled between the trees.

No, he thought. *Not stars... eyes.*

"Your talisman..." Belmorn said at last. "It didn't work."

"Huh? What? What do you mean it didn't work?" Kro almost

sounded offended.

"I mean if the crows noticed it, they weren't impressed. When I woke up they were sampling my face."

"Damn," Kro said with disbelief.

"Is that all you have to say? 'Damn'?"

"Sorry--would you prefer: Shit?" Kro turned away, began tapping his chin with one finger. "I've used this method many times and it's always worked. Timber crows scavenge, but they can't abide the reek of their own dead. Unless..." Suddenly, he brought a fist down on his leg, hitting it hard. "The herb-of-grace--I added it for the wolves but... somehow the aromas must have crossed. Become inert. Like liver and onions." This last part was muttered under Kro's breath. "Just like liver and onions. Shit. Have to make a note of that one. When we reach the moat, I'll have to--"

But the words trailed off into a stream of incoherent whisperings that made Belmorn wonder if Kro had forgotten he was there at all. For many minutes thereafter, the only sound was the dull clopping of hooves and the soft, unintelligible mutterings of a strange hooded man. Kro. If that really was his name. Until now, his words had been few, far between, and always a little left of direct. Consistently tinged with sarcasm and a wry edge that bordered on contempt.

Now Belmorn glared at the back of that hooded head and shook his own. As much as it frustrated him to admit it, he needed this man. Like it or not, Kro was the child's best hope.

As they rode on, much of Belmorn's concentration shifted to the ground. These giant's teeth came in all sizes. The blackfoot found his concern divided between the wounded child and his oldest friend. As the ground sloped upwards, Belmorn could feel the animal tense. He patted Magnus' neck, kneading his muscles as they moved up the hill. The adamandray was accustomed to resisting the punishing flow of their great, black river, but this country was a new challenge. One that called upon none of the animal's natural talents.

"Look," Kro forced the word out. "For what it's worth, I'm sorry. My actions after the crows... could have been better."

Could have been better?! Belmorn's thoughts roared but remained unsaid. At last, he simply muttered, "Forget it. The past doesn't matter. Right now, saving this one does." He lowered an ear to the girl's face. "Her breathing... it's getting weaker. I don't know why you saved me, wizard, but I do not trust you. So help me, if you've lied about where you are leading us. If she dies..." Belmorn's threat hung in the night air, incomplete but understood. He took a deep breath, just as both riders crested the hill. "How much farther is it to your safe place?"

Kro pointed to the landscape below. "See for yourself."

Belmorn peered out over the sprawling, moonlit waste. Though he had to concentrate, his eyes could detect something in the darkness that was darker still. Miles long, it stretched to the east and the west, circling where he knew the mountain to be.

"A wall?"

"Yes. One that separates the low Veld from the high. Most call it The Moat." Kro's voice was grim. His head turned, scanning the area. To the west, maybe another mile off, the path they were on led to a gap. As far as Belmorn could see, it was the only way through this oddly named wall.

"The giant's teeth are mostly behind us." Kro's voice sounded impatient, even eager. "Alright with you if we pick up the pace?"

Following a low grunt from Magnus, Belmorn nodded.

"Okay then," said Kro. "Follow me and mind the slope."

Cued by their riders, both horses raced down the other side of the hill. The adamandray was more than a third larger, but his was a breed not built for racing. The mare pulled out ahead, tearing like a silver ghost. Then, to Belmorn's surprise, Kro drove his horse from the path and began moving east--across an open field and in the exact, opposite direction of the Moat's only visible gateway. As if reading the blackfoot's mind, Kro turned back and waved for Belmorn to follow.

Wearing a fresh frown, Belmorn leaned in, holding tightly his precious cargo. And though he never heard it... the girl who's name he did not know, gasped softly.

Eyes opened but what they saw could not be rationalized.

A flap of shirt. A field of stars. The images came in flashes. A circle of light. Black fur.

The girl's mind was fevered--heavy with something like sleep that wasn't sleep. She was moving. That much she could feel. And there was wind, cold wind, on her face. But the girl didn't understand. Couldn't understand.

The sleep-that-wasn't... was calling again. Pulling her down and down.

The last she saw of that night was a snow-covered hill shrinking in the distance. And though it might merely have been the whimsy of a grasping mind, the girl imagined someone was standing on that hill. Standing and watching her go. In her state of partial-lucidity, for just a fraction of a moment, she imagined the man was none other than the hero of her favorite story. Charon himself--the defeater of the Teng-Hu and its three terrible children. The notion brought comfort as she faded the rest of the way out of consciousness.

Meanwhile, in the very spot Rivka had been watching, a man of dark aspect sat upon a gaunt horse. Watching the two riders with great interest, the brigand was quiet and he was patient. Once satisfied, Raigar turned his horse the other way round, then headed back down the way he had come. Straight for the ruined forest camp where an anxious Mannis Morgrig awaited his report.

6-2

Belmorn felt undeniably exposed.

He had never been in a place so open, yet so devoid of features. Though the darkness seemed thinner here than in the woods, there simply wasn't much to see. Hills, snow, rocks and a vast swath of open sky. Behind it all was a vague shape, ominous in its scale. The blackfoot couldn't see Mount Einder, not exactly. But the missing stars told him it was there.

Far closer though, was Kro's strange wall, the oddly named Moat. Why they weren't heading toward the opening he'd seen irked Belmorn. He considered asking whether Kro had lost his mind or not, but that would mean breaking the silence that had grown between them. Belmorn breathed in, filling his lungs with the frigid air. Letting it out slowly, he resolved to learn as much as he could with his own eyes.

Approaching the wall, Kro slowed his mare to a trot before dismounting in a flourish of cloak. At this distance, Belmorn could see that the moat was no solid thing but rather a tangled mass of prickle-vines. Memories of the vampiric rose flickered, but he pushed them away. In less dramatic fashion, Belmorn climbed down from his saddle, careful of the stricken child in his arms.

The blackfoot regarded the wall. Looking left and then right he confirmed two things. The structure stretched farther than he could see in both directions and there was no apparent way through the damned thing.

Turning around, he noticed a rather conspicuous rock directly behind them. Unlike the giant's teeth, this one was broad and flat. It was the only blemish on this particular swath of country.

"What are we doing here?" demanded Belmorn. "The way through the thorns was back there. I could see a road from the crest of that hill."

"I'm sure you could," Kro sounded preoccupied. "But I'm not looking for that door. I'm looking for mine."

Belmorn waited for further explanation, but none was offered. In frustration, he grumbled something under his breath.

"What was that?" asked Kro without turning from the thorns.

Belmorn sighed. "I said 'The Moat' is a strange name for a wall of thorns."

Kro appeared preoccupied. The man was clearly looking for something, but to Belmorn, there could be nothing to find. Wherever he set his eyes, the wall's surface was a uniform mess--tangled and overgrown.

"The name would make more sense if we could see the mountain," Kro answered after a bit. "Many have looked upon those peaks and seen a castle. And as I'm sure you'll attest, every proper castle needs a--" The man stopped mid-sentence, straightening his back. "Ah!" Kro drew his knife.

Belmorn had seen the weapon before. Had seen it pulled from the same old tree trunk that had been host to a creeping vampire.

Kro twisted the knife between a pair of hardened vines, wiggling, sawing, and eventually prying one branch away from the rest until it snapped with a crisp wooden sound.

Its breakage revealed something flat, metallic, and covered in rust. To the blackfoot's foreign eye, this object looked like an oversized hinge. Stepping back, Belmorn took in the section before them. The more he stared, the more he could make out a vague rectangular outline... close to six feet wide and taller than he was.

"A door?" His words formed an unintentional question.

"Only counts as a door if we can get it open." Kro's huffed. He turned to regard the child in Belmorn's arms. Her face was pale, but with an unsettling under-hue of yellow. With a flash of what might have been concern, Kro spun around and began hacking away with his knife. As he worked, wooden bits and thorns spun through the air to collect at his feet.

"This is it then?" Belmorn's voice was low. "Your safe place."

"It is." Kro's breath was getting labored from the exertion, but he did not stop. "Though admittedly, I've been away for a while. Too long, perhaps." He drew an arm across his brow. "These vines... They grow slowly, but they never actually stop." His speech was becoming truncated with short gasps.

Belmorn watched the man work a little more, examined what he was doing and what he was trying to accomplish. With a sigh, he made a decision. One he hoped he wouldn't regret.

"Kro."

The stern voice caused the alchemist to stop. Breathing heavily, he turned around and was struck by the eyes of the riverman. They possessed a steely glow in the moonlight.

Belmorn took a step forward, offering the girl who slumbered restlessly in his arm. "Take her."

For an awkward moment, Kro couldn't comprehend what was being asked of him. This business of clearing brush with a dagger was hard enough. Did the blackfoot expect him to do better whilst holding the girl in one arm? The proposition was ludicrous, of course, but Tenebrus Kro was exhausted and overtaxed, and it had been more than seven years since anyone had freely offered to lighten his burden.

He opened his mouth but quickly closed it. Putting the knife away, Kro accepted the unconscious girl, wrapping his long night-blue cloak around her.

Belmorn stepped pointedly to his gigantic horse, unfastened the clasps on one sheath and then the other--returning with those unforgettable axes in hand.

"Mind the hinges." Kro pointed, drawing a vertical line with one finger. "There are four. All secured to a single post... here."

Belmorn looked at the massive wooden column the vines had reclaimed. Without another word, twin axes sliced through air and bramble, ripping into the thorny mass.

As he watched the branches fly and fall, Kro's mind drifted inward, to that secret burden. The one question that had sent him halfway around the world, before finally calling him back to its edge. The unfinished task was all that mattered. The duty had been Kro's truest companion for so long he could hardly remember an existence without it. Now that he was so close to completing the damned thing--

Now

The word gave him pause. Its bitterness permeated his sleep-deprived body and mind. He had been so close then. Before the incident with the rose and the wolves. Nearly at the end. Nearly home. Nearly done.

But no more. Not since a single night of brash impulses nearly cost the man his life. And while he yet lived, Tenebrus Kro had paid for his foolishness with his one chance. The hope it had taken seven long years to find. Truly, the road ahead had changed much in such a short time. So much that Kro felt as if he had been thrust back to the start of it all--to that blackest of all his days.

How had he come to this? Standing out in the cold night, cradling an unconscious whelp, waiting for a strange man to finish hacking away the vines from his old door. This was not where he had pictured this week going.

Kro looked down at the face of the helpless girl, then at the blood stains. The filthy horse blanket she was wrapped in was filthier now by far. Marked with a large red patch that looked darker than any shade of black he had ever seen. It looked like a mouth, like a great yawning chasm in the cosmos.

With a hard shudder, Kro turned to look at the flat rock in the distance that had always served as his marker. It looked much the same as it always had. Oblivious to the horrors that had waged around it for so long.

Lucky bastard. He thought.

Saving one child was pointless. This was a fact blissfully unknown to the rock, but Kro forced himself to remember. He had no choice. He had to find a new way forward. There was no going back. The road behind was lined only with enemies--in the woods and half the cities in the damn world. In fact, enemies were all he saw anymore. Except...

Kro regarded the blackfoot. Watched as more of the wooden post and connecting door were revealed. He could picture this man Belmorn aback some giant river eel, slashing at its bucking, slime-slick hide. Unleashing every bit of primal ferocity that his black-river-blood lent him. But here, in this remote place was a riverman with no river. A blackfoot who had crossed leagues to the very edge of the known world.

But why? For what possible purpose?

The man did not feel like an enemy, but Kro had been wrong about these things before.

Looking down at the young girl who lay helpless in his arms, he denied the swell of affection growing in his chest. Kro had known the child for a girl straight away. Even under all the caked-on grime. He had girls of his own, after all--more precious than anything. And they were waiting. Waiting for him to be done.

6-3

Belmorn tried to control his breathing, but the frigid air raked the insides of his throat with every inhale. The moat's secret door now had a clear outline of newly severed branches. It was free, and for a series of cathartic moments, he had been free too.

Opening his hands, the axes dropped to the ground. Each landed with a dull THUKK, the bladed heads embedding in the hard earth so that the handles stuck straight up. The blackfoot set his large gloved hands upon one of the door's main timbers and pulled for all he was worth. The door heaved, but ultimately snapped back to its original position. Belmorn tried again, but the result was the same.

Admittedly, the door wasn't as free as he had assumed.

Still holding the unconscious girl, Kro spoke up. "There's too much on the other side. Let me--"

The blackfoot tossed over a glare that silenced the hooded man. After pulling his axes from the ground, he strode over to the adamandray. Magnus, who had apparently fallen asleep, gave a start.

"Easy, Old Man." Belmorn slipped the axes into their sheathes, and then produced a length of thick rope from one of the saddle bags. "Just one more favor tonight, okay?"

Magnus snorted a great cloud of annoyance.

One end of the rope was attached to a heavy ring on the back of Belmorn's saddle. Then, leading the horse over to the gate, he wove the rope in and out of the thorns and around the wooden frame. Finally, he tied a knot so large and so complicated, it looked almost as tangled as the moat itself. After checking the work, Belmorn stepped up and into his saddle.

"Ready?" he asked the horse, squeezing his sides with his calves. The adamandray lumbered forward, pulling the rope taught. The gate lurched, then stopped. Though it still refused to open, Magnus' efforts prevented it from snapping back into its original position. After a second's rest, the horse took another step. From within the thorny mass, green and wiry pops could be heard. Proof of the raw power of the gigantic animal.

Kro couldn't help but wonder how the rope could hold under such strain, but then remembered the size and power of the prey these river men pulled out of the rushing black.

His mind shifted to a monstrous beast he primarily knew from illustrations. The nautiloth was a shelled, tentacled behemoth, said to reach the size of a modest cottage, yet Kro had tasted its flesh on his last trip to the region. Even now, so many years later, thinking on it made his mouth water. The meat proved unforgettable, sharing characteristics of both scallop and the rarest venison. It had been served in a thick soup along with cabbage, leeks, and heavily peppered cream.

In all his prodigious travels, the alchemist had never tasted better. Unfortunately, reliving the memory only brought misery, as the man's stomach vibrated with an angry growl.

The adamandray jerked forward with another round of snaps and pops and finally, the massive gate swung open.

"There." Belmorn turned to Kro with a smug look in his eye. "Seems we've got a door after all." He led the gigantic horse over to where the other man stood. "Kro..." He reached out a long arm. "It's okay. I'll take her."

The hooded man looked up, dumbfounded and momentarily blinded by an errant moonbeam.

"Kro?"

With a slight nod, the alchemist handed the girl carefully up to the riverman. "Heavier than she looks," Kro said with a smirk, rotating his shoulders.

Belmorn said nothing to this. He was cinching a fold of his bear pelt over the girl's shoulders, around her face.

Kro climbed into his saddle. For a second, he just stared at his unlikely companion. Stared just like a child might at the pieces of a disassembled puzzle. "Tell me Belmorn. Before we go another step... tell me why."

"Why what?" the riverman sneered.

"Why here? Why all of this?" Tenebrus Kro walked his mare slowly, cautiously, toward the dark tunnel behind the gate. "The world lies that way." He nodded south. "Behind you. Here, all you will find is its ragged edge, so tell me, Lord Belmorn, why are we doing this? Why are you here?"

The blackfoot cocked his head as wild moonlight flashed in his eyes.

Before he could utter a response, a sound unlike any other crashed into existence. It was utterly non-directional and bigger than the sky. From miles ahead or only paces behind, it flowed like a poison torrent, carrying fear and spite, but also sorrow. Inside that enormous sound, there was a note of mourning... or perhaps just the mockery of it.

As Magnus grunted and stomped the ground, Belmorn's mind raced to tales of ocean-farers he had met some weeks ago in Fengaal. Men who spoke into their cups of great leviathans. Sea-dragons, the sort which typically lurk in the edges of maps. The sailors spoke of the songs these animals would sing. Claimed they could howl like underwater wolves for hours on end.

The tales had seemed tall at the time, but Belmorn supposed there were things a man who spends his life in a five mile stretch of river might never see. Never know.

As the sound reached its end, the blackfoot wrenched his neck to glare at the hills behind. He searched the shadows for answers, finding none. Then, before he could speak, another sound resonated. A series of gulping barks. One, two, three--then nothing. Nothing at all. Beneath him, Magnus stood stock still. To Rander Belmorn, the world felt much too quiet. He opened his mouth, forced out the only question he could manage. "What in Rinh's name?"

"That's Her." Kro was rubbing the neck of his mare who'd begun to dance in place, ears flat against her head.

"Her who?"

"What do mean *who*?! Didn't you hear?" The voice of the hooded man lashed out with quiet outrage. "The Veld has a witch!"

Again came the sound. Coursing through earth and sky and bone. First the wail, then the barks. One, then two, and one more.

Though Belmorn had heard mention of this witch since passing into the Veld, he hadn't dwelled on it. But these sounds were too big! Too monstrous! He searched the distance for any sign of what might be making them. "That doesn't sound like some bent-backed, old crone to me!"

"It's not," replied Tenebrus Kro. "That's a Hispidian witchwyrm you're hearing."

Heart beating wildly, Belmorn's gaze shot down the length of the wall of thorns, westward, where he had spotted the gap that surely served as a proper door. Deep grunts shook the body of his mount. His angry stomps threatened to escalate into hops.

"The horses!" Kro's eyes seemed to burn with strange hues--one of them, the color of madness--as he pulled one rein tightly to curb his mare into a tight turn. "We have to keep them quiet! she's close. Damn close."

"What in the hell is a Hispidian witchwyrm?!" growled Belmorn, pushing Magnus into a tight figure-eight to calm him.

"A curse." Kro sighed--his hood shifted slightly, revealing a pale face. "The nemesis devourer of countless. A gigantic patchwork thing able to straddle an unnatural line, each of its feet placed firmly in two distinct places. Life and death. The within... and the Without,"

"Damn it, Kro, I don't understand what any of that means. Speak plain, and do it fast or whatever is out there will be the least of your concerns."

"Keep your voice down, you idiot," the hooded man hissed in a hoarse whisper. "You want it plain? There is no plain. Not with this thing." Kro shook his head, letting out a cloud of resigned frustration. "Look... the species has been whispered about for a thousand years-- appearing in historical records, the world over. The Akkadians wrote of the sirrush, the great serpent what slithered upon the earth without dragging its belly. On their splendid gate, the Babylonians depicted the mushussu, An amalgam of feline and reptile that was said to devour any first-born child foolish enough to be female. It was the

Slavs who first noticed the animal's unique talents. They dubbed the beast drakvedma--the dragon witch. But the doomed people of Hispidia used another word: vanisher." Briefly checking the spanse behind, Kro steered the mare towards the secret door. "We have to get inside as quickly as possible."

Licking his lips, Belmorn reached a gloved hand and absently patted the somewhat calmer adamandray. Pulling the unconscious child closer, he asked, "Safety is in there?"

The hooded man held a finger to his lips and nodded. Taking slow, deep breaths, he visibly relaxed in his saddle and rode the nervous mare into the wall of thorns. After checking that the rope was still secured to Magnus' saddle ring, Belmorn followed, closing the gate behind him. Once shut, he tugged on a central bit of the massive knot, causing the rope to unravel. With practiced swiftness, he looped up the braided length and put it away.

Then, staring into a shadow steeped corridor lined with thorns and the unknown, he became aware of the silent fear in his throat and swallowed.

6-4

Both riders urged their mounts slowly, carefully.

Not more than a couple feet above their heads, the tangle of vines formed a thorny ceiling. The points were unnervingly close and the space, damn near suffocating. An inner battle raged within Belmorn. His rising panic was beaten back by reason, but only by the slimmest of margins. As one rider followed the soft hoofbeats of the other, no words passed between them.

Within the moat, time moved strangely. Moments no longer ticked away, but stretched. Both light and visibility were diminished, but that was just as well. The blackfoot reckoned there wasn't much to see beyond too many thorns and a horse's arse. The weight of his growing fatigue was becoming formidable. He needed rest. Needed it more than he would admit, even to himself. With a deep breath, Rander Belmorn relented. Closing his eyes, he did what every blackfoot had done since first mastering the black river.

He placed his full trust in his horse.

As the adamandray moved slowly along, a subtle change crept into the air. It was cleaner, cooler. Instinctively, Belmorn took a long draft and held it, reveling in the sensation. When he opened his eyes, he saw the silhouette of Kro on his silver mare.

There was a light at the end of the passage. Not very bright, but definitely there.

"Up ahead." Kro's voice drifted past in a carefully tended volume.

"Just where I left it."

The horses moved out of the thorn corridor and into an opening. Belmorn squinted, his eyes straining to adjust. They stood in roughly a quarter acre of cleared space. The thorny walls surrounded on all sides but here in this unexpected hollow, there were none above. He looked up at the blue September moon, happy for the added company.

Kro had dismounted and was already stomping toward a structure in the center of the glade. Belmorn stared until the dark blob became four walls and a roof. It looked to be a wagon--the sort that could be pulled by a single horse.

Kro shot a whispered demand behind him. "Wait here."

Hurried footfalls were followed by the creak of hinges. Then came rustling, rifling sounds. Glass bottles tinkled together, followed by a sharp chip-chip-chipping, like a knife stabbing rock. It was almost a minute before the warm glow of fire appeared. A suspended lantern swayed back and forth inside, painting the clearing in a subtle, swaying flicker. Following this, the glow of two more lanterns came into being.

Urging Magnus closer, Belmorn could see that the cart's broad side was covered in a large tapestry cloth. It was tied in place by unseen ropes and flapped in the breeze. It was through this the light of the three lanterns shone.

Magnus snorted, shook his head.

"I have no idea," admitted Belmorn. "But... I have a feeling about this place. This damned wizard. Maybe... we aren't so far off the map's edge after all."

Mindful of the unconscious girl, the blackfoot dismounted before approaching the wagon. The rear featured a wooden door. Through this, Kro appeared, holding one of the lanterns.

"Quickly! Bring her inside."

Three steps led to the open doorway. Inside, Kro moved from drawer to drawer, opening and then slamming them shut one by one. Belmorn lowered his head and stepped up and into the wagon.

The interior was lined with shelves and surfaces of all sizes, all filled with exotic bric-a-brac. There were bottles and vials, books and bones and other sundries too numerous to take in. Mounted on one wall was a wooden elephant mask. The surface was dry, covered in cracks and ancient yellow sap. Belmorn followed the thing's unnerving, vertical eyes to a shelf just below, where a strange collection of eggs was displayed. There were six in total, all unbroken, each mounted into its own little stand. The smallest was many times larger than that of a chicken. Before each, a tiny label had been scrawled out.

Rhea, moa, strige, lammergeier, impundulu...

The names meant nothing to the blackfoot. The largest bore a deep coffee color and the label of roc, but Belmorn could see there had been one more in the collection. The gap at the end of the shelf was not only conspicuous, it also held a seventh egg stand--empty and covered in dust.

The lanterns hung to his left, on a wall that featured an ornate panel with brass hinges. It was the sort of thing that would allow the fourth wall to open--transitioning the panel into a shelf where merchandise might be displayed. It was a common enough sight in the wagons of travelling merchants. Belmorn narrowed his eyes, remembering the cloth tapestry covering the other side. The color had been difficult to discern in the moonlight. Black? Violet perhaps?

"There you are, you son of a bitch!" Kro's whisper was triumphant. He pushed the current drawer shut and turned around in a flourish of cloak. He held a small, polished cylinder in his hand so Belmorn could see. The object was unfamiliar. Definitely made of rock, but possessing a strange metallic sheen.

"Do you know what a lodestone is?" Kro's eyes shimmered in the weird light.

Belmorn looked at the rock and shook his head in answer.

Kro held the stone closer, causing the lantern-glow to slink and slide over its surface. "If there are shards, more slivers of metal, the stone will find them and pull them out of the wound. But it will not be a pleasant process. If the girl wakes, the pain will be considerable. She won't understand. She'll scream--probably a lot." Pursing his lips, Kro shook his head. "We can't have that. She'll hear. She'll come."

"Your witchwyrm." Belmorn shuddered over naming her, as if he were tasting something foul.

Kro's expression soured--turning grim. His voice returned at a fraction of its previous volume. "Please understand, I will do what I can. All I can. But if she finds us now, it's over. For you, for me, and yes, for this little girl as well."

Belmorn glared back at the man in the hood. He did not speak, and no, he did not understand. Not by half.

"Listen to me," said Kro. "I don't know why fate has laid you across my path, but there is a hefty debt I owe you. Tonight, I have paid off some and will gladly do more but not at the cost of my own work."

Belmorn's glare hardened, but he chose to listen on.

"You are a stranger here. You have never glimpsed the beast. Have not lived most of a decade with its mark carved into the walls of your heart." As Kro spoke, furious passion came to a boil. Tears welled in his eyes, trembling, threatening to flow. "I will allow nothing to come between me and what must be done. Nothing. Do you hear me, Belmorn? If it comes to it, if she starts to wake," He nodded toward the child. "I will stop the screaming. I will not hesitate."

"What?" Belmorn could feel his own fury rise at the implication. "So help me, wizard, if I see that knife of yours..."

Kro turned, looking sincerely wounded. "I am no child killer!" His voice came in a low rasp but the offense was plain. "And for the last time, I'm no damned wizard." From the folds of his cloak appeared a vial of green powder. "Gorgon dust is science--not some magician's trick. I should hardly expect some backwater riverman to spot the difference, but I will use it on the girl."

Belmorn's eyes were already wide and wide they remained. He had not forgotten what a single puff of the substance had done to his body. Nor what it felt like to fall--arms immovable stone by his side. In that moment, he might as well have been plummeting off the edge of the world. It was a horrific sensation. One he was still not ready to forgive--and yet... if Kro was right about the Veld's witch...

Remember Sasha. Belmorn's thoughts came in a scolding hiss. *Your son still needs you. If you die, he follows but swollen and purple.*

"Put her there." Without looking, Kro pointed toward the opposite wall, at what approximated a bed. Little more than a wall shelf, it was mounted roughly a foot off the floor and covered in a patchwork quilt that looked as old as it was dusty. Belmorn crossed the floor in three strides, leaning forward to lay the girl down.

"You can go now. There's little enough room in here as it is." Kro knelt, looming over his unconscious patient. "Just remember, keep yourself and those horses quiet."

Belmorn frowned, stealing one final glance at the unconscious child. As he turned for the door, he could still feel the girl's warmth on his side, hanging there like an echo. Like the insidious memory of a missing limb.

As he stepped toward the rear of the wagon, glass bottles and jars and who knew what else softly shifted and clinked. Ducking his head, Belmorn slipped out through the door and he did not look back.

6-5

For the second time in as many minutes, the air outside was new. Belmorn breathed deeply, looking up at the moon and the stars, holding them until his head swam. He scanned the secret hollow within the thorns as pinpricks of starlight hung in his vision.

Belmorn winced--working a thumb and index finger over his eyelids. Dropping from exhaustion felt like a seduction. If for no other reason than to escape the memories of the past few days.

The Veld has a witch. Didn't you know?

A thin wooden snap pulled Belmorn from his thoughts. He saw stars in this hollow place. On the ground, in the shadows. But unlike the ones in the sky, these stars came in pairs.

The horses stamped their hooves, snorted, grunted, shook violently their bridles. Remembering what Kro had said about the dangers of noise, he rushed to the animals. They were backing away, back down into the thorny corridor and away from the glade. Away from the dozens of glowing eyes that had them surrounded--twinkling like tiny stars.

The hands of the blackfoot ached for their axes, but the weapons remained right where he had left them--secure and on the back of the retreating adamandray. Belmorn looked back toward the glade. He was utterly surrounded.

At first, the things remained on the perimeter, close to the thorny walls where shadows were thickest. Then, as if by some unheard cue, they shifted, moving like water from a burst dam to flow between the man and the horses. Belmorn's heart thrummed in his chest. There was nowhere to go but back to the wagon. He couldn't knock, wouldn't dare interrupt the surgery. Axes or not, this swarm of eyes was for him to handle. One more act for this endless gauntlet of a day.

One of the shadows broke away from the herd. Raising a pair of the hardest fists he could make, Rander Belmorn clenched his teeth and prepared for the absolute worst.

"Please..." The voice was a small, frayed thing. It came from a figure, slowly stepping out the dark.

As moonlight revealed more of the twisted, nearly-naked form, Belmorn could see the speaker was no man.

"Please," the hunchbacked creature said again. All around, more shadows were revealing themselves as members of the same strange race.

Magnus released a threatening squeal.

"Still your beasts!" said the thing.

Unable to move or scream, Belmorn watched as the creatures lay open hands upon Magnus and the silver mare. Rinh, how he wanted those axes.

Then, to his utter astonishment, the horses began to calm. Large, grayish hands spread over the animals' necks, backs, and legs, yet the horses no longer appeared agitated. Within seconds, the heads of both animals drooped until they lay down and went inexplicably to sleep.

Belmorn palmed his forehead, absently itching a spot usually covered by his missing haresh. He managed a weak "Huh?" before the creature whipped its head round, locking eyes. It held a long finger to a small pair of cracked lips, and Belmorn said no more.

The creatures were hairless, stood shorter than he was, but only because of a bent posture. Their upper body was bare, revealing mottled, grey skin that looked calloused, almost stonelike in texture. What Belmorn first took to be green fur actually seemed to be some kind of living moss. This covered their arms and shoulders while shabby pelts hung about their loins.

The arms and fingers of the creatures were larger than a man's. Due both to the limbs' length and the creatures' postures, the hands hung mere inches above the ground. Each face possessed the rudimentary building blocks of a human's but was distorted into something distinctly other. The eyes were luminous, set far apart and deep into the skull, creating a prominent ridge of brow. The small mouth was hidden almost completely beneath a nose so massive, it must surely have been a burden to support.

The nose struck a note of recognition in the man from distant Grael, though it was far from the drooping, wart-riddled organs Belmorn had seen in books. These noses were smooth, aquiline, creating a profile that in the low light, resembled birds of prey.

These strange, bent creatures could be but one thing: Trolls.

"Danger," said the leader in its frayed whisper. "But not in here." The troll made a gesture indicating the glade, and then it looked to the thorn wall separating them from the rest of the Veld. "Out there walks death. All our deaths."

There was a dull thud nearby, as if something heavy had just hit the ground. Slowly, the troll turned in the direction as more impacts resounded.

Footsteps? Belmorn thought.

As if by a crack of black powder, reality split down the middle. The wail--that wail--coursed through his body, through teeth and rib and seemed to go on forever. It was followed directly by a set of barks. One, then two, then one more. Each seemed to wield force enough to shatter bone.

Belmorn tried to swallow, but his throat felt lined with stone. Whatever vision he had once conjured of a withered old hag seemed quaint. His mind and heart raced--bombarded by thoughts and questions.

The walls looked to be roughly thirty feet high, perhaps more, but how thick were the thorns between him and that shrieking nightmare Kro called a witch? How long had the corridor been? An eighth of a mile? Assuming this hollow had been carved in the dead center of the Moat, the--

The wail sounded again, rattling the questions from his mind. It was too much. Was Belmorn not a blackfoot? Had he not faced and slain forty-nine greater eels and who knew how many salt-lions in over four and a half decades of life? Had he not faced and damn near defeated a dread nautiloth with only nine men as his anchor?

Yes. Yes he bloody well had.

Here was the sort of battle he was born for. Not man-shaped foes, but horrendous, unthinkable beasts the size of river barges.

Belmorn stormed across the glade. And the trolls shrank to let him pass. Vaguely he noticed females and children among them. One troll mother held a tiny babe to her naked breast. Upon reaching the sleeping adamandray, Belmorn reached for his axes but... a warm hand brushed his arm before he could unfasten the first of the sheath's leather clasps.

Turning around, his head felt heavy, thick even. The last thing he saw was the face of the only troll he had heard speak. And now, it spoke again. Just one word.

"Please."

PART SEVEN
THE HAG'S FOLLY

7-1

Henric Galttauer sat at the bar, quietly contemplating the first course of his supper. Past strands of blond hair, he stared into the cup, empty but for a last mouthful of pale, foamy liquid. After watching the remainder swirl and slide around the bottom, he finally swallowed it down.

BANG!!

A second cup was slammed down, splashing sudsy drops onto the dark wooden bar.

"Thing about teats, they go in pairs." With a smirk, the bartender and proprietor of the Hag's Folly, whisked away the empty cup. Ottma was a large, hard-faced woman, who happened to brew the coldest ale in Roon.

The captain didn't look up, didn't respond but to slide the new drink closer. Like the first cup, the ale was half frozen. The initial gulp slid down his throat like liquid ice, numbing him further.

Numb was exactly what he needed.

The captain of the Roonik Guard was not in the best of moods. He hadn't been in a very long time. How many years had passed since his brow had set in its current furl? Six? Seven? Seemed like hundreds.

Heralded by the chime of a small bell, the tavern door swung open and two new customers entered. The men received glares by all but the only man at the bar.

Exchanging nervous glances, the pair occupied one of the small round tables in the back, just as a half dozen others had already. The air in the Folly was more somber than usual, and that was saying something.

Galttauer took another long pull from the cup, chewing the small, tooth-sized bits of ice.

How could things have gotten so low? Fallen so far from right?

This was Roon. The last of the great shield cities. For over five hundred years, the city stood as a legendary example of what human civilization could achieve. His proud bloodline had always served, always protected the people and maintained the roads, ensuring travel safe and unplagued by vermin. For seventeen generations, no Galttauer had failed in this task.

Henric was the last of that line. Risen in the illustrious Roonik Guard to the rank of captain, he was respected, admired, and the most useless of all to bear his illustrious name.

"That bad, huh?" The voice of Ottma pulled at the captain's eye. Her voice was low, intended for an audience of one.

"Hmm?" It was the first sound the captain had made since sitting.

"Well..." continued the large woman "I always presume a measure of embellishment in the tales that make it across this bar. But based on that dark cloud you dragged in here, I'm thinking maybe, things really are as bad as all this."

The captain took another gulp of his drink. As he crunched on the ice, Ottma dipped his original cup in a bucket of water before toweling it dry.

"I have some stew left. If you're hungry."

"Hmm?"

"Stew," said Ottma more pointedly. "There's a bit left. 'Course it's mostly broth. Ran out of meat last week, and I can only recall what color a carrot is if I try really hard." she was smiling. On most days, any man would count himself lucky to receive a smile like that. Ottma may not have been the comeliest of women, but she was the genuine article, as honest as a summer rain.

"No," said Galttauer with a pang of guilt. "Thank you. I'll send out a garrison in the morning. Have them check the snares."

With pursed lips, the woman put down the cup and cloth. "Henric, you know as well as I do, there won't be any rabbit in those snares. Morgrig has--"

The captain's expression turned like bad milk.

"Sorry, Henric. Really. Not trying to rub salt in the wound."

The captain snickered and shook his head. "It's not you who should be apologizing, Ott. This is my mess." He took another long pull from his cup. "Mannis Morgrig is my fault."

The woman stepped back. To Ottma, the captain's meaning seemed clear. The news that had already spread through the city like a sickness was that of calamity. The convicted criminal known as the Red Wolf had escaped, aided by some unknown party, and, against all odds and logic, had once again slipped through Galttauer's fingers.

The fact that the escaped individual was not the despised criminal the woman--the whole town--believed him to be might have colored her opinion on the matter. But no one knew the truth beyond the good captain, and that particular bit of information was currently festering in his gut. As far as Galttauer was concerned, stew, even leeks and broth would be of better use in any belly that wasn't his.

What were you thinking?

Desperation changes men, even the good ones and Captain Henric Galttauer had committed an unthinkable act. He'd framed an innocent man--condemned him to a terrible death. And for what? To propagate yet another lie? That the threat of the Red Wolf was over?

The lone vagabond with no ties and no hope was marching off to die anyway, and Galttauer would not attempt to track down the true threat. Not again. His duty was and would always be to the people of Roon.

The witch of the Veld had killed or vanished too many of his men already. Twice he had endeavored to find the beast and to bring it down, and twice was enough. Locking his people behind their great shield kept them alive--withering slowly like grapes on the vine, but alive.

Of course, life alone is never enough. His people had grown gloomy and cold--colder than the wind. With that mummer's fart of a trial he'd hoped to give them the tiniest sliver of respite. An opportunity to turn from their woes and unite. Even if only for a moment.

Galttauer had no idea how to kill a witch, but bandits were another matter entirely. Unfortunately, his men were limited, and every time they left the safety of Roon, they did so at great peril, for the shadow of their true enemy was long. Despite having personally led numerous attempts to rout out the southern threat, the bandits had proved elusive.

Mannis Morgrig is my fault.

Ottma had no idea how off her interpretation of that statement was.

The so-called Red Wolf had only come to Roon's forest because the road had been left wide open, seeded with the red meat of Galttauer's own inadequacy. But too much time had been allowed to pass, and the bandits had grown comfortable. All too familiar with these northern woods and their absentee warden.

In trying to keep his people safe from one threat, the captain had invited a second to scratch at his front door. Not wolves, but vermin-- following near enough behind a lion to pick at scraps in its wake.

Scraps. That's all the once proud people of Roon had now--scraps of their pride and scraps for their supper. Last month, the stores had dwindled to the point where an old stallion had been taken from the stables and delivered to the city butcher. There had been a lot of meat, but appetites returned quickly. Already there was talk about which horse to choose next, but that wasn't what really gnawed at the captain's mind.

How have things fallen so far from right? The question wasn't difficult to answer, just difficult to face. Because you let them.

Galttauer lifted the cup to his lips and drank, drank until he could barely feel the other question gnawing at the frayed edges of his mind.

What will they eat... when there are no more horses?

7-2

The bell sounded again and there was light coming through the open door. It cast the entering figure in a stark staggering silhouette. Eyes collected on the man who ignored the only other sitting at the bar.

"Damn it, Graden." Ottma did not look pleased. "What do you think you're doing? I already sent you to bed once tonight."

Graden Kuhn, the city apothecary, was slight of frame. He dressed in a buttoned vest and glasses that made him look like a librarian. "Did you? I feel like that was yesterday."

Ottma frowned. "Yesterday too."

The man looked consternated at this. He placed one hand upon his face and slid it up to a crop of short, silver hair. He shrugged. "Well then. Must have gotten lost." After a snicker, he added, "Come on, Ott, don't be like that. I just want what all these fine gentlemen already have."

He tossed a pair of silver coins onto the bar and sat. The chosen stool was just two down from the captain, who had yet to react.

"I just want a taste of those lovely tits of yours."

Galltauer looked up. He tried to catch Ottma's eye, to gauge her level of distress. As far as he could tell, there wasn't any.

This was the Hag's Folly, the house of Ottma Steinholm, but it hadn't always been. For nearly thirty-two years, the place had operated under another sign. The Three Steins had been named for the trio of brothers who had opened the place, as well as the minimum number of pints typically consumed by its patrons.

Over the decades, three owners dwindled until only Ivan Steinholm--and his daughter--remained above the ground.

After the second failure to rout out the witch, the people of Roon had to acknowledge the shadow on their door. There was no denying the rumors or the ravings of that traveling merchant--of a thing on the mountain that had bested their finest warriors twice over. Unfortunately, the protector they looked to was revealed as no mighty storybook legend. Only a man who was out of options.

Ottma had inherited the bar from her father and uncles, and she could see the growing, infectious despair. All who walked through her door did so with black clouds around their eyes and in their throats. They came for liquid forgetfulness, and for a while, it seemed that this was all she could give. She was no soldier, no witch-slayer. She was a simple barkeep--brewer of the coldest ale in town.

But then came the day when Ottma had hung up a new sign over the door. The Hag's Folly was more than a name. It would stand as a statement. A bold assertion of courage for those who had forgotten the concept. Out there was a monstrous thing, but not in her tavern. In truth, hope was the thing. The most precious ware she could sell.

Renaming the half frozen ale from barrels stored outside had not been part of the plan, but a joke that stuck.

Witch teats. Served ice cold and always in pairs.

As with the dark wooden bar and every table and stool, she owned it. But every so often some horse's arse would twist the words. Usually just enough to piss her off.

"Come on, now, don't make me beg. One and two." The city apothecary slurred, stabbing a finger down on the bar. "Right here. Then, I'll say goodnight. I promise."

Ottma considered the request with a sour look, but started filling an empty cup.

"Oh." The apothecary sounded surprised but not nervous. "Captain! Didn't realize that was you."

Galttauer grunted in return as his grip tightened around the cup's handle.

"That was some business we had today, eh?"

In the following silence came the sliding of chairs as three of the patrons proceeded to hastily exit the Hag's Folly.

"Looks like Mannis Morgrig continues to escape the justice of the

Hraaf and the Vaarg. And right out of one of your goodnight cells, no less. Tell me, Captain, how does a thing like that happen? Right under your watchful eye?"

"Here." Ottma slammed a single cup in front of the city apothecary. "Be thankful that's all you're getting from me. Now drink up and get out."

Startled by the impact, Kuhn's face lit up. He lifted the drink to his lips, then paused. "The witch is one thing. But it seems like executing a simple cutpurse should be within the limited abilities of our mighty captain." The rank was slurred into something resembling an insult. With a lopsided grin, Kuhn gulped down a greedy mouthful. Immediately, his eyes went wide. "What is this?" The words were wet and garbled. As he spat them, clear liquid dribbled everywhere. "Water?!"

Ottma crossed her arms. "Don't like it? Feel free to go home thirsty."

Kuhn stood up so suddenly, his stool shot backwards. His face was all scowl. "You think you're funny? You ugly bitch, I should--"

But the man never finished his threat. With one great hand, Galttauer grabbed the back of Kuhn's head and slammed it down hard onto the bar. Then he spun the drunken man around--pinning him there.

"Whuh? Brgh--" The apothecary sputtered, dazedly trying to right himself. "You get your hand off me!"

The captain glared down at the man he was restraining. Then he pressed harder.

"Ahhggg!!" moaned Graden Kuhn. "So now you're gonna do something huh? This is what it takes for you to get off your arse?" The man spat out a broken laugh, and then winced. "Our people rot and starve with monsters just outside our doors, and you do nothing! Your guards are so stupid, they let Mannis Morgrig himself waltz in through our front gate and instead of bringing him to justice, you let him do exactly what he came for. To remind us all how pathetic you are. That he's no more afraid of you than she is--that fucking witch."

Galttauer released Kuhn from the bar and seized him by the shirt. Then, using two hands, he lifted him within an inch of his face.

"What's the matter, Captain?" the apothecary offered a crimson grin. "Don't like truth? Well here's some more: You killed this city. Not a monster or some filthy bandits, you. History will remember that. There will be no statue of you in the square, but don't worry too much because there'll be no square. Roon is done. Murdered on your watch.

Vanished off the face of the world. The only question is whether you'll be remembered as a failure or a coward."

Graden Kuhn searched the captain's face for evidence of injury, but Galttauer responded only via a weary glare. Then he looked at the woman behind the bar. The Hag's Folly certainly had a ring to it, but he knew that wasn't why she had chosen the name.

Captain Henric Galttauer turned his attention back to the drunk, bleeding mess in his hands. Rather than anger or contempt, something else stirred inside of him. Something he had once brandished so deftly, in a time long ago.

A time before wolves and witches...

PART EIGHT
BIRD MEN

8-1

Rander Belmorn opened his eyes but immediately wanted to close them again. To sleep for just a few minutes more. Or maybe a month.

"Your skin is really dark."

"Huh? I'm... what?" The man's voice came out a fractured rasp. He had no memory of lying down on the pelts that currently approximated a bed on the floor.

"Dark, I said. Well, darker than anyone I know." The high voice cut through the fog in his mind. "Are you a nobleman? Maybe a duke or a king or something?"

Belmorn sat up, still blinking away the lingering sleep. Not two feet away sat a young girl, her stockinged feet dangling over the edge of a wall-mounted cot. She was dressed simply. Wearing a cotton shirt that was too large and a pair of brown pants. In her hands, she was turning over a leather headband while inspecting the inside.

"This says 'Lord Belmorn'," said the girl, eyeing the inscription. "I can read, you know. My mum taught me. She also taught me that 'Lord' is something people call dukes and kings and stuff. So... are you one?"

Belmorn stared into the pale green eyes of the girl who stared right back at him and finally, recognition slid into place. This was the girl. The child he had been so desperate to save.

"No." He rubbed his head, trying to piece together the where and when of his current situation. "I'm no noble anything, girl."

The riverman peered through the dust hovering in the room. Through the particles that seemed caught in hazy light beams like flies in amber. All around were shelves full of small glass bottles, stacks of papers, and various bric-a-brac he could not hope to identify. And these caused more memories to fall into place.

The thorns. The wagon. The horses... They had been making too much noise, and there were trolls. They had been on all sides. Then came the colossal footfalls--the terrible, ominous stomping just on the other side of the wall. And there was the wail and barks that caused a chill to settle in the man's bones.

"Why does it say 'lord,' then?" The girl pressed, ignorant to Belmorn's unnerving recollections. Then she gasped, eyes going wide as saucers. "Oh! You stole this didn't you?"

The mix of excitement and reproach drew a lopsided look of exasperation from Belmorn. Without a word, he extended a hand.

After a few seconds, the girl relented, handing over the leather circlet.

"Thank you." Belmorn wrapped the object around his head, but without the haresh scarf between it and his skin, the leather felt cold. Frowning, he lowered the headband, looking to the inscription himself. At the delicate loops and curves of the hand-wrought letters. "And no, I did not steal this," he said, amused. "This band was a gift from my wife. The inscription is, well... kind of a joke. A bad one."

"A bad joke," repeated the girl, but not as a question. "I think... I'd like to hear that."

"Would you?" Belmorn shook his head, utterly unsure how he had managed to wander into the current conversation.

The girl nodded. "Sure. Been a long time since I heard a joke. Good, bad, or whatever."

Through his nostrils, Belmorn relinquished a long sigh. "Alright. But if I tell you... will you give me your name?"

"Depends," said the girl.

Belmorn raised an eyebrow. "On what?"

"On how good the joke is." The girl smiled behind her hands and Belmorn very nearly smiled back.

"The first thing to know is where I come from. Grael is a small village, one possessed of no storied history or reputation. It's just one of many such settlements built by my ancestors along the banks of the black river. The thing is... we river folk aren't quite far enough from the capital of Racallia to avoid paying the taxes." He exhaled through his nose. "But when it comes to protection, we are generally left to our own devices. Am I going too fast?"

"No," said the girl. "But so far, this isn't a very funny joke."

With a shake of his head, Belmorn pinched the skin between his eyes. "About four years ago, a group of riders came. Six of them. All Westerners. All wearing their intentions on their tongues and sleeves. I watched them from the bank as they rode in like a bad wind."

"Were they bandits? Did they open throats?"

Belmorn raised an eyebrow. "What sort of a question is that?"

"I don't know." The girl shrugged. "My uncle used to talk about bandits who would 'open your throat, as soon as look at you.' Never mind. Keep going."

"These riders, they... did not open any throats, but they were bad men. On that, you are going to have to take my word."

"We-e-e-l-l," the girl dragged out the word, sounding slightly dejected. "Did you kill any?"

"Of course not." Belmorn spoke quietly. "But as I was present and able, I approached them and had a conversation."

The girl's expression twisted to show she was not impressed. "That's it? A bunch of bandits ride into your village and you just 'had a conversation'?"

"Well..." Belmorn cleared his throat. "It was a conversation with axes."

"Ohhh, I get it." said the girl. "You kicked their sorry carcasses out of town."

Belmorn was once again taken aback by the child's colorful vocabulary. He shrugged his shoulders in something resembling an affirmation.

"Okay. Your joke is getting funnier," she went on "But that still doesn't explain the 'lord' thing."

Belmorn sighed. "It was just something one of them said. The men were very drunk, and I have no idea how, but one of them had learned my name." He lowered his tone and tried to mimic their accent. "'This must be the protector of this place, the illustrious Lord Belmorn.'"

"Oh boy." The girl smiled with nervous anticipation.

Belmorn smirked. It had been a while since he had just talked with anyone, and he would be lying if he said he wasn't enjoying recounting the exploit. "As for the title, I sure as hell did not encourage its further use. But it followed me like the linger off a murkwhiff. As I said, this band is a gift from my loving wife." He shook his head, snickering. "She thought it was hilarious."

At this, the girl pulled back. Raised a questioning eyebrow.

"I did tell you it was a *bad* joke."

The girl pursed her lips. "That's okay. I liked it anyway." she inhaled sharply, favoring her arm. "My name is Rivka Pesch."

"Well Rivka," Belmorn smiled, remembering why the girl was where she was. "My name is Rander. Rander Belmorn" He held out a hand, which the girl eyeballed but did not touch. "I'm pleased to say that you look a lot better than the last time I saw you."

The girl's expression was hard to discern. "Thanks. I feel okay. This arm hurts though--a lot. And the bandages itch. Also, the other guy won't let me outside."

Belmorn raised an eyebrow. "You mean, Kro?"

"Yeah. About the only thing he's let me do all morning is lay down and eat." Rivka shrugged, sighed. "Breakfast was fish. It was really salty, but good."

Belmorn measured her words. "Tell me, Rivka, do you remember what happened? Back in Roon?"

The girl nodded. "Most of it, I think. That man, he was going to shoot you from behind. But I didn't want that to happen so I yelled. Yelled as loud as I could. Then you turned and... I think... your sword exploded." Looking wistful, the girl seemed to be watching the events unfold again. Then, ever so slightly, she smiled. "It was worth it. I'm glad you're not dead, Rander."

"Me too. Thank you, Miss Pesch." Belmorn gave a sad sort of smile. "Would it be okay if I looked at your bandages?"

After a few seconds of consideration, the girl nodded. Carefully she pushed the cloak from one shoulder, and then she stretched down the collar of her shirt to reveal the wrappings beneath. With great care, Belmorn inspected what little he could see. The dressing was new. It appeared clean and well wrapped. When he reached the spot where the broken sword had pierced her, the girl drew a sharp breath.

"Sorry!" he blurted out.

The spot looked well-padded. Something had been placed between the wrap and the wound--something green. There was a bit peaking past one edge. Belmorn leaned back, carefully letting the cloak fall back onto her shoulder.

"It's okay. I'm fine." The girl was a tough one; that much was certain. "Besides, I'm the one who's sorry."

"Sorry? What for?"

"I bled all over your scarf." The girl's lips pursed tightly together, slowly twisting into one corner. "The other man, Kro..." she pointed. "He said it needed to be thrown in the fishing hole, along with anything bloody. He said the scent might draw 'unwanted attention.' He's been talking like that a lot. Talking like I don't know what's really out there." Rivka paused as a steely resolve washed over her. "He's wrong though."

"Is he?"

"Yeah. I've seen a lot."

Furling his brow, Belmorn considered this for a long moment. "Rivka?"

"Yeah?"

"How old are you?"

"Twelve, I think."

"Oh? That is a very good age. My son is going to be twelve. Next July, he'll..." Belmorn trailed off. After a while, he found the eyes of the girl again. They were bright, full of so much genuine concern the man's heart nearly broke in two. He redirected the conversation. "And where is your family?"

"Oh, them." The girl wiped her nose across the back of one arm but the automatic action caused her to gasp. Trying to hide the pain, she pushed on, "If you mean my Mum and Dad, they're back home."

"Back in Roon?"

"Roon?" she scoffed in disgust. "No. We were from farther up. Near Mount Einder. Small, mining town. Ever heard of Jayce?"

8-2

Jayce.

Hearing the name of the town ignited a blast of black powder in Belmorn's brain. For the girl's sake, he pressed on gently, careful of his tone. "Jayce... I have heard of it. Not exactly an easy place to find."

"No? Well I know where it is." Cinching the cloak tighter around her neck, Rivka shrugged, hiding another wince. "Last town before the world ends." her voice held a hint of pride.

"So I hear." The voice of the blackfoot was somber and warm. "But how is it that if your family is all the way back in Jayce, you were living under that statue?"

"I wasn't living under the Graveless, I just like sitting there. It's the only place I don't feel..." The last word went unspoken, but it might as well have been screamed as the top of the girl's lungs.

Alone

"I was small the last time I was in Jayce. Five maybe. Uncle Hebrecht, he was the one who took me to Roon. But that was after."

"After?" Belmon's voice was as small as he could make it. "After what, Rivka?"

"After they came." Her lips parted stiffly, not wanting to form the next words. "The bird-men."

Rivka hopped off the cot and shuffled across the floor. She stopped at a desk beneath two shelves that ran the length of one of the short walls. She began fiddling with what looked to be a clockwork music box. She picked it up, absently opening the lid, but instead of a dancer, there stood a figurine of a man with a long beard. His hands were up, his mouth carved in a silent scream. Upon seeing this, Rivka snapped the lid shut again, put the box down, and stepped away.

"Some say," her voice was quiet but held resolve. "... the sickness came from across the big water. That it blew in just for us, because the other towns, they were all fine. I still remember the day I left. I had been trying to wake Mum for a long time because I hadn't eaten breakfast yet, and the sun was already starting to go down. Dad hadn't gotten out of bed in a long time either. Even longer than Mum. And I was afraid to leave the house because everyone was supposed to stay inside, away from the bad air that was making people sick." The girl paused, looking not at the floor, but through it. She bit down on her bottom lip. "I heard the knocking," she went on, "But I didn't want them to come in and see Mum and Dad because then they would know."

Belmorn leaned forward a little. "What would they know, child?"

"That Mum wasn't sleeping. That she hadn't been for almost three days." her voice hitched. "Anyway, it didn't matter. The door didn't keep them out for long."

"I don't understand." Belmorn's voice felt very small in his throat. "Who was at the door?"

"I already told you. The bird-men!" she met Belmorn's eye with an edged look, but only for an instant. "There were three, I think. I heard them talking, but only one came inside. By then, I was hiding in the closet, but the door wasn't closed all the way. I had left it open, just enough to see. The bird-man was tall and skinny but he stepped hard like a horse. His body was wrapped all in black except for his ugly beak face. That was white--or almost white. Something like the color of old bones. It was like he had no skin there." The child paused, but briefly. When she spoke again, her tone was indignant. "I'm not a kid anymore. And I'm not stupid. I know they weren't really bird-men. Only the regular kind of men. Just doctors wearing masks. But they couldn't help us. Not Mum or Dad or anybody else because they all died anyway."

Silence hung in the wagon for some time. It was eventually broken by a rustle as the girl began sifting through a small wicker basket of cloth. She held up what looked like a skirt--dark blue with a line of small goats embroidered along the bottom. Considering this for a moment, Rivka frowned and kept looking until she discovered something that finally made her grin. The fabric was frayed at the edges, but quite supple. It was a deep, dark green, like forest leaves on a moonless night.

"Kro said I could have anything in this basket. I don't think these were all his. Some of them are girl-clothes. Here." she leaned forward, tying the fabric around the man's head.

When she pulled back, Belmorn reached up to inspect her work. The cloth bulged considerably to one side--but he smiled at her nonetheless. "My people call this a haresh. For us, it is very important. The cloth protects our heads from the hot sun out on the river."

"Really?"

"Really." He winked. "But that is not how you tie one." After removing the cloth, he folded it properly, pulling the frayed corners into a knot at the base of his skull. Then he pressed the leather headband to his forehead, fastening the clasp around the massive knot.

For the first time in a day and a half, Rander Belmorn stood up, tassels of dark green tapering down his back.

"So? How does it feel?"

"Very good. Thank you." Belmorn smiled again. "Tell me, Rivka... where is your uncle now?"

"Doesn't matter. It's just me now. Been that way for over a year. Once they kicked me out of the room we were living in, I tried to leave. I wanted to go back to Jayce. I tried to. I really did. But the gates... They never open anymore."

Belmorn took a knee and spread his arms wide. Without a second's hesitation, the girl shot forward. Wrapping both arms around his neck and squeezing until the man could hardly breathe. After that she sobbed into his shoulder--fully and without restraint.

The heat of holding the girl was poison that eroded Belmorn's cardinal rule. The primal, dauntless fury of love had him, and there was nothing that could be done. No argument, however pragmatic, would circumvent his fate.

Now, like it or not... Lord Belmorn had two children to save.

PART NINE

A PRICKLY RESPITE

9-1

The door to the tented wagon opened with a slow, wooden whine, and Rander Belmorn stepped outside. At a gust of mountain wind, he straightened his highwayman's collar, pulling the two halves closer together. With a shiver, he knew he had been right to locate his coat and bear pelt before stepping outside.

Kro's hollow looked very different in the light.

Until a few days ago, the blackfoot had never seen snow. Had, in fact, not been completely certain it was even real. Still, based on the tales he had heard along the way, Belmorn had expected this remote land to be buried beneath a foot or two of the stuff. The reality though, proved only partially true. While everything he saw was covered in white, the snow was gathered in inches rather than feet. But that's how things went. Every tale of the fantastic was one-part truth and nine-parts steaming horse shit.

As he thought this, a smirk pulled at the corner of his mouth.

Pointing his face toward the sun, Belmorn mused on just how long he'd slept. All night and half the morning, according to the girl allegedly resting on her wall mounted cot. He breathed in deeply, holding the crisp northern air until his lungs felt as though they might burst. Exhaling produced a great cloud which dissipated into feathery wisps.

The man Kro was tending to a satchel on his newly acquired mare. As for the adamandray, Magnus didn't appear to notice the arrival of his oldest friend. The large animal's attention was set firmly on the patch of snowy grass from which he was grazing contentedly.

Stepping from the cart to the ground, Belmorn spoke in a voice that carried, "So... where did you sleep?"

"Huh?" Said Kro, without turning.

"Well, the girl had the cot and I took up most of the floor. So... where did you sleep?"

After tightening a leather strap, Kro proceeded to secure it in place. "Don't worry about it." He said at last.

Belmorn plopped onto the cart's lowest step and started removing his boots. The first foot slipped free in a wave of near delirious bliss. The striped sock was so threadbare, the alternating lines of grey all blended together. "Could have taken my boots off."

The hooded man snickered as he slid a second strap through a metal ring and secured it in place. "Could have spared a blanket too," he responded with a shrug. "By all means, leave your complaints with the front desk." The man's tone was difficult to decipher. "Is the girl resting?"

"Probably not." Belmorn took off his other boot, hoping to distract himself from the weight of his mood. "Poor kid has been through a lot. Too much."

"Haven't we all." Kro gave a slow nod. "This morning, when I brought her a lavish breakfast of water and salted fish, I was able to pry free her name. But not much else. She seems quite interested in you, Belmorn--funny enough. I think you've got yourself a fan."

The blackfoot frowned gloomily. "Well, she's alive, and that sure as hell isn't because of me. I don't know how someone could survive such a wound, let alone be up and about the morning after. It's you she should be endeared to, Kro."

The other man shook his head and bent to collect a series of strange objects at his feet. Three pale crosses, each over a foot across and constructed from the cylindrical stalks of some strange plant. The arms were all equal in length and, most bizarrely, ribbed. Belmorn could not imagine their function.

Kro lifted the flap of his saddle bag--carefully inserting the objects, one at a time. "You're wrong about that, my friend." He gave a soft huff. "The lodestone cleaned the wound, but there was a sliver of metal resting directly on a vein, pinching it. When that came loose, blood came with it. Quite a lot, in fact." Kro's voice was strained as he picked up the silver mare's hoof to clean. "I shouted for you, Belmorn. Against my own best judgement, I yelled at the top of my damn lungs." He sighed. "I didn't know you were caught in the troll sleep."

As he listened, Belmorn's mind raced to picture the wagon's interior. To his recollection, there had been no traces of such a gruesome surgery. No lingering smells. Then he remembered what the girl had said earlier.

"He had to throw it in the fishing hole. Anything with blood."

"No," Grunted Kro, stepping away from the horse. "That girl doesn't owe me a thing."

"Rinh." The name of his river spirit was the only response Belmorn gave for many minutes as he once again relived the last night he'd been awake.

"Out there walks death. All our deaths." That's what the leader troll had said.

Belmorn scanned the glade again. The ground was uneven, covered in jutting, snow laden rocks and mounds of grass which shifted lazily in the breeze. "Kro. Where are they?" he asked. "The trolls. Where did they go?"

"The only place they can go." Kro smirked. "Open your eyes, Blackfoot. Look."

The perimeter of the glade was lined not with snowy grass but pelts, almost indistinguishable from the ground. Upon closer inspection, Belmorn could also see that slowly, subtly--the surfaces of these mounds rose and fell. His eyes bulged, transfixed on the patchwork of earthen-colored fur that concealed who knew how many of them. The trolls.

"You should know," Kro spoke softly, "...to them, 'troll' is an ugly word. Man's word. They are called the Pershten, and they have nowhere else to go." Kro scratched the mare's neck, and then patted her on the rump. The horse bubbled a surprised whinny and meandered over to where the adamandray was still grazing.

Not all of the grass in this hidden glade is counterfeit, thought Belmorn.

"I don't know what you've heard," said Kro. "But most is probably rot and fairytale nonsense. This much I can tell you for certain: The species is peaceful, nocturnal, and, fortunately for that girl in there, they possess a knack for healing that far surpasses my own,"

Belmorn stared at the sea of pelts. The man-sized mounds huddled together, lining the ground like a great slumbering quilt. "Last night-- the last thing I remember is one of them touching my arm."

"Yes, and then you went out like a candle." Kro looked at him, slightly bemused. "I can't tell you how the effect works, but it is definitely tactile. That was their chieftain who put you out. Bror is his name. We've met before. Years ago. Last night, he told me what happened. About how close she came."

There it was again. The she that began with a capital S. Belmorn knew now what it meant. It referred not to some cauldron-tending old woman but a monster who could make the ground quake under her very feet. Even now, he could hear her mournful howls and the barks that followed. Always three. Always in quick succession. He could still feel them punching his chest, striking his bones like the end of a hammer to a harpoon.

Last night, moments before the troll Bror had put him to sleep, Belmorn was about to do something very unwise. A cold realization clicked in his mind. "You're hunting it aren't you? This *Hispidian* witchwyrm."

Kro looked surprised, but only for a moment. Then he nodded. "With every ounce of will I have left."

"Why?" Belmorn frowned. "If the thing is so formidable... why you? Why does this task fall to a wandering whatever-you-are, when there are armored soldiers in Roon?"

"Soldiers do not hide like turtles in their shells!" The burst of sudden anger flashed bright but faded quickly. When Kro's voice returned, it was thin, hardly there at all. "I... am many things, Belmorn. But more than anything, I am a damned fool. And for this errand, that is something of a prerequisite." The smile of a man resigned to an unfortunate fate curled his lips. "Tell me... That night, before the troll sleep came, did you see her?"

After slipping back on the boots that were not his, Belmorn stood. "No. There were noises. Just footsteps and breath. I could hear her size and how close she was, but that was all."

Kro nodded and stared back from inside his hood. The riverman felt he was being sized-up, evaluated or at least, re-evaluated. After a moment, a genuine smile almost touched the lips of the man named Kro. Then there came an expression which Belmorn had not seen the man wear before.

It was a passing thing. Just a glimmer, a spark, but it looked an awful lot like hope.

9-2

"You risked a lot back there. Pulling me out of Roon," said Belmorn. "You didn't answer me last night so tell me now. Why? Why did you do that?"

Kro dismissed the question with a wave. "Don't flatter yourself. I wasn't in the city for you, Belmorn. You should know, sticking my neck out is something I lost the taste for a long time ago." He sighed. "If you think back to our clandestine meeting, back in the woods, you may recall that in addition to nearly becoming rose food, I had recently been robbed."

"I remember," Belmorn scowled. "Mannis Morgrig."

Kro nodded. "Morgrig, yes. Those *bastards*." A dark anger weighed on his voice. "They relieved me of much. My horse, but also the supplies that she carried. Irreplaceable things. That's why I dusted you. You may wear the trappings of a highwayman, but a life on the road has made me a talented judge of character. You are no villain, Belmorn. Quite the opposite, in fact. You were about to stop me from doing something very unwise."

Belmorn's scowl moved closer to a glare. He offered no disagreement.

"And you would have been right to do it," Kro said with resignation. "But, anger won out over sense I'm afraid. That bastard needed to pay. And I needed to make him."

"Well? Did you find them?" Belmorn asked.

"A blind man could have found them," scoffed Kro. "Morgrig has no fear of being found. He knows that in those woods he is not the hunted." Kro stopped. The absolute, epic disaster of that night pulsing in his brain. "I had a plan. A very simple plan. But sometimes, things happen that you couldn't plan for in a thousand years." He closed his eyes, pursed his lips. "In the chaos, a handful of those damned brigands died, but I recovered nothing. Accomplished nothing but a swift kick to the hornet's nest."

"What about your horse?" said Belmorn.

"Already over the fire when I arrived."

"Ah."

"Yeah," said Kro. "I really liked that horse."

"Kro," Belmorn's voice was low. "You're getting away from my question."

"Am I?"

"Yes."

"Sorry--what was it?"

Belmorn frowned. "Back in Roon. Why did you come for me?"

"Oh yes," said Tenebrus Kro. Belmorn's original question was a relief from his current thoughts. "As I said, I wasn't there for you. I haven't set foot in that city in years. Not since..." How much was he willing to share with the strange man he hoped would be his ally? How much could he share without driving him away with the awful truth? Kro abruptly cleared his throat. "The truth is the next closest tavern is sixty miles south. In Britilpor."

"Tavern?" Belmorn raised an eyebrow. "You were in Roon to have a drink?"

"To get pissed, actually. We did not meet on a good day, Belmorn." Kro moved his head from side to side, popping out kinks from bending and tacking the mare. Awkwardly, he met the gaze of the man beside him and cursed under his breath. The still-unanswered question bored from the riverman's eyes. The alchemist continued, "The Hag's Folly. The barkeep there brews a very fine ale. Stores the stuff in barrels out in the cold, so it will be half-frozen by the time she puts it to glass. The woman calls a glass of the stuff a Witch's Teat." Kro sighed. "I tell you that is the only thing I have ever missed about that damn city."

"A witch's teat?" Belmorn almost laughed. "Shame they arrested me before I got to try one."

"One?" said Kro, laughing in his throat. "They're only served in pairs."

Both men burst out laughing. Gloriously unrestrained, the sound poured forth like flowing twin rivers. Neither Belmorn nor Kro could remember the last time such a thing had occurred. It was many minutes before the conversation continued.

"The next morning, I woke up on the street. In front of the Folly," continued Kro, once he reeled himself back in. "I didn't know where I was going after that. Truth is I wanted another drink, but the place wasn't going to open again for hours. And so I decided to go for a stroll, get some blood flowing before it froze there for good. At some point, I must have stumbled through the center of town. By the statue of the Graveless, I spotted a few guards and what they were guarding. Or rather, wrestling. They were trying to remove the saddlebags and those axes from your horse, but I think you can guess who won that contest."

Magnus looked up from munching the short Veld grass and snorted a cloud of white breath. Belmorn looked proud.

"None of it made sense at the time," Kro went on slowly, as if relating the events as they were still unfolding. "I knew that sort of horse belonged in Roon about as much as I did, but my head was pounding too hard to care, so I kept walking. Eventually I heard the distinct sounds of a crowd gathering somewhere nearby. Your trial, as it happened. In my state, it was a few minutes before my head cleared enough to understand what was really going on. And as I stood there, looking up at the man who had saved my life--who's charity I had repaid so poorly--and listened as crimes that I knew to be those of another man, a motherless rat who plays at being a wolf, were pinned to his chest. Well, I suddenly found myself no longer thirsty."

For a few moments neither man said more.

"That's it?" the blackfoot folded his arms. Nodded slowly, scratching his beard. "You went through all of that because of chance? Some random flash of conscience?"

Kro shrugged. "There's no grand scheme here, Belmorn. I told you not to flatter yourself. Like it or not, you have your answer. And now I believe it's your turn. So tell me, what brings a man of your bearing to the edge of the known?"

Belmorn stepped forward as a gust of wind pulled the ends of his new green headscarf to one side. Right then, he looked like a force of nature.

"Desperation," he began grimly. "I am looking for someone. A travelling merchant whose name I do not know. For years he visited my village every spring. Just as our foals were finding their river legs. Though never to his face, the children started calling him the brushman." Belmorn cinched up his collar to block a gust that licked through the opening in the thorns. "This merchant sold horse brushes of unmatched quality, and we are people who live and die by the health of our animals, well... we must have exhausted his supplies every visit."

Kro snickered quietly, saying nothing.

Belmorn went on. "Unfortunately, we haven't seen him in almost seven years."

The statement hung in the air until Kro released the breath he had been holding. "Seven years..." he said. "... is a long time to wait for a horse brush. Where you are from, I presume such things are hard to come by?"

Belmorn raised an eyebrow. "This man sold more than brushes. Things no one had seen. Impossible things."

Kro looked at the riverman sharply for a moment, assessing the insinuation in his tone. "Where did you say you were from?"

"I didn't," said Belmorn. "But that doesn't mean you don't already know."

Kro lowered his hood, then glanced at the adamandray. As if aware of their conversation, the gigantic two-toned horse looked up from the grass.

Belmorn continued, "It was one of the first things you said to me back in Roon. You called Magnus by his breed. I have been on the road for almost five months. Do you know how many people have known an adamandray when they saw one? Do you? Those idiot guards, they didn't even think Grael was a real place, but you, wizard, you called me 'riverman'."

Kro stared at a patch of nothing in particular, somewhere between Belmorn and his horse. Then he turned his attention to the silver mare. As his jaw moved, it felt about as natural as rusted clockwork. "You say you are here looking for a horse brush?"

"I didn't say that at all. I'm not looking for a brush, just the man who sold them. I've been tracking him. Asking every passerby, in every city, town and encampment--inside taverns and outside stables. I asked merchants at their tables and men displayed in stocks and pillory. Even bandits unlucky enough to stop me on the road... I asked them all."

Belmorn turned to look south. His stormy grey eyes glaring with the accumulated fatigue of his journey. Standing there, Kro said nothing.

"This man," Belmorn went on. "I haven't learned much... but I believe I've discovered where he's from. An obscure town, missing on most maps." He stepped forward, closing the gap between the two men. "I may be slow recognizing a face I haven't seen in seven years, especially when it's kept so diligently beneath a hood... but I'm not likely to forget--that." Belmorn's head inclined towards the wagon's broadside, the tapestry that billowed in the now-gentle breeze.

On that faded purple field was a symbol used by alchemists to represent the circle of life and death. The Ouroboros. The serpent who devours its own tail.

9-3

Initially, Tenebrus Kro responded only with a subtle shake of his head.

"The brushman?" He said at last.

Rander Belmorn relinquished a nod.

"Huh," Kro chuckled. "Gone for a few years, and I'm reduced to a blasted brush salesman. Of all the things I sold from the side of that wagon." The man looked astonished but also deflated. For almost a full minute Kro stood motionless, eyes glazed over but shifting, as if he were reliving a dream. Or some other life.

"My boy is sick, Kro." Belmorn was standing to his full height. His hands were fists, his mouth a rigid line. "It is the purple sickness."

"What?!" For the first time, Kro's careful demeanor was shattered. "Your boy--but how? How long has he been stricken?"

"Three weeks before I set out," said Belmorn with an internal sigh of relief. "Twenty-two in all."

"Belmorn... that is..." Kro said in a low voice.

"A death sentence. Yes, I know."

"Belmorn..." Kro's words failed him. "Shit. I am sorry."

"Don't be," said Belmorn. "Sorry can't help my son. But your medicine can."

"What do you mean--*my* medicine?" Kro stepped forward. In his eyes, something bloomed, a notion, a realization, something profound enough to leave him visibly altered. "Oh, no..." He spoke practically in a whisper. "Belmorn, I know why you're here, what you've come for. But please, I beg you... Do not ask me for that."

The man's words ignited a fury that possessed the blackfoot. To have come this far, gone through so much.

"I have no choice!" Belmorn's gloved hand shot forward, grabbing Kro by the cloak. "I have come for the same medicine you once gave to a woman called Nikta Bergen. I was there when you gave her the white broth. It was almost nine years ago, but I can still see the writing on the label. Two words. Witch. Tears. It is the only substance I know of that might stop my boy's own throat from choking him to death."

The man shrunk deeper into his cloak, as far as Belmorn's grip would allow.

"Price is no object." Belmorn produced a pouch and rattled the contents. "There are six guilders here. Guilders! All yours. Just give me what I want."

There was much to process. Much that had been dropped so unexpectedly on his head.

As he backed away, Tenebrus Kro stared at the man-shaped cluster of raw nerves that loomed before him, wishing beyond all reason there were some god out there that might intervene.

The purple sickness.

The words pricked at a familiar pain in his chest. It was nothing new--the usual mixture of guilt and well-honed despair--but this time it did not come alone.

Lishka. Livinia.

He could still see their faces, as sad as they were heartbreakingly beautiful. Even now, as his eyes began to well up, they were waiting for him.

Witch Tears.

Kro looked to the mounds of grassy fur that covered his uninvited guests, the Pershten. He stared at them long and hard as a myriad of regrets rose to the surface of his mind. Things had changed again. A new plan had begun to rise in his mind, like a phoenix from the ashes of his original. And it had just been snuffed out.

Tenebrus Kro knew that he was alone again. Alone--his truest state.

There could be no hope of recruiting the blackfoot, not now that he knew what drove him. While a man might be swayed from the duties before him, a father was another matter entirely. Surely none knew that better than he.

At the appearance of a biting wind, Kro pulled close the sides of his hood--his fingers lingering on the fabric.

"Kro!" Hearing Belmorn's voice was like being doused by a bucket of half-frozen ale. "Damn it, wizard, do you hear me?!"

"I..." Kro began again in a more resigned tone. "I hear you, Belmorn. Half the Veld can probably hear you. And for the last time, I'm no damned wizard." The tears welling in his eyes itched into his nose, making him sniff. "Nikta Bergen." He could hardly hear his own voice. "So that was her name. I had forgotten. Though, nine years is a very long time." His body bowed, as if he carried the chains of a condemned man who was truly guilty of his crimes. "It pains me to tell you this but, the medicine you have come for is gone. Used up. And before you ask--*no*, I cannot simply make more."

The large riverman nearly doubled over, as if kicked in the stomach by one of his people's sacred horses. His mouth worked--open, closed-- though only a single word came. "No."

Rander Belmorn had found his quarry, the very man so many had told him was either impossible to track or dead. He, a simple riverman, he had done that. Yet contained within this accomplishment was the thing he had dreaded most. The knowledge that his time away from home was for nothing. Just as his wife had declared it to be, riding away from the side of his dying boy had proved the worst decision of his life.

Rand... He could hear Malia's strained voice. *Don't you dare. Your son needs his father. Now more than ever. Can't you see that? Can't you understand?! We both do.*

He had argued with her, restated the same case for the third or fourth time, but to no avail. Comprehension hadn't been the problem.

You think it is strength pulling you out that door? Real strength would be to stay by his side. To watch him and love him every second of every day he has left. Make no mistake, if you leave, it will not be because of strength. It will be because it's easier to set off on an impossible quest than to stay by his side. Tell me, husband, do you know what sort of man abandons his family in their darkest hour?

Belmorn tried to stop the memory from playing out to its conclusion. He shut his eyes. Shut them until he thought the hot tears might burn off his eyelids. But there was no stopping what he already knew. What he was and would be until his last breath.

A coward.

The word had been in him for a long time, hidden away, secretly brewing behind prickly walls. Now that it was free, it could never be put back in.

"The medicine," Belmorn's words cut through gritted teeth. "You made it once. You can make it again."

"Damn it, Belmorn, are you listening? No. I can't," Kro grumbled, shaking his head. "Listen to me now. The active ingredient in that tincture was something that I happened upon. An heirloom from a distant land--a gift. Might as well demand I turn those six Guilders you brought into soup."

The more Kro blathered on, the more Belmorn wanted to lift the one-time merchant high into the air and shake him until he heard the snap of every bone or until a little bottle labeled Witch Tears fell out. Whichever came first. When he unclenched his jaw enough to speak, Belmorn asked.

"This ingredient. What was it?"

"Something beyond rare. Honestly, I don't think you would believe me if I told you."

"Try me." Belmorn imagined his words were a knife against the hooded man's body. Why was he playing coy now? Had he not heard his son was dying?

"No."

"*What?*" the riverman balked. "What do you mean, *no?*"

"Belmorn, listen to me. You have a family. And that is a blessing among blessings. Believe me. Trust me. Go back to them. Now, while you're still whole and intact."

"How can I do that?" Belmorn exploded "That would mean that all of this--all of these weeks away have been for nothing! I cannot return like this. Not empty handed."

Kro appeared to roll this thought over before responding. "What the hands are or aren't holding doesn't matter. Your family just needs the hands, you big idiot. Don't you get it? All they really need is you."

9-4

The slow, wooden creak of the wagon door slid through the air.

The men turned to see the third member of their strange company. On the back of the wagon, Rivka stood, fully wrapped in a veritable mountain of blankets. Only her face was visible, a light shining in a multicolored sky.

"Pretty cold out here," she said.

Belmorn nodded in agreement, but privately, he continued to seethe. His shoulders rose and fell with heavy breathing that exited his nostrils like dragon smoke. He still had much to say to the man before him. Merchant, wizard, vagabond--whatever he was.

"Come." Kro spoke with a calm voice. "We should eat. You especially." He looked at Belmorn. "You must be starving."

Belmorn sneered but said nothing. He could hardly disagree. More than a day separated him from his last meal, and that had tasted of dead leaves and worm-asses. Without a word on that subject or any other, he trudged over to where the girl was standing.

"Interesting outfit," he said flatly.

"Thanks." The girl looked very serious. "I really hate being cold. Were you two going to fight? It sounded like it."

The question hit hard. Belmorn hadn't expected it. "No." He expelled a cloud of breath. "We weren't going to fight. Come on." He gestured to where Kro had walked.

"Because if you were going to fight," the girl whispered, "he'd be in trouble."

Offering no disagreement, Belmorn couldn't stop the grin pulling the edge of his lip.

On the other side of the wagon, Kro stood beside something inexplicable. In the ground was a hole filled almost to the top with water. They were standing on earth. A hard packed country of rock and soil, not some frozen lake. Yet there it was--a fishing hole. Perplexed, Belmorn turned to see that Rivka was grinning.

"That's where your *harsh* went. Your old one, I mean."

"It's called a haresh. Not a harsh."

"Oh. Right," said the girl. "Well, whatever you call it, my green one looks better."

Belmorn's smile managed to just touch his eyes.

Out of the ground protruded a long stick that had been threaded through the eye of a tall metal stake. Belmorn was silent for almost a full minute. His eyes flitting here and there as potential responses proceeded to bloom and wilt on his tongue. The stick, he saw, was twitching.

No, he thought. *Not a stick. A pole.*

With a heavy sigh, Kro slipped a pin from the stake's eye, releasing the fishing pole. He pulled it up slowly until the beginning of a long line appeared. The line supported at least a dozen sturdy hooks and, to Belmorn's surprise, live fish. Steam poured off the fish as they hit the air. And for the first few seconds they writhed and flapped before going utterly still.

"How is this possible?" Belmorn shook his head in disbelief.

"There's a river down there," said the girl. "Right under us. It runs along the thorns. The lower villages of the Veld pull these fish from it all the time."

"The moat," Belmorn muttered under his breath, remembering how strange the term had sounded for a wall of tangled thorns.

Kro nodded. "The Pershten tell of a great lake, deep beneath the mountain. Always hot, always teeming with these ugly fish. We know the lake feeds into this river. The evidence can be seen on especially cold mornings. Skáldi's Breath is its name. A great column of steam rising from the icy sea, just past the cliffs off World's Edge."

"Huh," was all Belmorn could manage. He snatched one of the still steaming fish--turned it over. It felt warm in his hand. The eyes were clouded over--useless and blind.

"That's a mab," explained Rivka. "They're ugly, but taste pretty good."

"Without roasting, good might be pushing it. But I've done what I can." A crooked smile grew on the lips of Tenebrus Kro. "According to what Bror has told me, his group has been living off them for weeks. Ever since they discovered this place."

"Mr. Kro?" asked the girl, looking around. "Where are we, anyway? I never knew the moat was hollow inside."

"It's not." With a grunt, Kro pulled the last of the mab fish from its hook, then began transferring them to a cloth. "I cleared this out years ago."

"Oh." The talking mound of blankets walked closer to where the men were standing. "That must have taken a long time."

"It did."

Belmorn exchanged a tentative glance with the girl. Covered in so many layers, she had taken on the shape of a wooden nesting doll. The notion nearly made him smile for a second time.

"Why did you do it?" asked the girl.

"Because I needed a storehouse that couldn't be plundered," he sighed. "This hollow... I used it for a long time. And then I stopped." Kro's words ground to a halt, looking miles away as he stared into the thorns.

"Oh," said the blanket mound.

Kro lifted the cloth, creating a sack for the steaming fish. He set it down beside one wheel of his wagon and a lidded utility box. From the box he extracted a small, flattish parcel of paper and twine, which he tossed to Belmorn.

"Prepared these during the night," Kro said, closing the lid of the box. "Should be enough there for both of you, but I do have more."

Having caught the thing, Belmorn fumbled to untie the knot with thick, half-frozen fingers. The opening folds of paper unleashed a most alluring smell that hit hard and fast, travelling from his nostrils down to his stomach.

"Fair warning, though..." said Kro. "The meat is salty as hell, and raw."

"That's okay!" blurted Rivka, who leaned closer to Belmorn, whispering. "A fire would be bad. She would find us."

She.

The word pulsed in Belmorn's brain, followed by another.

Her.

With a nod, he offered the girl first crack at the fish. From beneath the blankets, tiny fingers reared like pink worms, plunging hungrily into the cold meat. She looked up, smiling brightly as she ate. It had been a long time since the riverman had seen such happiness. The smile on his own face was a weak one, but it hung for almost four seconds before dissipating.

Belmorn popped a piece into his mouth. The meat was incredibly delicate--thin to the point of translucency. The saltiness burned his tongue, but it was an undeniable comfort just to be eating again. He took a deep breath and slowly let it out.

At the side of his wagon, Kro turned a well-disguised latch that unfolded a shelf. It banged into position, the sound loud enough to elicit a nervous scan of the thorns from the girl. After laying out the fish on the wooden surface, Kro began to remove the heads. Every time the knife connected with the shelf, it produced a dull THUKK that caused the walking blanket pile to flinch.

Belmorn stood, arms folded thinking, staring. For some reason, Kro looked suddenly, very old. The man's pointed beard was black, but streaked with a fair amount of silver, and his face wore many lines. He might easily have been fifty or more. Then again, the blackfoot knew, such trappings do not always come from age.

9-5

"Kro." Belmorn's voice was firm. "Thank you."

Tenebrus Kro studied the large man, but his eyes were difficult to read. "You like the fish?"

Belmorn snickered. "Er--yes. But that's not what I meant." He swallowed and gave the rest of the packet to the girl, who accepted the food with glee. "Whatever your reason was, neither one of us would be standing here if not for you. For that, you have my gratitude."

"And mine!" said Rivka with a vigorous nod. She smiled, her cheeks swollen with partially masticated mab fish. The sight prompted warmth to flush inside Kro's chest, but he said nothing.

Belmorn went on after a moment of silent deliberation. "These weeks on the road, one rule has been my constant companion. My compass. When Grael was freshly at my back, I swore to stay on task. To go and return as quickly as possible, and to never get involved in the business of others." Belmorn paused for a moment, looking regretful. "For nineteen weeks this kept me focused, safe. But in the last couple of days I managed to break this rule--not once, but again and again. And here we are." The blackfoot shook his head, chuckling. "Medicine or not, I am glad I found you, brushman. But if we are to part ways now, then tell me one thing. Is it merchant? Vagabond? Wizard?" He smirked at that last one. "What are you really?"

Kro stopped his arm, letting the knife rest where it was, in the center of a half filleted fish. Then, turning slightly, he finished the cut--laying the thin piece of meat next to the rest.

"The answer to that question is complicated, I'm afraid." The alchemist let a silence stretch as he began cleaning his work area, depositing the severed fish heads back into the well, which accepted them each with a small plop. Done with that, he pulled out a set of small jars from the utility box.

"These contain salts from the four cardinal banks of the Mazandaran Sea." After removing the lids, Kro pinched a small amount of salt from each jar. Then he sprinkled the seasoning--rubbing the mixture into the fillets. "You want to know me, Belmorn? Know that these salts are utterly inimitable, more precious to some than gold. No matter where you go, no matter what local chefs may say, you will never find a better combination of ingredients for preserving and flavoring fish. Trust me, I've looked."

For a moment, the alchemist inclined his eyes skyward. Above them, clouds of slate grey rolled in from the north--from the great drop-off men had named World's Edge. He did not like the looks of those clouds.

"Your people knew me as a nameless, travelling merchant who apparently sold very desirable brushes." Kro rolled his eyes, but a grin tugged at his mouth. "But this was only one life of many. I hail from a speck too insignificant for most maps. There, and also everywhere, my name is Tenebrus Kro." Offering his full name for the first time in years was not as difficult as he had imagined.

Kro continued, "Before the wagon, I fancied myself an alchemist." He paused, gazing inwardly, thinking, remembering. He continued as if reciting words scrawled on a page. "I think it was the searching that drew me to that incorrigible quest for the hidden. For a handful of years, this seemed my calling, but that all ended the day that I had my first epiphany. That the discovery of cosmic truths were never going to be found at the bottom of a mortar. The goals of the alchemic discipline are not true quests but excuses for those too inept or afraid to search past their own door. And so, I vowed to go into the world. To search as many shadowy corners as I could. And to become something more useful. Something I could never seem to find the right label for."

Kro stopped to draw in a long cold breath which he let out slowly. In silence, he replaced the jar lids, then set them gently back into the box on the ground.

"Livinia, my wife, she liked to say I was a seeker. But as it happened, my dearest, who saw and knew so much, was only half right. Seeking was never enough because I had to claim whatever obscurities I discovered. To dissect, to boil down, and to learn. And, yes when the item was deemed appropriate, it might be sold from the side of that wagon. After all, things that might improve the lives of many should not be hoarded by the few."

He turned away. As the man's hood fell back to rest on his shoulders, he could feel a sudden flash of cold. "Unfortunately, one or two of the treasures I brought home proved a hell of a lot more volatile than salt."

Belmorn and the girl watched with expectant eyes as Kro pulled an old rag and some thick paper from the utility box by the wagon wheel. He wrapped each piece of salted fish with all the care of a butcher. One by one, these were each placed into the box. After that, Kro plunged the rag into the fishing hole before wiping clean the shelf that had been his butcher's block. By the time he was done, the wooden surface was steaming.

"So..." Belmorn finally said. "What did you find?"

"That's the wrong question." Rivka spoke up for the first time in many minutes. Her voice sounded lower than before. Older too. "It's not what he found you should be asking about, but what he brought back." The blankets lay piled at her feet now, revealing a mismatched array of garments that made very little sense.

She was still wearing the brown pants, but now there was a skirt over that--dark blue with a line of small goats embroidered along the bottom. Over a cotton shirt was a brown jerkin with drab fur around the arm holes. More of this fur covered her boots and lined a deep blue hood which hung against her back.

Kro recognized the clothes right away. Rivka's eyes became lances locked on the alchemist. "You brought her here, didn't you?"

Kro did not answer. All his energies were focused on breaking free of the child's terrible, accusing eyes.

"My uncle talked about you," she said. "Used to say that the Veld carried the mark of that witch because the dark man with the wagon put it there. He also said the sickness that swallowed Jayce, started with just two victims." The words echoed out and into the sky. "A woman and a small girl who were both named Kro."

Taking in a long breath, and then shakily letting it out, Tenebrus Kro looked directly at the girl. Saying what she deserved to hear would not be easy. Then again, he didn't deserve easy.

"Your uncle was right, child. But it wasn't a sickness. Not

technically. Just another of the wyrm's adaptations. It seems there are spores in the eggshell, you see. Spores that are released by the very act of hatching. It is a defense mechanism unseen in the rest of the animal kingdom--intended to remove all threats to the newborn, while providing it with plenty to..."

The girl gasped. Her eyes darted back and about like a hummingbird at a rose bush. Just as her emotions looked about to boil over, Rivka's expression went flat.

"Why?" The question was tinged with neither anger nor judgement but her expectant glare did not relent. "Why did you do it? Why would anyone bring home a thing like that?"

"Because for all my accrued knowledge, I remain a fool." Kro shook his head and rubbed a hand over his face. "All my life, some part of me has puppeted these legs, these hands. Driving me to unearth and unveil, and I have been its willing slave. The damn thing was a gift. It was sixty years old, at least. I never could have imagined an egg remaining vital for so long." He sighed yet again. "She so loved when I brought her souvenirs--my Lishka. She was so smart, always so curious about the world around. When she first saw it, she assumed it was a rock. 'Only a funny rock.'" Kro's voice hitched. Despite his efforts to the contrary, tears welled and fell, tracing streams down his dark, wind-bitten cheeks. "Your uncle was right, girl. Plague didn't kill your family. I did."

Tenebrus Kro turned away. Then, laboriously--as if the thing weighed a hundred pounds--he pivoted the shelf he'd been using back into its original, upright position. Just as slowly, he secured it in place with a series of brass latches. Then he rested his head against his wagon, thinking dark thoughts, and for a long time, the man did not move.

They should hate you now. Both of them. And you deserve it, Kro thought this but was unwilling to turn and see the judgmental glares he could already feel.

Light flashed over the glen, casting the cart and thorns in cold, vivid light.

"Snow lightning," muttered Belmorn.

Kro couldn't stop a rueful snicker. "Bad omen."

"Yeah?" asked Belmorn. "Bad for who?"

Beneath a roll of thunder, there came another sound, as if the thing making it had been waiting for the perfect moment to strike.

The howl was long, ghostly, and upon hearing it, Kro knew that it came from neither dog nor wolf. Nor did it come from Her. No--this sound heralded something he had not expected. It meant that a swarm of vermin had finally found his door.

PART TEN
WOLVES AT THE GATE

10-1

Once the terrible sound had faded away, Belmorn stood enthralled by the whipping winds and tiny vibrations humming beneath his skin.

"The witch?" His head darted to his horse and the pair of Graelian axes mounted to the saddle.

"No." Kro's eyes were wide, but not with fear. "But, this is impossible! He couldn't have found me. Not here. Unless... we were followed out of the woods. Shit! I didn't even think of this."

"What? Someone followed us here? Who?" demanded Belmorn, wondering what fresh problem had laid itself across their path. "Damn it, Kro, what is this?" As he spoke, the blackfoot looked to the horses. Snorting clouds of panic and fear, both looked half ready to bolt.

"Oh, don't let the howls fool you, Belmorn. Those are just rats at our gate. Filthy, plague-carrying--"

But Kro's tirade was cut by another blast of sound. Somewhat like the call of a wolf, but only in basic terms. Hearing it a second time, Belmorn noticed it didn't pierce him to the bone like the witch's wail.

"We have to go," hissed Tenebrus Kro, running to the trolls, who were already getting to their feet. "Belmorn. I need you to trust me now! Just ready the horses! Please!"

Rivka backed away without direction. Her head was darting, her mouth a rigid line.

"Come on, girl!" Belmorn waved her close. When they were near the horses, he placed a hand on her shoulder. "Careful," he said. "They could hurt you without meaning to."

"He won't," she said without a shred of doubt. "Your horse. I stayed with him. When they took you away. I fed him too, and when the guards went home, I told him stories. Told him not to trust those idiot guards and he didn't. He's a good horse. He won't--"

The front hooves of the adamandray stomped in succession, shaking the ground. Rivka stumbled back, swallowing her next word.

"Whoa! Easy, Old Man. You're alright." Belmorn moved slowly with hands outstretched and his head low. "Just calm down. We both need to keep our heads right now."

The usually unflappable Magnus was not in a good way. His eyes bulged as he violently shook his bridle. From great gaping nostrils fired snorts of steam and fear, but the blackfoot remained calm. Slinking forward like a cat, the man slid a gloved hand up the animal's jaw line--willing his own resolve into the adamandray.

"Good man," said Belmorn, looping the reins around one hand. "Now I need you to stay with Rivka while I check your friend. Okay?" Magnus lowered his head and snorted, though his front hoof still pawed nervously at the ground. Not entirely satisfied, Belmorn spared a glance for the silver mare who'd backed herself against the thorns and was growing more frantic. "Rivka. If I don't calm that mare down, she's going to hurt herself. Will you stay with Magnus?"

The girl nodded.

"Good," The riverman gave a firm nod. "Thank you."

Rivka hesitated before thrusting her hand out to take the reins. As much as she knew the animal would never intentionally hurt her, Magnus really was enormous. Of such a size that the top of the girl's head didn't even reach his shoulder. It took a fair bit of courage gathering before she reached up to pat one of those long, striped tree trunks it used for legs.

Belmorn approached the mare, but his efforts were not required. The trolls had reached it first--were already placing open palms on the animal's neck and flanks, calming her with their strange talents. Rather than putting her to sleep, they gently led her away from the bramble wall. And when they did, Belmorn winced. He could see lines of blood dripping down her pale coat from where the thorns had scored her.

The troll leader opened his mouth to speak. Belmorn tried to recall his name, but that line of thought was shattered as the eerie howl filled the air for a third time.

"She is going to hear," said the Pershten chief. "Understand...

nowhere is left. Not for my people. Mountain roads all shut."

"I know," said Kro, taking the reins from the others and mounting. "Just stay down. Get back under those pelts, and whatever happens, Bror, keep your small ones quiet. Belmorn! Better get on that giant horse of yours! We have to ride!"

The blackfoot still didn't understand what was happening but could hardly deny the urgency in the air. With well-practiced movements, he climbed the series of square rings, grabbed the saddle horn and swung his leg over the top. Once in place, Magnus shook his massive head and snorted in the direction of the girl.

"Bror!" Belmorn turned, remembering the Pershten chief's name. "Look after the girl. Please, whatever happens, keep her safe."

"No!" shouted Rivka. "You aren't leaving me! I won't be left behind again. Not ever again! Whatever is out there, it can't be worse than that. Rander..." She looked up without a shred of doubt. "You'll keep me safe."

Belmorn frowned. "I'm not one of your legends, girl. In real life, if a sword goes through a man, he doesn't keep fighting for a couple of days after. He just dies."

"Well... I've already had one through me." The girl moved a hand to the bandaged side of her chest. "And I got better. Now, come on. We are wasting time!"

Bewildered, Belmorn looked at Kro, who simply shrugged.

With a weary sigh, the blackfoot took the girl's outstretched hand, pulling her into the saddle behind him. She gripped the man's waist so forcefully, he grunted. He had ridden with Sasha like this many times, most of which had ended in questions of when the boy was going to get a foal of his own.

But he couldn't think about that. Not now.

Turning the silver mare, Kro reached beneath his cloak. The sword he produced was long with a heavy, squared-off pommel shaped like the keystone of some ornate arch. The blade itself was wrapped in red velvet and secured with twine.

"I want you to know this goes against my best judgement," he said to Rivka. "But if you're coming along, you'll need something to protect yourself with."

"What?" Disbelief filled Rivka's voice. "Are you going to give me... that sword?"

"What, this? No, girl. I'm afraid not," Kro said with a smirk, clearly finding humor in the question. He pulled off the velvet sheath to reveal a long reddish blade. In the light of the oppressive sky, it looked as if it had gone to rust. "This is a Maldaavan blade."

Though the statement was delivered with gusto, neither Belmorn nor the girl looked very impressed. Clearly crestfallen, Kro went on.

"In the forging process, the smiths in Maldaav cool the metal with the saliva of giant bats. Buckets of the stuff. It makes the edge... thirsty. Even the slightest nick from this sword is a serious thing. It causes wounds that will not stop bleeding without the touch of fire. Trust me, this one's safer with me." With his other hand, Kro produced a familiar curved knife. With a flick, he turned it in his hand, offering the pommel to the girl. "Here."

Belmorn turned enough to see Rivka beaming. Then, with wide, disbelieving eyes, she reached out to accept the blade, pausing at the last second. "Are you sure you don't have another one of those rusty bat swords?"

"It's not rust," Kro smirked. "But yes, I'm quite sure."

She took the knife. Holding it up, the girl watched as light slid down its dangerous curve. "Thank you, Mr. Kro."

The girl's kind words went straight to his heart.

"Just understand," he said, sternly. "That's no toy. Keep it in your belt, blade pointing down until you intend to use it. Be careful. It's very sharp."

"I will."

"Good." Kro pivoted his mount in the direction of the tunnel they had rode in through. The mare's front hooves crossed the threshold from the glade just as a fourth howl blared. This time, the sound was followed by something else. Something that sounded suspiciously like the distant shouting of men.

"We'll lead them away." Kro halted the mare to look at the Pershten chief. "Hide. And whatever happens, keep hiding."

Bror nodded, then turned to his people, ushering them back under their goat pelts. Belmorn saw the panic in their eyes and the fierce love of one mother Pershten as she clutched her young one, pulling it back. For the briefest of moments, the two saw each other--a father and a mother each with something precious to protect. The responsibility carried a most primal emotion.

Fear, yes, but not for themselves.

And so, the father and the mother turned from one another. Each needing to face that fear as best they could.

10-2

Thorns whistling past on either side and above, the horses raced down the long corridor. In the tight space, the sound of hoofbeats was thunderous. Tenebrus Kro leaned harder into the silver mare. His eyes fixed determinedly ahead, but barely registered the passing blur around him. The haunting blare of the horn had yanked his insides into a massive knot with the distinct sense of an old debt come due. Back in the woods, the enemy had been too numerous and his own panic too fresh. Kro had done much in his colorful life, but the bandit's screams had affected him on a level he hadn't counted on.

The men were his enemies. His robbers. They had not only killed but eaten his horse, an animal he had ridden for almost three years and across two continents. They had found him in his most dire hour of need and they had left him for the rose. Morgrig and his men deserved to be mummified in thorny vines--to be pierced by a thousand pinpricks as their life blood was stolen slowly away. Such would be justice and irony distilled into a single moment. No simple, base vengeance, but poetry. Kro had reassured himself of this many times in the days since the incident. And while the logic rang true, it was all just too damned cold.

Questions of morality aside, the mechanics of what happened had been something of a flash in the pan, an unexpected chemical reaction. Poorly understood, even now. The heat, the smoke, the seeds... and the gland of the size-shifter. Even shriveled and dry, the thing was potent.

He had discovered the gland on a distant beach, extracted it from an animal most would assume to be some kind of eyeless seal. Tenebrus Kro however, recognized the thing for what it was based on one confounding detail. That the remains of a last meal was still protruding from an exploded stomach cavity. Laying on that beach and in full display was the mostly digested body of a small whale. An unfortunate creature more than twenty times the size of the animal who had eaten it.

Of course Kro had heard tales of strange things before. Sea serpents, leviathans that were there one second and gone the next. Once in Garrolvai, he had been privy to the drunken ramblings of an old captain who proclaimed the real reason such monsters were never hauled out of the deep. No such things as sea serpents, the man had said--only shifty things with the power to swell to a size large enough to make other things seem small. Things like ships and whales. The minute you kill them, they shrink back down--all the way to their original size.

Never one to discount the fantastic, Kro harvested and began to test every part of the seal-thing. Proceeding as ever, with the alchemist's creed held firmly in mind. Especially that part at the end--unearth, unveil and know.

Cognizant not to fritter away too much of the irreplaceable ingredients, Kro discovered a superfluous gland at the base of the brain stem. A gland that held nearly a pint of a dark, viscous oil that smelled peculiarly of wet dog.

Unfortunately, initial tests showed that the oil affected neither fish nor worms. But then, one very late night, after having drained an entire decanter of blood dark wine, Kro noticed something he hadn't before. Looking through his concentric lenses, a correlation slid into place. The animal's tissues were not arranged like that of any mammal, fish or reptile he had ever studied. As hard as it was to believe, structurally, the flesh of the strange eyeless thing had more in common with plants.

The revelation caused new hope to flicker but it wasn't until after Kro had successfully filled his tent with around a thousand feet of seaweed, that he knew for certain. Size-shifters were real. And the oils produced by that superfluous gland at the base of their brain stem was undoubtedly the key to their remarkable ability. Now he knew. Not just that, but the answer to the only question that mattered.

How do you kill a witch? The question had driven him for seven, hellish years. And there, on that distant beach, Kro could finally see that the answer wasn't force but rather, deception. A one-of-a-kind bait constructed from meat, size-shifting oil and one final ingredient. Seeds.

Providing he could get the witchwyrm to take the bait, the damage would be done. Stomach acids would dissolve small glass containers hidden in the meat, allowing the special oils of the size-shifter to mingle with the seeds of the vampire rose. Then would come the growth. The glorious, explosive growth.

Kro had pictured it many times. Thorny vines erupting glistening and red from holes where eyes had been and out of new ones in that long, serpentine throat. Had imagined the exquisite music of the witchwyrm's screams as she died, too stupid to comprehend the genius of her own undoing.

It was a perfect plan. One which Kro had ruminated over for many months, as he made his way back by ship and over roads to the region of his birth. Back to the pitiless edge of the world, where people were as cold as the wind. A good, well-crafted plan which had burned to ash, in the flash-bang folly of a single moment.

Back at the camp of Mannis Morgrig, something had happened. The heat, the smoke from the kindling boy--something unexpected. A chain reaction that could not be reversed.

Kro had lost it all. The components, the plan, and every shred of hope he'd cultivated--all of it, wasted on the wrong damned enemy.

Another horn blast shot straight through Kro's stomach. It made clear that however many wolves had been slain in the smoke-filled camp, their leader was very much alive. Mannis Morgrig was at his door, and the Red Wolf was hungry for blood.

The horses slowed, then stopped, at the end of the corridor. The gate was still shut, still latched and secured. Kro dismounted and peered through the thorns.

"Shit."

"What is it?" asked the blackfoot. "Damn it, Kro, who's out there?"

Kro turned around, wearing a guilty expression. "Do you remember what I said about what happened after I left you on the forest floor? About my big revenge quest?"

Belmorn looked annoyed. "Yeah. You said you kicked the hornet's nest."

"And so I did," said Kro, unlatching the gate. There was a ruckus going on outside--the jeers and ribbing of brigands. Kro peaked through the beams and the bramble. "Damn it," His voice leaked out, half a sigh. "I don't know how he found us, but that's him alright. Mannis shit-kicking Morgrig." Kro mounted his horse. Then he looked back to Belmorn and the girl. "This is all my doing. If there were another way, believe me, I would take it. But we have to fight this fight. Even if their damned racket doesn't bring the witch down on our heads, the damned fools brought torches. Belmorn, I-- "

Again the horn blared.

"Rose man!" the voice bellowed from outside, nearly as loud as the horn. "We know you're there! My man saw you. Followed you all the way up that hill. We haven't found your secret door, but I know it's close."

"How many are there?" asked the grim voice of Rander Belmorn.

"Less than ten, I think," said Kro, brandishing his Maldaavan blade.

"Wonderful."

"Hey, be thankful. There were more the other day." Kro smiled crookedly. "Anyway, I say they're outnumbered."

"What? Why?"

"Because, Belmorn, we've got *you*."

"Me?" Belmorn scoffed.

"This is no time for modesty. You're a man of the Black River, a blackfoot! You've probably ridden hundreds of giant eels to their graves on the shore!"

"Hunting and battle aren't the same, Kro. And eels are not men." Belmorn's scowl deepened. "You are going to get us all killed."

"Probably," Kro pulled up his hood. "But if we don't shut that damn horn-blower up, we're going to have worse at our door than a few unwashed bandits and I think you know that."

Belmorn didn't know, Kro realized. Not exactly. But by now, he must definitely have an idea. The man sneered.

"Rander, he said they have torches." The girl's hand touched his arm. Her small, unexpected voice was full of resolve, well past her years. "We can't let them set fires. The Pershten will die. Mothers, children--all of them."

Belmorn's mouth tightened into a thin, mirthless line. He reached back to touch his axes, and the act seemed to drape a calm over the riverman. He drew in a breath, letting it out in a slow plume that wreathed his face.

Another blare of the horn shot through the marrow in the alchemist's bones. Kro turned anxiously toward the shouting and then back to the blackfoot. Belmorn was fastening the last in a series of buttons. His collar was erect, obscuring most of his face, just as it had when the two first met. His grey eyes were set. Determined. The storm in them now seemed a hurricane.

"That damn horn," Belmorn glowered. "We have to get it. To stop them from using it before--"

A wail from behind answered the call of Morgrig's horn-man. The wail carried a note of mourning, clutching and gripping all who heard with finger-claws of ice and dread. Then came the barks. One, then two then one more.

The necks of all three riders snapped to look in the direction from which they had come. The tunnel was darker than it had been only moments before and seemed to twist in their vision.

Crashing, snapping, breaking sounds--as if twigs and thorny branches were being clawed away--echoed in their skulls and grew louder. Something big was coming from the other side of the moat. Judging by the sounds, they only had seconds.

"It's her," the girl squeaked.

Belmorn met the eye of Tenebrus Kro, who answered with a slow nod.

"What do we do?" the riverman asked.

"The only thing we can." Muted fury brimmed in his voice. "This is not a fight we can win, blackfoot. Not now. Not like this. We have no course. No path but away."

"But the Pershten," protested Belmorn. "By Rinh, we have to do something."

"We can't help them now. Pray or mourn, do what you feel is best, but do it later. If you really care for that girl or if you still hope to see your son again, riding away from that sound is our only option. Before anything else, we have to silence that fucking horn. Do you understand?"

Behind his collar, the blackfoot frowned. He addressed the girl, "Rivka."

"Yeah?"

"I need you to hold onto me, okay?"

The girl wrapped her arms around the man, weaving her fingers together on the other side. "Okay."

Alchemist and blackfoot exchanged another silent conversation. After an almost imperceptible nod, both maneuvered their horses in the confined space of the tunnel. As Kro backed his mare away from the door, Belmorn turned the adamandray the other way around. And when Magnus' back hooves connected with the old wooden beams, they did so with an explosive CRAKK!

The impact sent the gate outward and open--snapping old vines and sending thorny twigs flying and spinning through the air.

10-3

Roughly three hundred feet back from the face of the thorn wall, seven men sat on six horses. Aback the largest, a blood bay stallion, was Mannis Morgrig.

Even amongst the thick stock of men he surrounded himself with, the man was vast. Appearing, at quick glance, like a species of beast unto himself. A veritable pack's worth of wolf pelts hung from his shoulders and back. And where there wasn't fur, one could see an incomplete set of silver-white armor. The suite was Roonik, and it told the grim story of a previous owner. Around a central wound, the metal of the chest plate flared outward, as if some great monster had fought to get at the good meat beneath.

In a sudden gust, the man's bush of reddish beard blew to one side, but his eyes were unwavering. Morgrig regarded what was left of a gang he had spent over three years putting together. The two men who shared a painted mare both held torches and stupid expressions, but the one in front had a bow in one hand. Morgrig had never bothered to learn their names and would have gladly traded both for his good lieutenant, Alberg Voss.

Morgrig sneered--spat on the ground. If only his sword had accidentally found one of them instead.

To his left sat the tracker--a tall, thick necked man called Raigar who wore a scarred scalp in place of hair. Next to him was the idiot, Dirk, on his swaybacked, roan farm horse.

Further down the line was the one in the mask who rode a pale mare. Morgrig had come to think of the man in the plague mask as his personal butcher. Ugly, cleaver-like swords were strapped firmly to either side of his saddle. Though most assumed otherwise, not even Morgrig had seen the man's face. And in the thirteen months they had ridden and plundered together, he could count the number of muffled words he'd heard on one hand. When it came to the man called Slagter, only two things could be said for certain--he wielded those strange, pointless blades the way a poet wields verse and he was sure as hell no doctor.

"Scheepers," Morgrig addressed his seventh man and the horn-blower turned at his name. One of his eyes stared intently, but the other had been shut forever, sealed by flame scars. Over that eye was a generous swath of red paint.

"You need me to tell you every time?" Morgrig growled impatiently. "Blow the fucking horn!"

As Scheepers pressed the mouthpiece to his lips, something stole his breath.

From miles ahead or paces behind, flowing like a poison torrent through the air and over the seven men on six stolen horses, wailed a wave of pure mourning. But instead of inspiring sadness, the sound brought only one thing. Fear.

"Mannis?" The voice belonged to Dirk. The scrawny fool who had set his sights on the recently vacated role of lieutenant. Dirk was as much a coward as he was an idiot. Whatever he was about to say, Morgrig did not want to hear it.

Fortunately for the Red Wolf, before Dirk could say anything, a piece of the sheer thorn wall erupted outward, as a hidden gate was exposed and obliterated in one thundering impact!

All of the bandits gaped, staring, as the biggest horse they had ever seen galloped out of the newly made opening and onto the dale. Riding the animal was a man of dark and sinister aspect. He had the look of a highwayman--all black but for the green head scarf that flowed and snapped behind. Next appeared a second horse--silver, carrying a familiar hooded figure.

I see you Rose Man.

The Red Wolf had expected the son of a bitch to be alone. Not that it changed anything. Whoever this highwayman was, his presence would make little difference. Morgrig tightened his thick fingers around the grip of his long sword and looked around at what remained of his pack. Seven, including himself. Not much as numbers went, but these men had been through something. They had watched as their brothers were picked off and mummified, each of them food for a monstrous, towering thing more animal than plant.

That thing had been put there by a man who now occupied their every thought. A man currently riding straight for them on a silver horse.

"Hold fast, men," growled the Red Wolf. "This is it! Our chance for revenge is riding straight towards us, now! If you want to take it, best keep those weapons up and them torches burning!"

"Aye!" Came the collective roar.

The sound was more practiced than passionate but it would serve. Mannis Morgrig grinned and it was a dark, mirthless thing that creased an old scar on his lip. Red beard and hair billowing, he sat firmly on his blood bay stallion--readying himself. Wearing the practiced grin of a maniac.

10-4

Two horses thundered away from the thorn-wall and across the expanse in a matter of seconds.

Leading the charge was a fearsome looking man on a huge two-toned stallion. Though Kro had mixed emotions about Rivka being there, he knew Belmorn's side was probably the safest place for her. The man's axes were out--both of them. Incredibly, though neither of his hands were holding the reins, the adamandray moved in perfect sync. Straight towards the line of armed men as if animal and blackfoot were privy to each other's thoughts.

Kro snickered. If he had ever doubted it before, he could doubt no longer. Truly the stories of the river men and their horses had not been hyperbolic.

As expected, Morgrig's diminished forces wilted at the spectacle galloping their way. As Belmorn came within twenty feet, Kro saw him shift his legs. With no visible cue from his rider, the adamandray lifted itself to its full height and trumpeted. Magnus whirled then, threatening strikes with huge front legs as a bolt of lightning split the sky. And when those hooves came back down, the very ground shuddered.

The act caused the brigands to stagger back--one man even fell out of his saddle, but there was something else in the air. Something that prickled at Kro's last nerve. Unable to stop himself, he looked behind. Back to the secret opening in the thorns.

To his horror, something appeared in that gaping hole. Something long and glistening that flicked into view like the revolting tongue of a snake tasting the air. Kro's chest seized as he watched it appear. The thing he had remembered at the start of every morning and end of every night for the past seven years. And as more came into view he found that watching was about all he was capable of. His eyes wide, his teeth clenched hard enough to crack a shelled walnut.

First came the snout, then the eyes that shone like green embers. Polished gemstones the size of ostrich eggs, composed not of carbon and light but solid, undeniable hate. These details ran through Kro's mind as a snout and face became a full head and part of a neck.

Within seconds, jutting out of the thorns hovering a mere foot above the ground, was the head of an enormous serpent. Black with silver markings and crowned with a massive crest. Horn was the word that came to mind, but it was more likely just part of the skull itself. The structure was placed just behind the center of the head, just behind where the brain would be. It was a stout thing--pointed and back-turned, like the horn of a rhinoceros.

Frozen in abject terror, Tenebrus Kro stared into the face of his true enemy and with slitted, hating eyes, the Hispidian witchwyrm stared right back.

Move. The thought exploded in the alchemist's brain. *Move you useless idiot. Now!*

Kro's eyes snapped into focus. He drew in a sharp breath through his nose then, squeezing his knees together, he made the silver mare bolt. Seeing his old enemy face to face after so long was not unlike being struck by lightning. She had grown considerably in the last seven years.

Two nights before, she must have known they were there. Or at least near. Why hadn't she attacked then? Over his shoulder, Kro saw more than ten feet of neck had already appeared. And he knew that anyone else watching would surely identify the beast as a snake of titanic proportions. But, to his own dismay, Kro knew better.

A pair of appendages popped into view. Each of the creature's front legs ended in four clawed toes. These slammed into the ground, then began to pull the monstrosity free of its thorny birth canal.

10-5

Mannis Morgrig looked pale. His eyes, more frightened puppy than wolf, had gone bloodshot. The rest of the brigands were desperately looking to him for direction or possibly reassurance, but every single one came up wanting.

The monster's head protruded roughly twenty feet from the Moat's only viable opening. It swung from left to right, elegant in its motion. The fanged mouth at the end of that long serpent's neck opened wide. Then pushing upward with what appeared to be arms, a series of gulping barks was vomited into the sky. One, two, three, then nothing.

After this, more of the creature poured through the splintered gate and into full view. The head and neck of a colossal adder sprouted from an incongruous body--at least sixty feet long from nose to tail with two sets of dragonish legs. Based on spectacle alone, the horrendous silver and black thing had earned every whisper of its reputation.

Now fully emerged, the witchwyrm reared up on its hind legs-- standing like a bear and straightening its back to an amazing height. The animal's scales were long--flaring away from the body to give almost a hairy appearance. With a sudden shudder, a rattling sound travelled all the way down its long body and into the tail--moving like a shockwave through those long scales.

One of the back legs was lifted. It came down hard as the creature leaned in the direction of the men. With a flick of a forked tongue, once more the thing tasted the air. Then, with no discernable warning, the wyrm's head snapped in a new direction. Looking past the two galloping horses to lock eyes with the Red Wolf himself. Almost as if the thing could sense the presence of another mighty predator.

Mannis Morgrig swallowed the saliva that had been gathering in his mouth. He sat upon his blood bay stallion, utterly stupefied. His purpose, forgotten. His once burning desire for revenge, now as intact as a handful of snow.

After another flick of its tongue, the top half of the witchwyrm slammed down to the earth. Then, in a strange serpentine run, the hag used all four limbs to carry it over the Veld like some frenzied jungle cat whose spine bent the wrong way. And by whatever gods remained, it wailed as it came. Whether in fury or out of hunger, none dared guess, but all recognized the eager face of their own personal death.

Less than two hundred feet away, Morgrig stared, still paralyzed in awe. His brain worked furiously, trying to make sense of the signals it was receiving. Two horses raced straight toward him, galloping like the devil himself were at their heels. Only this was no devil; here came the witch. It was real, more terrible than all the tales, and it was coming straight for him.

The rider who pulled in front was an imposing highwayman type who Morgrig did not recognize. He was big and so was the horse that carried him and the pair of axes in his hands. But the stranger didn't matter. Morgrig was more concerned with the man riding just behind. The bastard who had been stupid enough to attack a band of wolves in their own den. The fucking Rose man.

With fresh rage, Morgrig turned and began shouting."This is it, boys. Weapons up! Set those teeth in a clench and keep 'em sharp!"

Unfortunately, the words came too late to do any good. Like a blast of wind from a hurricane, the highwayman thundered between the dumbstruck bandits, making straight for the one with the blowing horn. Scheepers, who was also brandishing a well-bent bow, loosed an arrow. The shaft sped through the air, its well-aimed trajectory sending it straight for the center mass of the massive highwayman.

PING! The sound came less than a second before a much louder CRACK!!

The speeding arrow deflected harmlessly off the broad side of a Graelian axe. Then, that same axe was turned--made to strike. Scheepers had managed to lift the bow but it was promptly split in half, both sides falling uselessly though still connected via string.

Absorbing most of the tremendous blow, the one-eyed horn blower reeled back limply. Somehow the man was still in his saddle, but now his hands gripped only air. The highwayman, showing remarkable mastery of the animal that bore him, turned in a great cloud of snow and dirt, sheathed one axe and began galloping once more. With one hand he held up the stolen blowing horn, before looping the strap around his neck. The final insult to this injury came from the rose man himself. As the bastard galloped past by in a second gust of sound and air, he flashed a lopsided grin. Morgrig watched all of this as if watching a dream. Of all the myriad ways he had seen this playing out...

With a guttural roar of hate and frustration, Morgrig rounded his blood bay and took off after the riders.

"Yaahh!" Bellowed the Red Wolf, jabbing his heels into the ribs of his mount. Leaning in to his horse, he did everything in his power to push the animal faster and farther away from the nightmare thing behind.

Morgrig had never believed the tales. The warning of a terrible Witch-Beast who was said to have ruled the High Veld for nearly a decade. The stories had been too fantastic to be real. Only now could he finally comprehend why a man like Henric Galttauer would slam shut his doors. And why bandits had been allowed to creep into the Roonik woods that had once been patrolled so staunchly. But Morgrig had to put the beast out of his mind. Just ahead, was the man who had caused all of this, galloping away on a silver mare. He unsheathed his long blade with a hateful sneer. Morgrig was gaining on his enemy. His blood bay was the faster horse.

The rose man looked behind. Then, from one of his saddle bags, he produced a strange object. Something that looked like a large letter X. The man looked at the object, then back to Morgrig as if he were working through some internal conflict. Then, after a slow shake of his head, the bastard tossed the thing--not aggressively, but the way one throws a ball to their dog.

"Catch!"

Without a thought, Morgrig snatched the thing out of the air. His eyes alternated between it and the road ahead. It was a strange, handmade looking thing--two ribbed cylinders, each roughly a foot long. They had been joined in the middle to make a cross. The four ends had been sealed with candle wax, and from the center extended a long black string. A fuse, Morgrig's instincts told him. He looked up from the unlikely thing, utterly dumbfounded.

The Rose Man nodded. With his free hand, he pointed back to the witchwyrm. Then, after making a brief fist, he opened the hand again, splaying five fingers wide.

The gesture's meaning was not lost on the Red Wolf, though he could not understand why his enemy would have just handed over a bomb. With another look behind, Morgrig saw the beast. It was coming fast, bounding in that bizarre slithering gait. It released more of those guttural barks. Then it pounced for the nearest horse--a painted mare with two riders--hind claws spreading like the talons of an eagle.

Morgrig didn't have time to look away. A rear leg sliced open the horses flank with three scythe-like claws. The mare screamed as it fell forward and down. And when it hit the ground, the animal's weight and momentum forced its head back the wrong way. After that, the only screaming was coming from the men whose names Morgrig had never learned.

The neck of the witchwyrm pulled back, arching like that of a swan. Then, flashing a pair of curved, ivory fangs, the head shot forward with the force of a cannon blast. The first man was bitten, then thrown high into the air. Straight up, he soared farther and farther from the ground.

Wasting no time, the beast fired again, snatching the second man in her mouth and swinging him round to meet the barbed tip of her tail. That follow up strike was marked by a loud scream that was cut suddenly short. For as soon as the barb touched that man, he became the first of many to vanish. Winking out of existence and without a trace, as if he had never been there at all.

Morgrig hadn't blinked, hadn't looked away at the wrong moment. His man was simply no longer there. Seeing this, the bandit commander felt the full, crushing weight of his folly. Not only was the damned witch-beast real, so too were her talents.

"Witchcraft," Morgrig hissed under his breath as he watched the first man careen back toward the ground.

As if it had been her intention all along, the witch caught the man she had thrown. And when she touched the tip of her tail to the body in her mouth, he too disappeared.

The witch reared up again and moved on two legs. Using its heavy, barbed tail as a counterweight, it leaned forward as it ran, neck and head parallel to the ground. It stalked over to its next closest victim.

Sprawled and unconscious, the man called Scheepers, had not recovered from the highwayman's blow.

Morgrig swore under his breath. Even with the distance he had put between himself and the fairytale nightmare, he didn't have long. The deaths of his men had bought seconds, nothing more.

Ahead, the hooded man and his tall companion were racing down a well-travelled road that led to a dense forest and, eventually, the ancient city of Roon.

The blood bay stallion was foaming at the mouth. The animal wasn't used to such a breakneck pace, and malnourished as it was, couldn't maintain it for much longer.

Morgrig looked down to the strange cross-like object in his hand. "Dirk!" he roared to the man who was riding at his side. "Torch!"

The idiot looked over with wild, bloodshot eyes. Though scared out of his mind, he knew better than to ignore a command.

When the horses were an arm's length apart, Morgrig looked back to see the wyrm was again on his tail. Running on two legs, it came like some undeniable force of nature. A tornado, a bolt of lightning. One hundred feet back... ninety... eighty. He could see its eyes now. Seventy feet. They glowed like green embers. Sixty. Morgrig thrust out the cross, fuse facing out. Idiot or not, Dirk understood enough. The man touched the flame of his torch to the bouncing length of fuse and by whatever Gods remained, it began to spark.

Reeling back, Morgrig gathered every ounce of his concentration and hurled the sizzling thing at his enemy. The cross flew, spinning end over end, splitting the air. As it did, the man who had thrown it pictured the rose man's hand and the violent reaction it had promised.

With light and a loud whooshing hiss, geysers of sparks erupted from the four ends of the cross propelling it faster and faster until.

Mannis Morgrig had seen bombs go off before, had witnessed the explosive rage and devastation of mortar shells.

This was nothing like that.

Not a single punching BOOM, but a series of crackling, snapping bursts of light and startling color spun with screaming fury. The cross narrowly missed the head of the beast and bounced off of its chest before whirling away.

In the end, seeing that no great damage had been dealt, Morgrig swore. The wyrm's ember-green eyes flashed with something that might have been pain or terror. Then they focused on a new target: the little man who had dared assault it.

Digging his heels in, Morgrig pushed his horse for all it was worth. The ground sloped into a slow incline. Three riders rode ahead of him: the rose man, the tall stranger, and his butcher. They were already near the top of the hill, exactly where he needed to be.

Morgrig had chosen his blood bay by the same logic that governed all of his decisions since taking up his current identity. It fit the brand. It had the right look. It was the biggest and strongest. Unfortunately, as he now learned, that particular horse was not the fastest.

Who are you? Morgrig thought. *Someone who runs? Someone who flees with tail between their legs like some common cur? Oh yes, I remember him. I just thought you were someone else now. Someone who clawed their way up from the muck and the mire to to become a king. No, not a king...*

Baring his teeth in a snarl, Morgrig brandished his good, long sword and pulled up the reins. He would run no more because he knew exactly who and what he was. Among other things, Mannis Morgrig was a wolf. And even at the bitter end, a wolf still has its teeth.

PART ELEVEN
BLOOD FOR THE ROSE

11-1

Rivka pressed closer into the blackfoot's back as she heard men screaming over the sounds of hoofbeats. Her heart dove from her stomach to her throat when the big man leaned back as they descended the other side of the hill. After a breath, she looked up and over to the man Kro who mirrored her action and nodded. Then he patted the saddle bags and did his best impression of a smile.

"It's a bàozhú cross." Kro shouted--clearly referring to the handmade thing that had just exploded in the witchwyrm's face. "Call it... a secret of the Orient. More importantly, we can't stay on this road. She has our scent. She'll follow us straight to Roon!"

Rivka's ears were sharp. In spite of the galloping racket, they managed to pick up most of what was being said.

"Agreed," Barked Belmorn. "Any ideas?"

"Maybe," A crooked grin lifted the edge of Kro's mouth. "Maybe a way we... kill two birds... one stone." He glanced at the two riders with a wild brightness in his eyes. Kro's hood was flapping against his back, but the blood red scarf was up and over his nose and mouth. That combined with his flickering hair gave the man an entirely different aspect.

"Maybe?!" Belmorn did not sound happy.

"Hey, best I got." Said Kro. "Listen! The wyrm... if she gets close, don't you dare attack her, Belmorn! Just give her space! Let her pass! She needs to follow me. That's what matters. Understand? Come to think of it, you better give me that horn."

Belmorn looked momentarily confused, then remembered the blowing horn he had taken off Morgrig's man. Slipping one arm out through the strap, he tossed the thing.

Catching it with one hand, Kro lifted the horn to his lips and blew. Though the initial sound was a pathetic squeak, his second attempt fared better. The howling carried out over the lower veld--rolling over land and rock and the hill behind. Looking quite pleased, Kro set his attention back on the road, barely managing to avoid a triangular rock. The first of the giant's teeth was small, but there would be larger specimens soon enough. Much larger.

"Come get us, you hag!" Shouted Kro, his hair flickering like a black flame. "Hey Belmorn... mind the rocks!"

"I see them."

Once clear, Magnus was veered to the left--following Kro down the hill and away from the clear path that they had previously taken. As for Rivka, she did not remember that path. She had been on death's door when her two companions had followed it through the dense woods on their harrowed flight from Roon.

As the adamandray rounded a larger, more threatening rock, something made Rivka look to the side. It was then that her eyes fell upon a rider not far behind. A rider who having already crested the hill, was gaining on them. But that wasn't the worst part. For this rider was wearing a pale mask--not pure white, but something close. A color like sunbaked bones. This rider, he was one of them--one of those bastards who had come for her mother and father, to declare officially what she was too afraid to say out loud.

"Bird man." Rivka whispered as a tear streamed from the corner of one eye.

The rider, and those others, walked like men but there was something off about them. Something inhuman. The ones who called themselves "doctors"--had worn hats and coats with high collars, anything to prevent the sickness from getting inside. But this one appeared to be unconcerned with such matters. Aside from the mask, the man was ill-dressed for the region. Tight wrappings covered most of his arms, but bits of brown skin showed--like Rander's, only much, much darker.

The man's hair was long and black, growing from his head in stiff ropes that bounced and slapped as he came. She had never seen hair like that before. And, though her mind might have been playing tricks,

Rivka thought could see feathers, long and black, sprouting from between those ropes.

"Go away!!" Rivka shouted at the rider, hating herself for it. She wanted to be brave. She had to be a grown-up now, not some stupid, scared kid. Rivka was twelve, and if there were any gods left to look down, they would know she had survived more hardship than most adults. And that she was too old to be afraid of some stupid mask.

Just look away, she told herself. But she could not look away. Even as the wind burned her face, Rivka Pesch held fast.

Noticing the girl at last, the man turned his long face. As he did, light reflected off glass, turning the mask's lenses into twin moons. Rivka tried to breathe, but the sight of those glowing, circular eyes had a paralyzing effect. Unreasonable terror clawed at her chest--had turned her lungs into useless wooden things. In fact, the only part of her that still worked was her hand. She knew this because it had already moved to the dagger in her belt. Mr. Kro had told her to leave it there until she was ready to use it, but the curved handle seemed to be pulling at her fingers. It felt good when she gripped it.

"Rander!" the girl bellowed, tightening her grip all the more. "Oh come on--Rander!" Urgency in her throat, Rivka leaned closer. In frustration she reached up and tugged at the man's whipping green headscarf. Finally, the blackfoot turned to look back.

"Look!" Furiously she tapped his arm on the side the bird man was approaching. Once certain that Belmorn indeed was seeing what she was, the girl re-gripped his middle and squeezed.

Belmorn narrowed his eyes. The man in the plague mask rode hard. In his hand, an ugly sword was drawn and poised.

Over the years, Belmorn had done much from his saddle--battling eels and other horrors on the brackish course. But now that saddle was not his alone. Unfortunately, the girl behind him wasn't just holding on for dear life, she was hindering his arm's range of motion. Wielding his axe in that direction would be impossible. There was only one course of action: They needed to go faster.

Belmorn put a gloved hand on the neck of his oldest friend. He was already asking too much, pushing Magnus harder than he ever had before--and with an extra rider. As the pale horse closed in, Belmorn steeled himself. The masked rider turned his curved, beak-like face locking eyes with the riverman. It was only a fleeting moment, but for the two warriors it was enough.

"Yah!" The masked rider's voice was deep and loud. He leaned lower and dug his heels into the ribs of his mount. The pale horse moved past the adamandray in a cloud of dirt and snow and indifference.

Bewildered, Belmorn glanced back at the girl. "Rivka! Are you okay?"

"Okay!" her voice conveyed similar surprise. He felt her nod against his back.

Then he noticed the direction the masked rider and horse were headed. He looked ahead at his hooded companion just as another blast from Morgrig's horn filled the sky.

"Kro!!" Belmorn shouted as loud as he could, unsure if the other man could even hear him. The masked rider was moving too fast. That pale horse of his, all wire and sinew, seemed to have been designed for this very task. In a matter of seconds, he would be in striking distance of his true target, and there wasn't a damn thing Rander Belmorn could do about it.

11 - 2

The mind of Tenebrus Kro was only half on the road ahead. It was also searching. Remembering. Hoping he really saw what he thought he had seen during his last visit to Morgrig's camp.

Upon reaching the clearing, before everything had gone to smoke and chaos, he had smelled it--the Veld. It had been too dark to see for certain, but if he was right, the brigand camp had been raised on the very edge of the tree line. And judging by how long it had taken Kro to walk from there to Roon, it couldn't have been very far from where they were now.

No need to hide if there's no one looking. Eh, Mannis? Kro shook his head. Musing on the brash success of the man who called himself a wolf.

It was then that a nauseating contemplation occurred. Even if Kro could find Morgrig's camp again, his insane plan would only work if the witch was following them. From what he had uncovered, the species was fiercely territorial. Usually only claiming an area of a few square miles, or the size of a small city. It was the real reason Galttauer's people were still alive. Because if she really wanted what was inside, doors weren't going to stop her. Even sturdy ones with big iron locks.

Likely, the hag had never ventured so far from her nest before. Having gotten used to feeding on the trolls and mountain goats, she probably had no idea Roon was even there. And that's the way it had to stay.

Reflexively, Kro urged the silver mare around another of the giant's teeth. This one was almost a foot high and pointed in his general direction. Once clear, he raised the horn to his lips and once again blew as hard as he could. Was it working? Was the witch going to follow the sounds, or had she taken her fill for the day and retreated to the high veld?

Suddenly, the sky was split by three loud barks that echoed and rolled over the Low Veld. Kro turned to see the front half of an enormous serpent looming above the hill's crest. Wasting no time, the witchwyrm scrambled down the slope all frenzy and rage. She moved on four legs, and she did so alone. Of Mannis Morgrig or his remaining men, there was no sign.

A surge of victory pounded in Kro's chest as he sounded the horn one more time for good measure. Looking ahead, he began mapping out the safest path through the treacherous field, but the sound of hoofbeats prickled his attention. The alchemist turned, expecting to see Belmorn and the girl. But instead, Kro saw that a strange man was racing straight for him at a harsh angle. The rider was one of Morgrig's--the one with the plague mask and long ropes for hair. He was coming fast and with an ugly sword raised above his head.

There came a downward flash of steel, but Kro had just enough time to lean hard and veer his mare to safety. The attack didn't miss by much. Gritting his teeth, Kro drew the Maldaavan blade from its red and gold scabbard. "Are you insane?" he demanded in naked outrage.

The masked rider shifted his head into a new angle. For a long moment, circular eyes of glass and darkness just stared. Then, the man's weapon answered for him.

A sparking clang resounded. The impact travelled down Kro's arm as Maldaavan steel bit into the crude, elongated butcher's tool. Another barrage of clashes immediately followed, resulting in both men pulling back their weapons for a moment of rest.

Somehow, Kro could feel it. The red sword wanted more of that. Not the rest, but the impacts, the cold bite of steel on steel. After so many years of disuse, it had worked up something of a thirst.

Giant's teeth, now almost three feet high zipped past on either side. After checking the rocks and judging that he was no more than a half mile from the tree line, Kro sneered. He turned back to face his enemy, but the masked rider was no longer there.

Panic rising, Kro's head darted from right to left and that's when he realized what had happened. In the few seconds it had taken to look away, the rider must have dropped back before pushing his pale horse into an attack from the other side.

Kro swung his sword around, but the angle was bad. The cleaver's force drove the Maldaavan blade into the tanned hide of Kro's saddle--slicing free one of the saddlebag's straps. The bag swung wide, spilling one of the remaining Bàozhú crosses.

"Stop!" Kro bellowed. "That thing back there... it has our scent! It's coming... for all of us!"

The masked rider swung his beaked face toward the man at his side and finally spoke. "The snake mother comes." His deep voice had a strange accent. "Nothing... can stop her. But she can't have... you."

Kro's eyes shot wide. Did he know this man? Or was he just so bent on revenge for what had happened at Morgrig's camp?

Kro looked away from the dirty mask, the ropes of heavy, black hair that cracked like whips with every undulation of the pale horse's gallop. Then, staring intently at the approaching trees, he drove his mare away from the last survivor of the Red Wolf's pack.

Calling from behind, the masked rider was shouting. His words resounded like the hits of a bass drum over the breakneck gallop.

"Today... is a day of reckoning, Mister Kro. For settling old debts. Fifteen years. I have thought of nothing. Nothing but this moment!" He released a stream of unhinged laughter. "All my searching. My patience. What I have become. It has all been... for you!"

Kro's mind reeled. He clenched tighter the handle of his thirsty, red blade, wondering how this person knew his damned name. For that was not a thing he gave out lightly.

"Ha!" The masked man lashed out again, but his eyes were not on the road. The cleaver swung out just as the pair came upon a huge giant's tooth. The stone passed between the two riders, but at the worst possible moment. The ugly squared-off sword connected with stone and was sent spinning back through the air behind them.

Kro wrenched his head around, taking in what he could. Enough to make sure the heavy weapon didn't hit Belmorn. Fortunately, the riverman was almost twenty feet back. And about a quarter mile farther off, the witch was still coming. Still moving down the hill in a strange slithering gallop, and going much faster that the tired Adamandray.

11-3

After a quick appraisal of the immediate landscape, Kro reined the mare into a tight barrel around one of the slanted rocks. Then, leaning in, he took off in the opposite direction--straight for the blackfoot.

Reflexively, the masked rider whipped his horse into a fast turnaround but Kro had managed to put a bit of space between them. Through fleeting glances, he saw the man produce a second cleaver sword. Like its twin, the preposterously large weapon was a tool of destruction that favored brutality and force, but an ill-conceived choice for mounted combat.

Riding the faster horse, the masked man caught up quickly and wasted no time getting back to business. In answer, Kro's Maldaavan blade swung out in a perfectly balanced arc, deflecting the blow in line with the strike's momentum. It was just enough force and in just the right direction to create an opening.

The rust-colored edge split both air and flesh--slicing away the wrappings that covered the man's upper arm. A stream of red sputtered, then gushed--falling like red rain that steamed when it hit the snow.

Somehow, despite a deep wound that looked to Kro like a mouth, vomiting blood. His attacker managed to hold onto the second of his cleaver blades. And after shifting it to his other hand, the man put his relentlessness on full display.

"Mister Kro!" He bellowed, pushing his pale horse to catch up with the silver mare. "Can't get away, Mister Kro!"

As the distance between Kro and Belmorn shrunk to nothing, a look of understanding passed between the two men. Leaning into his horse, Kro put his trust in the man he hardly knew--thundering right past him with full confidence, and a madman on his heels.

The masked rider behaved exactly as Kro had expected. Devouring the mare's footsteps as he came--both glassy eyes focused on one thing in all the world.

"Oh Mister Kro-o-o-o..."

KUNNGG!

The flat, hammer-end of a Graelian axe appeared out of nowhere and connected squarely with the rider's face. The beak crumpled into the headspace as a limp form tumbled from the saddle. The man hit the ground hard and did not get up--coming to rest beside one of the larger stones which Kro had called giant's teeth.

The pale horse ran wild. Panic-blind, it headed straight toward the monstrous thing lumbering across the rock-laden expanse. And though he felt a momentary pang of regret, Tenebrus Kro knew the horse's sacrifice would grant him and blackfoot precious time.

The adamandray appeared, though neither of its riders looked pleased.

"A friend of yours?"

"Hard to say... the face isn't ringing a bell." Kro shot another quick glance at the masked maniac. "Hey Belmorn, maybe it's safer if we stick together from now on, eh?"

"Yeah? Safer for who?" Belmorn turned to the girl. "Rivka. You okay back there?"

Kro's heart thrummed. He couldn't hear the girl's response but noted her overwide eyes, and near bloodless complexion. Barely keeping himself from looking back, Kro began to shout.

"Rivka!"

"Yeah!" She shouted back. "I'm okay."

"Good. Keep your eyes on me. "Okay? Just me."

Stiffly, the girl straightened her body and nodded, though she kept one hand on the hilt of the dagger he'd given her.

Rivka Pesch had never actually seen the witch. Whatever she had expected, whatever nightmarish visions had plagued her dreams these past seven years... Every imagining fell laughably short of the reality.

As she forced herself to look away, she noticed Kro's sword. He pointed with it toward the trees, and when he drew it back, the slick blood on the blade was nearly gone--almost as if the red steel drank it in.

Rivka tried to recall what he'd said about the weapon, but her mind was spinning. Cycling through images of a monster currently devouring their trail. To keep herself from looking back, she tried harder to remember what Kro had said about his sword.

Something about the spit of giant bats. About it being thirsty.

Now that she wasn't twisting back in the saddle, heat from Rander's back drew prickles to her right hand. Surprised at the sensation she looked down to see that her fingers were still wrapped around the dagger's handle. The spikes of hot and cold made her flex her hand, but not totally release the weapon.

If there were any Gods left up there, they knew why she wanted to use that knife. To stand and feel powerful instead of like the dirt on someone else's heel. And squeezing that handle made it possible to imagine the world around bending as she passed it by. It was just a knife, but in many ways, it felt like everything she had ever needed.

No--that wasn't quite right.

The girl pressed her face into Rander Belmorn's back. The stranger had shown more regard for her than anyone in Roon ever had. Warmth flushed into her face, and for the briefest of moments, she gave herself over to the feeling. To the idea of being... what was the opposite of lost?

Found. Her brain wanted to say, but somehow, that didn't seem right either.

11 - 4

As they followed the tree line, steam was billowing off the necks of both horses, as froth dripped from their mouths. Tenebrus Kro had begun to systematically look into the woods, which were now barely twenty feet to the right. Every few seconds, checking and rechecking. Clearly the man was looking for something.

"What--?" Belmorn began. "Are you looking for?"

The witchwyrm's wail and its barks, echoed from behind. Not for the first time, the sounds made the horses tense up. Their eyes bulge with fear.

"I think she's slowing down," said Kro. "Doubt she's used to working so hard for her supper. We can slow down for the horse's sake, but we need to keep one eye behind us."

"I can do it," shouted Rivka. Much to Kro's dismay, she was already looking at the witchwyrm.

"I said, eyes on me!"

"You did." Rivka shrugged. "But I want to help. Let me!"

"Watch her then," Belmorn nodded. "Kro, I asked you...?"

"What am I looking for?" Kro sighed, checking once again between the trees before looking up. The sun had returned, at least, melting some of the snow and giving a clearer sense of direction. "Something. It should be here somewhere."

"*Should*?!" Belmorn roared.

"Please, just trust me. We just need her to keep following us.

Following me, anyway."

"To what end?" Belmorn steered Magnus around two more of the slanted rocks. "What the hell are we doing?"

At last Kro finally said, "Morgrig's camp. I was there. I could smell-- could practically see the lower veld through the trees. It's here somewhere, I know it is. If we can just find it, there is something there that might be of some use. Something I left behind."

Just then, something dark caught Kro's eye--pulled it to a spot maybe seventy feet up ahead. It wasn't a rock, nor any one object but a collection of many. The discarded pile of random things was in full juxtaposition against the serene, otherwise untouched landscape. Discarded crates and empty bags, saddles, old boots and bones from a hundred meals--all of this and more spilled out of the trees from a single spot.

"Mr. Kro?" Rivka sounded closer to excited than scared. "She's moving fast again!"

"Good! Let her catch up!" Kro was shouting--pointing to the refuse that was spilling out of the woods. "Look! Right there! Morgrig, you son of a bitch! I knew it! He's left us a trail right to his front door!"

Another wail filled their ears as Kro stared back at the monster behind them. The sound had a distinct effect on the witchwyrm which the companions now witnessed. The thing shook its head like a wet dog. Then barking just once, the beast renewed her speed.

"Come on," Roared Kro, urging the silver mare back into a run. "Still Hungry? Still Ugly? Come get me, you fucking hag! I'm right here!"

Turning his silver mare, Kro entered the woods at the exact spot of the refuse pile. His blood was up. His hands ready. Looking back, he saw Belmorn and Rivka enter the forest too and another pang twisted at his heart. However unwise his new plan was, he did not have to see it through alone.

Once in the forest they did not have far to go. The bandit's garbage led to a clearing with tents and crates and the bodies of many men on the ground. Some completely encased in what looked like thorny green ropes. In all, the site looked to have been host to a fierce battle.

"This is it!" Kro shouted, drawing his red blade. "Steer clear of the center and stick to the perimeter! Hear me?"

Instinctively, Belmorn glanced to the middle of the ruined camp. In a circle of stones--what looked to be to spot for a campfire, loomed a large green mass. Shapeless and yet seemingly hunched over, he could see that the thing was connected to many of the strewn bodies via long vines.

Suddenly the eyes of the blackfoot went wide as the scene of he and Kro's dramatic introduction replayed in his mind.

"Hold on to me, kid." Belmorn felt the tiny arms squeeze his waist a little harder as he pushed the adamandray to follow. On command, the gigantic horse crashed over a trampled canvas that had once been a tent.

"Kro, you crazy son of a bitch," Growled Belmorn, too low for anyone to hear. Finally, he understood. Not only why they were here but what Kro planned to do.

The blaring howl of Morgrig's horn was deafening in the tight space. The sound of it left Belmorn's ears ringing. He didn't need to look to know the witch was close. Didn't need to watch as the moving brush behind him parted--giving birth to a horrendous thing. A patchwork creature. An amalgam of serpent and scorpion--all silver and black and hissing rage. He didn't need to see that. Not with the latest round of her barks still echoing off the walls of his stomach.

Shit. Thought Belmorn, after looking back anyway.

Kro had claimed this was Morgrig's camp, but what in Rinh's name could have happened here? The mystery tugged at Belmorn's curiosity but evaporated the moment his eyes returned to the camp's center.

If the mass had been hunched over before, now it was standing. Twenty foot high at least--twisted and covered in thorns, like some distant cousin of the wall they just left behind. Belmorn couldn't look away until a sliver of red caught his eye. Bright and proud, the color was incredibly out of place. A flower. Something like a rose with hairy structures coming out of the center. It was enormous--five feet across at least. Both inexplicable and beautiful, it was nestled amongst a series of green pod-like masses, each roughly the size of a man. Somehow, though the idea was utterly preposterous, the abominable rose looked content.

"Stay as far away from that as you can!" shouted Kro. "And watch those creepers on the ground!" He produced a bit of flint and, with a single attempt, sparked the fuse of the last Bàozhú cross. "Heads down!"

Belmorn and Rivka complied in unison--ducking as the cross was hurled overhead. Spinning, tumbling it sliced through the air, straight for the pursuing witchwyrm. Then, in mid-air, the cross ignited, spewing geysers of light and pain from each of its four ends, propelling it ever faster towards its target.

Ember-green eyes flashed with recognition. With a squeal, the beast planted a huge three-toed foot, turned in place, and swung its mismatched scorpion appendage like a flail.

The screaming cross was smashed with perfect accuracy and sent in a new direction with the approximate force of a cannonball. With a cracking burst of snow and splinters, the last Bàozhú cross was embedded into the trunk of a nearby tree, where it proceeded to shriek and spit until its impotent rage was spent.

For Belmorn's part, he couldn't believe the tree hadn't caught on fire.

The witchwyrm approached slowly to investigate the threads of smoke oozing from the cross' exposed ends. As it moved, its neck was postured in a reverse swan. The wedge-shaped head twitched to one side, curved fangs bared and ready. Once satisfied that the thing in the tree could do no further harm, the witch swung round to relocate its quarry.

By this time, the horses had reached the far side of the clearing. Though both animals pawed and stomped, the riders kept them steady. The head of the witchwyrm flicked into a new angle. Down came one powerful foot, then the other. The thing's prodigious bulk slithered and re-adjusted as its primeval mind was slowly made up.

"I'm right here!" The voice of the alchemist was ragged as he stood, shouting in his saddle. "What are you waiting for?"

Earlier, Kro had alluded to the fact that this plan wasn't a very good one; now Belmorn was fully questioning the man's sanity. But there was nothing to be done. The horses were spent and there could be no fighting such a beast. Could there? Rander Belmorn had fought living nightmares before, but this was different. There was no water rushing beneath him here. No river spirit to guide his hands.

Turning in his saddle, the blackfoot did the only thing he could to change the situation at least a little. Looking into the girl's frightened eyes, he wrapped an arm around her and squeezed. Rivka hiccoughed in surprise. Then she released a series of choked sobs. After holding herself tense for another moment, she decided to let it all go. Her muscles went slack. A cognizant allowance of her own need to be held and cared for.

"It'll be alright, kid." Belmorn said the words without believing them. Then he looked once more to the biggest flower he had ever laid eyes on. "I think I know what he's got planned here. If it works, we're in for a show."

A choked sound pulled all attention to the serpentine horror bounding toward them. Its mouth was open, full of teeth and a very human sort of hate.

"Kro?!" Belmorn turned the name into a complex question.

"It's alright. Just don't move," came an edged whisper only loud enough for them to hear. "Not a goddamned hair, do you hear me?"

Sprinting on two legs with heavy, clawed strides, the witchwyrm closed the gap via the shortest distance between two points. Not around the camp but across it. It stomped by the green mass at the center as if it were just another tree. With fangs out and ready, the thing lunged.

Rivka had already buried her head in the black fur of Belmorn's cloak. She didn't see the unlikely series of events that followed.

The head struck out, then elastically snapped back. Confused, the witch tugged on its snared back leg, but could get no closer to the hated prey. When the pulling failed, it coughed up a protesting bark and turned to investigate.

The thorn-laden creepers of the abominable vampire rose were tightening their grip. Sliding up that dragonish leg, scoring the scaled flesh as they went. The beast whipped its tail, thrashing neck and head from side to side. Jaws clicked and snapped. Even the forearms lashed out. But for all its primal rage and desperation, the witch had no power to free itself.

Already, one leg was almost completely covered. The coils tightened, constricting the appendage like a boa around a deer. More heavy ropes fell to strangle the beast's second leg, while still others knotted around the tail, gathering just below the meat of the hooked scorpion-barb, binding it.

Green eyes bulged. The creature who had inspired terror for so long was finally introduced to the concept. And so it was that in the ruined camp of Mannis Morgrig, a new sound was born. A single voice composed of many--high and piercing and horrible. For the first time in her entire life... the dreaded witch of the Veld was screaming.

11-5

"The tail!" shouted Kro without restraint. "Belmorn... while the rose has her, we have to sever the barb! Without it she can't vanish!"

Belmorn understood and pulled out his axes. Then he turned back to the girl with a fearsome tone. "Don't move."

Still clenching her dagger, Rivka nodded and offered no argument.

The blackfoot dropped from his saddle and shot forward. His fists gripped the leather-wrapped handles but loosely--spinning them so the blades were pointed out. He took in the scene: Two towering nightmares, locked in mortal combat. Studying every detail of the witchwyrm and this bigger, uglier cousin of the rose that had once held fast a stranger called Tenebrus Kro. Before him were horrors, to be sure. But as he took them in, he smiled.

River or no river... horrors were a blackfoot's stock and trade.

"The vines!" Kro warned. "We have to cut some away to get at the tail. Just be careful! Don't want to end up like them." He nodded toward the man-sized pods that had been arranged around the central bloom.

Belmorn frowned. His instincts were screaming. Demanding that he do as his father had taught him so many decades earlier. The way of the blackfoot was to hunt--not with bow or spear, but with one's entire body. To leap aback creatures, fist full of roped harpoons in one hand and a Graelian axe in the other. How many eels had he ridden? How many harpoons had he hammered in so that his fellows on the other end of the ropes might haul the day's catch onto shore?

As Belmorn reached the tail, he could see how fast this new and improved rose did its work. The back legs and scorpion barb were already close to mummified, but the witch was far from beaten. Front legs tore at the green mass that was the rose's body--spattering the camp with shreds of wet plant matter. As a large greenish blob hit Belmorn in the shoulder, he knew there was no telling which of the titans would be victorious. Kro was right, they had to act now. Had to sever the witch's connection to wherever she kept vanishing off to.

With two leaping strides the blackfoot launched himself forward. His twin axes were already swinging, already slicing the air and when they came down, a thick section of vines offered little resistance.

The Maldaavan blade moved in a coppery blur, severing its fair share of the unnatural plant. As Kro swung his weapon, righteous indignation flowed through his body. The mutated abomination was his creation. The smoke and the seeds, the gland and the oils inside-- the oil of the size-shifter. The strange eyeless seal which was, somehow, also that serpent-necked beast the skalds had named Jörmungandr--the world serpent.

WHIMM!! WHUMM!!

The red blade flashed twice more, singing as it flew.

Air and salt. Water and flame. The alchemist's creed returned. All that planning... for nothing. How could it have gone so wrong, so fast?

All of this could have been avoided. If only he'd been more careful when first approaching the rose. If only he'd brought a torch or better, a sword.

THUKK!!

An axe snapped another vine, finally exposing some of the witch's tail. The monsters struggled barely ten feet away. Belmorn looked up. The thorny ropes knotted and wound so tightly around the tail, the barb looked like it was suffocating.

As if it were turning purple.

The blackfoot lifted his axe and poured every ounce of strength he had left into a single perfect strike. But when the axe blade reached the tail, it bounced back--deflected as if by the clash of steel!

Rattled to his core, Belmorn stared. The tail was intact--unblemished. He couldn't believe it. His jaw opened and closed, but no words came.

"Belmorn."

Hearing his name made the blackfoot turn.

"Move."

The attack swung mere inches from Belmorn's face, moving in a coppery blur. He looked at the exposed section of tail. To the very spot that had refused his own strike so utterly. Kro's red sword had done what his axe could not. The tail had not been severed but by Rinh, it was bleeding.

Lashing with one of its front legs, the witch screeched and lunged forward. Its tail, weighted by the still-clinging vines, swung wild, smashing into a tree and sending a shower of splinters down on the men.

The eyes of Tenebrus Kro contained nothing beyond that gleaming barb, if perhaps the tiniest glint of madness.

"The tail!" he bellowed. "Belmorn! Cut it off! Now!"

Belmorn raised his axe, but it was too late. In a series of loud SNAPS, vine after vine gave way to the might of the silver and black nightmare. The two men backed away, realizing their folly. Too many vines had been cut away. The tail was no longer being strangled.

The head of the witchwyrm swung round fixing on the men with one bulging, hate-filled eye. That eye began to glow with a fiendish, ember-green light. Then, the beast vanished.

Heavy vines, no longer supported, fell and crashed to the ground.

"No!" Shouted Kro. "No-o-o-o!"

Seconds later, the beast reappeared on the far edge of the camp. With a cough of rage, it tried to stand, but fell flat. After a second attempt brought it close enough to upright, the beast heaved itself forward, scourging the ground with massive talons.

It turned to face the two men who had been the cause of all. The beast stared, seething with slitted eyes. There was nothing between it and them.

The witchwyrm took a step forward, teetering. Then it reeled back and coughed up a single bark that pounded the skin of the two men. Belmorn and Kro looked to the horses. They would never reach their mounts before the witch reached them. And the girl, the look on her face--volumes could be written on the true nature of terror and never fully capture that look. Belmorn's heart split down the center at the sight of it. After all they had done... to fail her like this.

The witch stopped its noise. It was ready. The chase was over. The game's final move, spent. Belmorn had managed to catch Rivka's gaze and he meant to hold it.

Look at me, girl. He thought with all his might. *Only at me.*

The arrow came from out of nowhere. From behind the men, arcing over their heads and down to stick in the witch's neck. Before the thing knew what happened, before even the pain had a chance to reach its brain, more speeding shafts appeared.

As if in a dream, Belmorn felt himself turning for an explanation. Everything unfolded in a strange, slower than usual motion. A garrison of armored men charged through the trees behind him, bows, swords, and pistols in hand. All weapons pointed directly at the horrible reptilian thing.

Before such odds, the witch shrank. Taking a step back, its eyes began to glow again. The edges of its silhouette rushed to meet at the center, and in the blink of an eye, the thing was gone.

Arrows plunged into the earth where their target had stood only moments before.

A loud unseen crash resounded from somewhere nearby. This was followed by shrieks and snapping, cracking branches. The sounds were moving away. Barreling clumsily through the trees, spitting unrestrained fury, the witch was retreating.

Belmorn's only response to this was to gape and stare as a rider appeared from behind.

The man's pale armor was more ornate than the rest. From his shoulders a pitch-dark cape draped down, flapping gently on one side. The garment was a stark contrast to man's crop of wild white-blond hair. Briefly, the rider turned to the two dumbstruck men on the ground and fixed them with a glare the color of ice.

Belmorn looked at the girl in his saddle. She was frightened, roughly twenty paces away and there wasn't a thing he could do to reach her. Admonished or not, the Roonik guard had them dead to rights. No amount of boiling outrage was going to change that. For now, all he could do was be still and keep squeezing those axe handles.

From high on his saddle, Henric Galttauer nodded in the direction of the writhing plant monster.

"Oil. Torches. Burn me that ugly thing to the fucking ground."

Belmorn watched as three of the Roonik Guards responded by producing bottles of dark liquid. These crashed upon the base of the towering plant--shattering on impact. Beautiful, terrible, the rose seemed to know what was coming. Petals slowly closed, while the man-shaped pods were pulled closer to the center. As he saw this unfold, Belmorn could not decide if the damned thing looked afraid or just unwilling to share.

Next came the torchbearers. In unison, five flaming batons were hurled--flying end over end like hand axes. The oil went up instantly and in dramatic fashion. Burning in a great roar of hot air and sound that pressed against the surrounding faces.

Belmorn, Kro, the girl on the giant horse, the men-at-arms, and their commanding officer, all stood in silence. Neither as enemies or allies, but as strangers in a crowd--with less regard for each other than for the spectacle before them.

The mutated rose burned, just as the good captain had commanded. Right to the fucking ground.

PART TWELVE
WITCH BLOOD

12 - 1

Rivka sat, frozen. Just watching, waiting. The violence of the scene had been replaced by a quiet, smoldering tension. Though surrounded, she was alone--a very small girl in a very large saddle.

Rander and Mr. Kro were on the ground--between her and a small garrison of soldiers. The Roonik men had appeared out of nowhere and much to her surprise, had driven off the monster. The witch.

The girl's eyes shifted from man to man as flames of the still burning rose creature danced upon her face and the curved blade in her hand. Rivka recognized the captain right away. He had passed her many times on the cobbles--once or twice even giving her a bit of something to eat.

"Tenebrus Kro." The captain glared down from the perch of his jet-black stallion. He had said the name as if it were the answer to some great and confounding riddle.

"Captain," Kro fired back without looking. "Finally found the knob to your front door, I see. What the hell are you doing here?"

Imperfect silence stretched in the campsite. For over a minute, the only sounds were the wind and the rustling of nervous hooves. Rivka didn't like this. She wished Rander was with her again. Wanted nothing more than to disappear into the black fur of his cloak.

"What should have been done a long time ago." The captain sneered.

"We are tracking someone. A villain. We weren't far when we heard... I don't know what it was. Shrieking." The captain was looking at Mr. Kro again. "Fortunately for you, we followed it here."

Kro waved this off. "Oh please, Henric. I had everything under control."

The captain's mouth curled into a smirk. "That thing there." He nodded at the burning mass of plant matter. "Your doing, I presume?"

"Hardly the most noteworthy of my sins, but yes." Kro clenched his jaw and released a weary sigh. "Figured I'd capitalize on a bit of bad fortune. Pit monster against monster and hope for the best. Believe it or not, it turned out alright... until the end there. Now if you don't mind, my friends and I have work left to do."

Galttauer looked to the man with the high collar--sparing careful regard for the strange axes he held.

"Friends, you say?" The captain raised an eyebrow, donned the beginnings of a wry smirk. "Thought you'd already killed all of those."

Furious, Kro lunged. And while Belmorn's arm stopped him from going far, it was too late. Rivka's ears were filled with a flurry of metallic sounds and the zipping whisks of arrows being pulled. Before she could exhale, the tip of the weapon had already settled upon their new target.

"Hold!" the captain's voice clapped like thunder. His cold eyes moved over his men in a slow, glaring sweep. "If an arrow flies, it will be that man's post. Clear?"

"Aye, Sir," the guards barked in chorus.

"Henric. Listen to me. We can end this right now." Kro's words fired like lead balls from a pistol. "You saw it. The witch is on the run! For the first time in its life, that bitch is afraid." He held out his red blade, allowing light to glisten off the yellow drops that had yet to be absorbed. "And better... she's bleeding."

Galttauer inclined his head and widened his eyes at the foreign weapon. "The color of the metal." Genuine awe touched his voice. "A Maldaavan blade? Is it possible?"

"I spent half my life traveling this world. You really think I'd have nothing to show for it?" Kro hissed through clenched teeth.

"I've heard stories of such weapons, but never seen one." Galttauer's eyes darted from the sword to the spot where the witch had crashed through the trees. "They say that wounds opened with Maldaavan steel are immortal things."

"Not quite. But let's just say that the cut on her tail is not going to be healing soon." A lopsided grin grew on Kro's face. "Don't you get it? We can track her now. But I smell a storm in the air. If fresh snow falls it could cover up the drops, which is why we must move fast. Unless of course you'd rather haul us back to Roon and give her plenty of time to heal and return to full strength. Then, who knows? Maybe she'll finally sniff out your precious shield city and the tasty treats inside before another seven years has a chance to pass."

"Kro." Belmorn dropped his collar, exposing his face to the cold air as well as too many untrusting eyes. "That's enough."

"Enough? Enough?!" Kro seemed at a loss. His fury was plain. He wanted to scream. To force the man in the black cape to confront all that his own cowardice had wrought. Kro's chestnut mare. His priceless, irreplaceable ingredients. A precious plan that had taken only moments to go up in smoke. And worst of all... the Pershten.

What had become of Bror and all the troll mothers and young ones after the blasts of Morgrig's infernal horn had summoned the monster straight to their hiding place? To the only sanctuary they had left?

None of it would have happened, if only the good Captain had done his duty, and kept the woods clear of scurrying things. Vermin. Rats that fancied themselves, wolves.

By the Gods, Tenebrus Kro wanted to scream all this and more--to spit his frustrations, right in the face of Henric Galttauer.

For a moment, the captain was quiet.

"Sir." The whisper came from one of the guards. "That's him. The one who escaped us. There stands the Red Wolf."

Slowly, Galttauer's eyes moved to the other man. The tall one with the axes.

Feeling like a painting on display, Belmorn's frown deepened. Part of him yearned for this to be the end. At least then he could go out swinging at the smug son of a bitch who had thrown him in a cell and paraded him through a humiliating, farcical trial.

Suddenly Belmorn's mind snapped back. Once again he was on Magnus' back racing away from her. She--the Hispidian witchyrm. Wind whipped at his face as he galloped toward the group of bandits he had heard so much about. Mannis Morgrig--finally he had a face for the name that had been hung around his neck like so much rotting albatross.

"Mannis Morgrig is dead." Asserted Kro. "I encountered him and his merry band the other day though we didn't part on good terms. Seems he didn't like my gardening." He gestured to the smoldering remains of the enormous rose creature. "He took what men he had left and tracked me and my companions. Caught up to us near the moat. That was when the witch found us. The idiot brought her down on our heads... with this."

Kro tossed the blowing horn which the captain caught.

"The Red Wolf has vanished, Henric. Just like so many others. Though we managed to pilfer his howl."

Listening, Galttauer turned the horn over in his hands, spotting a small depiction of a wolf. It had been carved rather crudely into the side and painted red. When he spoke again it was in a flat, matter of fact sort of way that left no room for questions.

"I am afraid you are mistaken, Guardsman. It seems Morgrig is no longer our problem."

"Aye, Sir," barked Guardsman Schmidt, straightening his back as an echoing wail cut the tension.

The sound was tragic, mournful--made by something in pain. Hearing it inspired no sympathy in Belmorn, but plenty of the opposite. His eyes went to a splatter of yellow green blood on the snow ahead. The result of Kro's final strike.

Galttauer urged his horse over to the conspicuous spatter, then dismounted. After dipping his fingers in the stuff, he brought them to his nose.

"This? This is *witch blood*? And you drew it with... a Maldaavan blade." This last observation held no question, only the acceptance of an unlikely truth.

"Yes, and a twinkle in my eye." Visibly exasperated, Kro pinched the skin between his eyes. When he spoke again, the edge in his voice was gone. "Damn it, Henric. Don't think I've forgotten what happened last time--don't you dare. Just... open your eyes! It is bleeding! That means we might have a chance! A chance we will squander if we stand around all night talking in circles!"

"You know he's right," the deep voice of Rander Belmorn came as a shock. "The question is, what are you going to do about it," this was directed at the man with the icy glare and the long noble bloodline.

Captain Henric Galttauer frowned so deep with such inward distaste, it might have been a new standard for the expression.

12-2

The group had swelled by five. Now, Belmorn, Kro and Rivka stood or sat beside four armed soldiers and their captain. The rest of the garrison had been sent ahead. On Galttauer's orders they were to ride past the thorn wall and into the High Veld. To locate any sign of the witch's blood trail and to stand upon it. Leaving a man behind every half mile or so, creating a chain which snow could not erase.

It had been the blackfoot's idea. A precaution, in case of snow.

"Belmorn!" Kro's impatience was becoming raw. "Now?"

"Not yet." The riverman patted the neck of his enormous horse. "I told you. Longer."

"Damn you and your doting, riverman. Even now she escapes us. You *know* this is our only chance!"

Belmorn lifted a ball of hard packed snow to Magnus' mouth. The horse's rubbery lips reached, pulled in the mass of snow and ice and happily crunched it down. "The horses are not the only ones who are tired, Kro. The witch ran just as far, just as fast. She will not be able to keep that pace on her return. Especially bleeding like that. The Roon men are fresh. If they do as they have been instructed, we will have no problem finding our quarry."

Hearing this, Galttauer sneered. "My men know how to follow orders, but I won't leave them out there for long. We rest for one hour. No more."

Belmorn set Magnus's giant saddle down on a log that likely served

255

as a bench in the camp. "Fine," He said, sounding not entirely pleased. "One hour."

"The witch," Rivka's voice came after a long silence. It was a tiny thing. "How does she do it?"

"Huh?" Kro spat, audibly frustrated. "Do what?"

"The horses, those men!" The girl was standing. Leaning against a tree. "She just makes them... disappear."

"Well..." Kro began poking around the camp, looking in tents and piles for his missing belongings. "Can't have a witch without a little craft."

"So it's... magic!?" The girl sounded awestruck.

Listening with only one ear, Belmorn accepted some feed from one of Galttauer's bags and poured oil and water over it. "Thought you said there was no such thing."

"Magic? Biology? If you want the truth, I have no idea." called Kro from inside a tent. "But I can tell you this... there is something important in the venom of that stinger. Something no other creature that walks or slithers on this rock can produce. That's why I had us try to hack it off while she was trapped. Something in that venom connects to another place. Belmorn, I told you... the witchwyrm's feet straddle an invisible line. A kind of boundary between worlds. One foot is anchored here, in the world we know."

As he continued to half-listen, Belmorn noticed his horse was still tacked, steaming with sweat, and had begun to shiver. He directed Rivka to make another bowl of food as he'd just done. When Kro was done talking, he called back "Don't be an idiot!" He began to untack the silver mare. "There is only one world."

"Ah... but when you look into your river, do you not see another man looking back?"

Returning to his own bags so he could groom the horses' coats, Belmorn snickered and shook his head. Then he pulled out the very tool he'd remembered the man for and glared at it. "Okay, Brushman. This other place. What is it?"

"Just, somewhere else. A place only witches and their victims ever see. The Akkadians had a name for it, the Without."

From inside her furry hood, Rivka's face went pale. Before she could respond, Kro was shouting again.

"She doesn't just make things disappear. She moves them. Secreting her victims away the way a leopard uses an acacia tree, where they lie placid and helpless with two separate types of venom in their veins.

The one in her teeth is unique in all the animal kingdom. It paralyzes and it heals. Reversing all manner of infection and disease, keeping her meat fresh and healthy."

Suddenly, the ears of all in the camp were assaulted by a series of distant barks--so loud they seemed to strike the very air like a drum.

"That's the one, Belmorn. What you came all this way to find."

"What?" The blackfoot spun to look at the hooded man, fires in his stormy eyes. "What are you saying?"

"The primary component in witch tears is her venom. What I once had was acquired by chance, in a land far from here. The stuff was old but potent as ever."

"You son of a bitch. You goddamned son of a bitch!"

Belmorn stormed over to where Kro was standing in five long strides. The four guardsmen bristled, but a gesture from their captain put them at ease. Galltauer was listening intently.

"You told me to leave." Belmorn shoved the hooded man. "My boy's salvation was right here, and you tried to send me away?!"

"Belmorn, please. I didn't want you to get any deeper into this-- either of you. Listen to me... this plan is not a smart one. I should be the one to bear its consequences. Please, just take Rivka and leave this place. Go back to your river and your boy."

"I can't. Not like this." The eyes of the blackfoot flashed. "Don't you see? Can't you understand? They are my everything. My heart. My life. And in their darkest hour, I left them."

"Only to find a cure!" The phrase exploded from the young girl. "Left them to come back! To save your son's life!"

"She's right, riverman." The captain spoke up at last. "What you did, coming here... going forward even after all you have endured... that is not leaving. That is sacrifice. True nobility."

"Noble am I?" Belmorn coughed up a mirthless laugh. "Bet you think I'm brave too. Thing is... courage isn't what drives a man so far away from where he is needed most. Fear does that. I may have been able to fool myself at first, but the truth of it was written on my wife's face as I rode away. This quest has been the actions of a coward and nothing more. One who would rather wrap both arms around a fool's errand than watch his only son wither away! To die a little more each day, swollen and purple!"

Regretting his temper and many other things, Belmorn spoke more softly.

"Kro... you once warned me about the people this far north. Cold as the wind, you said. But even they don't deserve to be taken one by one by that hag. I say we help each other now. That we kill this thing so I can take its venom back to Grael and save my boy."

After a few seconds, Tenebrus Kro turned his head, catching the stormiest part of Belmorn's eye. No more words were needed and none were offered.

Time passed in silence after that for a long while. For Kro's part, he continued searching the site. Scouring every bag and crate of accrued plunder with determined, if secret purpose, until finally...

"There!" Kro gasped, lifting a bag from a pile of discarded belongings. "If there are any Gods left up there..." The bag as the rest of the goods nearby had been trampled by the witch. With hurried, frantic jerks of his hands, Kro threw the top flap open and dumped the contents onto the ground. All present watched this intently though none could guess as to what madness had suddenly possessed the man.

"Where is it?" Kro muttered on hands and knees. "It had to be here. Has to be... ah!" From amidst broken glass and powder, sticks and shattered bits of clay, a small object was retrieved. Overcome with emotion, Tenebrus Kro dusted the thing off, then pressed it to his cheek. "I'm sorry. My loves. My life." He was close to tears--rocking as if alone in the ruined camp. "I'm so Goddamned sorry."

"Mr. Kro." Rivka stepped forward, placing a hand on the alchemist's elbow. "What's wrong?"

"Nothing, girl." Kro smiled as a tear fell down his cheek. "I just... thought I would never see this again."

He opened his hands to reveal a raggedy homemade thing. Something like a child's toy. It had been made of braided black hair--fashioned into the shape of a bird, with tiny buttons for eyes and a candle wax beak.

"It's a crow." Rivka smiled sweetly. "Like you."

Drawing one arm across his face, Kro nodded. "That night. I knew going after those bastard rats was stupid. Morgrig... everything he took was precious. Nearly impossible to replace. But this," he placed the tiny thing in his palm--allowing the wings to spread. "My sweet girl. My Lishka made this. Gave it to me the last time I..." Kro drew the back of one hand across his eyes. Allowed himself a moment. "Hold it every day, she said. And kiss it every night before bed. Do this, she said, and no matter how far apart we were... she would feel it and she would know."

Right then the man who's heart had been closed for so long, raised the raggedy object to his lips--leaving a kiss there. Then, standing up, Kro tucked his daughter's final gift away in his cloak.

"Of course you're right, Belmorn. The horses need rest. We all do. This is our one shot and too many lives depend on us now. Just too fucking many."

12-3

There were many riders coming.

As they moved over the low veld, the group stretched into something more resembling a line. This was a fortunate thing for the man on the ground.

The crescent knife felt good in his hand. Usually he kept the blade strapped to one leg and usually, that was where it stayed. But now that his cleaver swords had been lost, he was glad for the backup weapon. He had to be smart now. The man who had been calling himself Slagter may not have been sane, but he knew there would be no more chances.

This was it. Time at last for the settling of old debts.

In a long line, the riders approached the slanted rock in a gallop. Slagter was ready. Crouched beneath the giant's tooth--looking through cracked lenses for his hated enemy.

But these were not the riders he had expected. These were Roon men. A small Garrison of soldiers. Though why they were here, Slagter could not say. Mannis had proved time and again that the men of that blasted city were too afraid to open their door. And yet here they were, galloping straight for his rock--no doubt, chasing down the beast.

The snake mother had passed him already. Shrieking and stumbling--too frantic to notice that there was anything but shadows beneath Slagter's rock. She had collapsed not twenty feet away. Lying there for a time, her belly in the snow, just breathing and bleeding. He couldn't believe the size. That the accounts Mannis had dismissed as fish stories, fell woefully short of the reality.

At such close proximity, Slagter could see the beast had earned every word of her own legend. After a few seconds of respite, the snake mother scrambled abruptly to her feet, then vanished. Reappearing some fifty feet closer to the hill. It had all happened no more than ten minutes ago. And now it was riders who were about to pass his hiding place.

Inside his mask, Slagter's mouth curled into a grin. It didn't matter why they were here. These men had horses. Weapons too. In a straight fight, he could never take them all. But perhaps one at a time. So long as their eyes remained fixed on the trail.

One by one, they passed by. Each bringing a loud whoosh and gust of cold air.

One. Two.

He counted as they passed.

Three. They must be allies of Mr. Kro. Four. If even one lives, they might spoil everything. Five. Six. Seven. You have to kill them all. Eight.

As the ninth of the Roonik Guards galloped by in a great gust of cold air, the masked man made his move. Leaping, grasping, scrambling, then stabbing, slicing.

12 - 4

Horses tore through the northern woods and their count was seven.

The man in the very front wore a hooded cloak, the color of midnight. His beard was dark and pointed. His eyes focused. Hungrily they scoured both brush and path--yearning for the next fleck of yellow-green blood.

Decades of practice had honed his tracking skills but following this particular trail at his current speed was pushing those skills to their limit. The area past the moat was a wasteland. A vast, open swath under the shadow of a peculiarly shaped mountain. The High Veld terminated most abruptly at a massive cliff. The largest known to the civilized world.

World's Edge.

"There!" Kro's heart all but soared as he shouted, pointing to the yellow spattered on a small, flowered bush.

Riding just behind, Belmorn and Rivka met his eye. Both of them looked dauntless. Utterly set on the task of joining him to the bitter end of this damned nightmare.

It was wrong, Kro knew. Fundamentally unjust. This nightmare was his by right. So many innocent lives had been lost already. All for a singular, colossal lapse in judgement.

The egg had been beautiful, marbled with smokey trails of purple and grey. According to the man Kro had obtained it from, it was over a hundred years old. The thing could only be inert, little more than a curio. And his Lishka did always fawn over her father's collection of rare eggs.

"There!" Kro pointed to a tree with a cracked trunk. It bent as if something heavy had stumbled, lost its balance, and careened into it. Most importantly, running down it was a trickle of bright yellow-green.

Kro's legs squeezed together, urging his mare on even faster. The giant's teeth were just ahead. All of them slanted north, aimed in the same direction the riders were headed, as if pointing the way.

Weaving through and past the strange rocks both on and off the path, Kro was following a chaotic line of sliding tracks. A few steps here and a few over there. The trajectory was clear, but broken.

"Look at the tracks," Kro shouted to the man beside him. "The beast must have been vanishing as it ran. Slipping in and out."

Kro's eye caught a thread of yellow and he veered around another of the giant's teeth. There had been movement, a dark flicker behind one of the rocks. He recognized the area as roughly where the masked man had struck him. He squinted at the spot. Finding nothing, he turned his attention back on the road ahead. It was mental torture to keep their current pace. Slow and safe enough to travel over the treacherous ground.

"Racing falling snow and a setting sun to slay a witch," he called in a sing-song voice to the blackfoot. "Probably make one hell of a ballad."

"Yeah," said Belmorn. "If one of us lives to tell it."

Captain Henric Galttauer had not led his men away from Roon in a very long time. Before the Veld had been marked by a witch, his had been the name which kept the shadows from creeping too closely to the last of the great shield cities. Now, as he urged his horse and his men on and forward, he could almost remember what that felt like.

Wearily, he glanced ahead to the leaders of the expedition. The merchant man and his tall companion were about to disappear over the crest of the hill, but before they did, Galttauer was struck by a pair of eyes. The young girl who clung to the tall one's middle was looking back, staring, judging. Though she did not look familiar, the captain could not help but accept the brunt of that judgment.

He was glad to have those eyes pass out of sight, but the relief was short lived. As his jet black stallion summited the hilltop, Galttauer's breath caught in his throat.

An impressive collection of discarded clothing was strewn about the snowy ground. Cloaks, jerkins, and trousers lay beside and atop saddles, bridles and armor. Eerily, they mimicked the shapes of whatever men had worn them. Tracks, too, were everywhere. Horse, man, and other.

As Galttauer's mind reeled, one item drew his eye. The cuirass was old but definitely Roonik. It lay in a pool of dark red, and the metal around the neck flared in sharp, broken angles, as if pried from its previous owner with massive claws.

"Kro!" Belmorn's sudden voice made the captain jump. "What is all of this?"

The alchemist turned, but the dying light indicated no face within the hood. He shouted back. "Whoever she vanishes, wherever they really go, it is without the shirt on their back. What you see here are her table scraps. All that remains of Mannis Morgrig and his merry band."

"But this armor..." said the captain. "it looks Roonik."

"Of course it does. What's the matter, Galttauer? Have you forgotten the last time we rode together? It was up that same hill. Towards this same damned goal."

Seven years ago, the travelling merchant had arrived in a state, spouting nonsense about a monster in the Veld. Galttauer had relented to the pleadings of Tenebrus Kro, agreeing to follow him north with a small garrison if only to set his people at ease. Not for an instant had he lent credence to the man's ravings; Kro had been disturbed or drunk or mad, but he was certainly not to be taken seriously.

'Forgotten'? The captain scowled.

Even with the drumming of hooves pressing into his skull, Henric Galttauer could still hear his men on that blackest of days. Their cries still assaulted him at night and in the quiet moments, reminding him of the depths of his failure. Was it any wonder he chose to bar the gates of Roon? If the captain could not protect his people outside, he would keep whatever was out there from getting in.

"There!" The blackfoot was pointing at a thread of steaming yellow blood.

Some days ago, the man had claimed to be from Grael. An insignificant speck along a distant river most Velders would never see.

Back in Morgrig's ruined camp Galttauer had made a split-second decision. This man, Belmorn, had suffered enough--sentenced and damn nearly been put to death for the crimes of another. All for what? A deception aimed at the very people he had sworn to protect? Because if he could no longer provide true security then perhaps an illusion would serve?

This mental wallowing was akin to torture, though it had served one other purpose. In the captain's core, a fire had sparked to life--one stoked by unearthing and owning his greatest shames.

"There's more ahead!" Kro shouted. "Look there! The blood goes into the thorns."

The captain shifted his gaze to the man in the hood. Seeing Kro's face after so long had been like seeing a ghost. The man looked diminished and Galttauer knew why. But whatever animosity remained between the two men was a secondary concern. The witch was what really mattered and she was running scared. Scared and bleeding. That was something. It had to be. This time would be different. This time would pay for all.

"Into the thorns?" shouted the captain, approaching the ragged hole in the Moat. "What the hell is this? Surely the beast can't really have ripped a hole straight through?"

"Well... yes and no," answered Kro. "Technically I did most of the ripping fifteen years ago."

"But," Galttauer's eyes widened. "Why? How? Where we are, the Moat must be five hundred feet across!"

"More like eight," answered Kro with a shrug. "As for the why... Best to blame necessity."

The captain said no more. Discourse with Tenebrus Kro had always been the mother of his most legendary headaches, and their years apart had changed nothing.

With a sigh, Galttauer looked back to see a storm moving in fast from the south. The wind was kicking up snow, making it hard to see.

"There's a razor gale coming, sir." One of the four guards indicated the sky.

Without looking up, the captain turned to the guard, flashing his trademark expression. That quizzical smirk that had come so freely once. In better days. "I know," he said. "I can smell it"

But it wasn't the weather Henric Galttauer was smelling. That scent on the breeze was born of the sea. The end was near. Of the world. Maybe of everything.

12-5

It looked as if the wall of thorns was yawning. The illusion of an ugly, lop-sided maw was completed by broken timbers to approximate teeth. Kro frowned miserably. It was hard to believe that not so long ago, the entrance had been so perfectly camouflaged that most eyes would have passed right over it.

Most--but never those of the man who put it there.

Dread hung over the three companions. None wanted to go on but want had become a luxury.

Down the thorny corridor they plunged, six horses and seven riders, following the occasional fleck of bright yellow-green. As before, the light changed two times, first dimming under a bramble ceiling, then brightening as the corridor opened upon the secret glade. The one time sanctuary was such no longer. The wagon was destroyed. Crumpled inward, probably from a reptilian footfall or the lash of an enormous tail.

The purple tapestry that had covered the wagon's side flapped in the breeze. Anchored there by only a single point.

Upon his silver mare, Kro trotted over to the wreck. And as an errant breeze billowed the cloth up, he grabbed it. He held the faded tapestry, just remembering and regretting. Using both hands, he flattened out a portion to see the old symbol of the serpent devouring its own tail. The ouroboros had seen better days, but that was true for every man present, and the girl--perhaps her most of all.

"All journeys end at the beginning."

"What's that?" As Belmorn asked, Rivka peeked out, her eyes mimicking his question.

"Just... something my father used to say." Inexplicably, a faint smile crept into the corners of Kro's lips, behind his eyes. "Doesn't matter how long it takes, every journey is a damn circle."

Belmorn dismounted with a rude thud. Storming over to the still-attached corner, he ripped the tapestry free.

"What are you doing?" Kro couldn't help but feel outrage at this final and wholly unnecessary insult.

"Calm down." Belmorn didn't even look up. "Just putting this to some use."

Biting wind pulled the ends of the blackfoot's haresh. Without another word, Belmorn gathered the faded tapestry into one hand. Then he looked back at the girl.

Rivka was shivering. Her eyes were glassy, haunted. They swept across the empty glade, from wall to wall and then to the gaping tear ahead. The opening that had not been there before was wide enough to drive a pair of side by side wagons through.

"They're gone," she said flatly. "The Pershten. Just like..."

The sentence was left incomplete.

Upon riding into the clearing, the first thing Rivka understood was that the Morgrig gang weren't the only ones who had vanished that night. Bror and the rest were gone--utterly and without a trace. Surely forced through the witch-door, into that mysterious unknown Kro called the Without.

"I know, girl," was all Belmorn said. "I know. Here. Take this. You're freezing"

Rivka allowed the large tapestry to envelope her. After the process was complete, she cinched folds around her head like a second hood. The cloth was so large, it had to be wrapped around her three times. Peering out from the purple folds, she offered the blackfoot a faint smile. Then she pinched a bit in one hand and brought it to her nose.

"Smells a bit like fish."

Belmorn raised an eyebrow. "Smelly and warm or frozen. I'd say you're old enough to choose."

The girl hugged herself, pulling the old cloth tighter around her body.

"Good choice."

As he said this, she caught the briefest hint of a smile before he turned to face front.

Behind them, the captain emerged slowly from the dark corridor. The expression on Galttauer's face was consternation. She imagined it would have been no different if he had just ridden out onto the surface of the moon.

Again her mind went to the occasions when he had turned his attention her way. Offering her the odd bit of crust once or twice but never lifting her up. Never wondering if his sacred duty as protector of Roon's citizens might extend to her too.

She had learned many lessons out on the cobbles. All hard but necessary if she hoped to make it through another week, another winter. The world was rarely the way stories made it out to be. Perhaps that was why she had latched on to the one about the un-killable warrior who had battled a demon for days with a sword through his chest. Because real people never lived up to your expectations.

"Henric." The voice was Mr. Kro's. "Shouldn't the first of your scouts be here somewhere?"

The captain's black cape flapped like the wing of some enormous bird. He turned to regard the four men he had left.

"Not here, there." The captain nodded in the direction of the northern opening. "They are making a chain for us in the High Veld. In case the sky makes good on its threats." His icy blue eyes glanced at the darkening clouds overhead. "And I think we can all see that it will. Past here, the first of my men should not be far."

"Kro," For the first time, Belmorn sounded impatient. "Before we go, is there anything you need here? We could search the wagon. There may be something--"

"No," answered the grim voice of the alchemist. "Nothing." He looked to be tasting bile. "Henric," he said at last. "Storms in the High Veld hit hard and fast. If you do lose sight of us, I think I know where she is going."

"What?" The captain raised an eyebrow. "Kro, you insufferable thorn in my ass. Why didn't you say so before?"

"Because I wasn't sure before!" Kro pinched the bridge of his nose.

"I'm not sure now--but it makes sense. Why wouldn't she go back there?"

"Where, damn you!" The captain roared.

"Where this nightmare began. The first place she ever saw."

"He means Jayce." Rivka's voice was small but it rendered the three men who heard it, utterly speechless.

PART THIRTEEN
OLD DEBTS

13-1

Beyond the wall of thorns sprawled an alien landscape.

Those strange rocks Kro had called giant's teeth had been replaced by a flat ground, covered in a thick layer of snow. Beholding the whiteness was difficult. Especially with the cold, lashing winds.

"Razor gale!" shouted Kro from the back of his mare. He reached beneath his cloak and pulled up a maroon scarf. "Cover your faces!"

Wrapped in her massive, purple tapestry, Rivka shivered, tightening her fingers around the handle of her knife. She was yet unsure if she possessed the courage to use the thing, but the act of gripping it was a comfort. And she had lived long enough with too few of those.

Looking west, she winced as the wind slashed at her eyes. In the far distance, she could barely see the misty outline of the castle-shaped mountain. Far closer was a curved line, stretching from north to south. This of course was the real road. The path you were supposed to take through the Moat.

That road, she knew, led to the skeleton of a once bustling, mining town called Jayce. When Rivka's uncle was alive, he used to talk about going back. About how one day, someone would come to help Galttauer and his armored guards to set things right. And that together, they would wipe the witch's mark from the land.

Then, they could go home again.

Hebrecht Pesch had been a good man. A careful man. For a long time, Rivka had believed his every word. In the end though, he too had left.

There had been an argument, shouting outside her front door. Then sounds of an altercation--groans, the heavy SLAP of flesh on stone. After that, Rivka was alone. Good and truly. Right up until the night she was nearly killed with a piece of exploded sword.

"So that's it, then. Mount Einder." Belmorn shielded his face with an arm. "Damn thing does look like a castle."

Rivka looked past the storm clouds, to the tall spires stretching into the pre-dusk sky. Mount Einder. The road wound around and toward it, across the High Veld and eventually to the drop off. To World's Edge. Beyond that, there was only blue. A vast ocean--uncrossable, or so she had been told. Her uncle used to say that the sort of bravery it took to sail those waters had drained from the world. Abandoning it, just like all the Gods.

"You okay back there?" Belmorn's voice cut through the whistling gale.

"Yeah!" she yelled back, though only inches away.

The man turned in his saddle to face her. "Rivka, you know we are headed about as far away from safe as one can get. Are you sure you don't want to ride back to Roon with one of those armored guards?"

"Are you kidding?" she exclaimed. "I'd rather have stayed with that plant-thing than one of those inbred goons."

Wearing a faint smile, Belmorn turned back and said no more. Rivka took a deep breath and held it, pressing her cheek into the black fur of the riverman's cloak. The movement of the adamandray was rhythmic. The freezing air whistled past and over her, but Rivka felt warmer than she had in a long time.

Belmorn squinted, once again glad for his high collar. The powerful winds gave the snow little chance to settle, let alone accumulate. The gusting swirls also blew away things like tracks.

The witch blood was becoming nearly impossible to spot.

Belmorn turned to look back at the captain and his men, but saw nothing. It was as if a blizzard had swallowed them, except the snow no longer fell. The sky was a furious color as it gathered the most vibrant hues for the day's final hurrah.

"Kro!" shouted Belmorn. "You sure about this? I can hardly see!"

"Sure?" Kro shouted back. "Sure is for trackers, Belmorn!"

"That right? And what are you supposed to be again?"

"Told you before... I never figured that out."

"It's fine!" Rivka's voice joined the cacophony. She had a corner of purple cloth against her cheek. "Razor gales never last long. I know where we are. Just keep going!"

"She's right," called Kro. "Jayce isn't far, now."

Struck by the resolve of the young girl, Belmorn looked behind again, squinting through the gale. "Kro! I don't see anyone behind us," he roared. "Where is Galttauer? And where in hell are his damned scouts? We haven't seen a single man out here!"

"Don't know. Maybe a foot from our faces. Impossible to see in this fucking mess." Kro was shouting as loud as he could now. "Stick to the plan. If I'm wrong... if the witch isn't in Jayce..."

Belmorn said nothing. Not of their current predicament nor of the rising dread in his throat. The unthinkable possibility that the creature had not retreated to Jayce or any other place they could reach without the aid of witchcraft.

13-2

Henric Galttauer was alone. The razor gale had swallowed his men, the blackfoot, the child--even that blasted loudmouthed Kro.

It had been sometime since the group had set out from the hollow in the thorns. But the storm had hit fast--stealing sight and sound and all sense of direction. A blast of cold wind pulled the captain's cape from one side of his saddle to the other. It had been a long time since he'd faced the open fury of the elements like this, but Galttauer was no fool. Before leaving the thorns, he had ordered his men to put on their helmets before doing the same.

Away from the whipping wind, he turned. The captain's helm was a flat, unpolished steel and adorned with winged wolves on either side. The eye openings were large, fierce looking and connected via a V-shaped gap. Through this, he narrowed his eyes, forcing them to remain open. Searching for anything dark within the blinding white noise.

There!

Squinting hard, the captain pulled on the reins. Unless the gale had stolen his senses, there was a rider ahead! And for a single moment, Henric Galttauer's relief bordered on delirium.

"You there!" He waved, hoping beyond hope that the darkish blur would take the form of one of his men.

As the silhouette took shape, two eyes flashed in the white gloom. They were perfectly round, catching the light as if made of glass.

Without warning, the wind relented. Breathing, as these storms sometimes did.

The man ahead sat strangely in his saddle, seemingly favoring one side of his body. His face was hidden--not by a Roonik helm but a mask. The sort that doctors were known to wear. Over his shoulder hung three stolen quivers and a pistol. There was blood on his arms, across his chest. Red in its most vibrant form. As he beheld the color, Galttauer found that he couldn't breathe.

"You must be him. The man who used to protect the end of the world." The masked rider spoke in an accent Galttauer had never heard before.

"Where are my men?" Galttauer bellowed.

"Oh... around."

"Do they live?"

"Some did. When I left them, but this weather possesses even less mercy than I do."

"Impossible! Those men... they were thirteen of Roon's bravest. They could not have been defeated by one man."

The rider's head settled into a new angle before replying. "Thirteen you say? I admit, I did not keep count, but that is a very unlucky number."

"You lie! It's not possible!"

"Wrong, Captain. You see, a brave man will take on any foe, but a smart one will aim for the horse. Speaking of which, yours looks stronger than this last one I took."

The black stallion gave a snort. Right then, it was all Galttauer could do to force himself to remain calm.

"Who the hell are you? Morgrig? Or just one of his dogs out for blood?"

"I am no one's dog!" For the first time the masked man sounded angry. "Morgrig was a means to an end. A way to get close and stay close until my true enemy came home. You should have stayed behind your door, Captain. If you had, your men would still be alive." The masked man hissed, nocking an arrow. "Now... where is Mr. Kro?"

In his fist, the handle of Galttauer's greatsword seemed to be humming. Who this man was, he didn't know, didn't care. Everything that happened next, did so in a flash--the span of a single crack of lightning.

Galttauer charged. The speeding arrow shaft flew straight and true but connected only with the furious slash of Roonik steel before spinning into the haze.

After a surprised twitch of the head, the masked rider drew back his bowstring once again.

13-3

The first indication of a settlement was a single wooden pole. There was a strap of cloth nailed to the top--probably the remnants of an old banner or flag.

Belmorn tried to determine the color, but the razor gale prevented this. Suddenly and with all its remaining might, the storm exhaled. Voices were swallowed in the shrieking gusts, but the horses pushed forward as one. It had been Belmorn's suggestion to tether them. Connecting Kro's mare to the back of Magnus' saddle via a length of rope. This simple solution had kept them together as the Roonik men were swallowed one by one by the raging white void.

Reaching the pole, Belmorn dismounted, as did Kro.

When he moved to help the girl down, the vast cloth wrapped around her was pulled by the wind. Cloth billowed and flapped like a great purple wing, but as they had so many times out on the brackish course, the blackfoot's reflexes took over. His hand shot out, grabbed the cloth--stopping it from taking Rivka with it. Then he successfully lowered the girl to the ground.

With Kro's help, he reclaimed the massive purple thing and pulled it over the horses. Working quickly, Belmorn tied off the fabric, securing it to his saddle's many square rings. The three wrapped their arms around the pole and each other with the horses and tapestry for a shield.

They had become a massive purple blob possessed of not one

horse's ass, but a pair, utterly at the mercy of forces beyond their control.

Beneath the cloth, time passed strangely. For a quarter of an hour or more, all Belmorn, Kro and Rivka could do was hold on and wait. More than half frozen, each hung on to that wooden pole for dear life until the fury of the storm was spent at long last.

When the end came, it was abrupt. With a final lick of wind that faded out over the tundra.

Tentatively, Belmorn lifted a flap of cloth to peer outside. Fighting an onslaught of shivers, he said, "Looks like it's over."

"The storm maybe," said Kro, emerging from the cloth. "But not the day."

Belmorn took in his surroundings. There was no gate, no painted sign, nothing to mark the place that was omitted from all but the most complete of maps. Just then, he realized that the so-called razor gale had brought wind alone. Whatever snow had flown in the air had been ripped from the ground and all else. He could see shapes, great blocky things. Buildings.

Stiff fingers prodded at the various knots until the tapestry came free. Then, Belmorn lifted and bunched the cloth until a girl's face appeared.

"Are you okay?"

"Yeah." Rivka spoke through chattering teeth. "That... was longer than the ones I remember."

Belmorn smirked, then began gathering up the fabric. Making sure that there was plenty around her face, he wrapped the girl up as she had been when they left Kro's hollow.

"Thanks," she chattered.

"Alright, keep your voices down," Kro's warning sounded distant.

As the remaining snow settled, the buildings acquired features. Things like steps and doors took shape while various bits of clutter appeared on the street. Barrels, crates... a smashed cart lay beside the pile of stones it had once carried.

Belmorn noticed what looked like a small corral. The simple fence was badly damaged on one side.

"Goats," Kro offered an answer to the unspoken question. "This far out, you have to provide for yourself. In this case though, I'd say our herd provided for something else. Look there."

Belmorn saw a slash of bright yellow-green on one of the corral posts. Amidst the grey palette of the old mining town, the color gleamed.

"That's it then," Belmorn whispered. "You were right. The beast did come here."

Kro met the man's eye. "We should dismount. Find somewhere to tie off the horses. We have to be as quiet as possible. The witch may be wounded, but we've cornered her. She'll be desperate. Right now we have the element of surprise. I suggest we keep it."

"Agreed." Belmorn looked down at the girl with apology in his eyes. "Rivka," he said.

"No." she shook her head. "Don't you dare say it."

"I have to, girl. You know that."

"No!" Tears appeared and began to draw lines down her face. "I'm not going to go and hide in one of those buildings while the two of you fight that thing. Do you hear me? No! No more leaving!" At that moment, Rivka's chest wound pulsed with dull pain, but she hardly noticed. "Jayce was the only real home I ever had. But that thing took it away. Just by being born." As she spoke, her voice increased in intensity but also volume. "Don't tell me I'm not in this fight. Don't... you... dare."

"I..." Belmorn traded a wary glance with Kro. "I was going to say that you should keep your wits sharp. Watch. Listen."

Looking surprised, the girl drew the back of one arm across her eyes. "You... were?"

"Yeah," lied Belmorn. "Do you still have that knife?"

Holding the weapon up, the girl nodded.

"Good. Keep it just in case. But that knife must be your last resort." Belmorn reached back up to the saddle, pulled his Graelian axes from their sheaths. Then, looking as if he should know better, he handed one to the girl. With wide, hungry eyes, Rivka accepted the weapon. Grinning broadly, she bounced the thing in her hands, testing its weight.

"It's... not as heavy as I thought."

"Not so heavy, but the balance takes some getting used to. Feel it. Learn to anticipate it. And remember, only one side of the head is for cutting."

"And the other?" she swung the axe in a clumsy arc. The hammer end struck the ground with a ringing THUNNNGGG!!

The horses startled, and Kro turned with fire in his eyes. "For getting us all killed, perhaps?" He sounded annoyed. "You did hear what I said about the element of surprise, right?"

"Yes," said the girl, holding the axe as tight as she could. "Sorry."

"Alright, then." Kro shifted his cloak and drew the Maldaavan blade. It's length gleamed redly.

With that, the unlikely trio walked down the street, leading their horses. The first building crept up on the left. Like the rest, it was rectangle and scant of feature, utilitarian.

The blackfoot's blood surged hotly in his veins. Here at long last was Jayce, the proverbial X on the map. Of course, the true end of his quest had never really been a place.

He glanced at the man to his right.

"Remember," Kro's voice brimmed with quiet passion. "The hag could be anywhere. Around any corner. Jayce is meager as settlements go, but if she's nested in one of the residences, that's over twenty buildings we'll have to check. Keep your eyes open... for blood. For anything."

The sound of approaching hoofbeats kept him from saying more. Details of the rider were hard to make out, but there was no denying the large black stallion.

"Henric! Well, good you decided to join us." Kro's sarcasm didn't completely hide the relief in his voice. Stretching his neck, he attempted to see beyond the approaching rider. "Where... are your men?"

There came no response beyond a flap of dark cloak. The lone rider had a strange, slouching posture. He seemed to be sitting too far forward in his saddle.

"Kro." Belmorn's voice had a dangerous edge. "Something's wrong."

13-4

As he came closer, the three saw a pair of arrows fletched with black crow feathers. One stuck out of the man's collar; the other protruded from his chest--dead center, from that tiny stylistic hole in the breastplate.

"Henric?" Kro stepped toward the approaching rider, then stopped.

There was blood on the captain's face but his ice blue eyes yet gleamed with life. "K-rro," he sputtered, coughing. "I'm s-orry."

The apology was punctuated explosively as nearly two feet of sword burst forth--erupting from Galttauer's torso.

Like his men, the captain was covered in pale, ornate plates mounted upon an under layer of leather, allowing for a more supple range of movement in battle. The sword slipped through a gap between those plates, just above Gaulttauer's ribs, transforming the man into the living embodiment of his city's favorite statue.

"No!" Rivka's voice echoed down the snowy street.

With a sudden jerk, the sword retracted back through and out of the man. The body of Henric Galttauer fell from his horse. Landing in a clamor, as if someone had dropped an armful of cooking pots.

Still in the saddle, the captain's killer was revealed. He wore a crumpled mask--the sort doctors sometimes fill with dried flowers to protect themselves from plague.

"You!" Belmorn's accusation came with an expression harsh enough to give a salt-lion pause. "Are you blind or just insane? Your master is dead! Vanished by the same beast that we are hunting right now."

"Mr. Kro-o-o-o!!" The voice oozed like a slime, falling like steaming tar upon the ears in a strange, staccato accent. "The snake mother cannot have you, Mr. Kro."

Belmorn sneered, stepping between the masked man and his companions. "Insane it is, then."

The crumpled mask twitched, then shuddered as if shaking off a flash of cold, but the rider said no more. Kro and the girl were equally silent.

"If we battle, that monster is going to hear. Then she'll upset all our purposes." Belmorn brandished a single axe and a violent gleam in his eye. With a swipe of one hand, he ripped open his collar. "Whatever this is has to wait because right now we have a common enemy."

"I have only one enemy!" bellowed the masked man. "What the snake mother does is none of my concern. I am not here for her. Nor you, fool of a riverman!" The man's bloodied sword swung lazily through the air then stopped to indicate the man to Belmorn's right. "I told you, Mr. Kro. Today is a day of reckoning. For the settling of debts. I hope you did not think me a liar."

Belmorn and Rivka both turned in shocked silence to Tenebrus Kro.

"Kro?" Belmorn's voice held resolve. "What in Rinh's name did you do?"

"I... I don't know!" Kro's voice was low, but honest. He looked down.

On the ground, labored clouds rose from the captain's form. He wasn't moving, but for now, the stubborn son of a bitch was still alive.

"Kro?"

"Damn it, Belmorn. I said I don't--"

The man in the mask dropped from his saddle, hitting the ground with a hard crunch. He turned to regard the sword which he had stuck into the captain. It was different from those he had wielded initially. Long with an ornate, silver crossbar, it was the very sort carried by members of the Roonik Guard.

Without a word, the masked man inclined his head as clouds puffed and leaked through popped seams. Those clouds looked angry, like dragon breath. Stepping forward, the mysterious assailant thrust his blade into the ground. Then he reached both hands back, unlatching unseen straps within the thick ropes of his hair.

The mask landed like cast-off skin in a crumpled heap. Before, when Kro had looked upon that false face, his claim of ignorance to the man's identity had been true. But now, with his enemy's face revealed, memories resurfaced.

The man had dark brown skin and bloodshot eyes that looked yellow in the dying light of day. His nose was broad, his lips were thick, and he wore a partial beard. A section of his face--from just below one eye, down to the collar bone--bore horrendous, pinkish scars. The sort granted only by fire.

Though he looked older than when last Kro had seen him, it was a face not easily forgotten.

"The other Guards," Steam shot past Belmorn's teeth. "Where are they?"

"They were in my way." The scarred man offered a shrug--pulled the sword from the ground. "Now *you* are in my way."

"Stop." Kro walked slowly forward, posturing himself so that his thirsty red blade was behind his body. "Please... I do remember you. It has been a long time. Ten years."

"More than that!" the man roared. His voice rang between the buildings. "Lifetimes more."

Belmorn met Kro's eye. "Damn it, Kro, what did you do?"

"Much." Kro's voice was low. Barely loud enough for anyone but himself to hear.

"You were gone for a long time, Mr. Kro." The scarred man looked down at the crumpled mask on the ground. "But I knew that if I waited, one day you would come back." There was something mixed in with the man's hostility. Hatred, but also pain. So much pain.

"What do you want?" Kro's voice held resignation.

The man turned his back to the rest as he hunched over something which was slowly pulled from his belt. Something the others hadn't noticed. There came a sharp scraping sound and then the flickering of light.

"A small thing." The scarred man stood up, turned. In his hand was the Bàozhú cross that had fallen from Kro's pack when the two had tussled. The fuse of which now terminated in a furious, hissing spark. "I want you to say his name."

Kro's expression turned desperate. As if he were staring down the throat of a volcano, trying to comprehend its fury.

"Who's--?"

"The name of my boy!" The scarred man lunged forward. "You took him away! Used him up, piece by piece! Now you will tell me his name!"

13 - 5

Over the course of fifty-one years of living, Tenebrus Kro had been many things.

In the past three decades, he had uncovered much that was unknown and tried to put some of that to good use. In some cases, hope was administered, in others... lives were saved. Strange that whenever he looked back, none of that mattered. Only the mistakes. The regrets. The actions he would gladly give the better part of his body and soul to take back.

But there was no taking back, only moving past or burying deep.

Here he was, back in Jayce after so long. Trying to right his life's greatest folly, only to have a lesser one catch up.

When he found them, the remains of a young boy had been little more than charred bones--part of a finger, a few teeth. All accounts agreed that the boy's mother and infant sibling had perished in a blaze which was already hastening into legend--but the father had survived. And when a pale traveler had come from across the great ocean, seeking shelter and knowledge of hidden things... the still grieving man had confirmed the tragic accounts of what happened to his family.

The boy had not played with fire... the fire simply was. And whether it truly had been sent from their harvest god, or if fate had simply been in a particularly cruel mood, the boy had been the door for that fire. Its way into being. And his flesh?

So much kindling for the blaze.

The father, who had suffered such severe burns trying in vain to save his wife and infant, had pointed the way to his son's resting place. For the safety of all, the grave had been placed far away from the village. On a distant hill overlooking the sea, where the boy could do no more harm.

At the time, Kro easily rationalized the act of exhuming the remains as a necessary evil. Spontaneous combustion was beyond rare. The opportunity to study the bones of the unfortunate boy could not be passed up--especially when the secrets to one of the four elements might be contained within.

Air and salt, water and flame. Unearth, unveil and know. Such was the creed of the alchemist. All the justification Kro had required to still his conscience for the work at hand.

In the end though, the bones had not held the secret to the fourth element. Not fire, only smoke. A trick he had used a few times over the years.

"Well?" the scarred man's teeth and eyes flickered with the light from the dwindling fuse. "Say it!"

"I'm sorry," said Kro with real regret. "I can't. I... don't remember."

The scarred man bellowed a cry of frustrated rage. He lunged forward, sword in one hand, sparking cross in the other. Protecting his companion, Belmorn swung his axe in hard, devastating arcs, but the scarred man was fast.

As he pivoted, the long ropes of his hair swung in counterbalance. He grunted as they slapped his back. Out shot an elbow, then a well-placed knee. Belmorn stumbled back, grasping his stomach, coughing, fighting through the tears.

Kro's red blade appeared from the side, but the strike was half-hearted at best. The scarred man raised his own, deflecting the blow in a loud metallic clang. Then, with foam in the corner of his mouth, he looked into the eyes of Tenebrus Kro and spoke a single word.

"Babatunde."

The man's face was a hideous thing--marred by time and fire and years of incessant hate. The smile stretching across the ruined lips was the worst part of all.

"Say it!"

Kro stammered, trying to repeat the name.

"Baba--"

But it wasn't going to be enough. Could never be. He knew this as well as he had ever known anything, and so did the man with the scars.

"--tun--."

But before the final syllable formed on his tongue, the alchemist felt the cross pressing into his shoulder, across his collar bone. The sharp, white agony of an arrow, pinning it in place. He looked down just in time to see the last of the fuse disappear in a sickening, little hiss.

Once the flame reached the stores of refined powder inside, the fury of ten suns came screaming from four cardinal points.

The sounds that followed were of the air and of salt. Of water and flame. Yes--that one most of all. In his hubris, the man who was making them had unearthed and he had unveiled, but as countless prismatic embers scorched and melted and exposed the tendons beneath his flesh... only now did Kro finally understand.

He had never really known a damn thing.

A gloved hand shot forward, gripping the arrow still embedded into Kro's shoulder. With one mighty pull, the shaft and the cross came away. Belmorn, shielding his eyes from the light, hurled the shrieking thing like a tomahawk. The Bàozhú cross spun and screamed through the air, down the main street of Jayce and out of sight.

Howling, Kro dropped to his knees. His hood had taken some of the damage, but judging by his cries, not nearly enough. Belmorn ripped away the smoldering garment, tossing it to a patch of snowy ground where it could do no further harm.

Hands, twisted into claws, clutched and raked the ground. In vain, Kro began pressing fistfuls of snow into the open wound where his face had been until the man's consciousness gave out and he finally collapsed.

Belmorn stared in abject shock. Kro was not moving. Where his face had hit the earth, a wisp of steam now rose but by whatever Gods remained, he was not moving.

Remembering the axe in his hand, the blackfoot turned. Setting the storm in his furious grey eyes upon the interloper. This brown-skinned, rope-haired assassin whose scars seemed lacking when measured beside the ones inflicted upon his friend.

The assassin did not appear to notice the blackfoot thundering towards him. His arms were slack, his hands empty. Only when the axe cleaved the air did he move. Pivoting, thrusting out an elbow, he grabbed Belmorn's wrist and turned, twisting.

For a moment, the world upended. Belmorn landed hard, sliding a few feet. The scarred man shambled over to the nearest horse. He pulled a pistol from where it was strapped to the saddle and aimed it at the large riverman.

A series of clicks drew Belmorn's attention and his eyes widened.

"No! Stop," he said. "Get out of here!"

The scarred man turned his head at a curious angle, keeping the pistol pointed right where he wanted it.

"What's the matter with you?" Belmorn was close to pleading. "Do you hear me? I said go!"

"Pale skinned men..." sneered the man with the pistol. "The same everywhere. Always certain. Always so *above*. Even now, with you down there and this iron between us, you think you can decide what happens next, just by flapping your tongue." He lifted the barrel, stepping closer so that barely a foot separated it from its target.

"Hey!" Rivka shouted from behind the scarred man. "He wasn't talking to you."

Startled, the man wheeled round.

KUNGG!!

The second Graelian axe smashed into the man's skull, flattening his nose with such force a red stream shot through the air. The momentum pulled Rivka forward; the axe struck the ground hard enough to create a spark.

Dazed, the man stumbled a step back and then again, past the felled body of Henric Galttauer.

"That's what the other side is for!" Rivka shouted this as if it were the most venomous curse she could muster.

The scarred man who Morgrig had called Slagter, staggered backwards. He tried to speak, but his mouth no longer had the power to form words. Blood colored the few shards of his shattered front teeth. Then, in a blind rage, he lunged for the girl who had smashed his face.

A form clad in velvetblack rose up from the ground. Eyes burning like comets, the captain clawed at the side of his saddle, at the latches securing his greatsword. Then with a mighty roar, Galttauer called upon the very last of his strength. The long blade that had first belonged to his great grandfather lashed out in a furious horizontal arc.

There was a small, wet sound. And then, after a stumble, the scarred man fell to his knees. His hands raked the air like talons searching for a fish.

Belmorn's eyes widened again. His mind trying to string together the rapid succession of events.

Though the assassin's hands still twitched, the head that had driven them was no longer there.

PART FOURTEEN
A BLACKFOOT'S WORK

14-1

Belmorn and the girl stared though neither said a word. It felt like many minutes passed before the severed head returned to the cold earth--bouncing, rolling, carving a great pinkish arc in the snow.

Struggling to stand, Henric Galttauer also watched as the headless body lurched forward. The ragged neck, with nothing to support, pumped spurt after spurt of steaming red. Until it didn't.

Wearing a scowl, the captain straightened, then spat upon the body. He stabbed his sword into the ground, and still the onlookers said nothing. They watched the once proud man stand in victory--his own body still pierced with Roonik arrows. Captain Henric Galttauer looked more than victorious, more than heroic. He looked mythic.

"Galttauer," came the surprised voice of Rander Belmorn.

The captain coughed, winced. Then, using his sword as a crutch, he dropped to a knee. "I'm fine." His labored breathing carried an ominous rattle. "Help the girl."

Belmorn nodded. Getting back to his feet, he reached Rivka and kneeled. He placed his hands on the sides of her face and stared as if searching for something lost. The girl dropped the axe, and for the first time in years, she allowed herself to sob.

Belmorn pulled her in. He had tried so hard to close his heart to the girl. To remember why he was where he was, and who needed him most.

Sasha.

His boy might as well have been a million miles away, on an island surrounded by a lake of fire. If he allowed himself to love this girl, would his heart take the path of least resistance? Would it decide that what had been found was equal to what had been left behind?

No. Stop being stupid.

Belmorn looked at the dying sun. The orange sky gave way to hues of pink and indigo. He pressed the girl's face into his shoulder and hugged her tiny body.

When he released the girl, the first thing the blackfoot did was smile. "Are you okay?" He picked up the fallen axe.

The girl sniffed, nodded, drew the back of one arm across her face. "Me?" she waved her hand. "Sure. Been wanting to do that for a long time. Fucking bird-men."

Belmorn raised an eyebrow, surprised by the curse but in no way opposed to its application. In a swell of panic, he turned his gaze to the unmoving form of Tenebrus Kro. The man lay face down. For a few seconds, as dread rose in his throat, all Belmorn could do was remain nonplussed.

The sounds of horses reached him like a jolt. They were bristling and snorting--scraping the hard ground with their hooves. Fear rimmed the eyes of his oldest friend. He had seen that look in men before. And in the slime-slick beasts he pulled out of the churning black. He had never seen it on Magnus though. No matter how many times they had waded out from the shore. No matter what sort of monstrosity was breaching the surface. Clearly, the element of surprise had been lost.

"Captain," Belmorn shouted. "There are arrows in you."

Galttauer looked down. "Huh." He was still fighting to stand and yet, a familiar smirk appeared. "Forgot about those."

Belmorn pursed his lips, then shook his head. "Should I... ?"

"Take them out? No." The captain's tone was firm. "No point." He studied the riverman for a moment before turning away. "You have no stake in this fight, yet you're here, risking all to take down this monster. I can't say I understand why, but I know honor when I see it. At least... I used to." His speech fractured, then broke. After a fit of coughs racked the man, he spat a bloody wad upon the snow. "You're a good man, Belmont. For what it's worth, I regret hauling you up on that stage. Then, and every minute since."

The blackfoot wore a hard, stern expression. "I have a stake in plenty. And it's Bel-*morn*."

"Ah. So it is." Galttauer took a step. For a second it looked like his knee wasn't going to hold, but it did. "Bastard." He growled, looking down at the headless man. "Who the hell is this? Killed nine good guardsmen and their Captain for the bargain."

Belmorn paused, then grimly shook his head. "You'll have to ask him." He nodded at the unmoving form of Tenebrus Kro. "If he ever wakes up."

A distant crash turned their heads. Belmorn and the captain stared down the street as a strange sort of music reached them. It was tuneless, meandering between a shriek and whimper. Though far from the cacophonous barks of before, there could be little doubt of the source.

"Old Man!" Belmorn shouted. "Keep her safe! You hear me?" He turned to the girl, then pointed to the corral. "Stay on the other side. If that thing takes me, get her out of here."

The gigantic horse whickered before trotting over to where the girl was standing. Rivka however, made no attempt to climb into the saddle.

Belmorn knelt down so he and the child were at a height. "Rivka, please--"

"No! You said--"

"Listen to me, girl! On the river, every hunter, every blackfoot has a job. There are those who take the lead--who leapt aback the giant eels and pound in the stakes. But those stakes are attached to long ropes, held by others. Men and women. Hunters just as vital as the lead. It is their job to pull on those ropes, to haul the writhing beast onto the shore. But..." Belmorn held up a gloved finger. "They have to be patient. To watch. And wait for the right moment."

"And how do they know what moment is the right one?"

At this, Belmorn offered a lopsided smile.

The girl's lips were pursed. She looked to be considering a counterargument, but after a few seconds she just sighed. "Okay." she pushed forward the Graelian axe. "But you have to take this back now. It's too heavy for me anyway."

Belmorn accepted his other axe with mixed sentiment. He wanted the girl safe, and having both his axes in hand seemed like a good start. "Okay." He stood back up. "Now go."

The girl grasped one of the saddle's square rings while gripped her knife in the other. Then she and the horse headed behind the broken corral.

The riverman glared down the empty street, toward the approaching footsteps. The impact tremors shot through his body, hammering his bones and heart. Then came the wail. And the barks.

"Captain?" said Belmorn, a deep frown on his lips. "If you can still lift that sword, I suggest you do so."

14-2

Kro?" Belmorn shouted as loudly as he could, but the smoldering remains of the alchemist made no reply. "If you are still with us, I need you in this fight!"

The street ahead was empty. Laden in snow-covered cobbles, but empty. And then it wasn't. In an explosion of splinters from the side of a building, the monster appeared.

"Damn it, Kro! You're too stubborn to be dead, so wake the hell up!"

The beast of Jayce was frantic--seized by rage and frenzy. Her claws scraped earth and stone as powerful legs scrambled for purchase on the snow-slick ground.

Belmorn watched her come and he did not blink. The man stood tall, rigid, the long green ends of his haresh snapping behind him. Though his face was exposed to the elements, he could no longer feel them.

As he watched the monster regain its footing and shift direction, he tightened ten ardent fingers around the handles of two identical axes. The act summoned a stillness, a sense of clarity that reminded the man exactly what he had been made for.

"Belmorn." The voice was the captain's. He did not sound well. "Meet her. Buy me a few seconds to see to Kro. If I can rouse him, he may be of more help than an old fool who can't lift his own damned sword. Now go!"

As she moved in that strange serpentine scramble, the beast vomited forth a terrible shriek. Even from this distance, Belmorn could see the light of dusk gleaming off her teeth. Those curved, saber-fangs were unfurled, ready to strike--yearning, he knew, to be sheathed in his own flesh. And so, he too burst into action.

Belmorn's legs carried him down the street--not so much running but coursing. He had become like a bird of prey, but one too insane to know the difference between a blind mab and a white shark. Instinct and thought were one. His hands and axes shared a single course of action now: to collide with the coming nightmare.

Closer and closer, man came to monster until there was no gap left. The man roared, fangs shot forward and there resounded a deafening CLANG!

The witchwyrm reared up on its hind legs, changing its posture, arching its neck like a swan. Then it aimed that huge, adder-like head at the little thing who had dared to follow it home.

Henric Galttauer could barely believe what he was seeing. Somehow, the blackfoot was still on his feet! He had somehow evaded and struck the beast, which was now careening out of control!

The captain's strength was fading, and with it, everything else. He knew he'd never swing his sword again but that sound, that thunderous CLANG--it had stirred something. Stoking what few embers he had left.

Galttauer looked to the fallen alchemist. There was no movement but by whatever Gods were left, he had to try. Belmorn's bravery was prodigious, but in the end, he was just one man. If he failed--if that damned hissing nightmare made it to the horses and to the girl. Well, the good captain was going to be about as useful as a pair of shapely breasts on a corn snake. The alchemist, though... for the moment, he was an unknown quantity.

Keep going. Henric Galttauer spat red. *One more step. Another!*

Kro was maybe ten paces away. Lying face-first in the snow where he had fallen. Galttauer didn't know if the man was dead or alive, but he forced himself on. Gritting his teeth as fresh pain ignited with every step. He could feel three separate wounds, but he did not look down. The arrows still inside him were the least of his worries.

Not so far away, a battle raged, though the foreigner and the monster had eyes only for each other. As the captain stepped closer and closer to his last, neither seemed to notice him.

Finally, expelling air and flecks of red, Galttauer dropped to his knees. He placed a hand on the fallen man's chest and, for the briefest of moments, considered allowing this to be his final act. A welcomed relief, but one he hadn't earned. Not yet.

With an unintelligible curse, he flipped that damned loudmouthed Kro onto his back. Then, with pain throbbing in his every nerve, Henric Galttauer allowed himself to look down.

The blackened areas of flesh started at Kro's neck and went up to his cheek bone. Tendons were visible. Pink strings and oozing places caused the captain's stomach to lurch. Though the man's pointed black beard no longer existed, his lips were miraculously intact. And past them Galttauer could make the vague shapes of exhalations.

For better or worse, Tenebrus Kro was still alive.

The captain turned his head, coughing a fair amount of blood onto the snow. He plunged one hand into a pouch attached to his belt, one of many he had stocked before leaving his city.

Roon. Last of the great shield cities. The home he would never have a chance to fail again.

He retrieved a small glass vial, no larger than a man's thumb. With force he was not sure he had left, Galttauer squeezed until he felt the thing pop. Careful not to drop any of the glass, he held the crushed vial and its contents under the alchemist's nose.

Within seconds, Kro's eyes shot open.

Tenebrus Kro sat up with a jolt, looking everywhere at once. There was blood on Galttauer's shirt and on his face and more matting his mane of blonde hair.

"Henric?" Kro heard himself say. His words sounded distorted. Stiff.

Instead of a response, Galttauer extended a shaky hand. In it was a black powder pistol, the sort carried by the Roonik Guard. He offered the weapon handle-end first, making Kro feel as if he was expected to take the thing.

"How's your aim?" sputtered the captain, jerking his head toward the street.

Kro gasped upon seeing the clash of man and beast, which was now close to two hundred feet away. Understanding what was being asked, he took the weapon.

"On a good day?" Kro coughed. "Got to be worse than yours."

The captain smiled then. Just enough to reveal red teeth. "How about on the worst day?"

"Seems we're about to find out." In that moment, Kro had never felt more regard for the man. "Incidentally, where were you hiding this thing?"

"Up my ass." With blood dripping from his chin, Galttauer smirked, looking amused with himself. "Listen... I need a favor."

"Of course." Kro gave a nod. It hurt to talk, to even move.

"Back down the mountain... my men... That masked sonofabitch said some of them... might still be alive. I think he hobbled their horses and just rode past."

Kro frowned, then winced as fiery pain cracked his cheek.

"Please," Galttauer went on. "Roon is going to need a new protector. A better one. If there are survivors, get them home."

Kro curbed his instinct to fire back with something biting and sarcastic. Something about how the captain was greatly overestimating Kro's own odds of survival. Instead, he placed his hand on that of the dying man. "I will, Henric. I promise."

"Good. Now take this fucking pistol and get out there. One shot." The captain's voice had become a weak hiss. "Make it count."

Kro raised the pistol. He had fired many such weapons, just never at a living creature. As he looked to the battle being waged not a thousand paces away, he knew he would have no trouble breaking that trend. Just as he knew exactly what his one shot had to be.

14-3

Rander Belmorn wheeled round, using his momentum and catching sight of the beast's tail. It passed by like the end of a whip--close enough to feel a breeze.

The thing terminated in a hooked barb. Up close he could see that the thing was no scorpion stinger, but jointed, segmented--looking more like the leg of an enormous spider-crab. Kro had said that somehow, that organ was her connection to the place he called the Without.

Without a doubt, it had to go.

Belmorn's eyes slid up the tail to the yellowish-green opening left by Kro's Maldaavan blade. True to the man's claim, the wound had yet to heal. Flecks of the bright liquid were being splattered all around. The cut was small, but the red steel had done its work. Who knew how much blood had been lost already? How much strength? Between that and what internal injuries it had suffered in the clutches of that abominable rose, maybe, just maybe, there was still a chance for victory.

Raising both axes high, Belmorn moved quickly. Dodging a clawed swipe on the way, his eye never wavered from that bright spot on the tail.

Graelian steel sung, then clanged with a sour note upon the ground.

Belmorn looked around, left, right. He was alone. Left, right, right, left. The man spun around, both axes up, heartbeat thundering in his chest and behind his eyes, but the witch was gone. Vanished with no trace but the steaming blood on the ground.

As the witch reappeared, she was preceded by a strange effect, akin to a mirage. For half a second, reality quaked. Shimmering as if it had been brought to a heatless boil.

The serpent head appeared then struck, but Belmorn was already in motion. Twin axes clashed with a pair of enormous fangs. The beast recoiled, lashing a long white tongue while shaking its head.

The tail! Belmorn's thoughts exploded in his skull. *Stay on the tail!!*

He swung again at his target, but the tail moved unpredictably. He tried to keep eyes on it. Tried to anticipate, but...

Belmorn had only been horse-kicked once but that was enough. He had never forgotten the all-encompassing pain and heart-gripping panic of being knocked into the air before crashing back to earth.

This was a lot like that.

Gulping, coughing, needing to vomit, the blackfoot scrambled upright, realizing he had been hurled almost a dozen feet. Tears flowed onto his cheeks as he tried to regain his lost air. Stupidly looking to where the witch had been.

Gone again.

He looked around--gasping. His lungs burned, but above him, the air seemed to be boiling. The foot came down hard, slamming Belmorn to the ground. He was pinned, but at the last moment, he had raised both axes, blades out. Now they were all that separated him from the scaly flesh of the beast.

Wide eyes took in a darkening sky, but the sight was eclipsed by the head of a gigantic adder. Long, black-and-silver arrowhead scales flared away from the face.

The witch turned her head, pushing forward the bulging orb that was one of her eyes. It was green, marbled with veins and marked with a central vertical slash, undeniably reptilian. With a pulse, the pupil contracted, thinning down to a finger's width as it both considered and hated the man.

Out of its gaping maw flicked the pale tongue. Like everything else, the appendage was far worse up close--not simply forked but possessing many branches along its length. It flicked reeking saliva that steamed upon the man's cheek.

Belmorn focused on the pearl white fangs. They looked small on the beast--shorter than most daggers but hooked. What the teeth held was his prize. Sasha's only hope. He needed that venom like he needed air.

"Aggh!" Belmorn cried out.

Though the axe blades prevented the witch from pressing harder, Belmorn couldn't take much more. The man's eyes bulged from pressure and pain as hammers pressed into the sides of his collar bone.

Which will give first? He couldn't help but wonder. The witch's armored skin or your bones?

"Well?" The tiny voice in the dark was familiar. It was that of a young boy. "Can I?"

"Can you what?" asked the boy's father.

"Pick out a foal this spring?!"

Shapes began to emerge, and color. Little Sasha Belmorn. Not even nine and already a man.

"Oh my son," said the father. "I know this can be a difficult business, waiting to grow up. But do you remember what I told you about a blackfoot's work?"

The boy looked miserable. In fact, if his body language could be believed, the prospect of responding was a labor equivalent to emptying the river with a bucket. Finally though, he forced the word out with an exaggerated sigh. "Yes-s-s. It doesn't end when the sun goes down."

"That's right," said the father, privately brimming with pride. "A blackfoot's work follows him home. Sits with him at the supper table, lays in his bed, even colors his dreams. And do you remember why?"

"Because the river bites hard."

"And... ?"

"And it doesn't let go."

14-4

Belmorn's consciousness returned with a sense of extreme motion. It felt as if he were weathering rapids on Magnus' back. As if he was a fish caught in the mouth of a hungry salt lion who was playing with its meal.

"Let him go!"

He heard the voice but didn't understand. Sudden motion swung him up. Pain exploded from every corner, but such things were relative. He could see something round, orb-like. A black sliver in a sea of ember green.

It was an eye. Her eye. And, by Rinh, it was close enough to touch!

Belmorn tried to move, but this only resulted in more pain. His arms were pinned and useless... but how? None of what his eyes told him made any sense.

Unless he was in her mouth.

"I said..." came the voice of Rivka from the back of an enormous horse. "Let... him... go!"

The witchwyrm regarded this new nuisance with pupils that widened into ovals.

Galloping at full speed, Magnus lowered his head and rammed full force against the monster's long neck. The adamandray hardly lost momentum, trampling right over the beast with heavy hooves. The small girl bounced in the saddle, keeping her seat against all odds. The witch rolled, scuttered, shook its head, and then lashed out with its tail. But it did not let go of the blackfoot in its mouth.

Steam shot from the horse's nostrils. Squealing a deep trumpet blast, charged for a second time. Carrying a small, very angry girl on his back, Magnus galloped toward the cowering snakeish-thing who was hurting his oldest friend. At the last second, the animal turned its bulk, striking with both hind legs. The first kick was a mighty thing, but the horse did not stop there. Rivka clung to the saddle, barely hanging on through the attack. Again and again, the body of the witch suffered the bite of Graelian steel until the hooves passed through where meat had been, finding only open air.

The ground rushed up to meet Belmorn through shimmering, rolling space. Once again, the witch had slipped away.

The girl in the high saddle steadied herself and shouted, "Rander!"

Belmorn rolled over, forced himself up on one knee and then to his feet. His body thrummed with uncountable agonies, but he was happy to feel every one of them. They meant it wasn't over.

"Rander!" Rivka shouted from atop the towering adamandray, nervously considering the ladder of rings. "Are you okay?"

The man coughed, grasping his aching side. He didn't know how or why, but the beast had vanished and left him behind.

"Her fangs..." said the blackfoot with a slight tremble. "I felt them. They were like iron bars against my back but... they didn't go in!" With that, he reclaimed his axes from where they lay.

Rivka shouted once more. "There!" The girl's finger was indicating a shimmering patch of air.

Belmorn pivoted, swinging his weapons as hard as he was able. Tracing a circle around the man, the blades sliced at the boiling air, but connected with something undeniably solid.

The witch shrieked, pulling back and shaking its head.

Yet the beast suffered no fresh laceration. Even so, there was fear in those reptilian eyes. Faced with the tall man and the gigantic horse, the creature backed away. It stopped to rear back on its hind legs-- standing once more at full height. Then, like two leathery wings, great hood flaps shot out from the sides of its neck, making the front half of the thing appear more cobra than adder.

Looking more intimidating than ever, the witchwyrm proceeded to reclaim the step it had lost. In full display, it shot its head forward, all fangs and fury, to unleash a monstrous, hissing roar. Threads of hot saliva spattered the man, the girl and the gigantic horse. Then came the barks. One, two, three.

Down slammed a huge three-toed foot. The impact sent tremors, over snow covered earth, into the riverman. Two orb-like eyes seemed to glow--not with light but with waves of untellable, green hate. She could see the little man who had slipped from her embrace, but he wasn't the only thing that had hurt her.

The adder head lashed out--dodging around the tall man to hit the adamandray. Fangs sunk in, and the enormous horse was ripped off its feet, swung in a high arc.

The girl was catapulted but Belmorn did not see where. His eyes were on his horse. Proving too heavy to lift again, both Magnus and the witch's head crashed to the ground. Once released, the furious adamandray squealed, flailing its long white legs as the witchwyrm tumbled away.

"Old Man?"

Belmorn's voice was swallowed by an explosion of powder and light which cracked into being.

BANG!!

Shrieking howls filled the air and ears of all in proximity. The cobra hood snapped flush against the witchwyrm's neck as she thrashed about. Stomping, smearing her own yellowish blood in the snowy street

That was when Belmorn noticed the tail was only half as long as it was a second before.

Spurts of witch-blood were fired like water from the trunk of a mammoth. Slashes of startling yellow-green further painted the ground. Spattering rocks and snow and the sides and steps of buildings.

The snake head snapped chaotically, clicking its teeth over and over. Hind legs bent at the knees as the beast returned briefly to four-legged locomotion to scramble a short distance away.

Belmorn looked in the direction of the explosion. Though it did not explain the BANG, he saw someone standing there, one arm outstretched, holding...

"Rinh," he muttered in distant disbelief.

The hair of the alchemist was black and silver. Matted in places and burned away in others, sticking out on one side like the wing of a great bird. Without the cloak, Belmorn almost didn't recognize Tenebrus Kro.

The man's face had burned to a raw, blackened ruin. It was difficult to look at, but in that moment, all Belmorn felt was relief.

Kro closed his eyes, breathed deep the northern chill. The cool breeze was a relief as it blew through his hair and over his blistered skin. Right then, he possessed neither the will nor strength to do much else.

With trembling fingers, he found the scarf inside his shirt collar and pulled it up. The deep maroon stood out starkly from the dark blue of his tight-fitting patchwork ensemble.

"No more vanishing." Kro's shouts were misshapen--muffled behind the form-fitting scarf. "Not without that."

He looked to the bloody segmented stinger. Then down the length of severed tail to the raw, blackened end. He had one shot. Only one. So he had moved stealthily. Belmorn had the witch's full attention by then so approaching from behind was possible. Then, after tumbling over the adamandray, the thing had been stunned. Seizing his opportunity, Kro moved fast. Closing the remaining gap and pressing the pistol's muzzle into the wound as he fired.

"You hear me, bitch? You're trapped with us now!" Kro's words quaked with an unsettling elation that bordered on madness. "Right here with me!"

The witchyrm opened her serpent jaw wider than ever before, unhinging it for a throaty, tongue-lashing roar that seemed to go on for days.

PART FIFTEEN
OVER THE EDGE

15-1

"Rivka-a-a!!" Belmorn shouted at the top of his lungs.

His ears strained to hear through the witch's noise. In agony, the monster stomped around with the gait of a drunkard. Balance, it seemed, had been lost with the back end of its tail.

"Rivka-a-a!!"

The riverman's eyes passed over his oldest friend. Though Magnus lay still in the snow, Belmorn could allow himself to see no more. No matter how much it hurt, his focus had to be on the girl.

She had been hurled from the saddle when the witch retaliated. He'd seen her tiny, limp form fly almost weightlessly through the air towards one of the buildings. And now his eyes darted between that very structure and the shrieking, stumbling monster.

The building had two stories with a porch on the ground level and a balcony above. It was about thirty feet away, but infuriatingly, there was no sign of the girl. Not in the snow, on the steps, nor anyplace in between himself and there. He spied storage crates, stacked on top of each other, but these were frosted with fresh fallen snow. Undisturbed by any falling bodies.

"Rivka! Answer me!"

Belmorn clenched his jaw. It felt like a frozen hand was reaching up out of the earth, grasping his stomach. He'd known grown men who had their spines shattered from lesser throws than that. River men who'd lived the better part of their lives in a saddle.

"Damn it, girl," he hissed in a low voice. "Where are you?"

The girl snapped awake but her surroundings made no sense.

She was in a room she had never seen before. There were barrels and boxes, storage crates like the ones on the street. She remembered that miners stored their supplies in boxes like that. There were lamps and ropes and chemicals for leeching silver from the hard flesh of the mountain. Her father had taken her to a room like this once. In another life. Or perhaps only a dream.

Rivka inspected herself. On her chest was broken glass and splintered wood.

"What?" her voice was startling in the confined space, even to herself.

She moved to brush off the debris, drawing a sharp, stabbing pain. The wound in her chest had improved--far more than good reason would claim possible, given the time--but it was healing, not healed. Cognizant of the area, she managed to get to her feet.

"What?" She exclaimed. "What the hell is this? A storage room?"

Her eyes fell upon a window. Broken pieces of frame hung at wrong angles. Bits of errant glass trailed to where she now stood, but certainly not enough to fill the gaping rectangular hole. Slowly, she began piecing it all together.

She remembered being on Magnus' back. And she remembered the face, the strike, and flying. She remembered flying. But, if she had been flung here, why wasn't she hurt? Bleeding at the very least? Rivka patted herself, checking shoulders, arms, and back for protruding shards, but the only sore spots were those she remembered from before.

The tapestry.

On the floor where she had been laying was the purple cloth that had once covered one side of Kro's wagon. Earlier, it had sheltered them all from the razor gale and here, the tapestry had protected her once more. The cloth was thick, rugged, meant to insulate as much as to advertise the arrival of the wagon's driver.

Carefully, Rivka picked up one corner, lifted it to see the edge of a faded pattern.

Snake scales.

Sticking out of the fabric and lying on the ground were the missing window shards. Shimmering glass was everywhere in nuggets and slivers and triangular knives. The window gaped a mouth lined with horrible, irregular teeth that seemed to mock the girl. To remind her that she should probably not be alive. But she *was* alive. And based on the shouts and noises coming through the window, she wasn't the only one.

Desperate to get eyes on the only friends she had made in a very long time, Rivka rushed to the window. Judging by the commotion, the battle was very nearby but something blocked her view. Not the ground but wooden planks--old and covered in snow. Looking straight, then to the sky, the girl realized that she was not on ground level. The planks outside formed the floor and rails of a balcony.

"Is that even possible?" The words were small as they left her. "Across the street... through a second-floor window?

Frantic to escape her current surroundings, Rivka wasted no time finding a door. Unfortunately, years of disuse had frozen the internal latch in place and no amount of effort was making it budge.

With a grunt of frustration, the girl again considered the window. Part of her wanted to just leap through and face the consequences, but too much glass remained. It was a miracle she hadn't been hurt her first time through. Lucky indeed that the tapestry had taken the brunt of--

The tapestry!

After crossing the room, she lifted the heavy fabric. As she dragged it to the yawning window, she could hear terrible scraping noises coming from underneath--dagger-glass on old wood.

She heaved the thing through the window, covering the shards that looked so like teeth. Carefully finding places for her hands, the girl lifted herself up and through, landing on the other side with a resounding THUD!!

In seconds, she was across the balcony. Gripping the railing, she peered down at the street.

The witch wasn't far, and reared up the way she was, her head was almost at Rivka's height. From this vantage, she could see there was a pattern on the extended flaps that so brought to mind a cobra's hood. Stark hues were conspiring there--mimicking a pair of silver eyes that appearing to be weeping.

Something else she hadn't noticed at ground level--the monster was holding itself in a strange, asymmetrical way. Favoring one side over the other. Rivka's mind raced back to the glade in the woods. Along with visions of a towering rose monster, sounds returned to her ears: a dull cracking, as bones within the witch buckled in the terrible embrace of long, green tendril-vines.

Far below, two men came into view. Not in her memories, but right there on the ground! Kro was attacking the witchwyrm. Then he disappeared underneath it!

The beast looked like a cat searching for a mouse between its feet. Suddenly, it reared back up, and with a rattle of that wide weeping hood, it lifted one hind leg into the air. Rivka gasped. Her hands flew to cover her mouth because she knew exactly what it was about to do.

But Rander--he was already running, already diving.

He connected with Mr. Kro at the last second, pushing him out of the way of the clawed foot. In a single puff, Rivka released her breath.

This was no good. She could see her friends, but what good was that if she couldn't help them? She searched for something--anything that she might be able to use. Various supplies were strewn about the balcony, but only one caught her eye. Something conspicuous gleaming in the low light of dusk. In the confusion, she had forgotten all about it.

"My knife!" Rivka gasped. "Must have slipped from my hand when I was..." she looked at the window, then picked up the weapon. Gripping it she peered down at the thing that had murdered her parents.

"Your uncle was right, child. It wasn't a sickness." she heard the words of Mr. Kro in her head. *"Seems there are spores in the eggshell... released by the very act of hatching. A diabolical defense mechanism. Removing threats to the newborn witch while providing it with plenty to..."*

Kro had trailed off then. His thought, simply too terrible to finish.

"Plenty to eat." The words exited the girl in a snarl. Thinking of her parents as they lay bedridden, getting sicker and sicker--until sick was no longer what they were. Part of her still hated them for that, for leaving her.

"Plague didn't kill your family, girl. I did."

Rivka shook the memory away. It was confusing because Mr. Kro seemed like a good man. He had helped save her life. He'd given her fish, even let her take clothes from his wagon. And then there was the knife.

Just then she recalled swinging Rander's axe. The freedom. The feeling that her life might no longer depend on the whims of a cruel world. The axe had felt heavy at first, but as she'd smashed it into the face of that bastard bird man, it had seemed all but weightless.

Again the girl regarded the dramatic scene below. The beast was moving backwards. Away from the men but closer to Rivka's balcony. With a frown, she flipped the knife so its blade was pointing down. Then she renewed her grip, tighter than ever.

The weapon had been a gift from Mr. Kro. A way to defend herself or possibly just to placate her. Still, simply having it had made her feel better. Powerful even. And now, she finally knew what the damn thing was for.

15-2

Adrenaline. It had helped Belmorn through a string of moments already. But there were limits to all things. He had dropped one of his axes, employing that hand to cradle his left side, where the beast had bitten him. Breathing was difficult. Lungs ached for air, but the stabbing pains truncated every breath. Still, Belmorn had bigger problems. He would take a step, swing something, block something else. Adrenaline or not, this couldn't go on much longer and he knew it.

There were broken things in her too. That ugly hag. He could see from the way she moved and held herself. Or the way an attack might end halfway in a loud screech. Truly, they owed much to that strange plant creature--that damned abominable rose. Whatever the hell it was, it had given them a chance.

They were almost at one of the buildings. A big, boxy, two story affair with a second floor balcony. Had he imagined it? Was this where Rivka had been thrown? It was so difficult to concentrate on anything beyond the barrage of reptilian appendages being thrust his way. Belmorn looked up at the hideous adder-face, at the bulging ember-green orbs and their unrelenting hate. Then his eyes moved past all of that. To something inexplicable.

A small girl was up on the balcony--kneeling on the railing, then standing. Then, she jumped!

As she soared, Belmorn noticed that something was in her hands.

Something that flashed in the dying light. He wanted to shout, to extend his arms and catch the falling child, but it all happened too fast.

The witch never saw what hit her. The blow came from behind, forcing her head forward and slamming it into the ground. In its confusion, the beast might have seen a small person tumble from its back, might have seen one of the hated things race over to comfort this much smaller one. Yes, it might have done these things... if not for a strange and insufferable sensation. An itch--terrible, all consuming. It had blossomed quite suddenly, behind one of its eyes.

There was no thought process for what happened next. Only instinct and a lifetime of experience. The blackfoot saw his opportunity, just like he had a hundred times out on the brackish course. It was a small window, barely a second long, but he did not waste it. Sparing a final, momentary look to the girl, Belmorn leaped, straddling the neck of the witchwyrm as if it were one of his monstrous eels.

Rivka's knife had been driven directly into the witch's forehead. Just in front of that huge bony crest. Moving almost by itself, Belmorn's hand reached out and grabbed the handle--pulling as if it were a saddle horn. Then he abruptly felt his stomach leave his body.

With an ear-splitting shriek, the witch reared up. It stumbled, then spun around--flailing, stomping, scratching with twitching limbs and a stump of tail that had not stopped leaking.

Rivka looked up--catching the riverman's face one final time. His eyes, usually so full of storms, seemed calm now. She reached out for him, but the witch was already off. Running at full clip down the street and straight out of Jayce with a riverman on her neck and the tip of a long knife in her brain.

15 - 3

Hard and relentless blew the wind, but the blackfoot did not let go.

The monster ran with brainless abandon, wailing and bucking and trying to throw its rider. Belmorn had been jostled, had slid a fair bit down the neck and towards the body, but he did not let go.

The town of Jayce was behind them and the sky had become the world. Furious colors were everywhere, rendered in broader strokes than Belmorn had ever seen. Swept away on the back of a mount he could never hope to control, the man's eyes looked to a cloudscape of fiery orange. Just above the horizon he could see a great burning circle. The setting sun reminded him of a mouth. A yawning, gaping thing, eager to swallow both man and witch.

Belmorn's eyes fought to stay open in the wind, then focused upon the goal. The knife was some six feet or more away now. Still sticking out of the thing's skull.

Leg muscles squeezed the serpentine neck harder than ever. Scales longer than any snake's flared out and away from the witch's body, creating sharp protrusions--a far cry from the smooth, slimy skin of the greater eels.

What felt like a hundred points pressed into him. Their discomfort was exacerbated by the thunderous, plodding gait of the creature. The man winced. His every muscle was eager for this flight to be over. And soon enough, it would be. One way or another.

Jayce wasn't on most maps, but the one he had been following, put it right on the edge. World's Edge--that massive, legendary drop-off of sheer cliff face, beyond which stretched a vast ocean of ice and perhaps... a land of green-haired raiders, who once crossed aboard dog-faced ships. If one believed such things.

The blackfoot needed to climb and fast. Needed to reach the monster's head before they ran out of Veld. He shot out a hand but without consideration for his injuries. A shock of pain exploded in his side, sharp and deep enough to raise the question of whether he himself had just been harpooned. He hissed a cry through gritted teeth as the wind ripped a tear from his cheek.

More than anything, Belmorn wanted to let go, to let the end have him. But the faces of his loved ones would not allow this. Malia. Sasha. They were there, in his mind's eye. Even here, even now, the memory of their eyes grounded him, cauterizing his pain.

Regardless of what his conscience had to say on the matter, the actions of Rander Belmorn were most certainly not those of a coward. Fear does not drive a father to cross an entire continent in search of salvation for his dying son.

'Love does that'.

Even now, the emotion burned in him, throbbing angrily in every one of his wounds. Again, his eyes found the knife. It was roughly six feet away, still protruding from the top of the witch's skull. Just past the sharp, bony crest, right where Rivka had put it.

As the long green ends of his haresh buzzed behind him, he focused on the sound, used it the same way he would the roar of the black river. The noise became his anchor, a way to block out all the little things he couldn't control.

One of his hands was still holding an axe. And though he lamented dropping its twin, for the coming work, one would serve.

With a deep breath, Belmorn began ascending the neck. The movements were small, but far from polite. He used the axe's blade--thrusting it into the scaled hide as if climbing the sheer face of a mountain.

Stealing a glance at the road ahead, Belmorn's stomach sank. They were nearly there. Almost at the Edge. And though he viewed it all through the chaotic jostling of the witch, he could see something out there. Something like a pillar of steam stretching into the sky like smoke from a distant campfire. The sight sparked a memory.

This had to be Skáldi's Breath. Indisputable evidence of an underground river--hot and full of ugly, blind fish, just like Rivka had said. The steam stretched from the sea to the heavens like some strange, ethereal tether. And for some reason, Belmorn's mount was running straight for it!

Of course, the dreaded witch of the Veld wasn't thinking clearly. Not anymore. Not with the point of a knife in her brain. The knife. He had to reach it. Had to keep moving up the ladder of scales that got more and more spine-like, the closer he got to the head. Time slipped but the blackfoot didn't notice. His mind was on the work. On his footing and ensuring that each strike of his hammer-axe hit its mark. Finally, Belmorn reached the huge crest at the base of the monster's skull.

Up close, it was nearly four feet high--like the dorsal fin of some terrible fish but made of solid bone. Belmorn frowned, then turned to spit into the wind. Releasing a mighty roar, he pulled himself closer to that conspicuous bony crest. Close enough to wrap his arms around the thing and to hold on for dear life. For the next few seconds, the only thing the blackfoot concentrated on was breathing.

He could feel the cold, uneven surface of the crest against his cheek and in the palm of his free hand. Usually that hand would be holding a Graelian harpoon. Another of the blackfoot's tools--around two feet long with a devilish point on one end and square ring on the other. Flat, so it could be pounded, driven like a railway spike into the blubbery, slime-slick flesh of the blackfoot's natural prey. Those things that come up from the trench. The diplocaulus, the salt lion, seven species of greater eel (all longer than a man is tall), even the dread nautiloth--they had all known the bite of his steel. And now, so too would this damned, murderous hag!

Belmorn launched from the crest and out onto the skull. Dropping, he gripped the handle of the knife Rivka had put there and lifted his axe.

KANG!!

He brought the hammer-end of his weapon down with all his might. And again, as he had done so many times out on the brackish course.

KANG!!

Each blow pounded the knife's pommel like the flat end of a harpoon, driving it in, deeper and deeper.

KANG!! KANG!!

Finally. With the fourth strike, the witchwyrm stopped screaming. Less than ten feet from the cliff, it froze in place. Then it began to tilt. It leaned toward the Edge. In the direction of that rising pillar of steam.

Belmorn's stomach clenched. His eyes shot wide, and far below, the dark water gazed back, beckoning both beast and rider into oblivion.

Every shred of reason told the blackfoot to let himself go--but the work wasn't done. Rander Belmorn raised his axe once more. Clutching the images of his wife and son, he drove home that final inch of steel.

KANG!!

Like a newly headless chicken, muscles flexed and jerked, mimicking life in the throes of demise. Still upright, the slain thing lurched forward. A powerful hind leg kicked one final time, finding only open air. That was when both beast and rider began to fall--over the edge, through the steam, down and down and down.

And so it happened that Rander Belmorn, beloved father, devoted husband began to fall. Plummeting alongside the monster he had slayed--right off the edge of the world.

15-4

Tenebrus Kro leaned hard into the gallop, his hair in constant motion--flickering like a black flame. The lower portion of his face was obscured by a form fitting scarf once meant to shield his face from the world. Though from now on, it would be the other way around.

As he rode, wind conspired with the sunset as it blazed off the snow. Rimmed in tears, the eyes of the alchemist strained to remain open. Cold air penetrated the cloth, moving over his ruined cheeks and neck. This might have been a relief if not for the stiff tugging that told him the scarf and his recent wounds had fused.

What had happened with the scarred man and the exploding cross was too much to face right now. Real pain would arrive soon, but for the moment, Kro was thankful that the rush of battle was keeping such things at bay.

After the witch had fled with a large riverman attached to her back, Kro had wasted no time. The girl was a bit worse for wear, but she would live. Better than he could say for the adamandray, who he hadn't seen move. But this wasn't the time to think about them either. Kro had to clear his brain and focus on riding. To fight through still oozing injuries for the sake of a man he hardly knew.

The blackfoot had justified every tale Kro had ever heard of his kind. But this wasn't Belmorn's fight. At least, it shouldn't have been. This time, Kro's own life was supposed to be the only one on the line.

Why does everything always go so wrong?

Air and salt, water and flame. Unearth, unveil, and know. The creed of the alchemist ran through his head as Kro once again cursed himself a fool.

The stolen silver mare he hadn't bothered to name had retreated behind a number of stacked wooden boxes. Coaxing her had taken time. Too much damn time.

With Jayce far behind him, Kro stared ahead into the cloud of kicked up snow. He could hear distant bellowing but this was cut short by a choked sort of cry. The witch sounded as if she had found fresh pain, and that was good.

"There!" Kro shouted to no one in particular, his eyes catching the bright yellow splatter on the ground.

Raising an arm, Kro squinted until he saw a column of steam in the distance. Seeing the tracks turn in that direction, he smirked.

Like a moth to a candle.

Slowing his horse, he swallowed hard. World's Edge couldn't be more than fifty feet away. Heart in his throat, he turned to the east. The cliff stretched as far as he could see in either direction, but there were no more spatters of blood. And worse... as far as Kro could tell, he was alone.

He pulled the mare to a stop. "Bel-morn!" He shouted with one hand cupped around his mouth. Kro sat as still as possible, listening through the whipping wind as the name echoed away.

His call went unanswered.

With a frustrated grunt, he pulled down the scarf. The face revealed was a horror. A landscape of angry reds and charcoal black. Raw meat but with too many openings. Both cold air and adrenaline were helping to numb the chorus of pain, but ripping away the cloth had done fresh damage.

Kro lifted his hand, again cupping it around his mouth. "Bel-l-l-mo-o-o-rn!!"

Even shouting hurt as the too-tight skin around his mouth stretched and cracked.

God damn you, he thought. *I told you to take the girl and go home. You're not the one who earned this ending, you self-righteous son of a bitch.*

The alchemist allowed his head to roll back. The sky was everywhere. It blazed and churned and it looked empty, felt empty. A different man might have thought to pray, to beg whatever god might be listening for one last blessing. But Tenebrus Kro was a man who believed such acts to be pointless. The gods were gone, if they had ever been there at all. Ever since he could remember, he had always believed only in what could be touched and dissected.

Still, however unlikely it was, part of the man yearned for a miracle.

For some reason, Kro turned his head until the great pillar of steam was in his line of sight. Had he heard something--or... ?

He dismounted and led the mare closer to the edge. There was still no sign of the blackfoot or the witch, but something told him to keep going.

Ten feet from the edge, he heard it again. This time for sure. Something that wasn't wind or steam or his own thundering heart.

Releasing the bridle, he ran to the edge, sliding on wet ground at the end. Then, carefully, slowly, he peered over the edge.

Belmorn looked up. It was his only option. He had fallen quite a distance, though he wasn't dead. Not yet.

At the last second, his trusty weapon had saved him. When he leapt from the back of the falling witch, he swung the thing, hoping to catch the top of the cliff. In the end, though missing its mark, the weapon had dug into an errant jutting of the cliff's side some thirty feet down.

And so Belmorn looked up. Staring at rock and sky, wondering if he had the strength left to hang for much longer. Then in that darkening sea of pink and violet, a shadow appeared. A shadow that looked a hell of a lot like the silhouette of a man.

"Belmorn?!"

The voice sounded distant, but it rang with elation.

"Kro?" This exploded past the hanging man's lips. "How? I thought..." Just then his grip slipped an inch down the axe handle. "Tell me you have a rope!"

"A what?" Kro's voice sounded farther away than he looked.

"A rope, damn you!"

"Oh!" With that, the head disappeared.

Once again Belmorn was alone with his axe, his cliff, and certain death a thousand feet below. He had heard tales of daring men and women who were able to scale sections of the Karaggash Ridge with their bare hands. To a simple riverman, it had always seemed an improbable feat--a skillset which never seemed more practical than in this very moment.

He searched for a handhold, but the face of World's Edge was infuriatingly smooth. Clenching his teeth, Belmorn strained to pull himself up enough to place one hand on the flat top of the wooden handle. The small victory was a wave of hot relief in his shoulder. He searched the cliff with the toes of his boots, prodding and pressing for anything that might take a bit more burden away from his arm.

Nothing.

He looked up, hoping to see the return of his friend's face, but finding only cliff and sky. As he continued to hang, Belmorn wondered if his mind wasn't playing tricks on him. If he hadn't just yelled at an imaginary version of his companion, rather than the real thing.

His shoulder and arm trembled as much from cold as the continued effort of holding himself up, but he tried not to notice. Exhaling a puff of steam, Belmorn closed his eyes. He could almost see them again, his reasons for being.

Malia had been right. His impossible quest was indeed folly. He should never have left. Whether he survived the next two minutes or the next two years, the cure for the purple sickness lay a thousand feet below. The witch had gone to a violent, watery grave, and she had taken her special venom with her.

SLAP!!

The sound shot through the hanging man like a jolt of electricity. He opened his eyes, looked left. There, swaying in the breeze, was the frayed end of a rope.

Tenebrus Kro had his heels planted firmly and was pulling for all he was worth. Behind him, the silver mare stood, looking a bit confused. The rope was tied to a ring on the back of her saddle, but Kro was bearing his fair share. The man on the other end weighed far more than he had even guessed.

Still, they were making progress. Backward steps were being taken, slowly, carefully. Kro knew that if he slipped, it would mean all their deaths. If there had been more rope, he would have found something to anchor it to but... there hadn't been more rope.

After what felt like hours, a gloved hand appeared above the cliff, and then an axe.

"Come on, horse!" shouted Kro. "We're almost there! How about we both pull, eh?"

The silver mare turned with some degree of indifference, but a full-handed slap to the rump got her moving.

In one great heave the dark, damp, exhausted form of Rander Belmorn appeared and fell atop the cliff in a great, exhausted heap.

Releasing the rope, Kro ran to the man who had somehow become his friend. Placed a hand on his back. "Belmorn!"

"How... how did you find me?" The blackfoot was out of breath. He didn't look up.

"Tracks. In the snow. Also, she was still bleeding all over the place." After receiving no response, Kro took a deep inhalation and slowly let it out. He looked at Skáldi's breath. He had only seen it twice before, once as a boy and again with his little Lishka on her sixth birthday.

"Belmorn," Kro's voice was small. "Where is she?"

"See for yourself," said Belmorn, pointing at the steam.

Kro approached the cliff's edge. He peered over, through and around the steam. Before, his vision had stopped at the man hanging some thirty feet down. Now though, he saw the rest.

A thousand feet below--where the ocean lapped at the feet of World's Edge, there lay a spindly, broken thing. Rocks similar to the giant's teeth of the Low Veld cradled the lifeless body of a monster whose mark had been seared into the fabric of the region for so long. Her head lolled, locked in an endless, soundless scream. From such a distance, Kro couldn't see the fangs, but he knew they were there.

"This isn't over, Belmorn." Kro looked at his friend and then over the cliff again. "We can get more rope in Jayce. I think we can scale this--go down and bring back her head--" The alchemist stopped talking. His eyes widened as a wave dislodged the broken monster from the rocks and swallowed it completely.

After seven long years, his heart's desire was fulfilled and all he could feel was despair.

Belmorn stood, dusted himself off, and turned to look at his friend.

"You know," he said at last. "I've been pulling monsters out of the water for so many years, more than I can remember." He shrugged. "It was about time I gave one back."

"But..." Kro spoke softly. "Your boy."

"Rivka!" Belmorn's tone was sharp. "Does she live?"

It took a few seconds to process the question, but Kro gave a weak nod. "Yes. Miraculously, she appeared unhurt. If there are any gods left up there, I'd say one is keeping an eye on that kid. A hell of a thing, jumping from that balcony. That is the kind of seed that legends spring from."

"Yeah." Belmorn nodded, then fell silent. After a few long moments, he looked up again, blinked, and asked with a waver in his voice, "Kro?"

"Mmm?"

"Do I still have a horse?"

PART SIXTEEN
CIRCLE

16-1

Jayce was quiet, and it was still.

Cloaked in full night, the street would have been entirely silent had it not been for the girl. Rivka Pesch was doing the only thing she could for the enormous horse--sharing her warmth.

The adamandray was still breathing, but within its bulk coursed a strange venom. For some time Magnus had lay unmoving upon the cold street. His posture, his breathing, the steady rise and fall of his side, they all spoke of slumber. But Rivka knew better; the animal's eyes told a very different story. They were black and bulging with an unmistakable emotion.

Fear.

The girl had tried to close the horse's eyelids, but she could no more manage this than she could raise the animal to his feet. Alone and worried beyond measure that her other two friends might never come back, Rivka began to cry.

Through deep sobs, she stroked the horse's face. Then, leaning over, placed a kiss upon his cheek.

"It's okay," she said in the comforting tone of her mother. "We're going to be okay. Y-you were so b-brave tonight. And strong. N-no. Not strong, mighty. That's what you were. M-mighty. Just like Charon the Graveless." she sniffed. The shivering was getting out of hand. "I d-don't know if they make st-tatues of just horses. But they should." With a shaky breath, Rivka laid down her head, pressing a cheek to the animal's neck. "You know, if I was a st-tatue m-maker, I would make one of just you. Magnus the M-mighty. Witch-kicker. Bravest horse there ever w-was."

Her lips were closer to violet than red, but they held a faint smile. Very soon, she would have to take shelter in one of those buildings. Of course that would mean that Rivka was going to be alone. Truly and completely, all over again. Possibly forever.

More tears welled. She tried to fight them but lacked the strength. And so they flowed, tracing dark lines down her cheeks and disappearing into the striped coat of the adamandray, where brown and white mingled.

The town of Jayce was getting colder... but from inside, Rivka felt a warmth coming over her body. She wanted to keep looking--out there, past the buildings, down the street. In the direction where Kro had ridden off after Belmorn and the witch. More than anything she wanted to stay vigilant, to know the very first possible second that her friends were okay.

Perhaps... perhaps I can just rest my eyes for a minute. Maybe two. Yes, that would be all right. She could stay with Magnus the Mighty out in the street and close her eyes. The idea was insidious but more seductive than she could endure. Her body had no will to move, no strength. It needed this. To rest. To sleep. Just for a while.

The girl's mind registered sounds coming from behind. Shuffling footsteps. She remembered the captain. Perhaps, after so many months spent in squalor on the streets of Roon, he had finally taken pity on her.

Rivka's eyelids fluttered, then shut. With incredible effort, she opened them again, lifted her head, and turned in the opposite direction. The captain wasn't there. The street was filled, but not with men. Through her tears, the figures appeared blurry and indistinct, but she could make out their eyes. Tiny pinpricks of light.

They reminded her of stars.

The girl gasped and fell back upon the horse. Too weak and frozen to move again, she waited. One of the figures broke from the group and kneeled before her. The troll's eyes were tiny, sheltered beneath a prominent ridge of bone, but Rivka was not afraid. Aside from moonlight, there was true kindness in those eyes. Perhaps something like gratitude.

God, she wanted to keep looking, to say something. But then, in the inner darkness, the girl could feel a warmth that hadn't been there before. It came from everywhere, enveloping her like a blanket. Before unconsciousness took her, she felt the inexplicable notion of movement, of being lifted and cradled in unseen arms.

In that moment Rivka Pesch knew that she was far from alone.

16-2

Bror peered down at the human child. He was pleased to see that she still lived. With care, he cinched up the pelt she wore for a cloak around her already wind-bitten face.

The Pershten chief looked back at his people. He had tried to keep them safe for so long—only to lead them right back to the serpent's nest. It was what they had wanted. Every Pershten, young and old, had insisted upon it, for they had come to understand a simple truth. Whether Bror liked it or not, the time for hiding was over.

"Just stay down. Get back under those pelts and whatever happens, keep your small ones quiet!"

He could still hear the frantic words of Tenebrous Kro. The last he had managed before riding off with the other man and the child.

When the alchemist and his companions had raced out of the hollow place, the Pershten knew well what was about to happen. The hated beast was coming and she was coming fast. She had caused so many of their kind to disappear and had chased the rest from their mountain, from the mines and heated springs that had been theirs since time began.

Lacking the strength to fight or legs fit for racing, Bror did exactly as Kro had bidden. Ordering his people back under their pelts—to lie as flat and as still as the ground itself. The tactic, aided in part by the beast's rage, had worked perfectly. After tearing a new entrance in the bramble wall, the witchwyrm had stormed past the nearly two dozen trolls without a glance. Her slitted eyes had been fixed solely in the direction of the noises that called to her.

Soon, amidst horn blasts, there came the sounds of battle and of screams. A loud BANG had emboldened the Pershten chief into action. The alchemist had his sympathies, but Bror's people were peaceful. They were miners and shepherds and the catchers of blind fish, nowhere near equipped for joining the clash of men and monster. But they had to move--to once again flee from the snake-headed beast that would likely be back through this same break in the thorns.

Bror's mind had raced knowing damned well that there was nowhere left to go. Even if the beast hadn't blocked their way south, the world at large was not for them.

He had tried to convince the Chieftain of the cliffrook tribe of this very thing, but Schtell had led her people down that road many months before, hoping to live in the woods, where they might subsist on the noisy black birds that lived there. As far as was known, the beast had never left the High Veld, but there was another thing to consider.

Man had tried too hard for too long to convince himself that Bror's kind should be feared. That they were base, unnatural things who lurked under bridges or came at night to snatch swaddled babes from where they slept. Out there, trolls they had been labeled and trolls they would always be.

Their only chance was to hide. If not in their mountain then somewhere else. But there was nowhere else.

"Bror," came a voice in a tongue no human would have been able to discern. "The animal has been bitten. The beast's poisons are inside."

Bror regarded the adamandray. Then he looked over at the unconscious body of Captain Galttauer, which three more Pershten were inspecting. The man was riddled with holes and leaking a fair amount of blood.

"The Roon man?" Bror's voice was low and even.

"Almost gone," said one of the Pershten males, placing a very long sword on the ground, parallel to the man's body. The blade was covered in frozen blood. "There is another. There. And also there."

Bror's eyes moved from headless body to bodiless head.

"This was not the wyrm's doing." The other male continued. "Look there, the blood on the Roon man's sword. He did this. But why? Why would these men come all this way to fight each other instead of her?"

Bror frowned, causing the others to take on a sheepish posture.

"Because they are men."

Another nodded, stepped forward. "Bror, we did what we could for the wounds, but there is much damage inside. Schratmoss will not be enough."

Bristling, Bror shifted his focus from the man to the horse and then to the sleeping girl, still in his arms.

"Tonight we have more tools than schratmoss," he said in a firm voice. "Here... Gretch." Bror faced one of the gathered females. "Take the girl. There must be a bed in one of these dwellings." He pointed with his eyes at the nearby buildings. "Please find it."

The Pershten woman nodded, accepting the girl like a mother would her own child. Without a word, she headed off to the nearest structure. Bror kneeled at the horse. He peered down into its bulging, horrified eye and whispered softly, "Your fight is done. Now it is time to sleep."

The other Pershten nodded. They all placed open palms on various places of the horse's hide. Slumber came quickly and the animal was no longer afraid.

"Godnatt, brave one." Bror leaned in to inspect the puncture wounds in the animal's neck. Each was barely a pinprick. Far too small to have ever permitted such enormous fangs as those of the Witch.

Instead of breaking down flesh, witch venom restored it. The unlikely effect ensured that the victim remained fresh and healthy, allowing the beast to wipe out populations while keeping her cupboard stocked with fresh meat. Most bite victims were also hit by the second attack--the sting that caused them to vanish, to be whisked from this plain to wherever witches went. But sometimes an individual was left behind, bitten but un-stung, overlooked as the witchwyrm continued her gluttonous harvest.

If those bitten were reached by survivors, secreted away to lie paralyzed for many days, they awoke feeling invigorated. Experiencing something like renewed youth--their bodies healed from wounds both outside and in.

Bror frowned, cursing in his native speech. "Her poisons are working fast. These are nearly healed."

Letting the air out of his lungs, he pressed his mouth to the first puncture mark. The venom tasted like needle pricks. It froze and tingled until his tongue went numb. Again and again his cheeks caved, but most of the substance had been absorbed into the horse's bloodstream. The Pershten Chief lifted his head and spit carefully into a clump of a mossy substance, plucked from his own shoulder.

The others looked on as he lowered his head to repeat the procedure. When he was finished, Bror's lips curled into a grimace. Drawing a long forearm across his mouth, he looked woefully unimpressed at the venomous moss. In all, only a few drops had been removed from each wound... but perhaps...

"Bror?" asked the voice of a child.

The Pershten chief turned and looked down at the small one. "What is it, Nafti?"

"What are you doing?"

"What I can to save this man's life."

"But, these men... Didn't they do this to each other?"

"Yes but they cannot help it. Such is their nature."

"Then why save them?"

Bror took a deep breath. Then he placed a hand on the child's shoulder and simply smiled.

16 - 3

The trek back from the edge felt endless.

Kro had twice offered to share the use of his mount, but Belmorn had been cut from a stubborn cloth. His was a proud people who existed in perfect symbiosis with exactly two things--the river which sustained them and the gigantic horses which bore them into it.

Rander Belmorn was going the distance on foot. A gust of wind licked past as the tall man spoke. "You were wrong, you know."

Kro peered down, past his oxblood scarf. "Oh?" His voice was ragged. "About which part?"

"You said every journey was a circle. That no matter how far we go, we always end at the beginning. But that's shit. This--all of this--has been for nothing. I can never go back. Not now."

"I'd say that depends."

"On what?" Belmorn's tone was passing annoyed and circling angry.

"On which home you were planning to get back to. Seems to me there's more than one. That one you knew, with your pretty life that was? Healthy, happy family and little house? All your worries aimed at that damned black trickle? Well, that home, my friend, you were never going back to. They say time marches, but it's only in one direction." Kro took a deep breath and slowly let it out. "There's another one. A new home, right where the old one used to be. It's waiting for you."

Belmorn scoffed, shaking his head. He spoke with a measure of disdain. "Waiting for what?"

"For you to stop running away." The statement held an unintentional edge that Kro did not redact.

Rander Belmorn glared up at the man in the saddle, but he did not know what to say.

"I'm sorry we lost the teeth, Belmorn. And I'm sorry for your boy." Kro sighed, straightening his gaze. "But the witchwyrm is finally gone. Finally dead. Sinking into oblivion, and I am sure as hell not sorry for that."

After a while, Belmorn responded to this with a single nod. And that was enough.

In the distance, rectangular shadows became visible in the moonlight. The insignificant spec of a mining town should have been a welcome site, yet for the men who beheld it, there was no relief.

Kro drew a sharp breath, his hand shooting to the place where the masked rider had pinned an exploding cross. Though much of the man's face was hidden, Belmorn could see real pain in his eyes. It was not an easy sight to behold. It forced the riverman to remember that he was not the only one in pain.

"You know..." he started in a low voice. "You should see a doctor."

Amidst the discomfort, Kro managed to look genuinely surprised. "Right," he hissed through clenched teeth. "I'll look one up, next time I'm in Britilpor."

Belmorn looked up. He didn't smile, but he wasn't frowning either. "Who was that man?" he asked gingerly. "The one with the mask, and the scars."

"Morgrig's butcher?" Kro lowered his hand from his collarbone. "Don't recall a name... but..." Trembling fingers mimicked the curve of his hidden face. "I had this coming. " Kro's eyes grew moist. "As a boy, all I wanted to do was get as far as I could from this damned frozen waste. To see the rest of the world, maybe uncover a secret or two." Kro smiled then, sadly. "It was out there I learned about the craft of alchemy and about the code. Three words: unearth, unveil, and know. They were my map, even after I decided searching for eternal life at the bottom of a crucible wasn't for me. But no matter how long I was gone, no matter how far I went, this damn place always called me back. Every time." He turned. "Make no mistake, my wagon bore the symbol it did for a reason."

Belmorn could picture it. The serpent, eating its own tail, rendered in black. "The Ouroboros. Because all journeys end at the beginning," he said.

Kro nodded. "Like it or not, Belmorn, we all go back by pushing forward. Sometimes it's just hard to see. When too many steps are taken, we risk forgetting where we've been." He grew quiet for a moment, then said, "Babatunde. I had forgotten that name. Had gotten so used to thinking of what was left as just another what. Instead of a who."

"Babatunde." Belmorn looked confused. "The scarred man's name?"

"His son's." Kro shook his head. "The boy who went up like so much kindling--taking his mother and baby sister with him. I had heard the story in whispers and did what I always did. I located his grave, and I unearthed... unveiled." The man's voice quivered with emotion. "Just another curiosity to poke and prod. One more ingredient for my wagon--"

"An *ingredient*?" Belmorn snapped. The ends of his haresh changed direction with a sudden gust. "That man... Kro, you are telling me that you stole the remains of his dead son?"

Kro said nothing to this as the slow clops of his silver mare filled the silence. Finally, he continued, but as if the previous question had gone unheard.

"In that shallow grave there wasn't much left--a few blackened finger bones, some baby teeth. Little enough to keep in a single jar, and eventually a vial. Just another tool in my stock I employed to save my own sorry ass over the years. Yours too. Remember the night I broke you from that cell? When we were escaping, when I left you to make a distraction, did you imagine I was setting Roon on fire?" Kro barked a scornful, mirthless laugh. "The boy's bones were elemental things. They could create smoke in incredible quantities with the slightest kiss of an open flame." Kro stopped as his hand once again moved to his collarbone. "But those bones were a boy, once. Just a little boy. Cursed by some accident of birth. A cruel trick of whatever gods leer over that distant land. He was just a boy, Belmorn. And he had a name."

"Babatunde," whispered Belmorn with terrible understanding.

"Babatunde!" Kro bellowed the name, shaking in his saddle. After that, for some time... the tundra was silent. It was a long while before either man spoke again.

"Rinh." said Belmorn, his mouth turned in a scowl of disgust. "How do you live with yourself?"

"Oh?" asked the rider in a low drawl. "To tell you the truth, living was never the plan. You see, I was going to join them. My girls. They're waiting for me. You see?" Kro paused before going on "For seven years, there was only one true end I could imagine. Only one way to close the circle. I needed to return, not just here, but to them. To go where they had gone. But first I had to find a way to do what the people of old dead Hispidia never could. To answer the last question, the only question. How do you kill a witch?" Kro laughed, wincing in pain. "Imagine my shock in discovering that answer wasn't some elusive combination of whats. But rather a who." Another mirthless chuckle escaped the rider's gullet. "Maybe if Hispidia had a blackfoot, its history would be different, eh?"

Belmorn grunted. He did not appear amused. "So that's it then?" he growled. "You were going to kill yourself?"

"No. I was going to kill that fucking hag and use her tail and teeth to enter into that other place. Then I was going to find them, in whatever state. Even if it took a hundred years to sift through the bones."

Belmorn's feet moved on their own. His mind reeled, swirling with conflicting emotions for the man by his side, and for himself. "So do it then," he said with a frankness that surprised even him. "The tail barb didn't go over that cliff. You cut it off. That was her key, right? Her only way into the Without? You want to pick through bones until you die, there's nothing stopping you."

"If only I could." Kro turned, locking eyes with the blackfoot. "The barb is in Jayce, that's true." His fatigue sounded as if it went deeper than flesh alone. "But think back, Belmorn. Morgrig's men, when they were made to vanish, did you see the witchwyrm stick them with her stinger alone? Even once?"

Belmorn considered this. Summoning horrific images and forcing them to replay in his mind. It was always the same. Head first, then tail. Teeth, then stinger.

"What I said before was true. The tail is the key... but what is a key without a lock?" Kro's head tilted into a subtle angle. "Think of it like touching a lit torch to a bit of black powder. The two must meet if the desired reaction is to occur."

"Tail and teeth," Belmorn sounded distant, deflated. "The witch--she had two poisons, and you needed them both."

Tenebrus Kro looked down, said nothing. Though most of his face was obscured by cloth, the man's eyes held a resigned smile.

16-4

No longer in open country, Rander Belmorn and Tenebrus Kro moved over the cobbled rock of a street. The town of Jayce had returned with no grand announcement. Quietly creeping up before surrounding the two men, who hardly took notice.

Belmorn's mind dwelled on the face of his wife, Not as he last saw her--contorted with pain and anger as he'd rebuffed her argument and walked out the door--but as the young woman she had been. That girl had soft, copper skin and hair the color of midnight--stars and all. Malia Greyrain, she had been then. Even at fifteen, the girl had possessed a staggering beauty and quiet wit, sharp as any knife. And there had been stars in her hair. At least, that's what a seventeen year old Rander Belmorn had thought. The flowers she wore were so small, so perfectly white--even now they caused his heart to lurch.

He had made that girl a promise some years after, on their wedding day, to love and to honor. The first had come as effortlessly as the incessant thrums in his chest. But on that dreaded day, now five months gone--when he chose to leave his family in their darkest hour--Rander Belmorn had broken the second half of that sacred oath.

His boy, Sashander was dead. Or would be soon enough. The question that dogged Belmorn now was... had he been there, would it have made any difference?

Would it?

It was a question he had avoided for many nights, many weeks.

"Belmorn." The voice was so unexpected, so soft, it jarred the blackfoot to his core.

Feeling like he had been doused with a bucket of ice water, the blackfoot looked around.

There were people in the street. Dozens of them. Some were kneeling, others stood erect, but all seemed to be regarding something on the ground. A mass or mound--something big and dark. At first, they didn't seem to notice the two men coming down the road. Then heads turned and eyes appeared to ignite in pairs. To the men who approached, they looked like candle flies.

No, thought Belmorn. *Stars. They look like stars.*

His mind galloped back to another, more recent memory. His mouth was throbbing. His lip had been split, cleaved by the hungry peck of a timber crow. He had felt the fever coming, even then. The glimpse had been brief: lights between the trees, all in pairs.

And then he had woken up. Night was suddenly morning again. The fever he'd expected was nowhere to be found and his lip was inexplicably whole. Mended by unseen hands. The mystery had gnawed at the time, but so much had happened he had almost forgotten.

"Belmorn," the voice of Tenebrus Kro came again.

"I see them," the blackfoot's voice was a ragged thing.

As he gazed into the stars that weren't, he knew that they were eyes. Just not the eyes of men.

PART SEVENTEEN
LEGEND

17-1

"Rander."

The word drifted in on a lazy breeze.

"Rander."

Louder the second time, it came with a jarring sensation, as if the whole world were quaking.

The man's eyes snapped open. There had been dreams but holding onto them was like grasping at fog. He stared up at a wooden ceiling, and someone was shaking him.

"Rander!" The voice caused him to take a sharp breath. Belmorn threw aside the pelt which had been laid on top of him and sat up. Suddenly, he felt very cold. Kneeling beside him was the girl. Rivka Pesch. She was wearing various layers including a dark blue skirt that featured a line of small embroidered goats along the bottom. Grey fur topped her shoulders and boots and was lining the deep blue hood that hung against her back.

Despite looking very pale, the girl was smiling. She had been cleaned up and for the first time, Belmorn could see that her skin was far lighter than his own. The dirt of living on the cobbles had obscured many things including a field of soft freckles across the bridge of her nose. Most shocking of all though was Rivka's hair. What he had taken for brown was a stark, silvery blonde.

"I knew it!" she said in a reassuring tone, forgetting or ignoring that she was the child. "I could tell you were waking up! How do you feel?"

"Feel? I..." Belmorn began to answer, and then stopped. It was a simple question. His anxious mind raced to fill in the time between his last waking moment and this... but something was wrong. There was only then and now.

He lurched forward, gasped, shooting a hand to his ribcage.

The girl leaned closer, looking, in Belmorn's opinion, utterly unconcerned. She lifted his hand away and inspected the bandages that constricted his midsection.

It was then Belmorn realized something else. "Rivka?" he asked nervously. "Where are my clothes?"

"Over there," said the girl of twelve, with a wave of one hand. "They had to see if you were hurt. You're shirt and coat and everything is right over there." she gestured toward a chair where the garments in question had indeed been laid.

"They?" Belmorn drew the pelt back over his chest. "Who's they?"

"You don't remember?"

Belmorn shook his head.

"The Pershten! We were wrong! The witch didn't get them! They came back and have been taking care of us."

Belmorn looked on but said nothing.

"One of them, Gretch--she's really nice--she found us these beds!" The girl's face was practically beaming. "To tell you the truth, I don't remember falling asleep or much before I woke up this morning."

"Morning?!" Belmorn looked for a window, but the small room did not have one.

"Yeah. Gretch said there's usually lost time. You know that sleep-thing they do with their hands? Well, she said they had to try extra hard to get you to go down last night. I guess you lost more time than I did." The girl smirked. "What's the last thing you remember?"

"I..." Belmorn reeled. His mind fighting to reclaim what was missing. "The witch," he said at last. "I remember... riding it. Riding it... right over the edge.

"The edge of the cliff?" Rivka's eyes were nearly the size of saucers. "How?!"

Belmorn started to remember. Riding, climbing, pounding in that knife as if it had been a harpoon and of course, what it felt like to be five fingers away from oblivion. He looked to the girl and cleared his throat. Deciding to leave off the part about hanging off the edge of the world.

"Mostly dumb luck," he said. "but also... the witchwyrm wasn't thinking clearly. Not with that knife in her brain."

Rivka made a choking sound. Just once.

Belmorn smiled. Nodded. "That was an impressive thing you did. Not very smart, but impressive. I honestly don't know what you were thinking jumping off the balcony like that."

"I," The girl lowered her eyes. "Don't think I *was* thinking."

Hearing this Belmorn might have chuckled if not for his aching ribs.

"I mean," Rivka seemed to be searching for how to proceed. "It was like I skipped that part. Like my hands and feet already knew what to do. I know that sounds stupid."

Belmorn smiled. "Not at all." Placing a finger beneath her chin, he lifted her face. "In fact, to an old blackfoot, what you just said makes a lot of sense."

The girl appeared moved in ways she lacked the years to voice. Then her face scrunched up in thought. "Kro calls you that sometimes. Blackfoot. Is that the name of your people? Are they the Blackfeet?"

"What? No." Belmorn mused at the sudden turn of subject. "Blackfoot isn't our tribe. It's just a word some use to describe those who do what I do." He could see by the girl's expression, this wasn't helping.

"You're... a fisherman, right?"

"A fisherman?" Belmorn barely restrained rolling his eyes. "No, girl. Fisherman stalk minnows with worms and string, I--"

"You pull stuff out of the water to eat, right?"

"Well, yeah, but--"

"Fisherman." The girl sounded very certain. She even folded her arms.

Belmorn responded in a fluster. "No, no. It's very different. Anyway, you are completely missing the point. The water--the river--is thick with tiny plant life. Like bits of floating moss." Feeling like he had regained control of the conversation, Belmorn's tone shifted to that of a campfire storyteller. "So thick, in fact, you can't see anything, can't know what's swimming right beside, just beneath the surface. On the backs of our horses we wade out until the rushing water reaches halfway up to our knees." Belmorn checked the girl's expression before going on. "We do this barefooted, you see. And as the river moves over our skin and between our toes, we listen to it--communicate with it. After many hours, our exposed skin darkens with the moss. Black feet. Blackfoot. Get it?"

"I get it," the girl whispered, her eyes wide with expectation. "Do they stay that way? Black?"

"Rivka." Belmorn raised an eyebrow. "We do bathe where I'm from."

The girl frowned, unconvinced. Then she glared suspiciously at the blankets over Belmorn's feet.

"Rivka." Said the man from Grael.

"What?"

"Where is Kro?"

"Outside, I think. He left a while ago. Before you started to stir. He assumed I was sleeping, but I heard him ask where Bror was, and then he left."

"Huh." said Belmorn. "And what about Galttauer?"

The girl flinched at the name, then slowly shook her head. "I don't know. I wanted to ask, but..."

"It's okay." Belmorn started to rise from bed, then stopped. "Rivka."

"Yeah?"

"Could you wait out in the hall? For a minute?"

"What?!" she vigorously shook her head. "No! I don't want to go out there alone!"

Belmorn pinched the bridge of his nose. "Alright. Then I'll need you to turn around? Please?"

Rivka frowned, raised an eyebrow. "Is this because you don't want me to see your feet?"

Belmorn drew in a long breath, and then let it out through his nostrils. The air was cold and he had every reason to feel it. The hollow pit in his chest screamed and cursed, condemning him for his myriad shortcomings, but mostly for failing his son.

And yet...

"Yes," he said with a sigh. "It's because of my dirty, black feet. Now turn around before the sight of them scars you for life."

17-2

Followed by the girl, Belmorn stepped out into a narrow hallway. His highwayman's coat hung nearly to the floor. Aside from this he wore the pelt of a black bear, the green head scarf Rivka had picked out for him only the day before, and a look of consternation.

"What is this place?" He looked from one end of the hallway to the other.

"I think the miners used to come here if they got hurt," answered the girl. "When I was little, Jayce had a real doctor--one who didn't wear a mask. I think this was where he helped people."

Belmorn narrowed his eyes, looking to the next door down. As he stepped, it creaked slowly open until one of the Pershten appeared. Clearly one of the females, she was dressed in the same shabby fur the others had been--goat pelts, he now reasoned.

Gently, she closed the door behind her, but not before Belmorn caught a fleeting glance of someone lying in bed. Someone surrounded by many more trolls. The captain, he knew at once.

Rivka threw her arms around the woman, who accepted the gesture with some hesitation.

"Gotmorn, chylde." The Pershten woman spoke in a thick accent as her blue eyes nervously regarded the man. "Feeling better?"

"A lot. Yes." Rivka inclined her head, looking up past two heavy, moss-covered breasts. With a smile, she turned. "Rander, this is Gretch. She is the one I told you about. The one who has been taking care of us."

Belmorn's expression softened. "You have my thanks, lady."

The troll shook her head. "Chylde is over kind. Many Pershten gave care." her voice was low and thick with emotion. "But... your thanks are not needed, Witch Rider. We Pershten owe you more than can ever be repaid. Not with hands nor silver."

For a moment, Belmorn wasn't sure how to respond. Then, he managed a low... "Okay."

The Pershten woman stepped forward and placed a hand on his cheek. Belmorn half expected for everything to go black again. Instead, her striking eyes welled up with tears. He could see many lines on her face, framing certain features and crossing others in striking perpendiculars. Calling them wrinkles would be inaccurate. The lines looked like cracks in wood, fissures in stone. As he thought this, Belmorn knew that the woman was very old--not in the way men age, but by a scale used by trees, mountains.

"This..." Gretch's hand slid down to inspect Belmorn's lower lip. "This is Pershten work."

"It... it is?"

"Schtell's group happened upon you in the woods, yes?"

"I... don't know." Belmorn's voice was a wispy thing. "I can't remember what happened that night."

"Ah. They made you sleep." Gretch said this with a firm nod. "It is as I said. Schtell found you and gave aid. It is our nature, Witch Rider. At our core, my people are healers. Shepherds, miners, and fishers, but healers first. It is fortunate thing, you accept our talents so well." she laughed a little as Belmorn pulled his face away from her hand.

Rivka shifted in place, absently reaching for the still tender spot below her collar bone that had healed with an unnatural quickness.

Belmorn pushed his tongue into the lump where the two halves of his lower lip now met. He remembered the sharp taste of moss in his mouth. And the fear. "I... thought fever would take me for sure. I could feel it coming, starting to simmer." He spoke quietly with wide eyes. "When I arrived in Roon, the first thing I asked after was an apothecary, but... everything went sideways before I could get to one." He looked down. "The fever never took hold. Though I didn't understand why, or who, had come to stitch my lip shut. Or why I wouldn't have woken up while it was happening."

Belmorn stopped then--realizing something. That the night in the hollow had not been the first time he had been put to sleep by troll hands.

After patting the man's cheek again, Gretch's large hand slid to Belmorn's side, causing him to draw a quick thin breath through clenched teeth.

"Oh," said Gretch, regretfully. "This hurt?"

"Hurt?!" The man's eyes watered from the pain, but he forced his breathing to normalize. "Not much. No."

"Ah. Good thing bending bones do not sometimes break." she pointed to where the dressings were beneath the long black coat. "Keep this tight and still. This helps. Sleep too. No better medicine on earth or below."

"Somehow," The man raised an eyebrow. "I had a feeling you were going to say that." Belmorn smiled a bit more, allowing his edge to soften. But when he reached for the doorknob, Gretch stopped him.

"Gretch," he said. "I have to get in this room. I need to check on my friend."

The troll woman nodded. "The Roon man... we prepare him."

"Prepare him? What do you mean?"

"He is gone, Witch Rider. We must return what is left to his people."

Belmorn's face fell. When his voice returned, it was devoid of emotion. "Dammit, Galttauer."

With a solemn nod, Gretch spoke very softly. "His wounds were... too big."

Belmorn placed a hand on the Pershten's shoulder. Her lined face was rigid, but the sorrow in her eyes was unmistakable. "Tut mir leid. I am sorry."

"It's okay." Belmorn repeated the words, feeling immediately feeble. "Thank you."

"As for the other man. The Krähe." Gretch looked as if displeased that the name was on her tongue. "That one is outside." she pointed down the hallway, to a large exterior door. "Go, Witch Rider, and carry Pershten thanks with you."

The troll woman spared a final smile for Rivka before backing into the room she had come from and shutting the door. Again, Belmorn caught a glimpse of many Pershten around a bed, their attention solely on its pale-haired occupant.

Outside the sun was high and bright. It was a few moments before the eyes of the two adjusted.

More Pershten filled the street. Some were sitting on posts or wooden crates and standing in small groups. Still others explored the buildings across the street, inspecting doors and windows and whatever else Jayce had to offer.

"Belmorn!" Kro waved from where he stood next to a pair of familiar horses. One of which made Belmorn's heart shoot into his throat.

The stallion shook its head, causing the bridle to whip and jingle. Magnus was an exotic sight in all lands save the Black River region, where once he had dropped unceremoniously to the ground--an ungainly foal, blinking in the midday sun.

Belmorn rushed down the stairs and attempted to cross the street, but found himself mobbed. Having heard the man's name, the Pershten appeared from all sides. All grey and hairless and wearing grins.

"Witch Rider!" they shouted. "Witch Rider! Witch Rider!"

Belmorn's gaze darted from one approaching group to another. The trolls rushed to him like the surface of a lake moving to fill the space where a rock has been thrown. In waves, they reached him. Their faces beaming with adoration as they pawed at his shoulders--all with a single chant upon their lips.

"Witch Rider! Witch Rider! Witch Rider!"

"That's enough!" ordered Bror. "Back now! Give space!"

An immediate hush fell upon the crowd as every Pershten stopped where they were. Belmorn's heart pounded, sending adrenaline through every vein. His arms felt hard and ready, triggered by the crowd's reaction as if it had been the start of some new battle. This was ludicrous he knew, but then, Rander Belmorn was a simple man. He had most definitely never been worshiped before.

His gaze turned to Rivka, who was bracing herself against his leg. As she looked up, laughter bubbled up and out of her, warming the man. The sensation was fleeting, but he was glad for it.

17 - 3

"Belmorn!"

The crowd parted to permit two individuals--their Chieftain and Tenebrus Kro.

The alchemist wore a furry cloak of earthen hues, matching those of the Pershten. The pelt possessed no hood but hung long, nearly touching the ground. His black hair, long and unkempt, billowed in the passing breeze.

"Kro." Belmorn felt relief at the sight of the man. The upper portion of his face was all that showed over the scarf. The cloth looked much closer to red in the light of day, though dark enough to hide the fleshy ruins beneath.

After so much hardship, both men stood in failure. And yet, the faces around them held only joy and adoration. The Pershten were free to return home, back to Mount Einder. They could tend their goats and their underground lake of ugly, eyeless fish. That was good, Belmorn knew. But was it enough?

"It is good to see you," the blackfoot spoke the words awkwardly, wishing he had come up with something better.

"What's left of me, you mean." Kro stepped forward and slapped a hand on the taller man's shoulder. "Blue hell, you need to lighten up, riverman."

"Yeah. I... yeah." The ghost of a smile twitched at Belmorn's lips. "You sound like my wife."

Kro chuckled and bowed his head. "I'll take that as a high compliment." He might have said something more, but the eyes of the blackfoot looked beyond him.

The Pershten chief was leading the adamandray. Magnus whickered and pulled free to greet his oldest friend.

"Whoa there, Old Man!" Belmorn reached out with a high heart and a smile on his lips. He patted the animal's cheek and let him nuzzle his face. "How is this possible? The witch--I saw it happen! Saw what she did to you." He slid his hand up and down the neck expecting gaping wounds, but finding only what looked like, but could not possibly be very old scars.

Magnus stretched his neck out and demanded scratches as if he only had bug bites.

"Your animal is strong. He has recovered well," said Bror. "The wyrm's kiss is a curious thing, no? It's power to heal and to mend flesh is impressive. Because the horse is so big, we were able to take out some venom. Otherwise, this Old Man here would sleep for another day or two." Patting the mossy substance on his own shoulder, Bror smiled before continuing. "He has been fed, watered, and is well enough to ride. We have retrieved and packed your weapons, filled your bags with food and drink. Enough for many days. But this, all of this..." The troll hung his head. "Is a poor reward."

"No." Belmorn smiled, patting Magnus on the shoulder. "It is not." He reached out a hand.

For a moment, Bror looked at the limb like he didn't know what to do. Then he mirrored the gesture, tentatively shaking the man's hand.

"Bror," said Belmorn. "You have done much. You and your people. More than I could--" The man's voice faltered. He turned from one side to the other, scanning the sea of expectant faces. They might never remember the name of Rander Belmorn over another moniker.

"Witch Rider," said a small voice.

Surprised, Belmorn saw a Pershten child clinging to its mother's leg. Boy or girl he couldn't tell, though it appeared to be no older than four or five. He lowered himself to a knee, so that he was at a height with the child.

"Yes?"

"You look sad."

Belmorn looked up to the mother's face but found no concern there. He inhaled deeply, held his breath. "I do?"

"Ja."

"Oh... I was just thinking about my boy. About how much I want to see him again."

"But," asked the child, "why does this make you sad?"

"Oh... because," Belmorn paused, considering how to answer. "I'm going home now, but by the time I arrive, I don't know if he will still be there."

The troll child stepped forward but kept one hand on its mother's thigh. "Does he have to leave home?"

Belmorn smiled. "I hoped not. That's why I came here. I was trying to find a way to make him stay." He looked at Kro, and though there was no scorn in his gaze, the alchemist turned away.

"Did you?" asked the child. "Find a way?"

Another smile formed on Belmorn's lips. This one forced out a tear. The tiny bead fell, tracing the hard lines of his cheek before disappearing into the coarse hair of his beard. "I did. The only way. I... just couldn't hold onto it."

"Oh." The child broke from its mother to walk within an arm's length of the man. "I hate when I lose things."

Before dropping the last of his smile, Belmorn winked. "I think we all do, kid."

"Well, you could stay here with us. Herr Krähe said he would stay to... help us get back on our feet." The child leaned forward to whisper, "Strange thing to say. All of us can stand just fine."

Belmorn stared in awe at the child. Boy or girl, it was far too thin-- surely from who knew how many years spent moving, hiding, surviving. Home. Could this young one possibly remember what that meant?

For that matter, could an old blackfoot?

"I'm sorry," Belmorn rose, turning for his horse. "I have been away long enough. I don't know if my Sasha will still be there, but I have to try. I have been five months away, but the return will be faster. Perhaps Rinh will grant me this one thing at least. After all, the purple sickness travels slowly."

The young Pershten was looking up with eyes full of questions, but also empathy.

"Witch Rider?" The cautious question came from a Pershten woman with a tawny shawl wrapped around her head and neck, the mother of the child he had been talking to. "Your boy... He is very sick?"

Belmorn sighed. "Yes."

"Oh, this is not good." her accent was thicker than the rest. "So sorry.

So sorry to hear." The mother approached the man and his horse. "Please. This sickness... does it..." Unable to find the right words, the woman raised her wrist. Touched it to her forehead. "Is hot? Here?"

Belmorn turned. "A fever? No. This is not that kind of sickness."

"Ja." The mother's shoulders fell. "Schratmoss is good medicine." she brushed some of the mossy substance growing on the back of her arm. "Good for heat, for fever. And good for..." she gestured to the scar on the man's lip, the two halves which had been mysteriously made whole.

"Good, yes." Kro stepped in. "But not without its limits."

"Herr Krähe must know of another." It was the child speaking again. "He is wise. All Pershten know."

Kro and Belmorn exchanged a world-weary glance.

"Wise?" Kro laughed softly in his throat. "Knowledgeable and wise aren't the same thing, I'm afraid." He looked down at the confused child, and with a pat, sent it into its mother's arms. Kro's eyes were glazing over. When his voice came again, it trembled. "We almost had it though. In this very street. All I needed was a few drops."

Kro started as a jolt shot through him. He realized there was a hand on his shoulder.

"Excuse." Arms wrapped around her young one, the mother spoke again. "Drops? What few drops?" her face lit up. Releasing her child, the Pershten woman lurched forward, closing the gap between her and Belmorn. She was pointing to her teeth. "The--? The--? Vergiften!" she blurted out in frustrated excitement. "Few drops? Is medicine for your boy?!"

"The witch's venom. Yes," answered Belmorn, raising one eyebrow. "But... it's gone now."

"No! Not gone!" she backed away, not taking her burning gaze off of Belmorn. "Drops! Drops!" she grabbed the arm of Bror and spoke in their language to him.

"My friends." Bror spoke with an urgency. "This sickness that grips your boy, can it truly be cured by the wyrm's bite?"

"Yes," said Kro. "I've done it before. When prepared properly, a few drops can cure almost anything--even the purple sickness. Absolutely. Why? What are you getting at?"

"This..." said Bror to Belmorn. "Last night you returned... saw us with your Old Man. You misunderstood, felt we were doing harm. We tried to explain, but your blood was too high. So, again... we put you to sleep."

"Bror." Belmorn tried to recall the moments in question, but they were blurry. "What did I misunderstand? What were you doing?"

"Trying to save the Roon man." Bror said this with regret. "His wounds were too severe for our schratmoss, but I knew that there was another way. A better medicine."

"The witch venom." Belmorn nodded despondently. "Right. Unfortunately I just rode all of that over a cliff."

"Not... all." Bror waved over a younger Pershten male. Belmorn and Kro exchanged desperate glances as the other troll handed a burlap parcel over to his chieftain. With trembling hands, Bror opened it to reveal what looked like a small amount of icy moss--the same sort growing on the backs and shoulders of all his kind.

Belmorn looked confused. "I don't understand. I thought you just said..."

"The schratmoss is not the point, Witch Rider." Bror pushed the bundle closer. "What lies inside, I drew out of your horse with my own lips. What I hoped would save the Roon man."

"Venom." Kro's voice came muffled from behind the scarf, but hit like a clap of thunder.

Bror nodded. "There wasn't much. A few drops. But maybe... I hoped, enough." He looked Kro right in the eye. "But... by the time I finished, the other man was already gone."

Belmorn accepted the frozen moss ball as if it were his own newborn son. There were tears in his eyes. "Kro?" Belmorn's voice was a thin hiss. "Will it work?"

Deeply, the alchemist inhaled. He took the bundle of troll moss into his hands and inspected it thoroughly before exhaling a visible cloud through the dark cloth that covered what was left of his face.

17 - 4

Leaving the question unanswered, Kro shouted at the trolls. "Quickly! I need a surface. There! That!" An extended finger indicated an old wooden barrel. "Turn it over! Put it right here. Here!" His voice demanded urgency.

Belmorn could only stand and watch as two of the Pershten rushed to comply. They raised the barrel, dumped out what looked like coal onto the snow-covered street, and then stood it at the feet of Tenebrus Kro.

The alchemist wasted no time getting to work. First, he spread out the moss into a thin layer. Then, after rifling through one of what Belmorn had come to understand were many unseen pockets, he produced two small metal objects. Each was about six inches in length with a slight hook at the end. Tools of an unfamiliar sort. With these as well as great care, Kro set about sifting through the schratmoss.

"There!" Kro's voice quaked with emotion as he used the metal tools to extract a sliver of milky, yellow ice. As the seconds ticked past, he painstakingly harvested a small pile of the stuff. "That's all of it."

"Rinh." Belmorn's heart pounded in his throat. "Will it be enough?"

Kro locked eyes with the man from Grael and gave a firm nod. "Plenty."

The knees of the blackfoot ached, trembling from exertion as much as the cold.

"One problem," Kro went on. "I can't very well hand you a pile of the stuff as it is, can I? Of course not, it will melt before you reach Britilpor. We'll need something glass. Something--wait!" In a mad frenzy, the alchemist began to pat his coat. "Ah!" One hand vanished into a pocket, reappearing with a small green glass bottle. Kro regarded the thing for a second or two, looking almost regretful. Then he bellowed loud enough for all to hear, "Nobody breathe."

In one swift movement, Kro removed the topper and turned the bottle upside down. All at once, the gorgon dust flowed from the bottle in a great dark cloud that quickly dispersed. Piece by piece, the alchemist dropped the frozen venom into the green bottle and replaced the topper, securing it with an extra turn for good measure. "If he can drink, give it to him in a broth, any broth. It's the venom that matters."

"And if he can't?"

"In that case," Kro didn't dare break eye contact. "You will need to get it inside him another way. With a very sharp knife, make two incisions. Here and here." He traced lines on either side of his throat, from jaw to just about the collar bone. "If he can't drink, the flesh there is going to be hard as wood but be careful. Knick the wrong spot and nothing will stop him from bleeding to death. Make sure to cut vertically and not across. Understand?"

"Yes." Belmorn nodded, taking the green bottle. He marveled at the shards inside before tucking it into a pocket in his long, highwayman's coat.

"Good." Kro nodded back as a smile entered his eyes. "Very good."

Belmorn thrust forward a hand of gratitude, which Kro gladly shook. Not hand to hand but grasping the forearm as was the custom in the black river region. The blackfoot turned to the Pershten chief. "If you knew what this means to me. To my family." Belmorn's voice faltered.

The Pershten Chief moved his head in a slow, solemn nod. "Of course we know. You saved us, Witch Rider. Purchased the life of one boy with that of thousands. Pershten, men, all the Veld knows, and if they don't, they will. My kind lives longer than yours. Hundreds of years, if the gods smile. And our memory is longer still. Believe me, Herr Belmorn, what you have done here will not be forgotten."

"You know..." Rivka's voice cut in. The girl was smiling. "You really should build a statue. A big one with Magnus and everything. Put it right on World's Edge, pointing one of those weird axes down at the water. Just in case that thing ever thinks about crawling back up."

A smile grew on the Pershten chief's stoney face. "A fine idea," he said before reaching out to cup the girl's cheek. "Tell me, child... will you help us in this work?"

The girl thought on this for a second, briefly regarding Belmorn as the green ends of his haresh were pulled by the wind to point south. The only way out of the Veld.

"I can't," she said at last. "I'm leaving with him."

Bror's head crooked to one side, forming a question.

All eyes turned to the Witch Rider. There was no surprise on his face, simply mild exhaustion. He looked down at the girl.

"Rivka." The name hung in the air for a moment. "The road to Grael is long, and I will need to take it quickly. Riding hard and sleeping little. It will not be easy."

"Can't remember a time when anything was." The girl's brow furled in thought. "You know, I've been thinking a lot about the inscription inside your headband. And about your wife."

"You have?"

"Yeah. You said she was funny."

Belmorn's heart lurched at the implied question. "Yeah well... she certainly thinks so. Though I may be sleeping in the stables for a few years."

The girl raised an eyebrow. "I don't know what that means."

"Nothing. It means nothing." He suppressed a chuckle. "But funny or not, my Malia is a good woman. And an even better..."

The word mother went unsaid, though all in earshot heard it clearly. The moment of nervous silence was broken by the sound of hooves on stone. Wearing a very solemn look, Kro was leading his stolen silver mare.

"Please," he said. "There is no reason to go so far on one horse. Take her."

"Really?" said Rivka, her voice brimming with disbelief.

"Of course." He nodded, rechecking the belts on the saddle. "Take her and treat her well. Maybe give her a name."

"Oh I will!" The girl shot forward and wrapped her arms around the man called Kro.

"What will you do?" Belmorn's voice was low, hidden almost completely by the wind. Kro passed his gaze over the Pershten and the buildings and the street that had not been so full in many years.

"Well, I think it's about time I grew up, for one," Kro answered with a thoughtful sigh. "When Galttauer's body is ready, I will return him to Roon. And with the help of Bror and his people, search the high veld for the bodies of his nine guardsmen. Hopefully some will still be alive. I'll tell the people of Roon what happened here and that the veld is free. That in the end, their captain died well, that he helped save the lives of many... and of a little boy. After all, had he not been here... or hung on as long as he did." Kro paused. "The witch's healing venom would surely have stayed right where she put it. In the veins of that enormous horse of yours."

Magnus shook his head, causing the metal parts of his bridle to tingle like small bells. Belmorn patted the animal's neck, then relinquished a nod. Kro mirrored this, but looked back down the street--back to where the monster had first appeared.

"I went home this morning. Before you woke." Kro's statement hung between the two men--colder than the air. "Not much left. Part of a wall. Some rubble. It makes sense the thing would have made her nest there. Right where she hatched. Right there in the room of my little Lishka." The voice of the alchemist splintered and failed. Naked pain contorted the visible portions of his face as tears fell behind the blood-red scarf. "I still have much to answer for. More than can ever be made right in the meager years I have left." Kro spoke through ragged breaths. "I know this, and so do they." he glanced at the crowd of Pershten. At the parents and children and babes still at the breast. "But... today is not a day for wallowing in past mistakes. This morning is the first to dawn on a witchless Veld, and that is no small thing, Belmorn."

Kro bent down. "And as for you, Miss Pesch. Jumping from the balcony, right onto a monster's head? What do you think you are? A blackfoot or something?" He shot a fleeting glance at Belmorn. "The truth is, that was very impressive. I would never have been so brave. Of course, I am a sane person."

"Oh." The girl was momentarily flustered, before recognizing the smile in Kro's eyes. "Yeah. Well, I still lost your knife."

A smile touched Kro's eyes. "No child. You figured out what that knife was for." He winked. Then he picked up the girl and placed her atop the silver mare.

Rivka's face was lit by a mix of emotions. She patted the horse's mane, rubbed her fingers over the saddle, over the horn and down to one side. There was something there. Something secured by many belts. She looked, saw, but she did not believe. "You're giving me your sword? Your... Melvin blade?"

"Maldaavan," he corrected.

"But-but you said it was safer with you!"

"If you want to be specific, I thought that about the knife, too. Think you can prove me wrong twice?"

"Yes! Oh, yes please!" Just then, Rivka caught herself. Managed her exuberance. "I mean," she cleared her throat and straightened up. "Won't you need it?"

"For what?" Kro continued to fuss, absently tightening straps and belts he had already checked numerous times. "As I said, my adventuring days are over. It's time I act my age. Stop moving for a while. Maybe do what I can to help the Veld recover." He smiled. "Back to the blade, do you remember what I said before?"

"About the bat spit?"

"About the *edge*." He sighed. "This blade is thirsty. Always. Remember that. Respect it. Understand?"

The girl nodded vigorously, indicating that she did.

"Good. But--and this is just a suggestion--maybe you'd be better off training with something made of wood. Just until you get used to the weight." Kro looked at Belmorn who was checking his saddle bags and discovering something he did not expect. Several flattish parcels-- wrapped in paper and tied in string.

"These packages," said Belmorn with surprise. "More blind fish?"

Kro shrugged. "Just in case. There's a purse in there as well. Raw silver. One of the Pershten found it last night when they were figuring out where to put us. You should be able to sell it for serious coin in Britilpor. Go to the market and find the banner with a gold panther over silver and red stripes. Ask for Kiske, but don't take less than two hundred, understand?"

"Alright." Belmorn climbed up the series of square, iron rings to his own saddle.

"This is going to work, Belmorn. You are going to save your boy, Belmorn."

Kro stopped there, but there was more to the statement. Belmorn could hear it as clear as the chime of a morning bell.

As long as you reach him in time.

"Kro. I..."

"Save it. Just get on that improbably large horse of yours and go."

In that moment, a look passed between the two men. There was much that either might have said, but the look was enough.

"Well? What are you waiting for?" Kro stepped backward, shooing the two away. And though he was already walking between the

Pershten, he called back one last time. "Tell me, blackfoot, what was your son's name again?"

"Sashander," said Belmorn with a swell of emotion. "But we call him Sasha."

"Sasha Belmorn." Kro sounded as if he were turning the name over, examining it. "I like that. When he's better, you tell Sasha Belmorn, son of Rander, to find me one day. Tell him the brushman would dearly like to say... hello."

Belmorn smiled. "Count on it," he called back. "And Kro... thank you."

Kro lifted his arm and traced a simple shape in the air. A circle.

"Tell me about where we are going." The girl's voice was a tiny thing. "Is it cold there?"

"Sometimes. But... not like this." Belmorn took a deep breath, then released it in a puff of white fog. "Not enough to speak in clouds. Hell, I wasn't sure I believed in snow until I saw some a few days ago." He winked. "The river lands are sprawling and green. In the spring, tiny white flowers bloom."

"Tiny white flowers?"

"Yes. Sometimes, girls will pick them. Put them in their hair."

After a few seconds, Belmorn turned to find that Rivka was frowning.

"I'm not going to do that."

Belmorn couldn't help but smile as he glanced at the unexpected child who had found him. Lit by the morning sun, her green eyes shone like precious stones. Not emeralds, their color was far paler than that.

Hooves clicked on stone and bridles tinkled as both horses eased into a slow trot. The road ahead was long--the remains of a circle started on the day Rander Belmorn rode away from the two people he cherished most in the world.

"Rivka?"

"Yeah?"

"Are you ready?"

The girl sighed and spared a sweeping glance for the insignificant speck of a town where she had been born. She pictured Tenebrus Kro, the gathered Pershten, the buildings, the crates full of unrefined ore, the bend at the end of a snow-covered street that she recalled walking down with her father, her mother. She tried to visualize the loving parents whose faces had already begun to fade in her mind.

"Rivka?"

Heart pounding, she turned to meet the eye of the tall, dark foreigner who had found her by an old statue. He'd selflessly defended her against a cadre of guards and nearly been executed for the trouble. As she looked into those vast grey eyes, she saw that they were full-- not of storms but something else, something she had not seen there before. Hope, maybe.

"I'm ready," Rivka said at last.

Belmorn mirrored the nervous smile she was wearing. Then, reins in hand, he leaned forward and patted the adamandray's long neck. Magnus snorted, scraped the ground.

"In that case..." he said. "Let's go home."

The last word he spoke carefully, tentatively, as if the speaking of it might somehow spoil everything. To the girl though, it sounded wonderful. Possibly better than all the words she had heard before.

About the Author Person

Steve Van Samson is the author of the "Predator World" novels and has appeared in numerous anthologies including SLAY: Stories of the Vampire Noire, Wicked Weird and More Lore From The Mythos volumes 1 and 2. In 2019, his debut comic book story "The No Ware Man" was featured in the horror anthology series Gore Shriek Resurrectus: Volume 2.

For more mostly thrilling stuff, follow Steve online!
Facebook: www.facebook.com/SVanSamson/
Twitter: twitter.com/SteveVansamson

ROUGH HOUSE PUBLISHING!

Home of the not-so-funny books, music and pulp media!
For more information on the screaming mad publisher, roll up your sleeves and visit
www.roughhousepublishing.com/

CPSIA information can be obtained
at www.ICGtesting.com
Printed in the USA
LVHW051228180221
679381LV00007B/528